Revisiting the Undead

PUBLICATIONS

Printed in the United States of America

Lycan Valley Press Publications
1625 E 72nd St STE 700 PMB 132
Tacoma, Washington 98404 United States of America

First Printing

ISBN-13: 978-0-9987489-2-4

This book is dedicated to Michael Thomas-Knight

CONTENTS

INTRODUCTION AND DEDICATION   xi

X-RAY SPECS by Michael Thomas-Knight   15

MISSING BY Poppy Z Brite   30

DOING TIME by Rob Butler   40

HEARTBEAT by Nancy Kilpatrick   58

CHINGU by Todd Sullivan   68

BEAUTIFUL THINGS by Anton Cancre   88

THE NEIGHBORHOOD HAS A BARBECUE by Max Booth III   103

PUPPIES FOR SALE by Kurt Newton   110

THE ASSASSIN by Patrick Breheny   121

SLOWLY I TURNED by Kenneth Goldman   134

ACTIVE MEMBER by Ray Garton   152

DECOR by Michael Cornelius   158

PARTY TIME by Mort Castle   187

A DEEPENING HEART by Thom Brucie   190

HUMAN RESOURCES by Greg Chapman   206

THEY RESTARTED THE MILL AT KILLINGTON by Bob Moore   217

LORSCAPEDIA by Edward Ahern   232

BRIDGE OVER THE CUNENE by Gustavo Bondoni   247

KNOTT'S LETTER by Jason A Wyckoff   260

LIFECAST by Craig Spector   286

ABOUT THE CONTRIBUTORS   304

INTRODUCTION

Revisiting the Undead is about giving old stories renewed life, bringing them back in front of eager eyes, and into the hands of new readers. Some of these stories may be familiar, like an old friend who's lost touch. Others will appear as new and fresh as the day they were written.

The stories within, and their original publications, may have been forgotten, but they're not dead—they haven't outlived their usefulness or lost their entertainment value. We've dusted off a few tales and hope you'll enjoy revisiting them after all these years.

In the process of sorting through and blowing the dust off these undead tales, Lycan Valley contributor and friend Michael Thomas-Knight passed away after a long battle with cancer.

This anthology is dedicated to him, to all the writers who have gone before him, and to all those who will go in the future. Their stories, and their memories, will forever remain undead as long as there are readers to revisit them often.

Thank you to all the readers who help keep these stories alive, and thank you to the writers for sharing part of your past.

Lycan Valley Editorial
February 2019

MICHAEL THOMAS-KNIGHT R.I.P JUNE 18, 2017

MICHAEL THOMAS-KNIGHT

My name is Sarah Rose and I am Michael Thomas-Knight's daughter. Our family just wanted to thank all of his readers and followers for all of the kinds words, love, and support. Michael passed away on Father's Day, 2017. He was diagnosed with Multiple Myeloma, a rare blood cancer that attacks the bones, nearly a decade ago. He waged a tremendous war against this disease. Despite all of the chaos and sickness that he had to overcome, my dad was able to accomplish so much in those years. I, and the rest of my family, are so proud of him. We will forever remember and be inspired by his strength, his bravery, and his tenacity in the fight for his life.

Michael Knight, my dad, was not just a gifted artist but also a wonderful father. He was always imagining and creating. He was always loving and caring. He was always cheerful and making the people around him laugh. I was always astonished that he was able to keep his sense of humor and his optimism intact as he continued to be knocked down again and again. He always put his family first and made sure that we were taken care of, happy, and loved. He taught me everything I know—about horror movies, music, and life. Though he is now gone, he lives through his art, his music, and the countless memories we all have of him.

Sarah Rose
February 2018

X-RAY SPECS

MICHAEL THOMAS-KNIGHT

JIMMY SAW THE AD in the back of an old comic book.

> *X-RAY SPECS, THE AMAZING X-RAY GLASSES. PUT THEM
> ON AND DISCOVER A HIDDEN WORLD UNKNOWN TO OTHERS.
> SEE THRU WALLS, SEE THRU FLESH, SEE THRU CLOTHING!
> GET THEM NOW, BEFORE THEY ARE OUTLAWED. ONLY
> $6.95 PLUS $1 SHIPPING. CHECK OR MONEY ORDER MADE
> PAYABLE TO: NEW-DEAL DISCOVERIES.*

A mailing address followed. The picture showed what seemed to be an ordinary pair of dark sunglasses with squiggly lines emanating from the lenses.

The whole idea intrigued Jimmy's ten-year-old mind; secrets that only he would know, his own little world that no one could invade. He told himself that seeing through clothes harbored no weight in his interest for the glasses, but reluctantly, thoughts of seeing his neighbor, Cherry-Anne, through the x-ray glasses sent tendrils of unfathomable excitement through his body. Capturing a glimpse of her beneath the flowery sundress she always wore and gaining privy to the color of her panties seemed reason enough for the purchase. He pushed away the thought and regained his composure. Surely one of the great powers of Superman was his x-ray vision and that was why Jimmy wanted the glasses and not for any other reason.

Jimmy found the comic in the basement crawlspace, covered with dust, dirt, and spider webs. However, this was not your average superhero style comic—this magazine had visceral stories; scantily clad women being attacked by zombie hordes, murdered husbands rising from the grave to exact revenge, and diseased dogs devolving into hideous beasts and attacking their masters. In the back of the comic he found ads for rubber masks, model kits, and sinister posters, all of which he found interesting, but when he saw the ad for the X-Ray Specs, he could think of nothing else.

He had money stashed in the crawlspace, his private little hideaway from his dysfunctional family life. The crawlspace was filled with spiders and centipedes but Jimmy didn't mind, he would talk to them; most of the time they were his only friends. His alcoholic Mom became an angry drunk once she started her daily intake. His stepfather, Ron, was a gambler with a nasty disposition. He would abscond every cent that Jimmy earned from cutting lawns or helping old ladies home from the market with their bags. No doubt he quickly deposited the money with his bookie. If Jimmy protested he would get the back of his stepfather's hand, cracked skin and hard knuckles, across his young face. His parents never looked into the crawlspace, never mind entered it, so his prized possessions and personal belongings were always safe there.

Jimmy adjusted the flashlight under his chin and examined the comic again. It was old, the date read *May 1969*. He wondered if the company was still in business or if perhaps the X-Ray Specs were indeed outlawed. A brown centipede crawled out of the dirt and winded its way toward him. He picked it up and let it crawl around his hand; its hundred legs tickled his skin.

"What do you think?" he asked the slithering creature.

No answer. He placed his hand to the ground and the centipede crawled off and back into the dirt. He decided it was his money and it would be worth the investment for a chance to purchase the glasses. He got a money order at the post office before school, placed it along with a small note into an envelope and sent it on its way.

After several weeks, his excitement waned and he assumed he had lost his money. However, on Tuesday afternoon he stepped off the school bus and saw the postman walk to his front door with a small brown package and deposit it into the mailbox. Jimmy ran to his house, barely able to contain his excitement. When he got to the front walk he slowed himself and crept silently to the mailbox. The brown box was just the right size to contain a pair of glasses. He placed it carefully under his shirt and halfway down his arm sleeve.

A goblet clinked as his mom moved to see him come through the front door. She barely nodded as she looked up from the couch, the phone receiver under her chin, a smoke in one hand and the vodka tonic in the other. Oprah Winfrey's voice squawked through the television to the delight of housewives everywhere. His mother had nothing to say to him. All the better, Jimmy thought to himself. He ran to his room and closed the door. He admired the package. In a way, it was his first step towards independence. He needed something and he got it for himself. He hoped one day he would not need his parents for anything at all.

Slowly twisting the package in his hands, he noticed something strange. He looked closer at the postmark. The ink-stamped mark covered the original stamps. The first thing he thought to himself was, *these are the exact same stamps I used to send the letter with the money order*. However, it was the other strange fact that had him extremely curious. The post mark date read *May 26, 1969*. He tried to get a better look at the date but it was light and uneven. Had the post office not changed the date on the machine in all these years? He cussed himself for spending so much concern on the packaging and ripped into the box. He pulled the glasses from a clear bag and let the debris fall to the floor. He gazed upon the dark lenses with pride. A small triangular pattern on the lens surface reflected rainbow light as he moved them in his hands.

Finally, the moment of truth, he raised the glasses to his face and slid the arms over his ears. It took his eyes a moment to adjust. Everything looked squashed and distorted. Was this x-ray? It did look somewhat like a black and white negative but he couldn't even tell what he was looking at. He lifted the glasses and color flooded his senses. He saw his bedroom wall; the bathroom should be the next room over. He placed the glasses back down over his eyes. The world squeezed down again making him momentarily dizzy. Adjusted, he saw something but it did not look like the bathroom. It could be pipes he was looking at… is that what the inside of a wall looks like? He didn't want to see inside a wall, he wanted to see through it, to see what was going on in the next room. He pulled the glasses off and looked at them. Perhaps he was doing something wrong? Nope, there was nothing to them, you put them on, and you take them off, end of story. He did a few experiments, looking about the room. Things that were round or wide looked skinny, things that were skinny looked like line drawings. He turned on his lamp and looked at it through the glasses. The light completely blinded him, turning his field of vision a dull white.

He yanked them off his head and was about to throw them to the floor in disgust. Just then he heard playful laughter from outside sweep into his bedroom on a spring breeze and he ran to the window to have a look. Cherry-Anne wrestled a stick from her dog in her backyard. Another experiment, he told himself, but he would have to get a closer look. He took off for the backyard. She was a few years older than Jimmy and just starting to show signs of womanhood. She would talk to him sometimes at home but in school she mostly ignored him.

He climbed upon the metal storm doors, the back entrance to the basement, in order to get a view over the fence. She was still there, throwing *Bounder*, a small golden retriever, a stick and waiting as he fetched it. Jimmy placed the glasses upon his face. There was a moment of extreme disorientation and he thought he would fall, but then things came into some sort of focus, if you could call it that. Cherry-Anne became a skinny dark figure with a bulbous head and little blurry detail, as if he was viewing the shadow of a cotton swab. The wire figure bent over and retrieved the stick from the dog's mouth. *Bounder* was nothing more than a few fast moving, squiggly black lines. When she looked up she saw Jimmy. He didn't even realize she was looking in his direction until she spoke.

"Oh, hey Jimmy."

"Hey," Jimmy nodded.

"Cool shades," she said.

"Thanks."

He couldn't take it anymore; the glasses were useless and he'd been duped. He ripped them from his face. Cherry-Anne's hair, skin and eyes sparkled in the golden sunshine of the spring day. Jimmy felt dizzy again and fell backwards colliding against the wall of the house. He gripped the brick façade and steadied himself.

"You okay?" Cherry-Anne asked.

"Yeah, fine," he answered.

"Okay, gotta' go now, see ya' around."

Cherry-Anne tossed the stick for a final time and retreated into the house.

In the dark pit of the crawlspace, Jimmy dug a hole in the dirt floor to bury the evidence of his purchase. In it he threw the brown postal packaging and the plastic bag. He was about to toss the glasses into the hole and forget about them forever. He was scammed for eight bucks, so what? It was something to occupy his mind for a few weeks and expanded his abilities to deal with the world. He decided he should keep the glasses just for that merit alone and tucked them back into his shirt pocket. He kicked dirt back into the hole, grabbed his flashlight, and moved to his usual seat, a cushion from an old patio chair propped up in a car tire. He clicked the flashlight off and sat in darkness. He could see a little light where the hanging rug lay over the crawlspace entrance but not much else. It was at this very moment that he was possessed by an urge to put on the X-Ray Specs. It was ridiculous, what did he think he could possibly see? The urge pulled at his sensibilities until he had no choice but to submit.

It took a few moments to adjust to the darkness but this time there was no dizziness in the transition. Slowly, shapes began to form in his black field of vision. Something towered directly in front of him, its silhouette in a blur of high speed motion. Jimmy's body went rigid, his muscles sensing danger before his mind could comprehend it. The blurred vision cleared and Jimmy recognized the shape as the centipede that he often witnessed down here. However, it was different. It was big—bigger than Jimmy himself. The front quarter of its body stood erect. Thick tapering antennae arched forward from the top of its head. Its smooth eyes bulged from the sides of its head and two side-by-side mouth pincers opened and closed frequently just below the eyes, revealing an undetermined number of fluttering cilia that constituted a mouth. Jimmy could clearly see the segmented construct of its body, each portion housing two legs, one at each side. The legs aloft paddled at high speed as if the creature was swimming or the action somehow assured its balance.

Jimmy realized his breath had been locked in his lungs and let it out in short staccato bursts. He slowly pulled his legs inward, away from the thing and brought his knees up between them. A sound came to his ears, like a scream from somewhere far off, through a tunnel, finally reaching its destination. The voice was squashed, like an old radio, with static bursts and a flickering quality—small slices of sound as if someone was speaking from behind a fan.

"D-d-d-do not be frightened—*crackle*—young Jimmy."

The centipede's head moved with the expression of speech but the words were not coming from its mouth. The words were being heard in Jimmy's head, not with his ears.

"W-w-w-we will not hurt you.—*Sssss*—"

When Jimmy heard in his mind the word *we*, he realized there were other sentinel beings behind the centipede. Directly to the rear and left stood the spider. Its physicalities were more humanoid. Its head hosted many sets of glossy black eyes, fanning out in a pattern away from the two largest at the center. Large, hairy fangs, four or six in all, jutted down from the area of the mouth. There was no lower jaw as there would be on a human head, only fangs hanging like nasty daggers. The spider creature stood upright on what appeared to be the lowest set of legs, while the other sets contacted their opposites, pincer to pincer, in mock prayer. The spider's body was covered in coarse black hair. Beyond the spider were more beasts, standing quietly at different distances from one another, moving out beyond the dimensions of the crawlspace, into a vast area of gray darkness.

"What do you want?" Jimmy heard his own quivering voice question.

"W-w-w-we do not want anything from you specifically,—*crackle* —we are your friends," the chopped voice answered.

Jimmy slowly motioned toward the crawlspace exit and the centipede moved to block his advance.

"Please sit back," the voice commanded. "We have much to discuss."

Jimmy settled back into the seat. The spider moved forward and began to animate as if speaking, the voice forming in Jimmy's head as with the other and sounding quite the same.

"You have spoken to us for many years now. We seek cooperation… a partnership with you…"

"What are you?" Jimmy asked. "You are too big to be real bugs."

"W-w-w-we have lived here for eons, we have always been here. We assume this physical reality from you. It is your energy that makes us strong, that shapes us…"

As the spider thing continued to explain, Jimmy slowly reached up and raised the X-Ray Specs away from his eyes. The creatures disappeared as did their voices. When he replaced the glasses in front of his eyes, the creatures and voices returned and the spider creature was still speaking.

"…what your race would call dark matter. Your strongest emotions create this dark energy and we feed. Your biggest disappointments, your anger, your rage and your fear—your pain and your misery. Now for the first time in so many eons, we are finally able to make contact from beyond our dimension and into yours."

"Why… why do you need me? What do you want from this world?" Jimmy asked.

"Your world will be our sustenance. We have sensed it for so long, like an aroma drifting in from a far-off kitchen, our hunger and needs growing and yearning for it but always out of reach. Your race inflicts such misery and pain upon one another, enough dark energy to return us to our previous glory."

"How do I know you won't just kill me?"

A half dozen creatures stepped forward and hovered over Jimmy. He tensed up and gasped aloud. He shielded his face with his hands and arms, expecting a deadly strike to befall him and to leave him dying in the crawlspace.

"We praise you, you are our hero. Your communication was a homing beacon, the only way we would have been able to find our way to your world." These words seemed to be coming from a dark brown beast that resembled an earwig.

Jimmy let down his hands slowly. An array of chattering, snapping and clawing insectile appendages scurried before his eyes; mandibles, pincers, claws and an untold array of moving exoskeleton deviations. Despite Jimmy's tolerance for entomology, this was too much for him.

"Back away, please," Jimmy pleaded.

The centipede chattered something and the group retreated. Jimmy let out a sigh of relief.

"This must be a lot for your human mind to accept. I must apologize for the... eagerness of my comrades."

"How many are you?"

"W-w-w-we are many—*crackle*—we are..."

The creature's sentence was interrupted by a voice from outside the crawlspace.

"Jimmy!"

The creature looked over to the crawlspace entrance. Jimmy sensed that it was annoyed by the intrusion. It looked back to Jimmy.

"If you need us, just call. To help you is to help ourselves."

The centipede and the spider both retreated into the distance and the crawlspace became dark and returned to its claustrophobic dimensions. Jimmy removed the glasses and placed them in the front pocket of his shirt.

"Jimmy!"

His stepfather's angry tone let Jimmy know there was no waiting this out; he had to exit the crawlspace. He pulled the rug aside and peered out, perched upon the entryway a few feet from the basement floor. He saw Ron fuming in the dim light, waiting with folded arms for Jimmy to extricate himself from the hole. Jimmy jumped down and fell forward, losing his footing upon landing. He sprawled forward and the X-Ray Specs shot from his pocket, landing out in front of him.

"Your mama told me you were poking around in the mailbox."

Ron stepped forward and stopped, regarding the sunglasses. He lifted his foot; his worn work-shoe hovered over the glasses, intent on their destruction. Jimmy reached quickly for the glasses, knocking them forward and his stepfather's boot came down upon his splayed fingers, locking them to the ground with painful pressure.

"That's what you spend good money on? While I struggle to support you and your mother, sweating and breaking my ass in the ninety-degree heat, you're spending money on sunglasses?"

Jimmy's stepfather applied more pressure to the boot, pressed down harder on the boy's hand. Tears sprung from Jimmy's eyes as his fingers were crushed beneath the man's weight. A sadistic smile purged Ron's face, his gritting teeth a promise of more pain to come.

"I'm going to show you what insubordination brings you in this house."

Ron lifted his foot and Jimmy snatched his fingers back, covering them with his other hand. He curled up with pain, rocking back and forth, trying to ease the severity. Ron plucked a wire coat hanger from a metal clothes-rack and bent it straight as he advanced upon Jimmy. He reshaped the hanger into a metal whip.

"I am going to teach you something real good!"

Jimmy looked up to see Ron raising the whip over his head. The sadistic fury in the man's eyes made him wonder if he would even survive the beating. Through the tears of pain and the knowledge of this dismal reality, he questioned the validity of what he had seen in the crawlspace only moments previous. He made a quick decision. Now was the time to find out; he said only one word.

"Help!"

The sudden change in his stepfather's expression told a tale of terror all on its own. His eyes bulged in his head and his mouth changed from wicked grin to fearful grimace. Jimmy heard the sound of something breaking, a *crunch* followed by grinding. He saw, without the glasses, the insect mandible's crushing grip upon his stepfather's knee, and as the vice-like grip increased, blood splashed out upon the beast, making it visible as a giant red ant. With human hands and bat-like wings, the creature was a hodgepodge of unrelated and ill-conceived animal body parts. Just then the centipede rose up from behind and Ron turned his head to see it. The centipede snapped its mandibles and Ron's hand snapped off at the wrist, still holding the wire coat hanger as it fell to the basement floor. Jimmy sat up, nursing his bloodied fingers and looked into his stepfather's terrified eyes.

"No more beatings, Ron!" Jimmy yelled.

A feeding fury ignited as pincers, claws and hungry mouths seemed to appear from thin air, taking bites and tatters of flesh from Ron's body. Ripping and tearing ensued, snapping off chunks of flesh, undoing his physical makeup in an indescribable manner. Creature orifices pulled, chomped and sucked flesh from his bones, while pincers and entomological claws snapped and crushed his femur, spine and ribcage. It all happened at such a furious pace, Ron was still alive, eyes darting helplessly to and from, as his body was being dismantled. Blood rained down from where his body stood and worms with suction-cup like mouths appeared, vacuuming the hot liquid from the floor. Finally, from behind, a creature clamped down on Ron's heart, bursting it like a water balloon. Blood splashed out and Ron's eyes glazed over, no longer alive and searching for refuge.

They devoured his body in a matter of minutes; some pieces were dragged off by creatures into a tunnel of darkness that stretched out behind the melee, a path to a world of infinite horrors.

Without a word, the centipede chomped down a last morsel and turned, followed by a trail of suckling worms, into the black hole—the open doorway that connected its world to Jimmy's. Almost all traces of his stepfather were gone, except a bit of sticky fluid upon the basement floor where he had been killed and eaten. Jimmy stood, sniffing back tears, aware of his indifference to the fact that his abusive stepfather was gone. He wanted to question why he no longer needed the glasses to see what he had seen, but guessed the creatures were getting stronger. He picked up the glasses and returned them to his pocket, just in case he did need them later. He had so many more questions but his head ached and he felt indescribably dizzy. He decided he needed to get away from this scene, get far away from the basement and the incomprehensible horrors he had witnessed. He couldn't think right now, he couldn't sort through all that had happened this afternoon. He raced up the stairs, putting distance between himself and the events that had transpired in the cellar. He needed to get to the solitude of his bedroom.

His mom had passed out in her bedroom, empty bottle of vodka lying upon the rug at her feet, where her legs hung limply off the edge of the bed. Jimmy darted past the room; glad she did not catch sight of him and call him. He could not answer any stupid questions at the moment. He ran to his room and closed the door. Feeling ill, he threw himself on his bed and fell into a deep sleep.

In this sleep state, Jimmy had nightmares that reflected true life events. Every bad thing that had ever happened to him in his life was replayed in his mind, one on top of the other. Every bad day of his short existence was being revisited at high speed in these dreams and all the hurt and suffering he had experienced resurfaced as if those events had just happened. All the emotion; hatred, fear and pain, mounted in Jimmy's heart and soul.

Several incidents with his mother played in his mind simultaneously: *When he was four-years-old and his mother blamed him for his real father's death, a car accident—when he was in first grade, he had made a Mother's Day card in school and his mother barely acknowledged it when he gave it to her, then used it as a coaster for her beer bottle—When he was eight and she accused him of stealing her Vodka. For punishment, she grabbed the Christmas Tree and dragged it out into the backyard where she lit it on fire.*

Other images played out in Jimmy's mind: *His second-grade Gym teacher who berated him in front of the whole class for not being able to do even one sit-up—the class bully, Butch Langdon, punching him in the arm until Jimmy relinquished his lunch money—old man Fogerty, threatening him with a gun for stepping on his lawn.*

Then another incident played itself out in slow-motion: *In the school cafeteria, Jimmy walked back to his table with a tray of food, meatloaf with gravy and mashed potatoes. Someone tripped him with their foot; Jimmy went crashing down, face landing in the tray, mashed potatoes and gravy covering his clothes. He came to rest directly in front of the girl's table. Jimmy looked up and every girl in the cafeteria was pointing and laughing at him. It may not have been so bad but then he saw Cherry-Anne—her finger pointing at him, her laughing voice piercing his heart.*

The dark oppression of misery accumulated within Jimmy. Pain and hurt compounded to a self-loathing dread, a blackening of the soul, a hopeless surrender that was beyond tears, as images flashed in his mind at a feverish pitch. Then, Jimmy heard a scream.

He awoke in a sweat, tears dried against his cheeks, eyes squinting in the dark room. He heard the scream again and recognized it was Cherry-Anne.

He jumped up in the bed and pulled on his sneakers as fast as he could. He sensed something was wrong. Something had changed in the air, in the molecules of the world around him.

"No. Not Cherry-Anne!" he said, "Please, not her."

He tried to climb from his bed but felt weak. The oppression of misery that others had heaped upon him during his life sat upon him like a heavy weight. He shook his head and shrugged off the black cloud that restrained him. His head cleared and after a few moments, he was finally able to stand.

Jimmy ran from his room and down the hallway. He looked briefly into his mother's room and did not like what he saw. They were doing something horrible to her in there. She was naked, legs akimbo, arms held down by one creature at the head of the bed. Another creature laid on her, between her legs and over her body. Her face was frozen in the silent scream of a catatonic state. She was being raped by a human-sized cockroach.

He continued down the stairs then stopped at the bottom and debated going back to save her from the creatures. He decided against it. His mother had died many years ago, at the bottom of a glass, drowned in an ocean of vodka and thrown out with the trash. He ran for the back door and burst through to the backyard, hoping to reach Cherry-Anne in time to save her from an equally horrible fate.

Turning the corner of the house and seeing into his neighbor's driveway, Jimmy witnessed a terrible sight. Cherry-Anne was restrained by several creatures, each staking a claim to her with a tight grip of pincers or jaws, clamped down on her legs, arms, shoulders, and hair. Her blue eyes were wide beyond natural occurrence and her eyeballs darted back and forth to see the creatures holding her at bay.

Jimmy rushed toward the scene screaming. "Nooooo!"

The creatures, startled by the Jimmy's outburst, scattered in different directions, but none relinquished hold on their prize. Cherry-Anne's body was ripped apart in front of Jimmy. Arms and legs unexpectedly peeled in different directions, carried off by the fleeing beasts. Flesh ripped asunder and shredded. Her arms popped off her frame and her ribcage twisted and mangled under the strain.

Jimmy screamed, fists balled up in fury. His temples bulged with anger. Suddenly, he was hit from behind and forced to the floor. He felt the pain as something stabbed him in the back and turned his head to see a large scorpion with its stinger planted firmly between his shoulder blades. The centipede appeared and walked up to Jimmy. It used a feeler to touch his reddened cheek. The squashed voice entered Jimmy's head again.

"D-d-d-do not fight my friend, the venom is taking over quickly. You will be paralyzed in seconds."

"Why? Why?" Jimmy cried.

"W-w-w-we have decided that we do not want you interfering. The venom will liquefy your bones and you will be unable to move. We will keep you alive until we are done here. When we are ready to move on to another world, we will savor our last delicious meal in an honorable banquet to our hero, you Jimmy. Your organs will be deliciously tender by that time."

Jimmy rose up on his arms to protest but before he was able to utter a word, his arms began to bow outward as his bones softened. They folded under his weight and Jimmy's face hit the pavement. He spotted Cherry-Anne's solitary eyeball, popped free from its skull socket, looking back at him. Jimmy's misery and despair expanded beyond known limits of any human soul, holding no bounds. 🦇

MISSING

POPPY Z BRITE

IT WAS HIGH SUMMER and the breeze coming over the levee from the river carried a hint of cleanly rotting fish, a phantom of oyster shell still thick with silver glue. There was another smell on the breeze, something browner, from a deeper part of the river, a smell that might make strollers quicken their step and look away from the middle of the darkly shining water.

"Someone drowned a week ago," said Andrew, and Lucian answered, "Bullshit—it's sewage."

But it was the smell, along with the heat like a dirty, oily blanket, that drove them out of the nightclub. Notes descending on a saxophone followed them into the street like a string of colored beads. In the street the smell was still noticeable, but it mingled with the grease-dripping odor of frying oysters, the sharp scent of oil paints and turpentine left behind by the street artists who had all gone home hours ago. Jackson Square brooded behind dark curlicues of iron. Within, pigeons might roost, a needle might roll from one unhappy hand to another.

Lucian pressed his face briefly against the railing. It was cool against his smooth pale cheek, but when he turned back to Andrew, a dirty stripe bisected his nose and forehead.

Andrew spit on a handkerchief and dabbed at Lucian's face. "For god's sake, don't lick your lips now. A thousand diseases on that railing." Lucian twisted halfheartedly away from the sticky handkerchief, smiling.

Although they had left their nightclub, the club at which they listened to whatever might be new and sometimes played their own music, their night's drinking was far from over. On their way to Lucian's room they passed a lone, shabby man, bent over backwards, pointing a wailing saxophone at the sky. A crack somewhere deep inside the instrument made the notes rattle like bones, but Andrew dug out a quarter and aimed it at the shoe box by the man's feet. The quarter bounced out and rolled across the sidewalk, but the man didn't stop playing.

They passed a pizza parlor that reeked of tomatoes stewed in oregano and a foreign grocery which, though closed, wafted out a thousand mysterious, delicious smells, the smells of a kitchen in the Great Pyramid. Under it all they could still sense the wet brown river scent. Lucian's narrow nostrils widened imperceptibly.

They passed along the streets in silence, two white non-jazz musicians stirring up the air in the French Quarter. The buildings they passed grew darker, more broken. Feet padded along behind them for two blocks, then, deterred by Andrew's wide-shouldered bulk, disappeared down a side street that led toward the river.

A few minutes later Lucian passed a broken street light, turned down an alley, and nudged a heavy door with his shoulder. They ducked under a flapping black curtain, sending down a rain of dust, and emerged in a dark little shop lit by two kerosene lamps. Orange shadows licked at the walls of the shop, which were lined with shelves of tiny bottles and boxes. The bottles were queerly shaped, long-necked, and made of thick, ancient glass colored blue and amber, with stoppers instead of screw-on caps. Most of their

POPPY Z BRITE

contents were murky and indecipherable. The boxes gave off an odor of moldy cardboard. It was easy to imagine clicking, roiling nests of insects in the dark corners of the shelves.

Lucian stood slightly stiff-necked, embarrassed, staring at a spot somewhere to the left of the woman who sat in the corner of the shop.

"Good evening, Mrs. Carstairs. How's business?"

"As always. No one comes. No one wants magic anymore." The woman pulled a gray blanket more snugly around her shoulders. At her feet sat a bowl of colorless mush, perhaps oatmeal, in which a bent spoon was buried at an angle.

"Sorry to hear it. We'll just go on upstairs then." Lucian ducked through another curtain at the back of the shop. Andrew heard him clattering up a flight of stairs. He looked back at Lucian's landlady, who didn't appear to have noticed him. She was busily scratching herself under the gray blanket. His knee banged the corner of a long wooden box. He stiffened but couldn't keep from glancing down.

Under the glass top the thin little figure reclined, grinning up at him. It should have been a skeleton, but a thin layer of iridescent parchment still stretched over its face and the ratty framework of its hands, and he thought there were small, opaque marbles left deep in its eyesockets—he had never let himself look closely enough to be sure. A few dry strands of bone-colored hair twisted across a rotten silk pillow.

"It isn't hard to do," said Mrs. Carstairs, "if you love them enough."

Andrew stared back at her. She made no acknowledgment of what she had said, turning her head not an inch in his direction, but only huddled serenely, surrounded by vials of powdered bat's tongue, boxes which contained the fragments of the bones of saints and murdered men. And at her feet sat a bowl that might be oatmeal. Andrew swallowed the sour spit in his mouth and hurried up the stairs after Lucian.

Lucian had rummaged in his failing little refrigerator and found a bottle of beer for Andrew. For himself he pulled out a Donald Duck orange juice bottle half full of violet sludge. It was vodka mixed with a cheap Japanese plum wine that seemed to have about the same consistency as ketchup. It was vile and it filled the tiny room with a rotten fruity smell that stayed in Lucian's clothes. Lucian claimed the concoction could get him drunk faster than anything else on earth.

He sloshed some of it into a jelly jar that still had gray-white label scrapings on its side. At the first sip, his long eyelashes lowered in contentment; this was the taste he knew like the inside of a lover's mouth, the taste of his world. He took another gulp and lay back on his unmade bed, gazing past Andrew at the window. The moon's weak glow was diluted and made greasy by the dirty glass.

Andrew watched him. Lucian was languid now. In the street there was always a certain tension to his shoulders and slender neck, because Lucian was slight and exquisite-looking and wore silky little scarves and long black jackets that made him look rich even though he wasn't. When he wasn't being prodded for money he didn't have, he was being harassed for the European fineness of his face, and on the darkest narrowest streets his eyes took on a watchful look. Andrew, who was large and Aryanly handsome, usually walked home with his friend on late nights, not minding the long lonely walk back to his own apartment.

Lucian nudged his shoes off. He wasn't wearing any socks. He shook a few strands of feathery hair, dark auburn delicately frosted with silver-blond, out of his eyes and smiled at Andrew over the rim of his jelly jar. Andrew stood up, stretching, nearly knocking over his rickety chair. The ceiling of this room was unusually low. It was all right for Lucian, but Andrew, who was a foot taller, felt clumsy and claustrophobic here. "Do you mind if I open a window?"

"By all means, open a window—any window will do." Lucian's voice was heavy with plum wine and sarcasm; there was only one tiny window in the room. Andrew shoved at its smeary glass until it slid up. He hadn't heard Lucian move, but when he turned back to the room, Lucian was holding out a fresh beer. Their fingers kissed briefly and sweat-stickily as Andrew took the bottle.

Lucian's fingers were longer than the palms they stemmed from, very slim and clean, slightly flattened at the tips. The tips had been splayed and pressed out by Lucian's Juno, the only expensive thing in the room. It stood on four stilt legs in a corner behind Andrew, its black and white keys gleaming opaquely in the half-light from the window. Lucian's fingertips had crystalline magic, a sense of tone and pressure that could milk every spangle, every drop of color from a piece of music. He stayed in his room during the day, sleeping naked and innocent through the hottest part of the afternoon, then playing til nightfall, pulling spills and showers of notes from the battered little Juno to float out the window, to drift downstairs and be smothered among Mrs. Carstairs' bottles and packets. Once every month a check arrived from a faceless, sexless, relative in Baton Rouge. For a few days, Lucian and Andrew would eat in prettily decorated restaurants, drink in well-lit, airy bars outside the French Quarter. Then, it was back to dark clubs and sludgy plum wine until the next check came. Andrew could sing; the lyrics he wrote were attempts to capture in words the shimmering transparency of Lucian's music, and he could barely play guitar. They tried to expand the boundaries of all the music they had ever heard, composing intricate symphonies together whenever Mrs. Carstairs was too caught up in her rituals to bang on her ceiling with a broom handle.

Lucian stretched out his feet, flexing his toes comfortably. His toenails were the color of pearls, faintly shiny. He slurped down the last drops of violet sludge and filled the jelly jar again.

"That skeleton—" Andrew began.

"What skeleton?"

"The one downstairs."

"Oh. Mrs. Carstairs' corpse. Very charming."

"Why do you suppose she keeps it? Is it some kind of weird advertisement?"

"It's her husband. Was."

"No!"

"Something like that. It's too small to be a man's body, isn't it? Her child then. She told me about it at great length once. If I'd been sober, it would have shocked me."

"The skeleton of her child? In a glass box?"

"It died a long time ago. Her one and only, I guess. She couldn't stand to bury it and let it rot. She's a witch, you know, or calls herself one. She knew how to make it dry up. Mummify it."

"Didn't she have to take the insides out?"

"I suppose so. God, Andrew, forget it."

Andrew stopped talking about it but did not forget it. His eyes drifted and came to rest on Lucian's midsection. Lucian had unbuttoned his shirt, and the hollows in his slatted ribcage were full of silver shadow. Andrew watched the narrow chest expand and collapse again and again. His mind slipped back to the little body downstairs. Mrs. Carstairs would have gone to bed by now, so it was alone down there, keeping company with the dusty bottles and nests of roaches. Perhaps a faint phosphorescence lit the spaces between its bones.

Mrs. Carstairs had been unable to let go of the child completely; she had clung to the only part of it left to her, and perhaps if she pressed her forehead to the glass she could catch its sleeping thoughts. She had preserved the essence of the child, the cleanest part. She had seen parts of its body no one had been meant to see, but those parts were gone now. He imagined its chest cavity stuffed with fragrant linen, its skull scoured with dry spices. It was an ivory being, a husk.

Lucian pressed his lips together, stifling a yawn. It overcame him and his jaws gaped. Andrew glimpsed two rows of even teeth, a soft little tongue stained purple. "It's late," Lucian said. "I want to go to bed."

"Play for me first."

"It's too late."

"Please. Just a little."

Lucian's eyes flicked heavenward, but he was smiling. "Five minutes. No more."

He positioned himself behind the Juno, pressed buttons, twisted the volume knob to nearly zero. His eyelashes, black in the murky light, swept his pale cheeks. His hands moved and a flood of notes erupted, pouring away, cutting through the damp, heavy air in the room.

Andrew leaned forward, lips slightly parted. The music swelled and shattered. Each shard was a fragment of colored glass, a particle of spice. He closed his eyes and watched the music weave a tapestry across the insides of his eyelids. Its colors were streaky and bright, glittering.

When he realized that he was hearing nothing, he opened his eyes. Lucian had stopped playing and was sniffing the air. The tip of his straight nose twitched.

"There's that damn rotten smell again."

Andrew pulled in a noseful of air. The full, wet smell was there again, under the fruity odor of the wine and the tangy, private scent of their sweat. Andrew nodded. Lucian shrugged. "I can't do anything about it. It's too hot to close the window." He grew brisk. "There. You've had your music. It's late; go home. I'll see you tomorrow night." He pushed Andrew toward the door.

Andrew knew Lucian would undress and lie in bed with the juice bottle next to him, drinking until the needling heat became a faraway thing, beneath notice, and sleep was possible. At the door, Andrew turned back, not sure why he was doing such an unfamiliar and faintly embarrassing thing, and put his arms around Lucian. Lucian stiffened, surprised; then he decided to go along with it and slipped his arms awkwardly around Andrew's neck. It was a brief, clumsy hug, but when it was over, Andrew felt obscurely better. "I'll see you tomorrow then."

"Don't you always?"

A car ground by outside and in its shifting light a band of shadow slid across Lucian's eyes. Lucian's lips curved in a forlorn smile.

Andrew picked his way down the stairs. Lucian held the door open to give Andrew whatever light could be had; as he ducked under the curtain Andrew heard the door click shut. He stood in the dark shop for a moment, letting his eyes adjust to the light filtered and masked by Mrs. Carstair's heavy black draperies. When he took a step forward, his shoe struck the corner of the long wooden box. The glass shivered. He sensed something shifting inside, settling. If he pulled aside the draperies, let in the hazy moonlight, he would see—

He didn't want to. He headed for where he knew the door was, and had one bad moment when his hand found instead the thick moist velvet of the draperies; then he was outside looking up at Lucian's window, which was as dark as any other window in the sprawling block of buildings.

Back in his clean studio apartment, with a fan whirring at the foot of his bed and a streetlight glowing comfortably outside his window, Andrew brought his cassette player to bed with him and was lulled to sleep by a cascade of shimmering notes, the one tape

Lucian had allowed him to make of their music. The notes swirled around Andrew's room, looking for a crack, a hole, a route of escape. Eventually, they slipped under the door and floated away on an eddy of wind toward the river.

The next day was hotter and more humid; people gasped in the street like swimmers, and flies swarmed in glistening blue-green clouds above piles of garbage. The day smelled of coconut suntan lotion and seafood being deep fried in hot oil. As the shadows in the streets lengthened and the colors of the day deepened into smudgy blues and violets, Andrew made his way back to Lucian's room. The brown river smell had begun to creep back into the air. As Andrew nudged through the empty shop and climbed the stairs, the smell deepened and grew soft around the edges.

Lucian was still in bed. A sheet was twisted between his legs and pulled up across his body. Its corner touched on of his pale pink nipples.

Andrew knelt beside the bed. A warm dampness soaked through the knees of his pants, thick and sticky. He was kneeling in a puddle of vodka and plum wine. The fruity odor had grown sour in the heat. Lucian's long eyelashes were poised just above his cheeks, ready to sweep down. Andrew touched Lucian's hand. The fingers were stiff; he heard the sharp clean nails scratching delicately against the sheet under the pressure of his own hand. A bright cardboard package lay on the floor next to the bed: DozEze. Sleeping pills. Only two were gone. Lucian had not meant it then.

Andrew buried his face in the sheet, smelling cotton, a ghost of detergent, old sweat, all edged with the brown smell of the river. Neon patterns that swelled and burst behind his eyelids, resolved themselves into Lucian's face. The silky dark lashes, the dulling white glimmer behind the lowered lids, the parted pink lips were too lovely, too alone.

Andrew squeezed his eyes more tightly shut. How could he leave this room now? How could he give the proper authorities the signal to descend on this lonely little body with scalpels and death certificates and jars of formaldehyde?

After a few minutes he gently pushed Lucian to one side and lay down next to him.

* * *

This was a warm night, but they were beginning to cool off; there would be no more sweltering sheetless midnights, no more parched red days. Andrew rubbed at the smeary glass of the window and peered out. The man with the saxophone was still there, bending and writhing under the broken streetlight. Stupid place for a street musician. No one ever passed by here. Andrew had shut the window so he wouldn't have to hear the dying-cat wailing.

He switched on the Juno and poked tentatively at a few keys. The sounds they made were pretty, but there was no crystalline waterfall of notes, no undercurrent of magic dust. Still, he was getting better, already was better on the keyboard than he had ever been on guitar.

He crossed the room and sat on the floor at the foot of the bed, resting his forehead on the corner of the long wooden box he had constructed. The edge of the glass top dug into his eyebrow.

Andrew didn't have to remember to breathe shallowly anymore; he did it without thinking about it. He had none of the secrets of the woman downstairs, the witch, and the smell up here was very brown, very wet. That would pass in time. Lucian would be clean again; at last he would achieve a primal state of purity. Andrew thought of sticks of ivory, of dry perfumed husks.

He raised his head and looked into the box.

DOING TIME

ROB BUTLER

THROUGH A HAZE Geoff Brent could see figures in white coats, two of them, and a figure in a suit. It was the suit that worried him but his numbed mind was not sure why.

Slowly the haze began to clear. The white coats looked anxious. The suit was smiling but not the sort of smile you wanted to see.

"How are you feeling Geoff?"

"Really, you shouldn't talk to him yet. He needs time."

Time!

"Oh I'm sure Mr Brent won't mind. We're old friends, aren't we Geoff?"

Brent tried to speak but all he could manage was a cough. He was not at all sure who he was nor where he was. But the word *time* had made him shiver and he knew this guy in the suit; knew he hated him.

"You should wait until the drugs have cleared his system. He's very weak."

"I know, I know." Liquid grey eyes gazed keenly down. "Do you think he can recognise me yet?"

"He will do. Just give him time."

Time!

The suit continued to smile. The mists continued to clear. Brent could make out other features now, silvery thinning hair, a little moustache, a nose once broken...

"Carter!"

"Excellent. I knew you'd get there. Gregory Carter. Here to take you off your Death Bed."

Death Bed! Suddenly he remembered and Brent struggled to sit up. The white coats easily restrained him.

"A mirror. Get me a mirror."

Carter chuckled lightly and held one up.

"I thought you might ask for that. They always want a mirror."

* * *

An hour later he was sipping warm coffee in a cell. He felt terrible. Carter sat opposite, still smiling, one leg draped languidly across a metal table. He tossed a bunch of keys repeatedly into the air, catching them with ease.

"You should have known you weren't old when you saw me Geoff. I hope I don't look as if I'm in my late seventies?"

"I was confused. So would you have been."

"Yes I expect so. Is it good to know that you're still fairly young?"

"How old am I?"

"Oh, forty six-ish. You've been asleep for twelve years. Only twelve years of a forty year stretch. Not too bad eh?"

"I didn't do it you know. I was framed."

"Of course you were. They all are."

Brent sipped some more coffee and studied the white sterile room. Carter's keys flashed up and down in the bleak neon lights.

"So why have they woken me up early?"

"They didn't. I did. You have your old friend Gregory to thank for that." Carter smiled. "The bureau thought you might be interested in a deal."

Brent sighed. "That figures. What sort of a deal?"

"The sort of deal that gets you out of here if you do me a favour. Gets you out now. End of sentence. No more forty-year stretch. You get your life back. Sound good?"

"And if I don't do you a favour?"

Carter pretended to frown, tossed the keys and let them hit the floor.

"Ah, well, then I would have to get the medics back in. Pop go the injections and back under you go. You're seventy-four when you wake up. That mirror won't show your face so well the second time around. In fact, I might not even be here to say hello."

Brent put down the coffee cup. He didn't feel at all well.

"I'd like to do you a favour, Gregory."

* * *

They now moved to a more comfortable room with easy chairs, but Brent guessed there would still be a guard or two on the door. After being out cold for twelve years it was taking him some time to adjust, but the relief at being only forty-six was indescribable. It had only seemed like seconds from going out in panic to waking up in despair and now here he was with a chance of living again. Yet he knew the Government didn't let up on Death Bed lifers that easily.

"This must be quite a favour."

Carter nodded.

"Yes, I suppose it is. Do you want to hear about it?"

"I don't want to go to sleep again so I guess I want to hear about it."

Brent dropped into a chair and exhaled deeply with relief and tension. Carter wandered across to the windows where he stood for a while as if composing his thoughts. They were high up in a security wing with a view over South London. He swept an arm across the panorama.

"It's a dangerous world out there Geoff. It always has been of course but things have changed for the worse since you went under. There are new technologies, new wealthy nations, and new secrets. Unfortunately, there are more criminals too and the haves don't want the have nots spoiling their fun."

"Guess not."

"You should know. You used to steal from them."

"I told you. I was framed."

"So you did."

Carter again gazed out across London.

"Something had to be done. It was becoming just too expensive to guard what you owned. The great and good were unable to leave their houses and businesses without wall to wall security and expensive security guards. Even so, with the best that money could buy, they were still being robbed."

"Shame."

"Yes. Fortunately, technology itself came up with the solution."

"Yeah?"

"Yes. Now I don't pretend to understand the science but in the last couple of years it's become commonplace, and very cheap. Almost everybody, above the underclass of course, has it now and there's little left for the burglar to burgle. Once again the rich and famous can sleep soundly in their house in the South of France knowing that their houses in London and Rio and Paris etc. etc. are perfectly safe."

Geoff Brent twisted in his chair. "Nothing's that safe. There's always some way to break in." He noticed the sardonic smile creasing Carter's face. "Or so I'm told."

"That may have been the case twelve years ago but you cannot break into a building that is not there."

"What do you mean?"

"NDS. New Dimension Security."

"What's that?"

"From the consumer's point of view a simple little device. Rather like a remote control for a television but with unique encoding for each item you wish to protect. You point it at your house or office block, press a button, and hey presto, it's gone. Press another button and it's back."

"What do you mean, gone?"

"Gone. Vanished. No longer there."

"How does it do it?"

Carter shrugged.

"That's what I don't fully understand. Very few people do. They'd been working on it in secret for some years before you went down. When I got involved with this, the scientists at the firm who make these black boxes said that the simplest explanation they could make was that the buildings slide at right angles to our familiar dimensions and wrap themselves round into several other dimensions. It's something to do with Parallel Universes." Carter waved his hand and turned away as if embarrassed that he had to admit a lack of understanding. "All you need to hold on to is that the building vanishes. And since it's not there, nobody can burgle it. Quite neat I think you'll agree."

Brent got up and walked to the window too. He gazed out across the tower blocks.

"It doesn't look any different to me out there. Shouldn't there be open areas where all these buildings have been zapped?"

"There are a few, but it's at night when the effect is best seen. If we looked out then it would seem as if London had been largely wiped out with just those places that stay open all night protruding.

It's quite peaceful and dark too. They save on electricity as well. It's a really cost-effective device. Made the inventors a fortune."

"I bet."

Brent sat down again.

"So what's all this got to do with your favour?"

Carter chuckled and joined Brent in the easy chairs. He poured a glass of water.

"They've hit a problem."

"No, really."

"Yes. The manufacturers do a lot of routine monitoring of these devices to make sure everything's working properly. They have several test sites, for example, where everything is wired up for intensive study. Everyone wants to be the first to find out where all the buildings actually go. One of the things they do is weigh the building before and after the switch. And when I say they weigh it, I mean they weigh it. If you left a feather inside and it wasn't there when you went back in, they'd know all about it."

"And?"

"Well, ever since they started, they've been detecting weight losses. Very small amounts, almost zero in some cases. Not every building and not on every occasion but enough to get everybody worried. Apparently there's no way there should be any loss at all. Everything should come back exactly as it went. And it doesn't."

Brent ran a hand around the back of his neck. For someone who had been asleep for twelve years he was feeling suddenly very tired.

"So what's missing?"

"They don't know. They've checked everything they can think of. They've obviously put monitoring devices and TV cameras inside during transfers but they just don't work. They're stumped. They've taken full inventories and everything always comes back but the fear is that some smart operator is somehow working on a way to crack the security."

"Well, I did say there was always some way to break in, or so I'm told."

"It is a possibility. One that we need to investigate. If news of this gets out it would severely damage the industry and reintroduce a lot of security problems that governments round the world had thought were a thing of the past."

"What makes me think that I'm beginning to work out what this favour is?"

Carter chortled.

"I always said you were smart."

* * *

Now they stood in the control room opposite ESMRG Electronics, a building used as a testing ground by NDS Industries. Each place Brent went became ever more comfortable and, apparently, ever less secure. He felt a little as if he were on a runaway train. It was now going too quickly to jump off.

Dr Fenton, chief scientist on site, blew his nose in an embarrassed manner.

"So that's why we suggested a convicted burglar, Mr Brent. We felt that your experience and inside knowledge might be helpful in tracking down whatever is happening overnight when the buildings have transmigrated. Mr Carter suggested you might be the man for the job."

Carter simpered. "I thought of you immediately Geoff."

Brent considered the two thoughtfully. Carter was obviously enjoying himself enormously; Fenton was not.

"I rather think you haven't woken me from my prison term and offered me release just to give you a few pointers on how a thief is breaking into your building when it isn't even here."

Fenton looked startled. "No, of course not." He turned in some confusion to Carter. "You mean you haven't told him?"

"I think he knows."

"Yeah, I know," said Brent quietly. He stared at the building now dazzlingly bright in the setting sun. "You want me to go in and see what happens when you zap it, right. You want to flatten me into some other dimension and come back and tell you that some little green mice are coming in and spiriting off computer chips."

Fenton blew his nose again. "In essence, yes. The green mice are rather fanciful but something strange is happening and we need to know what it is. I must stress this is entirely voluntary. If you don't want to do it..."

"You go straight back to sleep," said Carter.

* * *

There was an air of tension around the control room as they prepared for the test. Brent had the feeling that this was normal. Although the trans-dimensional migration was now commonplace around the world it still seemed just too unreal to accept, even by those who had some idea how it all worked.

Fenton and an assistant hovered over a console while Brent gazed at the building. Carter remained silent in the background. An intercom announced that the building was clear. A hooter sounded four sharp notes.

"Right," said Fenton, "here we go. Watch closely, it all happens rather suddenly."

As commands were tapped in, the solid building seemed to dissolve and twist in the air; and was gone. In its place was a flat swathe of ground with the foundations and various pipes and cables revealed as if they had been smoothly sliced away by a sharp knife.

Brent blinked and shook his head.

"I didn't really believe you."

"It is weird isn't it" murmured Fenton.

"And you don't know where it's gone?"

"Well, it can be explained in terms of some very complicated mathematical models but on the human level, no. No idea."

"What about the pipes and stuff? I mean if a gas pipe were chopped it would be leaking wouldn't it?"

"No, not so. Remarkably the pipes, and indeed the brickwork, appear to remain connected to the building in its trans-migrated state. We cannot see the gas pipe any more but, apparently, it remains intact. All the mains services are the same but there is no contact possible through to the building."

"So we can't phone you when you're in there," chuckled Carter.

Brent tried to ignore him. "Tell me more about these animals you've sent."

"Lots of different species have been used. We've been doing it as a matter of course, even before any weight loss problem was detected. We started with insects and then on up to birds, dogs, monkeys. Absolutely no problem. They seem perfectly fine."

"But you can't monitor them while they're in there?"

"No. And any devices we've attached to do telemetry also don't work, just like the general measuring equipment we've put in. We've got no idea what happens in there. It really will be most interesting to get your report."

"Yeah, won't it just."

Carter clapped his hands. "OK, let's get it back and get on with it. Sooner the better, eh Geoff?"

"Yeah I guess so."

Fenton and his assistant turned once more to their controls. The hooter sounded again and a confirmation came in that the site was clear. Before Brent's still-startled eyes the building corkscrewed back into place.

"It just slots straight back. It's uncanny."

Fenton nodded. "There have been one or two problems with some retrievals. Not in this country. But occasionally there seems to be a slight displacement upon return and the foundations give way."

"They give way?"

"Yes." Fenton scratched his chin uneasily, realising too late that perhaps this was not a good subject to raise. "As I say it's very rare and it's never happened here. The suspicion is that the transmigration equipment is not quite aligned properly. As with all these hi-tech products you get rogue copies which aren't really safe. I can assure you all our equipment is very well-maintained. Some other countries are perhaps not so fastidious."

"What happens when they give way?"

"Well, I'm afraid the building collapses."

Carter broke in. "Don't worry about it Geoff. As Dr Fenton says it'll never happen here. It's as rare as an air crash."

"I was in an air crash once," remarked Brent bleakly.

"Well there you are then. The chance of being in two air crashes is infinitesimal isn't it? Now come on, let's get on with it."

"OK," said Fenton, "Let's get you into a survival suit, just in case, you understand. As this is the first test run we want you to have full protection with oxygen, emergency supplies, telemetry and so on."

"In case the mice run off with you," grinned Carter.

Brent continued to ignore him. "Did you put the animals in survival suits?"

"No, no, and they were fine, as I said. This is just a precaution. If the first run goes well and there are no problems you can try again without the suit, which will give you more mobility. But we must take every precaution on the first run."

"I thought telemetry didn't work."

"I doubt if it will but again we may as well try."

"Good." Carter slapped Brent on the back. "Come on then, let's get you into that suit."

As the three left the control room Fenton turned to study the data on his consoles from the previous migration. He looked worried and switched on a tape recorder.

"Fenton here. We are about to do the first human test. I'm looking at the data from the last run. I have a recorded weight loss of 4.2 kilograms. As usual, the computer can find nothing missing."

He flicked off the machine and leaned forward heavily on the desk, staring at the inscrutable building.

* * *

About an hour later Geoff Brent was escorted into the building by security guards. He was wearing a cumbersome suit. Accompanying him, unencumbered, was a parrot in a cage. Carter insisted on going along to make sure his man was safe.

When everything checked out he leaned close to Brent's helmet.

"Don't try anything Geoff. The place outside is crawling with bureau personnel. You'd never make it."

Brent placed a rubber gauntlet on Carter's arm.

"I've been wanting to ask you… have you seen Mary since I've… been asleep?"

"A couple of times yes."

"Is she OK?"

"She's very well."

"Can I see her?"

"Of course you can. After the test."

Carter removed his arm.

"See you later."

* * *

As Carter and the guards left, Brent felt the sweat trickling around the suit. He gazed at the parrot which seemed quite unconcerned. Fenton had told him the parrot had been there before and this fact was, indeed, quite a comfort, as Fenton had intended. His radio burst into life.

"Fenton here Geoff. Are you OK?"

"Sort of."

"Are you quite sure you want to go ahead? You have every right to pull out."

"I'm not at all sure, no, but I am sure I don't want to go back to sleep so pull the switch Prof. Me and Polly are go for launch."

Fenton chuckled but there was clear tension in his voice. "Right. We're doing a minimum run time of thirty seconds. That's as short as we can manage. Stand by and good luck."

The hooter sounded and man and parrot vanished.

* * *

Brent was surprised when the radio crackled again.

"Fenton here. Brent are you OK?"

"Yeah."

"Thank God for that. The guards are coming in."

"What do you mean? What happened? Aren't we doing it now?"

"Doing it? You've done it!"

"What?"

The guards arrived and bustled him out for tests before he could enquire further. The parrot watched lugubriously.

* * *

"So you didn't see anything?" Carter sounded suspicious.

"No. I tell you I was just sitting there, looking at the parrot and then Fenton came on the radio again. There was no sound, no movement. I didn't see anything. Nothing appeared to happen.

Fenton frowned. "Well, you definitely migrated, albeit for only thirty seconds. You've had two days of tests and these medical reports show no problems. I can only assume that everything was so normal you simply didn't realise anything had happened."

"So in that case we're clear to go again," said Carter. "No time like the present I always say."

Brent protested. "Hey, what about seeing Mary? You said I could see her after the test."

"You'll see her when I say so. If you don't like it you can go back where you don't want to be. Got it?"

The two glared at each other. Fenton coughed with embarrassment. "Right, let's prepare for a longer test this time."

Brent glowered. "How long?"

"We thought a ten minute run would be suitable next, again in the suit. That would give you time to move around the building and look out the windows. Following your report on that we thought an hour for the third run, unsuited. Then, if all continues to be normal, a full night."

"A full night? By myself?"

"Yes. It should be safe if we have completed the first three tests."

"Should it? Well, if it is, then I expect some of you guys would like to come in with me. We can take different floors and really scout around."

Carter shook his head. "Forget it Geoff. This is your trip. You're expendable."

Brent clenched his fists. The experiment had stressed him more than he cared to admit.

"So when can I see Mary?"

"She's on her way."

"When will she get here?"

"It's quite a trip. She lives in the States now."

"The States?"

"Yes. But she'll be here. Now let's get that suit on again."

* * *

This time it was different. Brent sat, and sat. He was motionless. He could move not one muscle. He could hear nothing. He could feel nothing. And all he could see was the parrot. That was where he had been looking as the building switched over and that was where he remained looking. He could not move his eyes. He could not blink. He just stared fixedly.

No less fixedly the parrot stared back.

* * *

Brent slammed his fist on the table again. "I tell you I was there for more than ten minutes. It was bloody hours! I couldn't move. I couldn't do a damn thing." He was shaking, trembling, his eyes twitching and blinking continuously as if making up for lost time.

Fenton spread out his arms. "Please Geoff, calm down. I know you distrust Mr Carter but I am telling you the truth. You were over for exactly ten minutes. No more, no less. I can show you the logs. It's obvious from what you've said that you had a frightening experience. If, as it seems, you had no movement or sensation once migrated then you would have had almost total sensory deprivation. That is devastating. Ten minutes may well have seemed like hours but it was only ten minutes. Trust me."

Brent's hands moved disjointedly. He clutched his hair, shirt collar, slapped his sides. His breathing was rapid. "Well, that's it. I'm not going in there again. That's it."

"Get some rest," said Fenton softly. "We'll talk again later."

He watched sympathetically as Brent was led shambling away to a rest room.

"He's right. We can't pursue the human observer approach any further."

Carter smiled unpleasantly. "Of course we can."

"But..."

"Don't be fooled by him. I know Geoff Brent. He's acting."

"The psychologists don't seem to think so."

Carter sniffed with the air of a man who had little to say for psychologists.

"He's a lifer. A con-man. He used to work at the bureau and stole from our clients. He's just pretending to be shaken up. OK, so he can't move for a few minutes. What's the problem? He shouldn't be in this state. He's faking it."

Fenton frowned. "It does seem strange that such a short time should have had such a bad effect but, if he is faking, he's doing it very well."

"He would do. He's a great con-man. Believe me. Get him in there again. You can talk him round. But this time let's get him sitting somewhere where he might see something interesting, like next to a window. I think even I might crack up if I had to stare at that parrot all the time."

* * *

Brent sat trembling by a window on the top floor. This time he had no suit, just headphones for the radio link. He stared down at the distant streets filled with traffic, dust and noise. The radio clicked. It was Fenton.

"Ready to go again Geoff."

Brent grunted. He felt sick.

"Remember we're only going for five minutes this time. That's all, I promise. Now are you looking out the window?"

"Yes."

"Good. Hold that view. Remember you'll only see what you are looking at as we switch. So don't blink!"

"No."

"OK, here we go. Good luck. See you in five minutes."

* * *

Brent stared at the ground. As he watched, the streets vanished and a new view opened up like land appearing from between clouds thinning below an aeroplane. It was sea. A mighty green ocean, an unreal green, an unearthly colour. Hanging impossibly above the foam-topped waves was the building he was in. It was on a slight slant such that he could see all the way down the various floors to the base of the foundations. As he watched he saw waves break against the concrete base. They broke again and again. As Brent continued to gaze the waves continued to rise, break and fall. Beyond his fixed vision other buildings flickered in and out of this strange scene like fireworks, some higher, some lower, almost in the water. Most were transient but a few persisted. The one in which Geoff Brent sat persisted longer than most...

* * *

Carter was pacing up and down. He stopped and looked at Fenton who was watching the computer screens with his assistant, Baker. "I never asked you. Have you had any weight losses on the last runs?"

"The first one, yes. The one we demonstrated to Brent. That was very large. 4.2 Kilos. But the last two, nothing at all."

"Weird."

"Very."

Carter gazed out of the window. "Still, I've had difficult cases like this in the past. You just have to keep hammering away. Eventually you crack it. Everything becomes clear if you just give it enough time."

Fenton started and stared at him. Slowly a look of sheer horror spread across his face. He turned to the computer, his fingers flying over the keys.

"The Foundations", he gasped. "Quick, Baker, stop the test. Get him out of there."

Baker looked up, startled.

"But Dr Fenton, we're only four minutes in."

Carter grabbed Fenton's arm.

"What's the matter?"

Fenton struggled against the stronger man to lever his arm away.

"You said it," he almost screamed. "Don't you see? It's time! Time is not the same over there."

"What?"

"That explains the weight losses."

"How?"

Fenton panted breathlessly.

"Time is not the same over there. In fact it may even be random. On one day you get no weight loss on a long run and another day you get a huge loss on a very short run."

"But I don't see..."

"It's erosion... don't you see? When you have a really long time period, the buildings get slowly weathered away. That's why nothing's ever missing. Nothing's being stolen, we're losing mass off the buildings' foundations. We never thought of looking there. It explains the collapses too. Don't you see?"

Baker now also looked white. Fenton escaped from Carter's loosened grasp and grabbed the controls.

"Four minutes," he muttered, "or four million years."

* * *

The rescue crew reached him quickly. He was still seated by the window, looking down. There were cars there again now, not the insistent green sea. But he didn't know that. He didn't know anything any more.

* * *

Fenton sat with his head in his hands. Carter looked thoughtful. Baker abstractedly stirred some coffee around.

"My God," whispered Fenton. "What must it have been like?"

"Like being awake on a Death Bed I suppose."

"A living death. And now still alive. A vegetable. And I promised him it would only be five minutes." Fenton looked up. "What will you tell Mary?"

"Mary?"

"His… he asked about somebody called Mary."

"Oh yes. She's my wife. Or was. Married her a while after he went down. We separated four years ago."

"Oh. I'm… I'm sorry. Is she here yet? You said she was coming."

"I lied." Carter stood up purposefully. "I suppose I'd better go and get another one off his Death Bed."

"What?"

"Well, we still don't know what he saw out of the window. We need to know that and if we're lucky enough to get a shorter crossing we should be able to find out. There's too much money riding on this to give up now."

"But you can't intend..."

"Listen, they're expendable. What happened to him would have happened anyway. He was just awake while it happened. That's all." 🦇

HEARTBEAT

NANCY KILPATRICK

IT WAS THE BEAT that got to him. Now, looking back, Greg tried to reconstruct what had happened, to analyze events. He realized he'd never heard rhythms like that before, not within conscious memory anyway.

It made sense. His roots, at least on his mom's side, were Haitian. But his mother had moved with his Irish father to Canada before Greg was born, and the ties to her culture and history were out of place in the lonely, yellow land of Saskatchewan.

Why they chose the dry, desolate, sparsely populated prairies, Greg did not know. Growing up in the tiny town of Tisdale, 150 miles north of Saskatoon—the small city where he had gone to university—Greg had not encountered music like this, even on the radio. Music that pounded through him as naturally as his heartbeat.

That morning at the harbor, Greg remembered turning, to glance at the glass and chrome skyscrapers behind him. This was his first time in a large city. He came to Toronto a month early for purely practical reasons: to find a place to live, to learn how the streets were laid out, to get organized with the university before starting on his PhD thesis. After breakfast, he'd decided to walk along the flag-stoned shore of Lake Ontario at the south end of the city. Out on the water he saw a long island, with an airport at one end. Expensive cruisers, and historic schooners sailed the water; he snapped pictures of the tall ships on display, with the gulls circling their masts.

Suddenly he realized that over the hours the lakeshore had become crowded. Droves of people headed in the same direction, seemingly drawn by a tinny-sounding music. He could see the parade route two blocks away, something colorful swaying above the heads of the throngs in the distance.

Women, gorgeous women, of all skin colors and ethnic origins, passed him, laughing, dancing to the rhythm of this sound, their long colorful skirts swinging as their hips moved so naturally. Some wore tight jeans or spandex, others shorts. Feet sandaled, midriffs bare, heads decorated with big straw hats or multi-colored bandannas. The men surrounding him seemed relaxed beneath the brilliant summer sun. Black-skinned and white-skinned walked together like brothers. There were Orientals, East Indians, South Americans, and even a few North American natives, all talking and grinning as though the United Nations had declared a day of world peace. It was astonishing to see so many people getting along well, and he decided to walk a little toward the sound to investigate what this parade was all about.

Of course, being a member of the only mixed-race family in Tisdale, a tiny, isolated community, Greg hadn't been aware of much prejudice. He had met with some once in Saskatoon, but then he'd been virtually cloistered there, living on-campus. Still, he read the papers, and subscribed to magazines. He watched the news on TV, and caught the gist of the larger world in movies. By the time he'd acquired his MA in quantum physics, he considered himself worldly. But nothing had prepared him for this.

"You a visitor, yes?"

He turned, startled. A short woman with very black skin walked in step beside him. Her midnight hair held fiery red highlights, strands braided and beaded, and her eyes were an arresting green.

What an odd combination, he thought. Intriguing. A bit unnerving. Her colorful cotton skirt hung to her thighs in front, and to her heels in back, and rustled around her as she moved so gracefully. A rope holding a carved gourd was slung across her chest—he suspected the gourd acted as a purse. A black, red and yellow African cap perched at an angle on her head, and a low-cut top composed of several silk scarves, wrapped and knotted in a creative fashion, allowed her breasts natural movement. He found her attractive but disconcerting.

"I'm... I'm from Saskatchewan," he said, adding, "I'm going to school. Graduate school." He wondered why he felt as shy as a freshman. "What about you?" he managed.

"Me? I be a witch, doncha know?"

The exquisite woman beside him smiled up at him, her knowing green eyes shining, teeth brilliant white, so white that the color temporarily blinded him.

* * *

Greg was aware of leaning against a wooden barrier, pressed in by people behind and on both sides. Across the street were more people, hundreds, thousands, eagerly waiting. Distant music wafted through the air like scent."*Caribana* is an annual event," he heard one woman explaining to someone. "Draws about a million people. Amazing lack of violence, considering the numbers."

He did not recall walking the last couple of blocks. How odd! Maybe it was this humid heat; he was accustomed to dry prairie summers. He shook his head to clear it and took a deep breath.

Across the asphalt, behind a barrier directly in front of him, he saw the gorgeous woman. Their eyes locked. She waved and smiled, her emerald irises glittering in the brilliant sunlight.

He waved back, wondering if he should run over there and join her. He'd like to. But they were together before; how did they get on opposite sides? Maybe she didn't want to be with him.

As a band rounded the corner to his right, the street exploded with sound and movement. Two skimpily-clad women, one black, one white, carried a banner that read "Music Mahn Records Presents:" and the name of their act, "Trinidad-Tobago—Drums of Fantasy."

Three dozen dancers wore silver and gold costumes, both the men and women in short skirts, or string bikini bottoms that exposed quite a bit of flesh. Their tops were shaped like twinkling gold stars. The hats glittered with stars or moons. The lead dancer, encased in a kind of costumed cart on wheels, carried an enormous headdress—half a story high—composed of both stars and a giant new moon in the center. The entire costume was a sky of gold and silver sequins, beadwork and feathers that sparkled and swayed beneath the hot sun.

They danced and thrust forward in the small-stepped style of Caribbean folk dance to the music of the steel band following on a flatbed.

Greg glanced across the street. The green-eyed woman's body gyrated so naturally to the beat. Suddenly she snapped her head in his direction and smiled.

He could not help but grin.

As the band neared, the music became ear-splitting and Greg had an urge to cover his ears. Sound pounded against his eardrums painfully. All around him people danced and strutted and clapped. He had never seen so many grinning fools! Not that he minded people having a good time. But exhibitionism bothered him. It lacked decorum.

He checked his watch. Nearly lunchtime. He had to find a store where he could buy a laptop before Monday.

The sound swelled to nearly overwhelming. He felt pressure in his chest, as though the bass shoved against his heart and forced it to beat at a different rhythm. Greg began to feel afraid. He was not used to this much stimulation. He turned to make his way through the jiggling bodies before the fear could get too much of a grip.

"Don't go. It's not yet begun." She was behind him.

"How did you get across the street?" he blurted.

Her hand lightly touched his arm. The feel of her warm, moist skin on his flesh was electric current through water. Each of her fingernails—well over an inch long—had been filed almost to a point, and painted blood red with jewels imbedded in each nail and he was not at all sure the color wasn't really black. His reaction to what his eyes saw was far different than to what his skin tasted.

When she took her hand away, he felt dismayed by the emptiness that hit in the pit of his stomach.

Her eyes brightened as she pointed one of those daggered-fingers down the street. Another band approached the turn off. The stars and moons band was almost past, and the sound had reached a level he could tolerate. He decided to wait a bit.

She leaned to the left, close up against him, her body both soft and firm. She smelled of exotic sweet flowers, and the scent filled his nostrils, cutting out the odors of ginger beer, meat patties, sunscreen.

Two heads taller, he looked down at her hair flying from beneath the cap that could not restrain it, streaking her smooth dark shoulders. He wondered at the red strands. Of course, women color their hair. The red highlights were probably from a bottle.

She snapped her head around and up. Those green eyes narrowed, and her full lips pressed together tightly. "My mama, she

Irish, my father Haiti. I know the pagan practices from both lands. It make me special. Like you, mahn."

He could only dwell briefly on the fact that she seemed to have read his mind. And that she was going on about this witch nonsense. What startled him was her ancestry, the same ethnic mix as his.

Before he could say or do anything more, she gripped his arm, sending more shocks through his skin that left him speechless. "This band for you," she cried through the increasing sound surrounding them, gesticulating lavishly at the approaching dancers.

As the band turned the corner, the crowd roared. More than with the previous group, these costumes were spectacular on an entirely new level. The dancers, in black and white, each wore a thin two-toned mask, nearly obscured by a hood attached to a long cape. Only the feet shuffling forward to the beat betrayed race, and again it was a mix. Greg wondered how they could stand to wear capes in this heat.

The lead's headdress draped behind in a long train carried on two carts with wheels. It reached higher than the others, at least one story of a building. The crowd went wild, screaming, clapping, cheering, bodies swaying. As the band neared, Greg saw that this masterpiece of a headdress was dotted with many small masks, made from sequins and beads, duplicating the obscured faces the caped dancers wore. Long black and white plumes alternated and movement let these feathers sway and bend like the leaves of a palm tree, or fingers beckoning. Black and white, black and white, black and white. Each mask depicted a different emotion. The opposites glittered and sparkled, the satin shimmered, all of it blended together to weave a hazy world between light and dark, one that had the crowd ecstatic.

The flatbed truck pulled up; steel drums sang and horns blared through ten enormous speakers. "Haitian Drums—Synergize."

As the music swelled, Greg felt almost knocked off his feet. The vibration pounded in his head, his chest. He lost track of his heartbeat, which capitulated to this intense beat. The relentless sun, the scent of exotic flowers, the volume of sound like a tidal wave. Greg felt himself slipping down, slipping away...

Warm flesh curled around his bare arm like five strips of fire. He glanced down and saw the blood-red claws pressed into his skin. The woman with the green eyes smiled in the most seductive way, a smile that visually represented the sound that made his body quake. As sunlight hit those emerald orbs, the dark dots in the center shrank to pinpoints that transfixed him.

Before he could stop her, she pulled him beyond the barrier and into the midst of the dancers.

She faced him, shoulders rotating, hips swaying, head bobbing, her smile luscious. Her body began to undulate. He could not feel his body moving. He could not feel his body at all. But when he looked down, he saw his feet step forward one at a time, imitating the slow shuffle happening all around him.

The music controlled him, turning him into only sound. Around him, the crowd had moved into the street and the line between observer and observed vanished. People of all skin tones trembled violently, as if throwing a fit. Several couples did an erotic dance, a kind of hopping close together, the woman in front, the man behind, their faces joyous as they melded with the music. Before he realized it, he was doing this dance with the green-eyed woman.

Her dark hair with the beaded red plaits whipped his chest as her head snapped back and forth to the beat. The sultry scent of her permeated every pore of his body. He felt her body meet his, from head to toe, as if they were one flesh, not two. It was no longer just the music. He was losing himself, blending, disappearing...

Greg broke and ran!

The music of steel drums dogged him. He tripped and fell, got up and raced down the street, fighting unconsciousness. Another band was turning the corner. He saw the sign "Jamaica—Black/White Mahn/Womahn Reggae" and felt desperate.

People barely parted as he rammed between them, stumbling over curbs, running into traffic to blaring horns, falling onto the grass, getting up, running against the curious faces coming toward him, until finally the crowd thinned.

The sun pressed him down. The air felt dense and he could not breathe easily. He gulped in breaths and felt hot sweat trickle down his face, sticking his clothes to his body. He looked around—he was at the spot along the harbor where he had begun. A semblance of normality was returning. But the music's rhythm that had invaded his chest still beat where his heartbeat should be. And the ringing in his ears cut off the outer world.

He slowed, gasping, wiping sweat from his eyes. His heart did not slow. The steel drums felt imbedded in there, pounding a tinny rhythm that was too voluminous and too fast. This was too much life for him to contain.

A thought gripped him—he needed to get to a hospital. Maybe he was having a heart attack. Or a seizure.

The next few hours were a blur, like a nightmare that leaves a taste of terror afterwards. He remembered hailing a taxi. Sitting in the emergency room. Undergoing an EKG. A young resident, an Oriental woman with ancient eyes, telling him nothing was wrong, handing him a prescription for Adivan. Greg heard the words, "Heat stroke" and "Call your doctor."

The drug helped some. He drifted into a dream, of warm weather and hot physical sensation, his flesh sliding along dark flesh, his lips finding hers. He fell into a place of green pleasure, one that felt like home to him, where he faced himself as surely as if he looked into a mirror, but here he saw his soul, swirling in a pool of erotic energy, alive with desire.

But in the middle of the night, the pounding of his heart jerked him away from the dream. His body vibrated and throbbed. Yet when he looked at his hands, they were not shaking. In the mirror he could see his body was not trembling, although it felt that way inside. His eyes looked desperate, frightened, and he had never felt so alone.

By instinct, with no plan to guide him, Greg made his way to the lakeshore, to the parade route. Traffic gone, the street was eerily silent. Sanitation workers had removed all but the odd sequin and feather. The barriers had disappeared.

Greg did not know why he had come here, but the memory of her drove him, of that he was certain. Above, the moon shone full and expectant. It was quiet enough to hear water lapping against the dock when a boat passed in the harbor, although the ringing in his ears continued. The air felt hot and heavy for this late at night, and a slight mist rolled in off the lake. He caught the scent of flowers and turned.

"What... what are you doing here?" he asked, startled. Delighted. Somehow relieved.

"I live there." She pointed out across the water to nowhere in particular, the surface glinting in moonlight like jewels. "I walk by the water at night, to be calm. You feel the same?"

"What have you done to me?" he blurted out.

The green-eyed woman swayed toward him like a shadow in the night, her eyes dancing with life and passion. With promise. When she reached him, she raised her arms, as if to caress him, but he pulled back.

"You fear me, you fear you, doncha know?" she said softly.

He watched, paralyzed, as if what was happening occurred in slow motion. She unbuttoned his shirt and lay her black palm against his bare chest.

He watched her fingernails make impressions against his skin, and it was as if he could feel her nails enter him and scratch his heart.

Her touch exaggerated the pulse of the muscle on which his very life hinged. Suddenly, the beat of the steel drums settled in again, as strong as it had been in the afternoon.

"Make it stop!" he cried, his chest heaving. Tears spilled over his eyelids; he could not recall the last time he had cried.

"It not stop now, mahn. No, never," she said, moving closer until her body pressed against his. "You grow used to it. This drumbeat, it be your heartbeat, and these tears you weep so sadly, they will seal them beats together. Oh, you get used to it!"

Instinctively his arms encircled her. He inhaled her scent, a memory, a promise of things to come. Her beautiful eyes danced, sparkling like green stars, like the Caribbean ocean, like the Emerald Isle. Like a home he had never known but wanted to claim. Like the color of his steel-drum heart.

CHINGU

TODD SULLIVAN

THE GRAY SMOKE from Kim Jung Hyun's cigarette drifted up from the burning ashes to curl around her neck. She sat opposite her superior, Song Ji Hun, in the Café Bene in Nohyeong Rotary. The days had grown longer as March fell to April, the snowy winter giving way to a rainy spring. Already, it was almost eight o'clock, and Jung Hyun checked a sigh of impatience as she waited for her superior to tell her why he'd called the meeting today.

"The *Gwanlyo* has given you a new assignment." Ji Hun took a slow pull from his cigarette, and turned to look at Jung Hyun as he blew a long funnel cloud of smoke from his nose. "We need a human."

"Ah." She thought about it for a moment, but nothing she'd been told in the last year and a half of her undead life could explain away the comment. Laughter suddenly burst out from a group of high school students behind her. Jung Hyun had noticed them when they'd come in earlier to sit out on the patio in the smoking section. When she'd started smoking in her teens, she would have never been so bold, and she had grown up in Seoul, the capital city of South Korea. On the small rural island of Jeju, she'd been slightly surprised that the kids had decided to flaunt their nicotine habit so.

Most of the tables in the Café Bene were filled, and she and Ji Hun also sat on the wide patio, though in the corner by themselves. It had been drizzling moments ago, but that'd stopped, and the air had been left with a sharp chill. Jung Hyun wore a vest and short skirt with stockings, and with her long black hair falling down her shoulders, she looked like a university student out on a date with the impeccably dressed Ji Hun.

Except she wasn't a university student, and Song Ji Hun wasn't her boyfriend. Taking a deep drag of her cigarette, she asked him, "So what kind of human do we need?"

"The *Gwanlyo* will fill in the details later." Ji Hun took off his fedora, placed it on the table, and leaned in closer as he lowered his voice. "This is tricky business, acquiring a human. You've been given a high level, high risk assignment." He patted her hand as he gave her a bright smile. "You should be proud. The *Gwanlyo* must feel you've excelled in your last tests. Your star is rising, Kim Jung Hyun."

Jung Hyun returned his bright smile with one of her own as she bowed her head to him. What's the angle, she wondered. She glanced at her superior through the strands of her hair, but he wasn't giving anything away. Reaching for a fresh cigarette to have an excuse to withdraw her hand away from his, Jung Hyun lit it as her smart phone jingled. She checked the text message, and when she looked back up at Ji Hun, he reached into his pocket and produced a colorful business card.

"You've never met him, but it's time you did. Set up an appointment with him as soon as possible."

Jung Hyun took the card. A digital image of a tidy little shop appeared on one side. On the other—the address, telephone number, and man's name in blocked yellow letters: Moon Jae

Young—Electrician.

"The *Gwanlyo* has a local mart in Hallim, and the freezers have been disabled," Ji Hun said. "Tell Mr. Moon that it's an emergency job, that the drinks and produce will spoil in days. He'll want to charge more, but don't let him up the price too easily. Ultimately, though, money's inconsequential. Tomorrow evening, you're to open the shop. A key will be left in a slot by the door."

Jung Hyun slid the card into the top of one of her boots, then waited until Ji Hun finished his Americano. She stood when he stood, and he said, "I'll call you later."

They parted after leaving the Café Bene. Wisps of gray clouds hung in the dark sky promising more rain. Jung Hyun went to the corner and hailed a taxi. Telling the driver, "City Hall," she called her best friend, Ha Seung Yeong, who'd texted her earlier, and they set up to meet at the bar, Factory, in twenty minutes.

She got out of the taxi in front of *Shi Cheong's* bus terminal. The city hall area bustled with people and scooters and buses. Uniformed middle and high school students walked the streets in flocks of striped skirts and gray pants, and young adults filled drinking *hofs*. Jung Hyun crossed the major intersection and went down the block and around a corner into a narrow alley. Small *galbi* restaurants ran along the alley, and voices poured out from open doors as patrons fried pork over grills and downed soju from tiny glass cups. The Factory was on the second floor of a two story building. Jung Hyun climbed narrow wooden steps to throw open a heavy door, and entered a dim lit smoky bar. The Factory had a handful of tables, and a small stage.

Jung Hyun took a seat at a small square table against the wall, and ten minutes later, Ha Seung Yeong walked in.

"Oh! You're already here." Seung Yeon sat down beside her and clasped Jung Hyun's hands. "Have you been waiting long?"

Jung Hyun shook her head. "I just got here. So, who's this boy

I'm sharing you with this evening?"

Seung Yeon lowered her head so that her long hair obscured half of her pale face. She had small, sharp features and a very slim build. She could pass for one of the high school students outside if she ever wore her old uniform again. But Seung Yeon had finished high school several years ago, had already completed university, and worked full time at an elementary school as she attended graduate school in the evening.

"Stop being so pretty," Jung Hyun scolded her, playfully punching her in the shoulder, "and just say who he is."

Seung Hyun slapped Jung Hyun's arm back. "You will be so surprised, that is all. I won't tell you anything about him, I just want you to meet him."

"Uh oh."

"What *uh oh*!" Seung Yeon slapped her again. "He is a very interesting guy!"

"I worry about your taste. Your last boyfriend, he was a little possessive."

"Possessive?" Seung Yeon shook her head. "I don't remember him being possessive. What do you mean?"

"Nothing." Jung Hyun smiled even as she kicked herself for saying that. They sat so close that their legs touched, and Seung Yeon's body heat warmed Jung Hyun's cool flesh. Seung Yeon's smell, the berry scent of her hair, the flowery aroma of her facial makeup, made Jung Hyun nestle closer. Beneath the artificial scents were Seung Yeon's more natural ones, the faint musky smell, and of course, the heavy perfume of her blood. Jung Hyun's incisor teeth tingled as she lightly massaged Seung Yeon's wrist, as she gazed at her friend from behind the mask that she wore, the façade all vampires wore when out amongst humans. Jung Hyun's pulse did not quicken because her heart no longer beat in her chest, but something deeper inside of her became inflamed by her lust for her friend's body, by her desire for her friend's blood.

"Oh, there he is!" Seung Yeon said. "You will be nice to him, won't you?"

"Of course," Jung Hyun lied easily.

A dark skinned foreigner had entered the bar, and sitting at the table, said to Seung Yeon with a heavy Dutch accent, "You're so early! Aren't we meeting at nine?"

"Oh, David, not nine o'clock," Seung Yeon replied in English. "Don't you remember, eight-thirty o'clock, not nine-thirty o'clock."

"I'm sure we decided on nine. Ah well, we're all here now. And who is this beautiful lady?" He reached out and took Jung Hyun's hand in a gentle, yet firm grip. "I'm your Romeo."

"Kim Jung Hyun." Jung Hyun noted his solid build and great physical shape for what she guessed was his mid-forties. Quite older than her friend's twenty-three years. David wore an old cap perched on a bald head, and had thin, black rimmed glasses and a nice sports coat that fit his muscular frame well.

"I humbly apologize, I didn't bring a friend," David said, "so it looks like it's just going to be the three of us." He still hadn't released Jung Hyun's hand, and when she attempted to finally break their initial handshake, he held on tighter. With a grin, he asked, "You running away from me so soon, darling?"

"Oh David, no one would run from you," Seung Yeon replied, at which David immediately released Jung Hyun's hand to take hold of Seung Yeon's. His eyes, though, were a bit slower to move from Jung Hyun to Seung Yeon, and when he said, "Why, you're looking lovely tonight," Jung Hyun couldn't tell if he was talking to her or her friend.

"Oh, thank you! Why are you late, are you coming from gym?"

"I'm not late, beautiful, I'm early," and he winked at Jung Hyun. "I was just with a couple of mates at the Indian restaurant around the way. But as a gesture of my sincerest of apologies, first round on me!" And with that, he got up, hustled over to the bar, and came back a moment later holding three foreign beers between the fingers of one hand, and three tall shots cupped in the palm of his other. He placed them all on the table.

Seung Yeon giggled. "Oh, I love Budweiser!"

"Excellent. I love a lady who's easy to please."

Again, Jung Hyun was confused as to whom he was referring, as David's eyes had lingered a beat too long on her as he'd spoken. He put a shot in front of each of them, and Seung Yeon, picking hers up and sniffing, asked, "But what is this?" She wrinkled her nose at the smell.

David put his finger to his temple, a puzzled look on his face. "Tea?" He lifted it up to his nose. "Honey for my sweet ladies?"

"It's tequila," Jung Hyun said.

"Give the Misses a prize!" David held his up, and motioned for the two girls to follow. "Cheers to spending a beautiful night with beautiful ladies!"

They clinked glasses, and David knocked his shot back, with Seung Yeon following suit. Jung Hyun took hers last, and she kept the grimace off her face as the familiar nausea swept through her when consuming anything except blood.

David brought the next round also, three more beers and three fresh shots of tequila. Seung Yeon excused herself to the bathroom, and since the Factory didn't have one inside, she had to go outside and around the corner to the public restroom. After she'd left, David pulled his chair closer to Jung Hyun and took her hands under the table.

"You're quite the mystery." He stared intently at her from behind his black glasses.

Jung Hyun gave a coy smile. "More a mystery than my friend?"

"Seung Yeon is a lovely, lovely girl," David replied. "And extremely bright. She was the top of my class in Comparative

English."

"Ah. You were her professor?"

"Visiting this year from Daegu. But Seung Yeon's not like the rest of the kids. She didn't need me at all!" David gave Jung Hyun's hand a squeeze. "She's a genius at languages, you know. English, Japanese, Chinese, Russian. I think the girl's even on French and Spanish now!" He freed one of his hands to lay it on her knee. "And what are you brilliant at, Kim Jung Hyun?" He gazed deep into her eyes, gazed long and deep, perhaps too deep, and his face went slack as his hand crawled up her thigh.

"My brilliance?" Jung Hyun leaned in closer to David. "Loyalty." And she laughed at the perplexed look David gave her. "It's just a joke. So you're an English professor? Do you tutor privately?"

"Of course, and my hourly fees are reasonable." David sat up straighter, focus returning to his features. "Just give me your number, and we can set something up."

"Of course."

David fished for his phone, and when she'd given him her number, the door to the Factory opened again, and Seung Yeon came back in. "It's drizzling again," she announced, frowning. "So much rain! Why must it always be raining?"

"It'll be clear skies soon enough," Jung Hyun replied as her friend sat back down next to her. "Just wait and see."

* * *

Early the next evening, Jung Hyun showered and changed into a hoodie, black tights, and jean short shorts, the white pockets peeking out from the cut off. She took a taxi down into the Namwon neighborhood, and waited in a Paris Baguette bakery on the next block from a bright yellow apartment building, Mideum

Hanaro. Without any proper description of Mr. Moon, she would have to probe deeper for him. Clearing her thoughts, Jung Hyun slipped into the minds of those around her. She skirted through the scattered fragments of broken images of classrooms, teachers, *hogwons*; offices, deadlines, endless reams of paperwork; tangerine farms, narrow streets, wandering strays. She tensed under the effort of maintaining a normal outward appearance as she surfed through the mental data streamed from the people moving around her going about their daily lives.

A small flatbed truck pierced her thoughts, and she blocked out everything else to focus upon it. In the driver's seat, she saw a man wearing a sports cap. Unusual for Korean men, the man sported a several day growth of bristly gray hairs over gaunt cheeks and an angular chin. The man fell into a fit of coughing, and taking a tissue from a box on the passenger seat, he cleared his throat long and harsh before spitting into it. Tiny clots of blood mixed with the phlegm, and balling the tissue, the man tossed it on his dashboard amongst a collection of wadded tissues. As he reached for a pack of cigarettes in the nook of the passenger seat, he abruptly stopped. Perking up, he looked to his left and right, then peered out the truck window, and Jung Hyun gasped because, across the telepathic link, he seemed to be staring directly at her.

She broke the connection and stood. What was that? She'd never heard of anything like this happening before, and considered calling her *superior*. Why wouldn't Song Ji Hun warn her of what this man was capable of? Jung Hyun frowned. Ji Hun always hid surprises up his sleeve, and she'd walked into yet another one unprepared. Her hands curled into tight fists, her frustration made greater because of the futility of her anger.

Ji Hun wanted her to fail, she knew. But she'd outmaneuver him, figure out this mystery on her own. She watched with normal eyes as Moon Jae Young's blue flatbed truck rolled to the intersection, and after he parked, he got out and entered his shop on the first floor of Mideum Hanaro.

Jung Hyun left the bakery a moment later, and crossing the street to the apartments, stepped up to the door. She steadied herself, preparing for whatever she'd encounter on the other side. When she realized she was grinding her teeth, she forced herself to relax, pulled open the door, and entered the small shop.

Moon Jae Young sat behind a brown desk directly opposite the entrance, and only three short steps placed her right before him. Sparse gray hairs covered his gaunt cheeks, his breathing labored. Heater, printer, air condition, and other machinery parts littered the shelves. A collection of wires and knobs, small and big screw drivers and wrenches, cable cutters and a black solder gun, cluttered Jae Young's desk. A trash bin at the foot of the desk overflowed with wadded tissues, several of which had fallen onto the stained tiled floor.

Jae Young had his cell phone to his ear while he spun a black switchblade on his desk with the other. He nodded at her in acknowledgement, and mouthed to her, *"Jaka mayeon,"* as he raised a finger. Jung Hyun gave a brief smile as she waited. He ended his call, but immediately fell into a coughing fit, and spit a clot of phlegm dotted with blood into a tissue.

"Ashi," he muttered, tossing the wadded tissue onto the pile filling the trashcan. Then he stood and looked at her, his breathing a wheeze in his lungs. "Most people just call for an appointment," he began, his eyes roving around the closet-sized shop. With an apologetic wave, he added, "I don't get many visitors."

"I was seeing my friend upstairs," Jung Hyun lied. "She lives right here in Mideum Hanaro, and she said management recommends you. I am in big trouble. My father's store in Hallim." She shook her head. "The freezers. They are dying."

"Ah, I'm sorry." He fished around his desk, the veins in his hands a blue spider web beneath his pale flesh. Finding an old account book, he grabbed a pen and came around to her. "Tell me where your store's located and when you want me to come out."

Jung Hyun bit back a flinch as he stood right before her, so close they almost touched in the cramped space. As she recited the address Ji Hun had given her, she noticed a framed photo on a shelf behind the chair. She hadn't seen it with Ji Hun sitting. The photo showed a soccer team posing on a game field at a nearby high school. The sun shined brightly on the green grass and the players in their clean white and yellow shirts with black shorts. Studying the picture closer, she realized one of the players to the left resembled Jae Young. He looked younger there, though, healthier, his face clean shaven, his body strong. How long ago was this? At the top right hand of the picture, she saw the digital date embedded in the image. Only a little more than two months ago?

"You smell nice."

Jae Young's sudden comment startled her. He hadn't looked up from his worn notebook, hadn't stopped writing down her information.

"My good friend always told me I have a nose like a hound. You smell like him." Jae Young inhaled deeply and let out a long sigh. "*Ahh.* I haven't seen him around lately."

Color seeped back into Jae Young's face, and the gray at his temples seemed to darken as his greasy hair filled and became thicker.

"The girl you were visiting upstairs was smart to recommend me," he continued. "Most people here on the island don't realize that I went to Kaist University in Daejeon. One of the best technology institutes in the country. I always tested in the top five percent of my class." Pride filled Jae Young's voice, and though he'd stopped writing, he still didn't look away from the notebook. Jung Hyun stared, amazed, as he stood straighter, his body filling out, the wheeze falling from his breathing.

"I was going to go into nuclear energy. Had it all planned out." Jae Young tapped the notebook with the tip of his pen. The blue spider web of veins had disappeared, and his hands no longer trembled. "But then, it just seemed like the best idea to move to Jeju. Fresh air and beautiful scenery. Never really thought too much about the decision before, but I guess I followed my friend here." He shook his head. "Why hadn't that ever occurred to me before?"

Jung Hyun had had enough, and she took a step back away. Yet as she moved from Jae Young, it seemed she took some light away with her, for Jae Young seemed to dim, the blue blushing into his hands, his hair graying, his breathing labored again. He stooped over more, the stronger visage dissipating with her distance.

"Now that I haven't seen my friend in a while," he wheezed out, "I've had so many weird thoughts. So many strange dreams. Bad dreams." His eyes had remained in the pages of the notebook as if glued there. Jung Hyun took another step from him, and at the door, she put her fingers on the handle and pushed it slightly ajar.

"For almost twenty years, he's been a constant in my life." The burden of standing seemed too much, and Jae Young stumbled, catching himself on his desk. "Haven't I been a good friend?" Tears moistened his eyes, slipped down unchecked into his scraggily beard. Jung Hyun took a step outside, her confidence shattered.

"Tomorrow," she said. "I'll see you tomorrow evening."

But she wasn't sure he heard her, and as the door closed behind her, she caught the unmistakable sound of Moon Jae Young sobbing.

* * *

Minutes after Jung Hyun awoke the next evening, the sun having just fallen behind the wide blue ocean surrounding Jeju Island, someone rang her door intercom. The buzzer brayed, and she checked the video link to see Song Ji Hun standing outside. She let him in, and offered him sweet instant coffee. He carried a black leather messenger bag, which he placed on the floor at his feet when he sat down at her table. After fixing two cups of coffee, she joined him, and they sipped the scalding liquid in silence until her superior asked, "When are you meeting with Mr. Moon at the mart?"

Jung Hyun had been waiting for this question. She'd never heard of anything like what occurred yesterday happening before. Ji Hun hadn't warned her, yet she knew he knew the danger. He had to, he knew everything.

Jung Hyun made a pretense of looking at her watch. "In a little more than an hour."

Ji Hun nodded, and took a loud slurp from his coffee. Jung Hyun counted the seconds in her head until she felt the pitch of her voice would be perfectly casual, and then she asked, "So is he a vampire?"

"He's human." Ji Hun spoke simply as if answering a most typical question.

"I'm not sure what I'm supposed to be doing with him." Jung Hyun took another sip of coffee.

After a moment, her superior responded, "You're supposed to have him fix the mart's freezers."

Jung Hyun's hands tightened on the cup. When Ji Hun finished his coffee, she asked him if he'd like another, and he shook his head. She would have thrown him through the window of her five-story apartment if she could, but instead she sat silent until he finally unclasped his messenger bag and withdrew a silver thermos. Several runes emitting a faint protective power had been carved into its surface. Ji Hun spoke soft words as he placed the thermos on the table, and the runes slightly glowed to fade away.

"And now this," Ji Hun said. "The *Gwanlyo* has decided to acquire your human, Ha Seung Yeon. They have been watching her for a while and believe she has the right temperament to serve us in our day needs."

Jung Hyun gazed ahead, her false breathing even, her poise controlled. Her superior stared directly at her, his eyes seeming to peel away layers of her façade as he sought out her reaction. Because of this, she gave him nothing, and pushed her thoughts deeper down into herself, so deep that they fell into a hole where she hoped even Song Ji Hun wouldn't be able to follow.

"What's in the thermos?" She asked.

"Does it matter?"

When she did not respond, he said, "It's blood from the forty-six resident vampires on the island. You're to add yours now, and give it to Ha Seung Yeon to drink. It's already been mixed with several other liquids, and she'll find it quite delicious."

Jung Hyun remembered to blink her eyes, and so did. Outside her apartment, the sounds of humans going about their evening drifted up to her: doors opening and closing on the other nine floors of the building; a truck rumbling by on the street; voices of kids and teens and adults on the sidewalk below, all living their lives without knowledge of the monsters making monstrous plans right above their heads.

"What will the potion do to her?"

"Bind her to us. She'll never learn of our existence, but when we need her, she'll obey." Ji Hun tapped the side of the thermos. "You'll have to give her a fresh dose monthly to keep the effects going. Don't worry…"

"I'm not worried." Jung Hyun's interruption came smoothly, and she realized she meant it as she smiled at her superior again.

"Don't worry," Ji Hun repeated, "she won't notice the difference." He unscrewed the cap and slid the thermos over to

Jung Hyun. With a swift motion, she sliced into her own wrist, and let a stream of blood flow into the mixture until her fast healing closed the wound.

* * *

The small town of Hallim stood about twenty minutes from the central city, Jeju-si. The main road to Hallim went through farms and fields, and *olleums*, tall hills common throughout Korea, dotted the landscape. Jung Hyun found the mart easily, as there were few other buildings around for kilometers. She opened the door with the key stashed in the window, and entered a small store with four aisles filled with candy and chips, ramen noodles, and household items. She went to the back and placed her hand on the soda, beer, and ice cream freezers. The glass compartment doors were room temperature, and she nodded. She had been briefly worried. She'd left her apartment later than she'd expected, and she'd fearing Moon Jae Young would arrive at the mart first and manage to get inside the store to start working. Keys left in easy to find hiding places was a common practice on the island, and someone with his job would have had no trouble discovering where this one had been.

Jae Young pulled up in his blue flatbed truck several minutes later. Jung Hyun stood behind the counter, and when he entered, toolbox in hand, she started to greet him,

"An-yeong-ha-sep-nika," but the word caught in her throat. Jae Young looked worse than before. He labored to breathe, and he moved clumsily, as if he might keel over with each slow step he took. He had made an effort to shave, but obviously it'd been half-hearted, and uneven patches of gray fuzz covered his chin and cheeks. He shuffled over to the freezer, and placing his hand on the glass compartment door, grunted.

"I don't even hear the motor running," he muttered, then fell into a fit of coughing that forced him to place his hand flat on the door to hold himself up so that he wouldn't collapse.

"Do you need something?" Jung Hyun still stood behind the counter watching him, her feet rooted to the spot. Clearing his throat long and loud, Jae Young spit a glob of phlegm and blood onto the floor, then rubbed it away with the heel of his shoe. Jung Hyun grimaced, her stomach twisting.

"Pardon me," Jae Young muttered, and knelt down to the belt fans at the foot of the freezer to pry loose the panel with his black switchblade. Peering at the machines with a thin flashlight, he asked, "Do you mind if I smoke?" He sat back up to look at Jung Hyun, who nodded. Fishing a pack out of his pocket, he shocked her by offering her one.

"No, thank you," she started to say, but Jae Young motioned for her to join him, his bloodshot eyes locked on her face.

"I can smell it on you. I know you smoke." He offered her a reassuring smile with crooked brown teeth. Biting the bottom of her lip, Jung Hyun nodded politely and went around the counter to take a cigarette. She kept as much distance as possible between them as he lit it. Then she crouched down several paces from Jae Young while he lit his.

He took a raspy inhale from his cigarette, and asked, "You been smoking a long time?"

"Since high school, I guess."

Jae Young barked out a laugh, and blood stained spittle flecked his ashen lips. "I guess we all start in high school. I didn't really get going until compulsory service in the army, though. Great time to pick up lifelong habits."

"Well, no army for me," Jung Hyun said with a smile, which Jae Young returned. "My best friend in high school smoked. She's the one that got me going. Whole groups of us would sneak off into the bathrooms between classes for cigarette breaks."

Jae Young barked out another laugh. "The teachers never caught you all!"

Jung Hyun shrugged. "They knew. If they found us with cigarettes or lighters, they'd confiscate them and give us a solid beating with the rod. My friend had a knack for never getting caught, but me." Jung Hyun shook her head at the memory and rubbed her backside. "I guess I wasn't so clever."

"Friends," Jae Young said. "They'll lead you to Hell if you let them."

The comment caught Jung Hyun off guard, and she came out of the past to glance back at Jae Young. He'd inched closer as they'd talked, and now she almost leapt away in shock, but training to maintain the façade of being human instinctively kicked in. The years had melted from Jae Young, and he gazed at her with clear eyes, his hair full and black, his body strong and muscular. He looked at his hands, opening and closing them in amazement.

"Why?" He whispered, and caught Jung Hyun's eyes, but she couldn't offer him an answer that'd make sense. Ultimately, it seemed he didn't need one. Face contorting with desire, Jae Young scooped up the switchblade and lashed out at Jung Hyun with the quickness of a vampire.

Jung Hyun barely managed to twist from his attack so that instead of her throat being ripped from ear to ear, Jae Young only caught her on her left side of her neck. The blade sliced through a major artery, and blood sprouted from the gash. Jung Hyun issued a pained gurgle as Jae Young flung himself on top of her. He fastened his lips on the gaping wound.

Jung Hyun struggled under him, but with each gulp he took, she felt him become stronger as she weakened. She beat on his back and sides, but her blows were futile.

Jae Young moaned long and low with pleasure, his body

grinding against hers, his legs intertwined with hers. He shivered uncontrollably, and Jung Hyun felt the multiple orgasms course through his body like a heartbeat, one after another after another.

Almost like a lover, Jung Hyun reached her hands up to Jae Young's face as her sight dimmed. She touched his chin, ran her fingers up his cheeks to his closed eyes. With one last desperate act, she shoved her thumbs under his lids and gouged out his eyes.

A howl erupted from Jae Young as he fell back from her, his palms pressed tight against his face. He crashed into the freezer, shattering the glass. Still he screamed as he threw his body back and forth, and Jung Hyun dimly feared that someone might hear him though their closest neighbor was at least a kilometer away.

Jung Hyun struggled to sit up, but the gray world spun round and round her, and for a moment all she could do was flop around in the pool of her blood.

Finally, she just dragged herself across the tiled floor towards Jae Young, who still screamed, his tongue extended from his wide open mouth. Picking up the switchblade, Jung Hyun focused her strength, then plunged the knife right below Jae Young's ear and ripped it down to his collar bone. His cries abruptly cut short into a strangled gurgle, and Jung Hyun immediately slashed the other side of his throat, from ear to collar bone, leaving him almost decapitated.

With a fatigued sigh, Jung Hyun bent down to drink from the now silent Moon Jae Young.

* * *

Two days later, Kim Jung Hyun stood at her window looking down at the city streets spread out below her. She wore a gray miniskirt, her legs bare, and a black and red long sleeved shirt. K-pop played from her laptop speakers. On her table sat two crystal glasses and a bottle of wine that she'd filled with the potion from the thermos. She waited, counting down the seconds in her head.

She'd called Song Ji Hun after she killed Moon Jae Young, and told her superior that she needed assistance in cleaning up the mart. Another vampire would come by to help, he'd said, and though he'd seemed like he wanted to get off the line, she had abruptly asked him, "The *Gwanlyo* had stopped giving Mr. Moon the potion, hadn't they? That's why he was dying."

"He wasn't dying." On the other side of the line, Ji Hun took a drag of his cigarette. "Not yet, anyway. He was going through withdrawal. But he needed to die, which is what your assignment was."

Jung Hyun had kept her voice emotionless, refusing to allow her superior to know how furious she was. "Why didn't you tell me?"

"Jae Young had become too proficient at picking up thoughts. Especially from us. Perhaps the binding had become too close over the decades. We don't know for sure. But if you had known why we sent you to him, there's a good chance he would have picked it up and ran. And if he ran..." Ji Hun took another drag of his cigarette. "It would have been very difficult to locate him. He would have been loose in the mortal world with power unchecked by us. We couldn't allow that to happen."

Jung Hyun could almost see Ji Hun shrug wherever he was that night. "So we didn't."

Staring out the window today, Jung Hyun swore to herself as she had after getting off the line with Ji Hun. *Bastards!*

The intercom buzzer in her apartment rang, and she jumped, startled, even though she'd been expecting it. Composing herself, she looked in the mirror one last time before going to the door and opening it to a widely grinning David.

"Wow," he gushed, his eyes going up and down her body. "You look marvelous! Absolutely stunning!"

Jung Hyun smiled, but before she could step out of the way, David entered, brushing his body against hers. Jung Hyun bit back a scowl, and simply bowed to him. "Thank you," she replied in English. "Please, sit down."

"Well, what do we have here?" David motioned to the wine and glasses set up on the table. Turning to Jung Hyun, he gave her a sly wink. "We are here just to study, right?"

"Of course." She flashed a coy smile, and sat down in one of the chairs. David briefly checked out her legs as her skirt rode up when she crossed her legs, and with a grin, he sat down opposite her. Jung Hyun uncorked the wine, and poured two glasses.

"So what do we toast to?" David lifted his glass, and she followed suit.

Jung Hyun thought for a moment before saying, "Friends?"

"Friends." David brought the wine to his nose and sniffed. "Friends," he repeated. "They'll lead you to Hell if you aren't careful."

Her grip tightened slightly on the crystal stem at those last words spoken out loud. *"What?"* She hissed.

"Kim Jung Hyun." David put down his glass and leaned in towards her. All pretenses fell from him as he stared directly at her from behind his black rimmed glasses. "We've been proud of you so far. The *Gwanlyo* gave you this high level assignment because we thought you could handle it, and you were doing so well. But to do this." He waved at the wine bottle containing the potion in disgust. "If I had been human and you'd given this to me, you would have not only infused me with power, but you would have also driven me insane. Only exceptional humans are ever offered the gift of either becoming a vampire, or being bound to vampires."

Jung Hyun couldn't stand his hardened gaze, couldn't deal with the way he looked at her, all false lust expelled from his expression. She turned away to keep her tears from showing, and looked out her window at the dark city.

"I can't do this to Ha Seung Yeon," she whispered. "I can't condemn her to Moon Jae Young's fate."

"You don't have a choice." David shook his head. "Like you, we started watching her not long after she was born. In time, we determined her to be too weak to become a vampire, but she could still be bound." David paused. "She *will* still be bound."

David leaned back in his chair, lit a cigarette, and slid the pack across the table to Jung Hyun. "This violation of a *Gwanlyo* directive muddies your, up to now, stellar record. You will rectify this. You must."

Kim Jung Hyun hadn't cried in a year and a half, not since they made her into the beast she was today. Yet now, as she thought of her *chingu*, of her friend, her tears slipped down her face to stain her pale flesh red. 🦇

BEAUTIFUL THINGS

ANTON CANCRE

PREPARING FOR DEATH is easy. It's the one thing we are guaranteed, something programmed into every molecule right on down to our DNA. It's even easier in the face of Armageddon. When the outcome is inevitable, all you have to do is lie back and let it happen. You walk out into a field of groping, moaning, tearing rot and just hope it won't hurt nearly as much as you know it damn well will. You stop struggling and surrender yourself to something you can't fight and it all goes away. The hard part is figuring out how to live.—*excerpt from a journal found on a body during Cleanup and Reclamation.*

* * *

"Why the hell are you doing this, Frank?" Tim asked. Five minutes outside and the sweat was already running rivers down his face, filling in the crevices and cracks that lined his eyes and mouth. If anyone thought to ask, he'd have given just about anything to get back into the house where there was at least some shade. Anything but this. "You know he's gone. Been this long... one way or another, he's out of your reach. You *know* that."

"Don't know what you're talking about, Timmy, old boy," Frank said, with a smile that didn't completely touch his lips, let alone reach his eyes. Unable to meet his old friend's gaze, he focused on his fifth cataloging of items in his backpack. "I'm just going to do some reconnaissance, see how far out I can get from here before running into too many of the bastards. Pick up some extra supplies if possible. Maybe meet up with another group like ourselves."

"Don't 'Timmy Old Boy' me and don't for a second think I'm falling for your bullshit. He did a damn fool thing and now you want to feed yourself to whatever stinking, shambling piece of shit happens to stumble across you out there because of it? I'm telling you, let him go."

"I can't," Frank said, "He's my son, dammit. The only job I have, the only one that ever mattered, is to look after him and I failed. I failed him, I failed whatever is left of the memory of his mother and I failed the most basic functions of nature. I fucking failed," Frank's voice finally cracked, eyes filled with more water than it seemed possible. Great gleaming lakes teeming with anger, guilt and fear threatened to break and drown the world.

Tim didn't bother responding. Instead, he relaxed, waiting for the silence to fill itself in. Sometimes you had to let a man have his say, get it out of his system, and then hope he would listen to reason.

"Did I ever tell you about the night I finally decided to leave the house?"

"Yep. Wife dead, then not. Growl. Moan. Bite. Screams, crying and eventually a crushed skull later convincing you that it was time to take the kid for a road trip. I don't want to sound calloused, but we've all told our tales enough that I could recite everyone's verbatim."

"I didn't tell you everything."

The only thing Frank could feel was a numb throbbing in his foot. Everything had taken on a cloudy haze, like he was living in a Lifetime movie of the week. His heart was beating far too fast. His head was pounding. The house was dead quiet but there was too much internal noise for him to focus. A muffled thump at his right caught his attention and, after what seemed like a Herculean struggle against the independent will of the muscles controlling his eyes and neck, he noticed a malformed lump shining dimly in the scant light.

Whatever it was, it was squat, lumpy and of a shape that vaguely suggested some long lost intention of roundness. The irregular turquoise gloss, bare clay randomly showing through like bits of exposed bone, caught the light filtering in through the slats in the boarded up window.

Finally, something his mind could wrap itself around: a present from Johnny, a school project from earlier this year when the schools were still open. But he didn't remember the bottom of it being so dark, almost black. Mind still too fuzzy, too empty to be sure.

He could remember the first time he had seen it: a mutated aberration as heavy as a Volvo and just about as ugly. Then there was Johnny's face, twisted up in a mixture of anger and shame bespeaking the end of all that is good and pure in existence. The boy had wanted to destroy it on the sidewalk right there, though Frank was pretty sure it would have done more damage to the concrete than vice versa. In swooped Eileen, stern face carved in granite, sharply demanding that he do no such thing before settling into a dissertation on abstract art and the importance of imperfection as the highest form of beauty. Any mother could placate a sad child with smothering hugs and sloppy kisses but nobody could commit to a line of bullshit like she could and Johnny fell for it whole-heartedly.

On her next birthday, it held a place of honor in the middle of the dining room table.

Now that table was in pieces around the room and as much as he needed to get up off the floor, he couldn't. Couldn't pick himself up. Couldn't move. What good would it do? Everything was falling apart out there. The repeated assurances that, as long as everyone remained in their homes, the authorities would sort it all out weren't worth the gas they were propelled on. He'd always laughed at the unwashed, dreadlocked buffoons that constantly circled the Plant screaming about the end of humanity's reign on earth, but it looks like they were right all along.

When he had come down to investigate the moans, he was struck by the raw, gamey stench that rolled in waves from the dining room/kitchen combo at the back of the house. None of them had bathed for far too long, but only an idiot and a dead man could mistake sweat and dirt for the slaughterhouse reek of fresh spilled blood. Running into the room, he almost slipped ass over teakettle in the thick crimson pool on linoleum that had always been a bitch to keep white and never would be so again. His immediate thought was that one of them had broken in, that the boards and scrap wood scavenged from furniture had been no match for the patience of something with nothing else to lose. He had to get Eileen and Johnny the hell out of there before more caught on and their sanctuary became a sepulcher.

Then he noticed the writing on the wall.

These things were sloppy eaters, there was no arguing that, but he had never known one to take the time to write 'sorry for the mess' in blood before. He recognized the ragged haircut on the groaning monstrosity that had started shuffling toward him, even though the hair was the wrong color, no longer the shining gold that always caught the morning sun in its own gleaming furnace. Just yesterday, he had managed to convince her to get rid of those long, flowing locks that hadn't seen a pair of scissors since she was a little girl. She finally agreed that it made far too easy of a hand-hold and they had all seen too many times what happened once one of them grabbed you.

With the thought of that deadly grip in his mind and time compressing around him as if the world was suddenly trapped in drying amber, he noticed that its hands and fingers hung loosely on its wrists. Old Universal Mummy limpness, instead of the usual rigid claws, drawing attention to the torn flesh running from the inside of the wrists up to the elbows of both arms. Even though nothing had managed to breach their defenses, death had wormed its way into the house.

Suddenly as a tiger pouncing from among the high sugar cane, the flow of time returned to normal and the luxury of rational thought was beyond him. Running on instinct alone, he grabbed the nearest sturdy object and began pounding. Untrained, undisciplined, no style or form whatsoever. A flurry of fear and rage over before he truly understood what was happening.

That had to have been hours ago; long enough for the sun to start its morning crawl over a lost world. Half the night spent standing in the same spot, staring emptily at anything except the mess on the floor directly beneath him. He wasn't sure if he'd been crying or if it was just blood drying on his face but he knew there was a choice being made here. Perhaps it already had been. He took one last look down at the piece of Avant Garde and went to get his son.

It was time to get the fuck out of Dodge.

"I know it's a cliché, but then let it be a fucking cliché. He was the only reason I bothered to move from that spot," Frank said. "She had been unfailingly upbeat, constantly telling us it would all be over soon and we'd be able to move on with our lives, but she just couldn't fool herself anymore. That was what cut it for me, what tore the survival instinct right out of my heart: if the queen bullshitter couldn't believe her own line anymore then there really wasn't any hope left. Better to sit there and starve, or even be eaten, than waste yourself fighting what couldn't be fought. I was done.

"But that ugly ass hunk of clay reminded me that I wasn't alone in this. *I* may not have seen any reason to continue, but I didn't have the right to make that decision for *him*. I had to at least try to keep him alive long enough for him to decide his own fate and that's the only reason I'm here today. I owe him my life."

"There are people here that need you, too," Tim said. "Just as much as he did then."

"My ass they do. Never would've made it here in the first place if they didn't know how to take care of themselves. They'll be fine."

"OK. We both know better than this stupidity, but there's no convincing a fool when he's determined. You understand that the only way we're likely to see you again is limping, moaning and smelling like year old Limburger left to ripen in the back of a Pacer in August, right?"

"Yep."

"Then I won't stand in your way. But you're going to wait an extra day and I won't hear any arguing against it. There's no way in hell I'm going to let you leave me alone with those whippersnappers."

* * *

They were working their way down the freeway when they heard the first one moaning. Pretty pathetic display, even for a dead man, but it was enough to put them on guard. With no sightings, Tim and Frank became more paranoid each day. In some ways, they were a bit relieved to hear one simply because the sound let them know where it was.

They held back and waited on top of what once may have been a lime green Ford Escape. Neither of them quite liked being so exposed but at least the highway offered plenty of obstacles to slow down any attackers. Guard rails on the sides would have to be clambered over and the cars piled into and over each other every foot or so provided few paths and set up marvelous choke points. As long as they didn't run into any large hoards, it was workable.

A hundred yards off, he saw them coming. Five. Mobile in their own way, but pretty far gone: not a single hair to split between them, flesh sloughing off in greasy chunks as they squeezed between rusting, jutting pieces of metal. One that Frank certainly hoped had been a woman back when it mattered still wore a moldering, yet screaming red vinyl skirt that cut into the meat of her stomach and legs as she slouched along.

"Would you look at that," Tim exclaimed, pointing out an enormous hulk of a former human being. "I do believe he has a good bit of his large intestine hanging out of his ass. Gonna need himself a hemorrhoid donut."

Worrying about silence once those things started calling out was pointless. Once some started in, any others within range to hear it would follow. At that point, being quiet was just an exercise in stubbornness.

Frank didn't say anything.

Both of them unshouldered a bludgeon. Tim slowly swinging the Morningstar they'd found in an abandoned storefront and Frank's simple, but reliable crowbar hanging lazily by his side.

And they waited.

And waited.

And waited.

Until the first one, the one with a ragged stump of shit-snake hanging out of its ample ass, finally waddled into range.

"I guess it'll be age before beauty," Tim said, dramatically gesturing toward the maggot meals-on-wheels tank.

Swinging in a wide arc, he landed a well-practiced hit into its temple and the results went well beyond his expectations. The grapefruit sized ball hit with enough force to cave in half of the thing's skull and the spikes slid in like butter. The beast slumped to the ground.

Frank, impressed as he was with Tim's skull-o-matic, opted for the straight-forward approach with the tart in red vinyl. As she began to claw and scrape at the side of the vehicle, bits of bone and flesh tumbling beneath her, he shoved the point of Ol' Reliable into her eye socket. With a squelch and a pop, it broke through the thin bone behind the eye cavity and punctured the brain, taking the little light that remained out of her other eye.

When someone has done the same thing enough times, their muscles begin to know what to do before they have the opportunity to consciously think about it. The body acts on its own, doing as it has been trained and too much interference from the brain only gets in the way. One good side effect is that this allows the mind to wander off to ponder any subject it wished. A negative side effect is that the mind tends to enjoy focusing on the things that do the most damage.

"Take a deep breath... Line up your shot. Breathe out slowly and fire," Frank said, shaking much more than Johnny was.

He couldn't help being nervous dragging his son out here among the lost. The roof was clear and the building was long enough to make it highly unlikely that any of them would crowd the back fire escape. As long as they moved quickly once the swarming started, they should be able to miss out on any serious concentration. He'd taken worse risks with Tim and even some of the other youngsters out on scavenging raids without the slightest worry but he couldn't get past the fact that this was his son and he was putting him in danger. If something went wrong, if they had misjudged anything at all and Johnny died out here today, he would have no one to blame but himself.

At the same time, he knew that this was necessary. The days where a man could coddle and spoil his child were long gone. Living forever had never been an option and his chances of making it back seemed to get slimmer each time he left the two-floor, one acre compound they called home. Taking him out into this might possibly kill him, but hiding him behind those walls would definitely do it just as surely as if he had ripped his son's steaming guts out himself. The boy needed to know how to survive on his own out here and training on a dummy could only take him so far. Frank knew well enough the difference between shooting paper targets and taking aim at a wailing, flailing, biting mass of rotted flesh that was once a regular human being. Worse was feeling the throbbing pain pulse up to your shoulder and the wet splatter of old blood and congealed putrescence across your face as you smash a brainpan up close.

"Holy fuck!" Johnny shouted after nailing one directly between the eyes. "Did you see that? I swear that splatter looks just like a butterfly's wing." He giggled just a little before lining up the next one.

Frank was a little surprised by how quickly and easily Johnny was taking to his work. He didn't flinch at the violence or hesitate with any of the worry about the monster's former humanity that had so plagued Frank early on. He also didn't seem to possess any of the malice or hatred that often arose as a way to combat the inevitable guilt. They were just things that needed to be destroyed.

He almost envied his son for having grown up in this world. The boy would never get to see a game at The Great American

Ballpark or marvel at how tiny everything looked from the window of an airplane. He wouldn't have the opportunity to know the feeling of true and complete safety. He wouldn't even get to endure the embarrassment of dancing with his mother at his wedding. But he would never be held back from doing what survival dictated by memories of the way the world once was.

"Lori keeps going on and on about Jackson Pollock paintings," Johnny said while reloading, now having to shout over the growing din of the moaning multitudes below. "I wonder what she'd think of the patterns I'm making."

Watching his son perfectly comfortable in his work, Frank felt a level of pride that disturbed and calmed him. He knew that his time as mentor, coach and father was nearing an end. He also knew his son would be fine.

* * *

"Shit, Frank," Tim said, trying his best to keep from meeting his friend's blank stare. "I don't know what the hell to say. I told you this was a damn fool thing to do."

Frank didn't bother to respond. Wasn't sure he could even if he wanted to. Couldn't breathe, couldn't think straight from the shock. He had finally come to his own personal Armageddon.

They'd been following the signs for about two weeks since their first sighting on the highway. A simple name, destination and date spray-painted directly on the asphalt every mile or so. It was something they had worked out for scavenging runs, a demand drilled into everyone's skulls. The idea was to allow for the possibility of rescue in case of injury or becoming surrounded, giving a search party a regular update on location and travel time. Seeing Johnny's name was a two-fold relief to Frank, not only reassuring him that his son had at least made it this far but also that he was still thinking, despite his temper tantrum. Maybe it meant that he actually wanted his father to come after him. He wanted to come home and stop acting like a jackass.

For some idiot reason, Johnny had gone into the city, the first place everyone with any sense left. A high population crammed into close quarters meant a quick and easy spread, like ripples through a lake. Even if the local hoards had migrated to somewhere else in search of food, there were still the blockades to deal with. Worthless walls, thrown together during the early stages to block off the street, made of whatever crap could be found in the nearby buildings: old mattresses and bed frames, bookshelves, ovens, washing machines, tables, etc. Not only was there no way in hell such a slapdash job could work, but now the materials were mostly rotten or rusted and they posed nearly as much of a risk as the occasional creepy crawly still trapped within.

After squeezing their way through one of these death traps, Frank and Tim had noticed a pulped mass of putrid flesh on the concrete. What they could only guess had once been a human had been utterly destroyed. Bones hadn't just been shattered, but pulverized and what meat remained had been beaten into a thick soup. This wasn't the typical M.O. for a flesh-hungry beast, only your garden variety human was capable of this kind of savagery.

That was when they saw him.

The hair was what clinched it. Who else would wear the long, tightly bound braid of a Chinese monk from the cheesy kung-fu flicks they had watched together so often? Certainly no one else with the delicate blond he somehow managed to get from his mother, glimmers of gold shining through the dirt and grime it had amassed.

Not having sensed their presence yet, he simply stood there. Still, relaxed, probably the calmest Frank had ever seen him. He looked malnourished. Bones jutted at every angle under pallid skin.

He was missing his right hand from the wrist down. Jagged threads of skin and sinew dangled like tinsel from the nubs of bone.

Tim knew what had to be done. No father should have to do this shit, even though they all had. He unslung a dented and crusted aluminum baseball bat, the Morningstar having proved a tad too unwieldy to be practical, and walked towards *it*.

Until he felt a grip as solid as granite on his shoulder.

"I can't let you do that, Tim," Frank said to him as he turned around, locking his gaze with eyes that practically blazed with regret and resolution. He should have known it was going to go this way.

Frank had been on his way to relieve Johnny of the much despised night watch a couple hours early. He couldn't sleep and, after the fight that afternoon, he hoped maybe it would calm the boy down a bit. Besides, they hadn't heard a single moan or scrape for months so it wasn't going to be a particularly stressful watch.

This lack of recent contact was precisely what had started the argument earlier in the day. Johnny was certain that any real threat was over and that it was time to start long-range scouting expeditions in hope of finding other survivors. He wasn't the only one, but everyone else had agreed to wait through the next winter freeze and spring thaw since those processes would speed up decomposition of any remainders out there. Their compound was completely self sufficient thanks to the supreme luck of a working well and a garden fertilized by their new waste disposal techniques. There was no reason to push their luck and risk any more than they had to. But Johnny wouldn't hear it. If they continued to wait, they could be damning another group of holdouts to starvation. They were being selfish.

Frank immediately saw this for the con it was. Johnny felt cooped up. He wanted to get out and meet new people. Mostly, he was horny. He seemed to honestly believe that he would ride into another compound on a glittering white horse to thunderous applause and accolades from women simply dying to get a hold of his cock.

So there had been a fight, with all of the petulance and anger that accompanies any argument with a teenager. Where logic and reason had failed, demands had been laid out in the face of grumbling and pouting and you-don't-understands. He had spent the night locked in his room but had at least gone out on watch peaceably enough.

As Frank began a perimeter walk along the wall, he heard the earnest whispers that could only mean another argument. It came as no surprise to anyone that the teens were the first ones to adapt a form of whisper that conveyed the tone and intent of top-of-the lungs, throat shredding screams. Determined to keep his distance, he stuck to the shadows as he checked out the situation.

As it turned out, Johnny was in a bit of a spat with Lori, the only girl in the compound near his age. When they hit puberty, there had been plenty of speculation about the possibility of a relationship between them, but nothing developed.

"Come on Lori," Johnny insisted, "I just want a kiss. Just for good luck."

"You're so full of shit, J," Lori spit back. "We both know you wouldn't want to stop there. I've told you over and over again: I… am… not… interested. So keep your dick in your pants."

There was no question in Frank's head about what was going on here, but he didn't step in. Sometimes a boy needed to be shot down. What he didn't need was to know that he was being shot down right in front of his old man. Still, boys have been known to do stupid things in these moments, so he wasn't going anywhere.

"Why do you have to be such a bitch about this?" Johnny said, pressing in on Lori's personal space. She was obviously uncomfortable, but holding her ground. There was no room left for any damsels in distress in the world and she had earned her bad-ass wings out there just like everyone else. "I'm the one who always risked his ass while you got to jaunt around on your little shopping sprees. Don't you think you owe me a little?"

That was when he decided to pounce, pushing her to the ground and throwing himself on top of her. Frank couldn't believe that Johnny was actually stupid enough, asshole enough to try something like this. He couldn't let this continue.

But before he could do anything, Lori slammed her elbow into Johnny's nose, breaking it. Taking advantage of his momentary pain and confusion, she pushed herself out from under him and stood up.

"I don't owe you a damn thing," she growled. "I've done my fair share, just like everyone else. Hell, I've killed more of them close up than you have from the safety of your little rooftops. If you ever touch me again, I'll use your nuts to flavor our next soup." After kicking him in the side twice to hammer the point in, she stomped off back toward the house.

Frank didn't know what to do or how to deal with the situation. Behavior like this couldn't stand but now didn't seem like the time to address it. For the moment, Johnny wasn't going to be doing anything and a lecture wouldn't leave nearly the impact of that broken nose. He decided to slink his way back to the house and spend the night considering what to do in the morning. Maybe, given time to think about it, Johnny would realize what he had done and apologize on his own. In the meantime, Frank would leave his son with whatever little dignity he retained.

By morning, Johnny was nowhere to be found. The house was alive with the groanings and mumblings of its residents. He had left no note, no explanation and not much food. The shit had taken about a quarter of it with him on his temper tantrum and he didn't bother to close the damn gate on his way out.

It was time to go through the whole hackneyed bit. Wasting time they didn't have, explaining something both of them already knew. It was pure fucking stupidity, but Tim went ahead with it anyways. What else were friends for?

"Frank, he's not your boy anymore."

"*Tim*," Frank responded, the fury in his eyes dying down to the rough glaze of poorly fired pottery, "he hasn't been my boy for a long time."

The reassuring weight of Ol' Reliable firmly in hand, Frank walked over to meet his son.

THE NEIGHBORHOOD HAS A BARBECUE

MAX BOOTH III

IT WAS JONAH'S WEEKEND, and the neighborhood barbecue was going wonderful. Practically everyone had shown up, except Bryan Campbell, who was still in the shop being repaired. The neighborhood valued Bryan's presence. They eagerly anticipated his return. Surely he'd be up and functioning by tomorrow.

Jonah Watson stood behind the grill, sprinkling lighter fluid on a pile of charcoal. He dropped a lit match onto the rocks and smiled when it erupted into flames. He could only stay there a moment or two before needing to step back and let the grill burn in peace. If he'd stayed there any longer, he'd risk melting the plastic off his face.

Jonah's son, Timothy, was playing a game of Frisbee with his best pal, Henry. Jonah waved at him. Timothy waved back.

"Five minutes," Jonah called. "Then it's time to sit down."

"Okay, Dad!" Timothy shouted, throwing the Frisbee back at Henry. It flew at a rate of two hundred miles per hour. Henry caught it while in the midst of a conversation with his own mother.

Gerald Brown, the man from the house across the street, clapped his hands. "Your boy has one hell of an arm on him."

"Thanks," Jonah said. "He's going to try out for Little League next year. Wants to be pitcher."

"Well, he definitely has the potential," Gerald said. "My own boy was thinking of trying out too."

"Best of luck," Jonah said. "Dinner in five minutes."

He left Gerald standing there on the patio and walked into the house through the back door. His wife, Nancy, was standing at the kitchen counter with her friend, Helga. They were each holding an empty salad bowl, stirring large wooden spoons through the air.

"Honey," Jonah said, "dinner is almost done. I trust you will inform the rest of our guests."

"Of course, dear," Nancy said. She set the empty salad bowl on the counter. "Helga and I will finish setting the table."

"Thank you," Jonah said. "I will join the rest of you shortly. Now I must go use the facilities."

"See you soon, husband."

"You too, wife."

Jonah exited the kitchen and passed a group of partygoers in the living room. They were huddled around the coffee table, simultaneously playing five different board games.

"Hello, everybody," Jonah said. "At the table in five minutes."

He left them in the living room and walked upstairs to the bathroom. He locked the door behind him and turned around to face the large outlet in the wall. He unbuckled his pants, reached inside his zipper and pulled out the end of his life-cord. The moment when it first slid into the outlet was always the best. The initial shock that powered through his body was the closest thing he would ever know to euphoria. He only recharged for a few minutes, but it was enough to get him through another two or three hours. He'd come back up and completely fill his battery once the barbecue was over and everybody had gone back home.

Back downstairs, Jonah found the house empty. Everybody was outside now, sitting at the long picnic table set up in the grass. The fire in the grill had already died down. He tossed a bucket of water on the last remaining flames. Satisfied that he'd successfully gone through the motions, he sat down next to his wife at the table. There was already a plate in front of him. There was a plate in front of everybody. Ceramic, white. The only thing on any of them were the words "MADE IN THE U.S.A.".

The same message was written on the back of their skulls, hidden behind their patches of hair.

"Today has been outstanding," Luna Sunflower said, gripping a fork in her hand and twirling it around invisible food. "You have really exceeded our expectations."

"Thank you, Luna," Jonah said. "We gave it our all. I couldn't be more proud."

"Impressive as always," Allen Taylor agreed.

"Thank you, Allen," Jonah said, and noticed someone he hadn't expected sitting at the end of the table. "Bryan? Bryan Campbell?"

Bryan looked up from his empty plate, wide-eyed. "Uh, hi. I just let myself in; I hope that's okay. I hate missing the barbecues."

"You are supposed to be in the shop," Jonah said. "You are supposed to be under renovation."

Bryan nodded. He looked off, almost. Sick. "They released me early. I don't understand either."

Jonah stared at his neighbor for a moment, weighing the possibilities. Why would the Maintenance Men go against their original word? When they said something was so, then it was so. There was never any change. They'd originally issued an order notice to the entire neighborhood that Bryan Campbell would not be allowed back into the public until Monday at noon. But here he was, at the table, on Sunday.

"Well, what did they tell you?" Jonah asked. Now the whole neighborhood was staring at Bryan. They expected answers.

Bryan opened his mouth, then closed it. He dropped his head and looked down at his empty plate. The fork in his hand continued to twirl invisible strands of food. "They... they just told me that their job was complete, and I was free to go home. Then they led me outside, and I walked over here so I wouldn't miss the barbecue."

"What was it like inside?" Jonah's boy, Timothy, asked. "What was it like inside the Tool Shed?"

Bryan stopped twirling his fork. Frozen. He did not move for several minutes. Obviously the Maintenance Men hadn't done such a good job after all. He was already combusted again.

"Hello? Mr. Campbell?" Timothy said again. "I asked you a question."

Bryan twitched slightly, then slowly raised his head to face the boy. He stared at Timothy intensely. His eyes seemed to sparkle in the sunlight. Not only his eyes, but his cheeks as well.

Several silent alarms started going off in Jonah's brain.

"Why is your face all wet?" Timothy asked. "What's happening?"

"Maybe it's raining," suggested Donna Portugal. She raised her face to the sky to check.

"It's Sunday," Jonah said. "It doesn't rain on Sundays."

"Then why is his face wet?"

"I... I don't know."

Bryan began shaking. He gripped the plate in front of him and squeezed. A strange noise omitted itself from his mouth. Something like an animal squeal.

"Father," Timothy said, not taking his eyes off Bryan, "what is happening?"

Jonah did not answer. He did not know.

Jonah's wife, Nancy, stood up. "Something isn't right," she said. "I'm going to call Maintenance."

She was halfway toward the backdoor when Bryan spoke. It was so faint they could barely hear him. But she still stopped, nonetheless. She turned around.

"What did he say?" she asked.

Bryan's face was completely soaked now. The animal squealing was rising in volume. He opened his mouth again.

"I said... *NOOOOO!*" he screamed, and the plate shattered in his hands.

The skin on his hands also seemed to shatter. But beneath the skin, instead of the typical wires and electronic boards, was...red. Dark, moving, animated *red*. Water? No, not water.

"Father," Timothy said, "is...is that blood?"

"Oh, no," Jonah whispered.

Bryan leapt from the picnic table and backed away from the neighborhood. He stared at them, afraid, and they stared at him, also afraid.

"Please," Bryan said. "I don't know what to do. I'm so scared."

His hands were dripping blood all over Jonah's recently mowed grass. Jonah stepped forward. It was his weekend, which meant that he was in charge of the situation.

"Bryan, what did they do to you?"

Bryan leaked more wetness down his face. The animal in him squealed.

"I don't know. I don't know. *I don't know.*"

"It's okay, Bryan," Jonah said. "Come here. We aren't going to hurt you. But we do need to look at you, to see what they did. Don't be afraid. You are one of the neighborhood."

Bryan paused, unsure. He held up his bleeding hands. "You should all be disgusted by this."

"Oh, we are," Jonah admitted. "But we are also fascinated."

The rest of the neighborhood were on their feet now, right behind Jonah. They all chanted, "Don't be afraid, Bryan. Everything is okay now. Don't be afraid."

"My hands," Bryan said. "My hands, they *hurt.* They hurt so much. My whole body does."

The neighborhood fell silent. Things simply did not *hurt.* Not with them, at least. Maybe with animals. But the neighborhood did not embrace pain.

Pain was a pure fairy tale.

"Father," Timothy said from behind Jonah, "what is happening to him?"

"Why do my hands hurt?" Bryan pleaded. "I don't like this. I don't like this at all."

Jonah tried to concentrate but he wasn't prepared; he wasn't prepared for any of this. "Maybe you just need to plug in and recharge for a while," he suggested. "You've just gone through some intense repairs. This could all be a peculiar side effect, something that'll go away once you're walking around with a full battery."

Bryan did something completely unexpected. He began laughing.

"Father," Timothy said, "why is he laughing? What is funny?"

"I don't know, son," Jonah whispered. "I don't know."

He moved in closer to Bryan. He tried to keep eye contact but he couldn't stop staring at the blood dripping from his neighbor's hands. Something was terribly, terribly wrong, and he didn't have the first idea on how to fix it. He was just a citizen. Whether it was his weekend or not, he was not qualified to handle this kind of situation.

"Bryan," Jonah said. "Please stop this."

"Plug in?" Bryan said. "*Recharge?*" He laughed louder, waving his hands in front of him. Blood flew across the lawn and splattered across Jonah's face. "Don't you understand, Jonah? Don't you get it?"

"No," he said. "I do not understand at all. Please."

Bryan's laughter was out of control. Jonah no longer could tell if he was laughing or crying. He just wanted to sit back down at the picnic table and continue the barbecue. It had been going so well until now.

"I can't *recharge*, you idiot," Bryan said. "Can't you see that I am *bleeding?* Bleeding! I'm bleeding here and you want me to go plug myself into an outlet."

"You will feel better," Jonah said. "I just know it."

"Plug in with *what?*" Bryan asked.

"What... what do you mean?" This time, Jonah took a step back. So did the rest of the neighborhood.

Face wet and maniacal, Bryan unbuckled his belt and let his pants fall down to his ankles. He pulled down his underwear, then stood straight up. He stared at the neighborhood and the neighborhood stared back.

"Okay, Nancy," Jonah said, without taking his eyes off Bryan. "It's time to call Maintenance."

Bryan laughed again. "Go ahead and call them. They're the bastards who did this. And guess what? They're going to do the same thing to each and every one of you. Is that what you want? Is *this* what you want?"

The neighborhood began to flee.

"Father," Timothy said, "where is his life-cord? *Where is his life-cord?*" 🦇

PUPPIES FOR SALE

KURT NEWTON

WHEN IT WAS TIME for Ellie to kiss her husband goodbye, she tried to hold his lips against hers longer than their usual stay, keep them there by sheer force of will. But they departed too soon. Always too soon.

"Bye, Daddy."

"Bye, Daddy."

Two voices from behind, shouting in unison. Two blonde, smiling-faced boys, age three, pushed through Ellie's legs to get at their father. Awaiting them were the big hugs, the big kisses, the big voice that told them he was just going to work and that he'd be home as soon as he could to play with "You two rascals." All of this went on like ritual as Ellie stood by, smiling her patient smiles, happy for her husband's happiness. Although, over the past three years, the ritual had worn thin. Seeing her husband's face twinned and then tripled was a bit much at times, like standing in a crowded hall of mirrors with no avenue of escape. Ellie longed for the days when it was just her husband's face she saw, those long, wonderful looks he used to give her that were hers and hers alone.

"...and Mommy will help you with the puppy sign. Right,

Momma?"

At first, Ellie didn't understand what they were talking about, but she quickly realized her husband was referring to the For Sale sign they were going to make to advertise the puppies their dog Jenny-girl had had.

"Right Momma?" A tug at her bathrobe on one side.

"Right Momma?" A tug on the other.

Ellie glanced at her two boys, their curious faces wondering what her answer would be. "Why, of course I will," she said with mock gleefulness, her eyes growing large, her smile wide. And the two boys matched her expression exactly. "Well, I have to go," Ellie's husband said, backing down the front steps. "Now, you two boys be good for your mother."

"We will, Daddy."

"We will." Again, like stereo.

Ellie waved as she watched her husband's car leave the driveway, and the smile on her face wanted to go with him, but she held it tight.

* * *

After breakfast, Ellie dressed herself in jeans and a sweatshirt, and she helped the two boys get into their own clothes. Outside, the weather was bright and warm, unseasonably warm for October, but the sun occasionally disappeared behind a bright puffy cloud and the chill of autumn reminded Ellie that winter would soon be upon them. Overall, a nice day for the puppies to spend a little time outdoors advertising their cute, furry faces to whomever should drive by.

There were six all together, Golden Retriever pups, all a picture perfect tawny brown, the color of butterscotch pudding with a little whipped cream on top. Jenny-girl had outdone herself, her first litter and, according to Ellie's husband, her last. Out of the six, there were only two males, but they were identical, right down to the white circular tip on their tails. These two they intended to keep. Ellie's husband said it couldn't have been more perfect: a perfect puppy for each of their two perfect boys.

But, right now, there was a sign to make. There remained four other pups unspoken for that needed a good home.

As Ellie searched the garage, the two boys followed close behind, hanging on her every word and movement. Each tried to help Ellie when it was best that they just stay out of the way. For Ellie, the world was just too small sometimes. But what could she do? The man she loved had given her twin reminders of his love and adoration.

Finally, she found a piece of plywood large enough to make the sign, and she hauled it out and laid it flat on the cement floor of the garage.

The boys crowded in.

Ellie had also found some old ceiling paint left over from when she and her husband had first moved into the house, and as she knelt over the blank piece of plywood she thought back, remembering the fun they had had, just the two of them, paint splattered and arm weary, but still finding enough energy to make love among the still unpacked boxes. Life had never been better...

"Let me..."

"*No, let me...*"

"I can..."

"*No, I can...*"

Twin voices burrowing into her ears.

Ellie tried to paint the letters as neatly as possible, but with the two boys "helping," her letters came out crude and child-like. The only thing missing were the misspelled words and the backward letters. But it was important for the boys to feel like they were helping. Always for the boys. "Think of the boys," Ellie's husband was fond of reminding her, as if she herself were a spoiled child.

"There!" Ellie announced, trying to summon some brightness back into her mood.

"There!" the two boys repeated, their competitiveness momentarily forgotten. The three of them stared down at the sign: PUPPIES FOR SALE, AKC GOLDEN RETRIEVERS, and below that their home phone number. Simple, straightforward. Four years spent educating herself in the field of marketing didn't all go to waste, Ellie thought dryly. But then it was her choice not to seek a career, choosing instead to start a family, wasn't it? She did know her husband had wanted children right away, didn't she?

"Now, who's going to help Mommy carry the puppies?" Ellie spoke in a perfect nursery rhyme voice.

"I will!"

"I will!" came the duel responses.

"Well, go ahead and get them!"

And around the house the two boys ran. Ellie followed after them, breathing the fresh morning air and admiring the splendidness of her property. Maybe she was selfish—look what she had: a beautiful home, on two beautiful acres, surrounded by tall shade trees which, at this time of year, were the envy of the neighborhood. She could have anything she wished for in the way of jewelry or clothing, all she had to do was ask. What else was there?

Ellie supervised as the puppies were transferred to the front of the yard, making sure the boys handled them properly. Awaiting the puppies was the old playpen the two boys no longer needed. What better display case? Ellie thought when she saw it in the garage, proud of her resourcefulness. Jenny-girl paced nervously the entire time, perhaps wondering what was going on. Why were her babies being removed from her custody? What was wrong with the perfectly suitable hay-lined doghouse she had given birth to them in, had licked their blood-wet bodies clean in?

Ellie wondered what Jenny-girl would do when it came time to hand over one of the puppies to a total stranger. Would she chase after the car? Worse yet, would she try and bite the offending intruder? How would any mother react? Ellie decided then it would be a good idea to bring Jenny-girl out back and tie her up. She didn't want a lawsuit on her hands.

With Jenny-girl safely out of the way, Ellie sat on the front steps and focused her attention on the two boys as they played in the autumn sun, chasing leaves and each other in lazy circles. She watched as her husbands' faces giggled and frowned, displayed rapt concentration and careless abandon. So much like their father. But it wasn't enough. No, it wasn't enough.

It was a good thing Ellie had tied Jenny-girl up when she did, because it wasn't long before the first car slowed, then pulled over in front of the house.

It was an elderly couple. Retired, comfortable, Ellie thought. When they got out of their car, Ellie got up to greet them, ready to answer any and all questions regarding Golden Retriever pups. But as they approached, Ellie noticed the camera around the woman's neck.

"Hello," the woman said, her voice possessing a strong, grandmotherly tone. "We were passing by and I couldn't help but notice. Would you mind if I took some pictures of your two boys?" The woman's husband stood sheepishly behind her, looking embarrassed by his wife's forwardness.

"Oh, no, not at all," Ellie said, smiling. "Go right ahead."

The woman wasted no time in approaching the two boys. She talked to them briefly, then squatted into a photographer's crouch and began snapping off picture after picture.

"Beautiful day, isn't it?" the elderly gentleman said, standing alongside Ellie.

"Yes, it is," Ellie replied, watching the woman's immediate rapport with the two boys. The click and whir of her camera was distracting.

"Ever since we've retired she's had that thing around her neck," the elderly gentleman said, trying to make conversation. But Ellie wasn't listening. Instead, she watched as the two boys soaked up the attention like two professionals. First one would throw a handful of leaves into the air, while the other one sat waiting to be covered. The first one smiled innocently, the second one acted surprised. Ellie saw the rest of her life laid out before her in those twin faces, always the proud mother, always the patient wife, the nurturer, the care-giver, each camera click a snapshot seizing a piece of her future...

"Any luck with the pups?"

Ellie blinked. She realized she had been smiling all along, and her face hurt. "Oh, no, you're the first to stop."

"I'm sure they'll go quickly."

"I hope so."

"People need pets, nowadays... helps to take their minds off the world and its problems."

Ellie turned her head to where the puppies sat in the playpen. All six faces peered out from between the nylon mesh as if through a pet shop window. They too watched the two boys as they shrieked and wrestled in the leaves, receiving all the attention.

The camera finally stopped. "Well, I thank you very much," the woman said, breathing heavily as if it were she who were diving in the leaves. "I bet you have your hands full with those two."

"Oh, they're a handful all right," Ellie replied. She heard herself then and realized she sounded every bit the dutiful mother.

"Well, I hope we didn't impose on you too much."

"No, no, it was my pleasure." *Anything for the boys.*

Ellie watched as the couple returned to their car. "Good luck with those pups," the elderly gentleman called to her before getting behind the wheel. "Thanks," Ellie shouted.

They waved as they pulled away, leaving Ellie almost in tears.

* * *

When lunchtime arrived, Ellie called the boys in and made them both peanut butter and jelly sandwiches, and gave each a tall glass of milk. She even made a sandwich for herself, but didn't have the appetite to finish it. She just sat and watched quietly as the two boys hurried through their meal, eager to get back outside. This time, Ellie brought a lawn chair with her and sat beside the playpen as the two boys resumed their play.

The day was still warm, but the sun was now making fewer and fewer appearances, sending whispery chills across Ellie's skin. The puppies slept peacefully, one atop the other, their little bodies heaving with each quiet breath. Ellie rested her chin on the edge of the playpen and stared down at them. Animals are so adaptable, she thought. So trusting of the life that went on around them. Ellie knew if she were to pick up one of Jenny-girl's pups—one of the perfect males, perhaps—and gently squeeze the life from it, the others would carry on as if it were something that was meant to happen, like a brief spring rain, or a sudden gust of wind.

The two boys whooped and paraded beneath the showers of leaves. They used their hands and feet to shuffle the leaves back into a pile, then they burrowed like sweatered animals, burying themselves and giggling with each newly invented game.

Ellie leaned over the pen and ran her hand along the puppies' soft fur, caressing their thick ears and muscular legs. One stretched, all four legs straightening; its open mouth revealed a tongue curly and pink like a piece of ribbon candy. *So soft. So trusting.*

"I'm tired, Momma."

"Me, too."

The two boys came over to where Ellie sat and nuzzled up against her. They had leaves in their hair, twigs stuck to their clothing. She unfolded the blanket she was sitting on and laid it on the grass for them, and they climbed aboard. In a matter of minutes, the warming sun and the fresh, scented air worked to put them both to sleep.

The afternoon turned late, the sky grew overcast. School buses came and went, but no one else slowed as they drove by. The two boys slept. Ellie watched, and waited. Only another hour and her husband would be home, pulling into the driveway, getting out of the car with that face she loved so much. Soon, her day would be complete.

The telephone rang.

Ellie was nearly asleep herself when she heard it. She slipped off the chair and hurried into the house, taking a quick look over her shoulder to see if the two boys were still asleep.

It was her husband. He was going to be late tonight.

How many times did that make? She had lost count. Didn't he know how much his absences hurt her? Couldn't he see the yearning in her eyes when he left each morning? Didn't he know that it wasn't the same just to have his face in miniature staring up at her wherever she turned, pulling on her, asking her questions; that it only served to remind her of his absence? Couldn't he see that?

"No, no, that's okay... I'll be fine, really... I love you too... Bye..." *Goodbye*. She closed her eyes and pressed the telephone receiver to her lips and thought of the kiss he had given her that morning. One one thousand... two one thousand... three one thousand... She could almost feel it. When she opened her eyes again and looked through the picture window, she saw that a long black limousine had pulled up alongside the road in front of the house. Near the playpen a strange man stood.

Ellie dropped the phone and rushed to the front door, her heart thumping in her chest. She tried to walk calmly out to the playpen.

"Puppies for sale... how charming," the man said. His voice carried an air of sophistication. He was dressed in a dark, expensive-looking suit, and his hair was black and neatly trimmed. An older man, but of an age Ellie couldn't guess. He gripped the edge of the playpen and appeared to be staring down at the puppies.

"Can I help you?" Ellie asked the man, closing the gap between them. Jenny-girl's barks could be heard in the back yard, but the two boys slept undisturbed near to where the man stood.

"I'm sure you can. You see, I'm in the market for some... company." He looked up. His eyes were like two black pools. "It gets lonely where I reside, and I thought..."

"The puppies—yes, they make excellent pets," Ellie offered.

The man smiled at this, leaning his head to one side, as if weighing the validity of what Ellie had just said. He inhaled deeply, then sighed. "Beautiful creatures, aren't they?"

Ellie looked down into the playpen. Most of the puppies had awakened and were staring up at the man. Ellie hadn't realized it at first, but all the puppies had backed off to one corner. "Their mother—the one you hear barking out back—is AKC registered. Their father was supplied by a local stud service, also AKC. He has championship bloodlines," Ellie recited, remembering what her husband had told her to say. She had no reason to fear this man. But then why did she feel so ill-at-ease?

"I'll take them," he said suddenly, as if he had had his mind made up all along.

"Oh! That's wonderful! But first, you should know, we're asking two hundred and fifty dollars—"

The man waved his hand in a gesture that meant money was no object. He reached into his coat pocket and pulled out a billfold. He handed Ellie five crisp one hundred dollar bills. Ellie took them with a wide smile. Wait until her husband got home...

"Have you decided yet which ones you're going to take?"

The man grinned. His eyes locked onto hers. "The two boys," he said. His voice was almost a whisper, but Ellie heard it as if it were voiced from inside her own head.

Ellie hesitated. "The two males...?"

"Is there a problem?"

"Oh, no..." She wasn't thinking straight. Her mind seemed slow to comprehend. The two boys... the two boys... What was it about the two boys she needed to remember?

"No, everything's fine," she heard herself tell the man.

"Good. I'll just need a receipt and I'll be on my way." His eyes... his eyes seemed to penetrate her very soul.

"If you'll excuse me for just a minute, I need to go inside."

"Take your time," the man said, smiling charmingly.

Ellie turned and walked toward the house. She felt the man's eyes on her back, and with each step she knew she was risking something. The hairs on the back of her neck bristled, her stomach fluttered; it was a feeling she remembered from her childhood—the pond behind her house—walking out on the first ice of the winter with a nervous excitement that told her that what she was doing was dangerous.

She gripped the bills in her hand, their thick papery feel rough between her fingers. $500.00! It was like found money. What some people will pay...

Jenny-girl still barked out back, perhaps sensing that two of her offspring were about to be taken away. If only Jenny-girl understood the value of money, Ellie thought, maybe she wouldn't be so quick to protest.

Once inside the house, Ellie filled out the necessary papers. Male #1. Male #2. Distinguishing marks: white-tipped tail, etc. Ellie signed her name. She also took a blank piece of paper and wrote up a receipt, then realized she hadn't asked the man's name. But it didn't seem to matter. What mattered was that she take her time.

When she stepped back outside again, the long black limousine was pulling away. Ellie, stunned, simply watched it go, her arm not even attempting to flag it down. Her heart began to race in her chest and she grew suddenly weary. Slowly, her eyes scanned the yard until they came upon the blanket beside the playpen. She knew it would be empty. She walked on numb legs down to the chair beside playpen. She had to sit down.

* * *

The sky was now completely overcast; it would be dark soon. The puppies lay sleeping, all six of them cuddled together as before. Ellie kept expecting to hear shouts and shrieks and little boy laughter coming from the pile of leaves off to her left, but she knew there would be none forthcoming. She still had the five one hundred dollar bills in her hand and she began counting them. One hundred, two hundred, three hundred... over and over. She kept counting even as shadows crept across her vision, and the air turned cold. One hundred, two hundred, three... What some people will pay...

She kept counting even as her husband pulled into the driveway. She couldn't wait to tell him, to turn to his face—that face, the one she had always wanted, the one she couldn't wait a lifetime (or two) to have all to herself again; that tired, lovely face—she couldn't wait to see the happiness that was sure to blossom there once she told him the good news.

THE ASSASSIN

PATRICK BREHENY

ANDRE WAS HIDDEN behind garbage cans in the alley, and he sat in a puddle of slush, listening to the hail pinging on the lids of the cans. His legs had gone numb from crouching during the long wait, and he was so wet anyway that he finally sat on a folded newspaper. He couldn't see it in the dark, but he knew well what was in all the newspapers these days, that the Germans were France's benefactors, they distributed food to the poor, provided clothing, medical treatment, in their efficient way saw to it that Paris ran smoothly They were under orders from the wise and kindly Fuhrher himself to behave as gentlemen, be polite to the locals they weren't rounding up, act in a civil manner, to not rape or plunder as they did elsewhere, to take photos as if they were tourists, to enjoy the cultural life of the music halls and live theater, the museums and the fine art of Paris (at least that which Hitler and Goebbels themselves hadn't taken.) On directions from Hitler, the Weirmacht were what France had always needed, if you weren't a Jew—or a Gypsy or a homosexual, or mentally or physically impaired.

Andre's rifle was cradled across his legs, and from between the cans he watched a German convoy moving down the darkened boulevard. He was waiting for the last vehicle, and he wondered if there was any end to the procession. He remembered headlines in papers like the one under him had also been about yet even more benign German soldiers coming to Paris to help solve the problems of the French. Not involved himself at that point, Andre had still thought, send more troops, get more resistance. It was a human equation.

They were here now. He peered down the street sixty feet to the cellar door front of a boucherie, with a short iron railing intended to separate the beneath-street entrance from pedestrians, though there were no pedestrians tonight. No movement, no sound from the doorway; no hint of Marcel and Msr. Paul. Who would expect to find, under that drenched cardboard box, invisible in the dark, at the top of the steps, a positioned fifty caliber machine gun? The military minds had ordered searched the buildings and cellars, and the doorways and the alleys, and then blackened out the neighborhood. And as the convoy rolled through moonless, starless gloom, two assassins emerged from a trap door in a sub-cellar below the basement storage room of Msr. Paul's butcher shop, with the machine gun. The box, folded, was in the basement. Marcel the young student was with M.Paul, the rotund middle aged butcher. Andre himself had pushed back a manhole cover on an adjacent street, and reeking from the putrid sewer, bitten on the legs by rats, he had traversed alleys to get to the back of a selected restaurant, intentionally left unlocked. He went though it out to the recessed entry where stinking cans of uncollected food waste had been checked and quickly left. Two other men, Msr. Jean and Msr. Pierre—no last names—laborers in their sixties, had pushed back a vent and climbed out of an air shaft onto the roof of an apartment building that had been vacated of tenants yesterday by the Germans.

The old working men on the roof across the street had no ideology, nor did Andre. Marcel and Paul the butcher, teamed together, were socialists. Andre just wanted the Germans out of France That was ideology enough for him, enough for Charles de Gaulle, leading the resistance in exile from London. Enough for Jacques, the young commander, Jeanette's husband who they had killed in front of her and her small daughter Mimi. Enough for Henri, Jeanette's father, the gangster. Before there was an underground there was an underworld. Vice and corruption were as old as invasion.

Mid-ranked Nazi officers were getting tired taking pictures, visiting landmarks. How many times can you see the Eiffel Tower, the Mona Lisa? They couldn't slaughter indiscriminately as they did elsewhere, were under directive from on high to be "nice" They were bored. And Henri could get them things they couldn't find on their own, didn't want known they got, under risk of disobedience to Hitler. Some risked their reputations as "officers and gentleman", and therefore their lives, to sample Henri's temptations—a little opium here, a little boy there, a little of this, a little of that, what would you like? And to keep continued access to Henri, they needed him safe. To keep their transgressions secret, they needed him satisfied. He received gratuities from them, while he inquired about their family's welfare, their personal health, hoped they slept well—a little opium will soothe a guilty conscience —and as he catered to their dark wants, took the proceeds that were rendered to him and gave them to the resistance. Most gangsters joined the Carlinque, the French Gestapo, but then stopped being gangsters, they were Gestapo police, and while as Frenchmen they could do nothing about German transgressions, they reported to the German Gestapo that could. Henri was bonded to Nazi officers in avoidance of detection by the Gestapo, even as he channeled their money to have them killed.

Henri had preferred to remain a freelancer, a gangster who was still a gangster, somebody special , but now, in 1943, Henri went over, joined the Carlinqe the French Gestapo, giving his miscreant mid level Nazi officers what they needed most besides being a provider for their needs—an insider who could cover for them, warn them. And being inside, Henri had information for the resistance, like this convoy movement tonight that was transporting a German general, and was thought to be secret.

To Andre it didn't matter if Henri was a patriotic Frenchman, or just upset that some other well organized gangsters had wrecked his operations. It didn't matter that the mismatched pair in a doorway with the machine gun—a young student and a chubby middle aged butcher—were communists. It didn't matter that he, a young student, and the old codgers on the roof had no ideology. It only mattered that they were united in getting the bastards out of France.

Andre looked up at the tenement rooftop. It was his job, and the job of Msr. Jean and Msr. Pierre up there—after M. Jean and M. Pierre dropped the flares—to draw fire to themselves, and of course their fire itself might do the job, but it was intended as diversion so the machine gun in the doorway could fire accurately. It was a suicide mission, and all five had cyanide capsules, with orders to take them rather than face capture.

Andre ached for a cigarette. With a start, he realized he would never smoke another cigarette. Why can't they hurry, he thought. Why can't we get this over with? The street was all too familiar. He hadn't known before they took up preliminary positions last night —his in that sewer—that it would be this boulevard. You didn't know ahead where you were going. He hadn't imagined before joining that guerilla security could be so tight. He hadn't known much about it at all. He had been naively excited by patriotism and potential glory the night he told Jeanette, and was shaken with dejection at the horror in her face. Still grieving for Jacques, who was executed in front of her and Mimi, and terrified for Mimi's safety after their imprisonment together, she begged him to never come back to her house. That image was with him now, Jeanette clutching Mimi to her legs. He thought of how it would be in the morning, when she found out he got killed on her street. She couldn't mourn him openly, but perhaps a private wake or memorial, certainly a prayer or two.

This was his first mission, and was to be his last. He thought about how he got involved with the movement. It started the afternoon he ran into Marcel, the first time he'd seen him since the occupation. He and Marcel had been going to the university together before the Nazis came, as had Jacques and Jeanette. Andre had been a rival of Jacques' for her, and Jacques won out. Young as they were, and still in school, they'd married and had a child. Hernri'd had the means to see that they'd get by and finish school, or he had until…

He had heard whispered reports that Marcel was part of the resistance, and the day he met him on a street, Marcel invited him to a bistro for wine. When they were seated at a table with their drinks, and the garçon had left, Marcel asked, "So, what have you been doing?"

Andre had been defensive. He knew the question wasn't like Henri's "How's the family?" to the Germans.

"I've wanted to help. You know how quiet things are kept. I didn't know how to go about it."

"You seem to think I'm into something?"

"I have heard…"

"I'm meeting some friends here, and I'll introduce you. If you're interested, this will be your chance."

That was how it happened. It seemed he had no choice at all. Msrs. Jean and Pierre and Paul arrived, all sizes, shapes, ages, ideologies and absences of ideologies, economic levels, interests, represented in an unlikely gathering at a bistro, as diverse as was the resistance. They explained their plan to him, in what seemed to be in public but wasn't—the bistro was resistance, and therefore closed to anyone else at the moment, unless the Gestapo happened by.

Andre knew then he couldn't back out. He knew too much, and if they didn't kill him, they'd call him a coward and a traitor. He knew now there was nothing accidental about his meeting with Marcel, but he had no regrets. He would die for France, and the deterrence of a villain. And the resistance was growing. He'd heard that even some of the artists and intellectuals, who had been so accommodating at the beginning, were joining. A few, at least.

The aching for a cigarette was hunger, he realized. He hadn't eaten since last night, hadn't missed it before, the stink of sewer on his clothes, and these foul garbage cans now, not piquing his appetite. How good some boulli would taste. Boulli and a cigarette. He shivered along the length of his back with a trembling chill. Warmth and boulli and a cigarette. And Jeanette with Mimi hugging her legs, the line of her dress across her hips, with the incline suggested beneath the taut cotton, and the hunger was hunger and something else, and couldn't they move that convoy faster, or was it really endless?

Now he knew why field armies kept two men in a foxhole. He wondered if M. Jean and M. Pierre were whispering to each other on the roof, maybe talking about old campaigns in the first Great War. Certainly Marcel and M. Paul in the other doorway weren't, but they at least had each other's company. Another 'never' occurred to him. He would never talk to anyone again. But he would. He would scream dying profanities at the murdering dogs. When it started. He wondered how it would be getting shot. Fast, he hoped. Cyanide was fast, but he also heard it was painful.

Which would be worse?

Maybe he could get away with a cigarette if he kept it covered. No, he couldn't chance it. But if they couldn't see him, he could ensure they wouldn't see his cigarette. He slipped one from his chest pocket, turned his back to the street, and lowered his chin to his chest. He struck a match in cupped hands, quickly lit the cigarette and blew the match out, keeping his hands over the glow. I could be shot for this, he thought, and almost laughed at the absurdity of it.

His teeth chattered and his nose kept dripping. He was cold to his soul and feverish, and the cigarette brought on coughs and sneezes he almost choked stifling. He had rats here too in the garbage cans, and he wanted to shoot them for the ones that bit his legs in the sewer, trying to eat him alive. No wonder he was sick. Did he have flu or plague? What couldn't you get from bites by sewer rats? He had to urinate, and got on his knees in the slush, holding back so he wouldn't make much noise. Releasing liquid reminded him his canteen was almost empty, and he was thirsty with illness. The cigarette tasted like rope, and he threw it under the torrent. I must at least have pneumonia, he thought, if not some viler disease, and tucked his penis away, wishing he could use it while he still could for what Frenchmen were supposed to be famous, though, national reputation or not, he really hadn't had much experience yet with that.

Jeanette only lived a block away. Andre had lived there, working for Henri, while she was being held by the Germans, and after she was released, continued to stay, sleeping on a cot in the basement—until he too joined the movement.

That was in 1941, six months after the invasion. The Germans took her prisoner after they killed Jacques. Even if Henri's daughter, she was the wife of a resistance fighter—he in charge of a unit of students and former students, men and women, all under his young command—though the Nazis, in their eagerness to execute all adversaries, never learned that, nor who they were. The officers who were Henri's clients had to be careful with their own about showing any favoritism. Why was Henri's son-in-law in the resistance? Misguided youthful idealism was the answer. Free Jeanette and Mimi, and you'll get her support. But Henri hadn't been allowed to visit to tell her that. What was needed from Jeanette was a written and public oath of allegiance to the Vichy Armistice Agreement, a pledge that she could not contradict later, and a denunciation of the resistance and her late husband's zealous foolishness.

They kept her and Mimi together, and stopped feeding them. Mimi, smaller of course, would starve before Jeanette, and she'd have to watch that. Andre knew that for herself alone, with the grief for Jacques so fresh, she probably would not have given in, but she was a mother. Germans don't last forever, and her small child's life was just beginning. By luck, her specific assigned interrogators were compromised by association with Henri. Her signature could mean a lot if it could be construed to deter recruitment in the resistance, and would justify freeing her. She had to say convincingly that she'd had a change of heart. The Nazis were good, they were civilized and kind, and France had always been in need of them. Every time she wanted to change an outrageous paragraph, the captain awaiting her signature placed food in front of her hungry child, but physically restrained her from eating it.

She signed to keep Mimi alive. Andre learned about her ordeal during conversations in the parlor in the evenings, after he'd eaten dinner with her and Mimi. He didn't want to feel attraction to her, she was still a grieving widow, she was a victim, she had chosen Jacques over him—but it was there. He just couldn't indulge it. Not yet, he thought, when he lived there. Too soon after Jacques. And then he'd become resistance and had to leave. And now—never. He remembered the scent that was always with her, the sweet hormonal fragrance of a young woman, and how beautiful she looked at the dinner table, with her long, brushed, black hair, her brown eyes, and classic French features.

Andre had been living there because he worked for Henri. Worked for him after the occupation, had not before. He was a messenger. He'd pick up a brown envelope at an address, and deliver it to a concierge at another address. He never knew what was in the envelopes. Little diversions like opiates, or information on where to go to get other little diversions? He was almost certain nothing related to the resistance. Henri's involvement was not logistical nor tactical, totally clandestine, passive and contributory. And what Henri himself might have done to other Frenchmen before the invasion—well, that wasn't Jeanette's fault. But Andre knew he would not have been working for him back then. Just not an enforcer type. What he was doing tonight did not come easily nor naturally. He'd make a better altar boy than construction worker.

He was sitting in urine and slush. God, he longed to spend just one night with her, to forget about wars and invaders and death. He imagined how she'd look now were he to rap on her door without the rifle in his hand. He could see himself dispelling her fears, comforting her, telling her truthfully they were gone, it was over, and inevitably taking her to bed. If he could just spend one night in her bed, and be warm and secure and in love, he might be ready to die.

The dark night came suddenly alive with a glowing red. Rifles cracked from the rooftop, and Andre, off balance, jerked to his knees . The fire would come from the roof first, of course. They triggered the flares, they knew when. Peeking between the cans, he saw the jeep. It was not the last vehicle. There was an open two and a half ton truck behind it, and one in front. Soldiers scurried over the sideboards, returning fire to the roof, and ran in the open to protect the jeep. Both trucks were mounted with machine guns and they too fired at the roof. Andre had to shoot also, attract fire to himself. He saw two of the soldiers lying in the street, and a razor of fear slashed through him.

He brought his rifle up and fired. He'd aimed everything at the jeep, hit two of the soldiers protecting it who were also now lying on the ground, but his bullets that hit the jeep had bounced off. He could see the pock marks. Something new by the Germans? The machine gun in the doorway opened up now, fired a full volley of fifty caliber bullets at the jeep. He couldn't tell if they penetrated or not, had no way to know, if the bullets had, if they'd killed the general inside.

The German machine guns blasted bullets into the boucherie doorway, and they threw grenades at it. The rooftop was silent now, but they kept machine gun and rifle fire directed at the building, and shattered every window. Andre heard cries of fear and anger from the apartments, so despite the eviction, there were squatters or former tenants in there.

He suddenly realized nobody was firing at him. Nobody knew he was there. In the chaos, they'd only realized they were being fired at from two, not three positions. They had at first been turned toward the roof, and he had been firing at their backs. Had he been late? Distracted by his thoughts and needs and reverie, an undisciplined untrained recruit? Had he let his compatriots down? No, he had fired on time. He couldn't know when to fire until the flares ignited, and then he had done so. Of course fire came from the roof first. They initiated the attack with the flares. But if he'd been kneeling, ready, not sitting down, would he have fired sooner?

He didn't know if they'd succeeded or not, but nobody knew Andre was there. Jeanette just lived down the street. Surely she'd let him in this one time. He could make her house through the alleys, and they wouldn't even be looking for him. The cyanide was to avoid capture. They weren't trying to capture him. What good was one more dead Frenchman? Live to fight another day.

He drew his rifle away and took a second glance to be sure that no one could see him. The flares were almost out; they cast just an ember of light. But then a door of the jeep on his side—the safe side, they'd think—pushed open, and he got a glimpse for less than a second of a figure with a beaked officer's cap, and a jacket with shoulder straps regaled in insignia. The bastard was not only alive, but seemed uninjured, and was immediately surrounded and protect by a dozen troops. A shot by Andre would have to go through two of them, and if it did, would be spent or almost. He had no target he could see. But if he ran, the mission was a failure. Marcel and Paul, Jean and Pierre died for nothing. If he shot enough German soldiers before they realized where he was, before they could stop him, he might get a shot at the general.

He raised the rifle again. The huddle of soldiers separated, made an opening. The general was shooing them away, demonstrating his confidence, his authority, being a general, in charge. He was in the open, arrogant, walking with the dignity of a parade toward the alley of Andre's doorway. He wore glasses. If the Germans had innovations like bullet proof jeeps, could the super race see in the dark too? Or were they just spectacles? They looked like sunglasses, but in the night he couldn't tell. Feeling extremely self conscious and vulnerable, Andre thought the general was looking right at him. He was looking right at him—he could not be completely hidden by the garbage can—but did he see him? Andre knew night vision existed. He'd seen drawings of the goggles, but they looked like submarine periscopes on each eye, gave a man-from-Mars look to the wearer. Could these technological krauts have refined them to look like sunglasses?

Maybe they were just eyeglasses, because he now shone a thin flashlight, about the size of a small dinner table candle, the beam passing over Andre, who was bent as low as he could be and still able to shoot. He stepped onto the sidewalk, shouting, pointing, probably ordering the doorway and alley searched, walking toward the cans. Andre sucked in to hold his breath, and the muscles in his rectum tightened. He was sure he could see him now, magic vision or not. But no, he was pointing beyond Andre, looking down the alley, the light going there, and shouting more orders. He was six feet away.

Andre took a careful steady aim, under the beak of the cap, above his nose, where the lenses of the glasses were joined. Right between the eyes. Slowly, quietly, he squeezed the trigger. Coming from explosionless silence, the only sound there had been the general's loud voice, amplified by the narrow alley and doorway, that single thirty caliber shot sounded like it came from a cannon.

Andre saw him lash backwards and fall. The flashlight flipped, did spins, giving a crazy montage of lit images—the general's soles in the air, the cans with rats fleeing, the restaurant door, the alley pavement, and then the light stopped moving. The flashlight lay on the general's chest, shining back at his head, which looked like a tomato that had been squashed with a hammer.

Andre dropped the rifle and ran headlong through the alley. If he could only make it to Jeanette's. No, he couldn't go there. Where could he go? Nowhere. He had taken no more than five strides when he heard the machine guns behind him. Then everything slowed down. He'd remember it in slow motion, but he wouldn't remember it. The bullets tore through him, and he fell into the melting sleet. The ground felt so cold and good because he felt it and it didn't hurt. The bullets did. He cried out in an anguish of physical pain, he cried out in grief for Jeanette for what had never been and had been, he mourned those fallen with him,

Marcel, his peer, and Msr. Paul, and Mrsrs. Jean and Pierre who had lived long lives, but still not long enough. His spirit was abandoning his body, and knew he was leaving this world for a waiting unknown, if such existed. He was going to find out. Or find out nothing.

He had one final thought: His young life had not been a failure. He had done everything he should. He had not let his comrades down. He had accomplished his mission tonight.

SLOWLY I TURNED

KENNETH GOLDMAN

"Action alone—not words, not thoughts, but action—this is the Behavioral therapist's only guaranteed method of achieving his patient's positive change. Thoughts and feelings will follow, but action must come first."
— Dr. Martin Steinman Speech to The American Psychological Association.

THE BOOK TOLD HENRY to get up and dance. Henry didn't feel like dancing. He didn't even know how to dance. He had never tried it alone, let alone with a woman. But he figured it would be easy enough with no one there to see him make a fool of himself. And *One Hundred and One Tasks To Happy*, replete with smiley faces, was insistent. Those smileys wanted him to dance right now because doing so would make him feel good. Henry wanted to feel good. He needed to.

The tasks appeared simple, good-natured chores anyone could accomplish. Carefully placed in sequence, sometimes an easy task followed a more challenging one, so you never felt much pressure.

Therefore, each new page came as a surprise, an opportunity to experience success by the simple act of doing. In under two months Henry had made it to Task 66, sometimes pulling off two or three assignments in a single day. But the ultimate result wasn't what he had hoped for. Since Jamie, true happiness proved even more ephemeral, and in the end he didn't feel happy at all. He didn't feel much of anything. Henry turned on the radio. It didn't matter if he had music on, but real dancing—the kind people did when they hit the dance floor—*that* required music, otherwise he would feel like some idiot suffering an epileptic seizure. He tuned the FM dial of his old Sony. Donna Summer was warbling about some girl working hard for the money. Now *there* was a sign! Henry remembered Jamie's first words to him, last month in Radley Park when the performing mime broke character and suddenly sang out those lyrics. And now, here was Donna Summer warbling her bouncy '70's disco number about some poor working girl either waiting tables or prostituting herself, Henry was never certain. Probably the song's intent was to remain ambiguous like that. Dancing couples could smirk over the innuendo of Miss Summer's words while the women shook their firm little asses and wiggled their hips, as if they too were working hard for the money. Okay, then, Donna's song would do for Task 66. It certainly had got him through number 32 on the day he met Jamie.

Henry danced. Like a man possessed he bounced around his studio apartment, his motions awkward and a little bizarre. Arms waving in meaningless gesticulations, he jumped and hopped in mad improvisations as if palsied. If this were meant as interpretive dancing, anyone watching Henry's movements would have the impression that here was a man on the verge of complete mental collapse. He figured three minutes ought to do it, pretty much the length of the song. He worked up a sweat and maybe he did feel a little better for the experience. Not enough to cancel his sessions with Dr. Steinman, of course, but enough to attempt a smile. His goal accomplished, he checked off Task 66 in the book's 'Task Accomplished' box that followed each exercise. *His 66th task to Happy...*

"Henry, I have something for you," Steinman had told him eight appointments earlier. "I want you to think of this as a kind of homework assignment between our sessions. Will you do this for me? And for yourself?"

Henry had held out his hand for the therapist's gift, nodding like a boggle-head doll. "Yes. Yes, I will, Dr. Steinman. I will. Thanks." *[Yes yes, I will, I will, I will...]* His quick compliance had set off an internal alarm. Wasn't that what Steinman said was his problem from the start? Insecure and uncertain of his ability to make correct decisions, craving approval, Henry never questioned others' demands. His father wanted him to work full-time in the storeroom of Womack's Men's Clothing, the business he had run seemingly forever, no questions asked? Henry had asked none and spent years checking endless stacks of pants for imperfections and stains. 'Inspected By Number 6' read the small label scruff he tucked inside the pockets of newly stitched men's pants, the dutiful son watching his identity reduced to a number. Schoolyard bullies had tried their own brand of torture. *"How about wearing your tighty-whitey underpants on the outside today for all the girls to see, Henry? Will you do that for Joey Botta, your best bud who otherwise will kick the snot out of you where you stand?" "Sure Joey. I sure as shit will! You feel like throwing in a wedgie with that order?"* Even God had his demands. *"Will you eat the flesh of Christ, Henry? Will you drink his blood?" "Slip that cracker my way right now, Father, and pour me some wine. Yum and slurp! Just like Dracula, eh, Father? Geeve me a bite of yourrr neck, Jesus!"* Dance, Henry, dance!

...But Dr. Steinman wasn't Henry Womack Senior or some school tyrant insistent on tormenting him; he wasn't a full-of-shit priest or a hundred other control freaks trying to run his life.

Steinman's motivations were not guided by greed or the need to feel better about himself at his expense. Martin Steinman concerned himself only with Henry's best interests. It was okay to say 'yes' to this man. You had to trust *some*body or you would wind up trusting no one. And then you really *were* alone.

"My book hasn't officially been published yet," Steinman had informed him. "I wanted you to be the first to have it before it's on the shelves later this spring. These are exercises in positive bombardment. Technically it's a bit more complicated than that, a cart-before-the-horse approach if you listen to my critics. But we Behaviorists believe positive thoughts follow decisive actions, not the other way around, and where the ass goes the mind will follow. Are you game?" The book didn't contain much writing. *One Hundred and One Tasks To Happy* its title read, the two upper case O's consisting of have-a-nice-day smiley faces. At first glance it seemed tacky and simplistic, maybe even stupid. But if any of the tasks worked, Henry would feel satisfied with just one way. The pages were enclosed in brown wrappers so you couldn't read any single page without tearing off the sheath that hid its words. "To keep the element of surprise," Steinman told him, as if each page's instruction contained its own special gift. "These are daily assignments, Henry. Don't ask anyone—including me—how to complete them. Trust yourself and do them in the order in which they appear without skipping any. You may complete more than one each day, if you feel like it. Will you do a few of these for our next session? Will you commit yourself to doing them all?"

"Yes," Henry said. *I will... I will...* It beat wearing his underpants on the outside.

* * *

YOUR HAPPY TASK 1: For Today Only, Treat Yourself To A Large Sundae. If You Are On A Diet, Don't Count The Calories. The Flavor And Toppings... Your Choice! Enjoy Every Mouthful! And Remember... Today Belongs To You!

The doctor's book started with an assignment no one would refuse, probably to get a lethargic reader off his ass. The tactic worked. As instructed, Henry didn't think about the roll of belly flesh almost popping through his shirt buttons even while hot fudge veined his chin. The book told him to enjoy every mouthful. He sure as hell did. "Today belongs to me," he said aloud. And at that moment he felt it did, although soon those dark feelings of worthlessness crept back into his brain. Ice cream, like alcohol, provided only a temporary respite, any idiot knew that. He figured tearing off the second task's wrapper might make him feel better. The doctor had mentioned two tasks were fine if he chose to tackle a second or even a third in one day's time. Tearing the wrapper, he read the contents of the page beneath.

YOUR HAPPY TASK 2: Say Hello To Someone You Have Seen Often But Have Not Said Hello To Before. Talk If You Want, And Walk Away Smiling.... And Another Day Belongs To You!

More yellow smiley faces, a variety of them, adorned the page. One wore a tiny top hat and carried a cane, a legless toupéed Fred Astaire incapable of dancing but still smiling away. A second offered its broad toothy smile to a third and obviously female member of genus smiley. The ubiquitous little suckers almost coaxed a smiley face from Henry. Almost. *Positive bombardment, just like the doctor ordered. Okay, then...* Henry grabbed his baseball cap. Not quite a top hat, but it would do. Down the block he saw Mindy Wilson. He had known the girl since she was a scabby kneed little kid. Now here she was, a fetching high school cheerleader he sometimes watched in Starbucks with a hundred of her closest friends. She was walking her designer dog, some well-coiffed miniature breed of something-or-other whose pink ribboned ears seemed entirely appropriate for a canine accompanying Mindy. Henry always shuffled past the girl without uttering even a grunt. Since elementary school, pretty girls like Mindy Wilson scared the hot piss out of him. *Think of the little kid with the scabby knees...*

"Hello," Henry said. He smiled. Not a broad smile showing teeth, not something to cause the girl to run screaming for home. Just your basic 'how-ya-doin' today' smile that wouldn't tag him as some kind of leering psychopath headed for the school yard. For one terrible moment Henry felt certain he had screwed up big time, that once out of sight Mindy would dial her cell phone to report a neighborhood pervert named Henry Womack.

But then *(infuckingcredible!)* she smiled back. "Well, hello yourself, Henry. How have you been?"

Walk away... just walk away smiling, like the book says. "Fine. Just fine, Mindy. Thanks for asking... Mindy." Henry walked off, but he kept smiling, all right. For the next three blocks. The feeling didn't last. Like the first assignment's rush had worn off, so had this one. Steinman's tasks felt like some kind of drug he craved to reach a behavioral high whose dosage Henry needed to increase to maintain whatever euphoria he had achieved. The therapist had told him that some of the tasks might seem simpler than they really were, while others would not produce the desired effect right away, but Henry should remember to stick with the tasks because the completion of them was the most important part. Maybe today *was* his. But he would have to do it all over again tomorrow.

YOUR HAPPY TASK 9: Call Someone You Haven't Seen In A Long Time. Thank Them For Something They Did For You.

"Hello?" "Miss Procopio?"

"Yes... Who is this?"

"Miss Procopio, this is Henry. Henry Womack Junior."

"Who?"

"Henry Womack. You probably don't remember me. I had you for tenth grade English." Silence. "Fifth row, last seat. You seated everyone alphabetically, so I sat in the back. I never raised my hand so you probably don't remember. I was pretty shy."

More silence. Then, "How did you get my number?"

"Online. You're listed among Carver High's retirees of 2003. Phyllis Procopio. A few Googles on my PC and there it was. Your number, I mean. Anyway, I wanted to—"

"Listen... Henry, is it? It's past ten o'clock and you shouldn't—"

"Miss Procopio, I just wanted to say thank you, is all. I've been thinking of you, because I read my first book because of you. I read it on my own because you once mentioned it in class. *The Catcher in The Rye* by J.D. Salinger. I don't read much, but I loved that book even though you told us it was the book Mark David Chapman said made him shoot John Lennon." Henry thought he heard the woman gasp.

"Mr. Womack, you really ought not to be calling me so—"

"—That's all I wanted to say, Miss Procopio. You have a good night, okay? Thanks again. Really. A book can mean so much to —"

The woman hung up before he could say more, and Henry wasn't sure he felt so good about this task. He probably had scared the loose turds out of the old woman, his call coming out of nowhere like that. But he had completed his ninth task and that *was* good, so he checked off his 'Task Accomplished Box,' even added his own smiley face to the page. Another day belonged to him and he went to bed satisfied.

YOUR HAPPY TASK 15: Put On Your Best Clothes And Go Somewhere You Have Never Been. Walk Around And Enjoy The Sights. Another Day Is In Your Pocket!

This one proved difficult because it rained hard and Henry had selected to take the bus to Atlantic City. The assignment became an all day event and he told his father he would not be making it to the store. This did not put the old man in a terrific frame of mind. But Henry wanted to see the famous boardwalk, maybe spend a few dollars in the casinos and enjoy a foot long hot dog too. He left before dawn to make the three hour trip. It probably would have been a better idea had this been the summer instead of the early spring when it was still chilly, and the rain didn't help. He felt foolish soaking wet in the only suit he owned ('Inspected by Number 6'), walking the boardwalk while chowing down on pizza and hot dogs. But tasks had to be completed in their proper order, and Henry would never cheat on Dr. Steinman. His wallet emptied of fifty-three dollars swallowed by Donald Trump's slots, his clothes still damp, Henry returned to his apartment late. But he checked off the book's box while managing to feel he *had* accomplished something. And wasn't that Steinman's point?

Tonight Henry wore his own smiley face. Measured against his results, *Happy Task 32* outshone the others.

Make Someone Laugh Today And You Will Make Today Yours. The World Is Your Audience!

He had no clue where to start. Henry's sense of humor resided in the same barren territory as his social skills. People sometimes laughed *at* him, sure. He had proven adept at this more often than he cared to admit. But to share a laugh *with* someone, to coax hilarity from another person in the spirit of shared joy or even momentary camaraderie, that talent completely eluded him. Everywhere people were laughing at *some*thing. On TV women were in stitches over some asinine remark Regis muttered to Kelley. On the school bus little kids snickered and hooted when someone farted; on street corners the older kids entertained each other with cunt jokes. A punch line was doable and easy. People told jokes every day. He could do this, dammit!

The answer came to him in Radley Park. Its paths teemed with strollers enjoying the first real burst of spring weather. Henry spotted the young girl in pancake makeup, watched for a moment as she performed. Mimes annoyed most people. They weren't funny and were only minimally entertaining, and this girl proved no exception. Yet here she was on the promenade, her face painted white except for red bow tie lips frozen in a perpetual frown and eyes deeply shadowed, doing her damnedest pretending to struggle against an imaginary wind on a perfectly calm day. A small useless umbrella served as her only prop, and a tin can sat nearby with nothing inside. No one offered even polite attention to her desperate mimics. The scene bordered on pathetic. The mime approached Henry, stopping him as he tried walking past. In wide arcs she drew an imaginary box in the air surrounding the spot where both stood.

Henry watched. He didn't know what else to do. The box wasn't real, but he was trapped inside. The girl beat against the four imaginary walls of the box inside which she had enclosed the two of them while Henry remained in place feeling a complete fool. And then, inspiration! *[The world is your audience. Make someone laugh...]*

"Talk!" he cried out. "There's nothing here! Can't you see that?? No box! No walls! Nothing! You're trapped inside your own imaginary box! So free yourself! Talk!!"

The girl looked at him as if Henry were insane. She pointed to her mouth, shook her head with exaggeration as if to say "I'm a mime, idiot! I *can't* talk!"

"Yes you can!" Henry shouted, and now people began to stare. "It's easy. You just open your mouth and words, they come out! See? I'm doing it right now! So *talk!!* "

Playing along, the girl mimicked trying to speak. She spat soundless syllables, she opened her mouth very wide as if to shout. But still nothing. Again she shook her head.

Henry turned to the passersby, then to some old people sitting on a bench. "We can make her talk!" he shouted. "Come on, say it with me! Talk! Talk! Talk! Talk!"

A miracle followed. First a pimply kid holding a skateboard chimed in. Then a young couple walking by did the same. Almost everyone surrounding him joined the chant directed at the young mime. *"TALK!... TALK!... TALK!... TALK!"* People laughed loud and hard.

Whether encouraged or frustrated, the girl pretended to make an effort to speak. Her mouth contorted and the crowd roared, waiting... waiting...

"They think this is some kind of bit," Henry whispered to her. "They think I'm in on it. Let's give them something to see!"

He saw the mime's wink. She understood. With exaggerated drama the mime stepped forward, cleared her throat. Passersby nearby watched as she sang out Donna Summer's song. Like the girl working hard for the money in those lyrics, so was this young mime. She added an impromptu soft shoe number, using her umbrella as a cane prop while dancing her heart out like some vaudevillian on speed. *"Voila!"* she shouted when through, arms high, seeming astounded at her burst of inspired showmanship.

Henry picked up his cue, pantomiming the release of an imaginary door exiting the imaginary box. Taking her hand they walked through the invisible door to freedom—and to unexpected applause from the crowd. The girl bowed, and Henry, his smile now in full bloom, bowed too. Coins clinked into the girl's tin can for the next two minutes. Some bills got tossed in too.

"You're a hit," Henry whispered.

"*We* are," she said. "We're Martin and Lewis. Laurel and Hardy. Clinton and Obama!" Together they snickered like school kids. Had he tried a thousand times Henry could not have repeated the extemporaneous routine. But it worked this one time, and walking by the duck pond with the girl it turned out that she *did* talk. She talked a whole lot.

Her name was Jamie and she was a student at the College of Performing Arts. The mime routine had been her assignment, similar to but more structured than any of Steinman's tasks. She admitted worrying she wasn't any good at acting before a crowd and might have called it quits after today. Then along came Henry and he changed everything. That night they met for a movie. With the white pancake makeup washed off, Jamie fell short of pretty, but she didn't fall short by much. They laughed at the same scenes, although sitting near her Henry couldn't care less about the lunatic antics of Robin Williams.

Walking back to Jamie's apartment he already was a man in love. "I'm glad you decided to talk," he told her.

"You won't be. Now that I've violated the mime code of ethics we're bonded forever. We're fish and chips, a burger and fries." She was flirting with him, but that was okay. Another incredible moment had passed. Somehow Jamie managed to create a hundred of them.

* * *

"...a hundred of them?" Dr. Steinman seemed impressed, but skeptical. "Henry, I'm happy for you. This is a good sign. But—"

"'But' is never a good word, Doctor. Not unless you're spelling it with two t's." Henry saw the therapist smile. He had not often revealed his lighter side to Steinman.

"Some things aren't always as they appear, Henry. Good feelings are great, of course, but they can also blind you. You're making progress, but keep your eyes open and your feet on the ground for a while, okay? We're after lasting happiness here, the real thing, right?"

"I *am* pretty damned happy, Doctor. Jamie, she has these famous comedy routines she does for her acting class at school, and I help her with them. 'Who's on First?' 'Niagara Falls.' You know, The Three Stooges. Abbott and Costello. Old vaudeville bits. I laugh all the time with her. Sometimes it's like we can't stop. I have some of her routine memorized. Want to hear?"

"Why not?"

"I'm a homeless guy, see, and I'm a little crazy, and I'm telling my story to someone, I'm saying… 'We were very happy, my little family. One morning we were seated around the breakfast table and a knock came at the door. There stood a man. He was broken in health and spirit. I bade him enter, I welcomed him into my home. I said *'Make my home your home'*… and he did! One day I returned from work to find that my home was no longer a home. My wife and the stranger had fled! Then one day at the banks of the *Niagara Falls* I found them! Suddenly my brain snapped. All the years of pent up emotion of years suffering welled up within me. I knew I would never be satisfied until I had my bony fingers wrapped around his throat. So with murder in my heart...

slooooooowly I turned!! " Henry acted this out, eyes bugged, turning in exaggerated slow motion.*"...step by step, inch by inch* I crept upon him and when I saw the stare in his face I struck and I grabbed him!"

"Okay, Doctor, here I'm supposed to grab you and slam you into the wall, start beating the crap out of you. Then I say, 'My poor friend, I'm sorry. But every time I hear the word Niagara Falls, I just want to kill!' And throughout the bit somehow someone keeps accidentally saying 'Niagara Falls' and I keep losing it worse and worse and beating on you. Funny stuff, huh?"

Dr. Steinman looked like he wanted to laugh, but for some reason therapists always kept that same blank expression. He didn't laugh. He didn't even smile. "Real funny stuff, Henry. And I'm glad you're on your way. Jamie sounds great. But feet on the ground with this girl, okay? Go slowly. It isn't difficult."

* * *

...But it *was* difficult, more difficult than any task in the doctor's book. Henry managed three weeks before he caved. "I think I love you," he blurted out as they sat on Jamie's stoop. Unlike his daily assignments he said the words because he wanted her to hear him say them.

She tried for a joke as if he had said nothing. "'Say goodnight, Gracie.'" She managed a terrible impression of George Burns. Henry didn't laugh. "Come on, where's your sense of humor? Your line is 'Goodnight, Gracie.' Burns and Allen. Remember?"

"I think I love you. No... I *do* love you. This is no bit, Jamie."

She fell silent, reverting again to mime mode. Henry felt like a bad stand-up comic dying on stage. "I'm really sorry, Henry. I like you, you know I do. We're friends. Good friends, I'd like to think. Franks and beans. Smith and Wesson. But that's all we are. Is that okay?"

"There's another guy, isn't there? We never talked about it, but
—"

She touched her finger to his lips. "No other guy. And no more
talk. Friends. Simon and Garfunkel. Piss and vinegar. Okay?"

It wasn't okay, it was nowhere near okay. "Okay," Henry said.

* * *

No happy task followed. Henry could not open Steinman's book.
Still, he spoke to Jamie every day, even laughed with her, or
pretended to. If acting was her talent, he could do it too. But
whatever smiles he wore, they disintegrated during time spent
alone when the sadness wouldn't let go. He couldn't eat, had
trouble sleeping.

Dr. Steinman advised he try more tasks, attempt to regain what
ground he had lost.

One night over coffee Henry blurted out, "I forgive you, Jamie."

She looked at him confused."Forgive me? For what?"

Behind the smiley face mask Henry swallowed hard. "It doesn't
matter. Just know that I do." He didn't tell her that offering his
forgiveness had been his 56th happy task.And he didn't tell her that
he had lied.

* * *

A favor for a stranger.

A pat on a puppy's head.

A loving note written to his father. These were among Henry's
next tasks. He completed them—check, check, and check—even if
his heart no longer was in it. Now, having danced like a maniac to
Donna Summers' ditty, he needed to peel another brown wrapper
from the next page to keep from screaming. He read *Happy Task 67*.
For a moment it didn't register. He read it again to be certain.

There Is A Person Who Makes You Feel Very Happy. Maybe You Smile When You Think About This Person. Maybe You Feel Sad When This Person Is Away. Kill This Person Today! Carpe This Diem!!

Smiley faces filled the page. Some had blood dripping from their mouths, but the crimson smiles remained. Henry's own mouth fell open. *[Don't ask anyone—including me—how to complete the tasks, Henry. Trust yourself...]* Kill this person???

"This is crazy..." he said.

["Eyes open... feet on the ground... we're after lasting happiness..."] Happiness... Happy... One hundred and one tasks to... Happy!! Step by step... inch by inch...

"Trust myself," Henry muttered. "That's what's important here..."

(...and trust Dr. Steinman, of course. Trust someone or you trust no one.)

Maybe it wasn't so crazy. Not if you thought about it. Maybe it wasn't crazy at all.

Because Jamie made him happy. But Jamie also made him sad. Really sad. The doctor knew it, even warned him. Happy... that was the goal. His only goal. There were one hundred and one ways to reach Happy. He had tried sixty-six but he wasn't there yet.

"I'm not happy... not happy..." He read the page again. Dr. Steinman's words echoed inside his brain.

Kill This Person Today!

Steinman would never steer him wrong. Never. *["Are you game, Henry? Let me hear you say it!"]* The smiley faces on the page lined up together as if in some Broadway chorus line. They sang out to him in a hundred cartoon voices united in their aria like operatic Disney characters, a hundred animated bloody mouths open in song yet still smiling, smiling, smiling. *"Kill her, Hen-reee... Hen-reee... Hen-reeeeeeeee...!"*

In the end Jamie had made him sad, so sad he never wanted to leave his bed. And Dr. Steinman knew what was best. The therapist knew because he cared when nobody else did. And all those smiley faces, they wanted him to feel happy too! *["Let me hear you say it!"]*

Henry's lips quivered. "Yes... I'm game..."

* * *

He hadn't called, he just showed up at her apartment and rang Jamie's bell.

She appeared in her robe with her hair still wet. She looked so sweet, like a little kid at a slumber party. "Henry? I'm not even dressed. I just took a shower. It's kind of late."

"This won't take long. Promise."

He closed the door behind him. The smile never left his face.

"Were you playing baseball?"

Henry looked at the bat he held as if noticing it for the first time. "It's for a bit I've been working on. You've got me motivated to act, Jamie. I have to show you!"

"A comedy bit? 'Who's On First?' That's great, Henry! Let me see!"

His smile widened. He shook his head. "It's not 'Who's On First?' It's kind of short. 'Niagara Falls,' remember? The one you acted out for me? I haven't got much yet."

She sat on the couch, curled her legs under her. "Show me what you've got."

Henry stood before her, cleared his throat. "I'm a little nervous."

"That's okay. Just do it."

He took a moment to get into character. Then... "Say 'Niagara Falls,' okay? I need the trigger to set me off..."

Jamie played along. "Okay... *'Niagara Falls!'* How's that?"

Henry's eyes bugged and his body stiffened with exaggerated derangement. *"Ni-a-gara Falls!! All the years of pent up emotion of... suffering and pain. Sloooowly I turned. Step-by-step! Inch-by-inch...!"*

Approaching her he raised the bat like a slugger preparing to smash one out of the park. Showing teeth and hovering over her, his forced Cheshire cat smile broadened. Somewhere inside his brain a smiley face sang out his name.

"There's no baseball bat in this routine, Henry."

"There is now!" he said, tightening his grip.

Jamie managed only an aborted scream, more of a squeak.

Henry took one mighty swing and connected with her skull. He felt the vibration of shattered bone and heard it crack, went for a second swing and watched her head explode.

Swinging the bat again and again, half blinded with blood he kept swinging it until Jamie slumped to the floor, and still he kept swinging counting sixty-seven times until her face no longer was there. He studied what raw pulp remained, lowered the dripping bat. "Say goodnight, Gracie…"

* * *

Martin Steinman luckily had caught the error in time. He was on the phone that same minute. "Jesus, Lloyd! How could you make this kind of mistake? Did you read Task 67? Did you?? Thank Christ I decided to double check the printer's copy tonight! Hell, man, what am I paying you for?"

"Take it easy, Marty," his editor answered. "Sometimes these things slip by us. The printer screwed up. But your book isn't on the shelves yet. We caught it, we can fix it. No harm done. All your other happy tasks are fine. We'll fix the smileys so that it looks more like lipstick, not blood. Promise."

Martin lit another cigarette, a sure indication the man was pissed. The therapist usually wasn't the type to lose it, but tonight he verged on a shit hemorrhage. "Fuck the smileys, Lloyd!! Buy a dictionary! Task 67 is supposed to read 'KISS,' idiot! That's spelled *K-I-S-S...*"

ACTIVE MEMBER

RAY GARTON

STANDING IN THE DOORWAY of the small apartment, the big detective puts his hands on his hips and looks around. "Jesus Horatio Christ," he says quietly, "there's enough blood in here to drown cattle."

* * *

He hurried down the wet sidewalk, not wanting to look suspicious, but wanting to be far away from the park as soon as possible. His hands were deep in the baggy pockets of his long green coat, pulled together over the front of his pants. He was crying; his twisted face glistened with tears, his thin chest hitched with sobs.

He had done it again. *They* had done it again. He hadn't wanted to, he really hadn't. But he never realized that until it was too late, until afterward. He never thought about it before, when he could stop it, keep it from happening. How could he think with that voice hissing at him, stabbing upward through the center of his body like a steel barbed spike, up and up, straight to his brain. He could only think afterward, when it was quiet, satisfied, resting. Growing.

He *knew* it was growing. He hadn't thought so at first, but it soon became obvious, impossible to ignore. He wanted, *needed* to tell someone, but he knew he couldn't. After all, even *he* hadn't believed it at first. And if he told someone about the growing, he would have to tell about the voice, too. They'd put him back in that place, give him back to the twitchy-lipped doctors, the stiff-necked nurses. He could almost hear the door locking behind him again, smell the sterility, the stinging, artificial cleanliness of the halls and bathrooms. No glass or metal objects. Guarded showers. Jigsaw puzzles and pottery classes. Questions answered with questions. He wouldn't let that happen again. He knew what to do.

He had known the moment he rolled off that girl in the park. She was tiny, young. He'd had to beat her to get it inside.

He knew what he had to do and he was going straight home to do it.

He was surrounded by the city, in the very center of it now. All around him, great god-like erections rose toward the dirty night sky. Cars drove by, their tires making moist panting sounds on the wet pavement. A few yards ahead of him a bus, long and fat, grunted to a halt at the curb and he hurried to catch it, his hands still in his coat pockets, his tennis shoes splashing through puddles. He saw a pretty face, blonde, big tired eyes. Looking up and down the length of the bus, he saw that she was alone inside.

The doors opened.

What if it awoke? Told him to follow her, *made* him follow her, forced him with its ugly, insistent pounding?

"Hey, buddy," the driver said, "you coming, or what?"

He backed away, turned, jogged down the sidewalk, away from her.

Never again, he thought, *not after tonight. Tonight it ends.*

* * *

The woman in the robe and curlers walks in behind the detective, arms folded over her fat, soft breasts. "I knew he'd be trouble," she says.

"You the one that called, ma'am?" the detective asks.

"That's right. I'm the landlady."

He watches her standing there, soaking it all in, ogling the mess. He knows she can't wait to tell her friends. "You received a complaint?"

"I heard the screamin' myself," she says, pressing a liver-spotted hand to her chest. "Hell, I'm alla way down*stairs* and I heard it myself." She looks at it some more, all the blood, the knife, and shakes her head. "Yeah, I *knew* he'd be trouble."

* * *

He was cold even though he was sweating and gasping from his rush to get home before it stirred, before it spoke.

It began years ago at the boarding academy where his father had sent him after his mother had killed herself with a shotgun blast to her face. "Get you some good Christian teaching," the tattooed man had said. But he knew it was *really* to get him out of the way of his father's woman friends. There had been a lot of those.

The dean had caught him one night. He hadn't even heard the keys rattle in the hall. The little man had just walked into the dorm room and found him sitting on the bed with the magazine, masturbating.

"It's evil," the principal had told him the next morning. The man had glared at him over the big oak desk, leaning forward, his pockmarked face hard and burning with righteous anger. "It hangs there to remind us of sin and the only good that comes of it are urine and children. It's dirty. Filthy. Why do you think little boys are taught to wash their hands after they touch it?" Tiny gems of perspiration had sparkled beneath his razor-like nose. "It must be fought, trained, or it will make you do things you have no business doing."

He'd heard it that night for the first time, when he thought he was asleep. Just whispers. Unintelligible. Dream-like.

But over the years it got louder, clearer.

Then they had put him away, punished him for the things it had made him do. Horrible things. Nasty, wet things that had brought him no pleasure—not really, not afterward—and had even made him throw up and lose consciousness at times. But they were things that had pleasured it, that had quenched its thirst and sated its hunger and, most importantly, silenced its incessant *hissing*.

I'm crazy, he'd thought with giddy relief. *Just crazy, that's all. Now I'll get better and it'll go away*.

And it did. For a while. Long enough for him to feel, to *seem*, cured.

Now it did not hiss. It screamed. It scorched the inside of his skull with its hot breath and made his eyes water with a voice that sounded like the end of the world. It was enraged, perhaps, by the sores that had appeared on it, swollen and running with milky fluids.

And dear sweet merciful Jesus it was *growing*.

His hands, still in his coat pockets, covered it now, pressing over the denim crotch that had grown tight, that would not hold it much longer. The sores, probably draining again, stung. Beneath the pants, he was still wet from its copious vomiting earlier.

I'm not crazy, he thought frantically as he hurried across a street, around a corner. *I never was. I'm not, no, I AM NOT CRAZY!*

He thought of that poor girl, limp beneath him, whimpering, and cried some more.

* * *

"Why do you say that, ma'am?" the detective asks.

"Huh?" She turns to him jerkily with wide eyes, torn from her lurid thoughts.

"Why do you say you knew he'd be trouble?"

"Oh, he was a nutcase," she says with a wave of her meaty hand. "A week or so ago I come up here for the rent and he answers the door with his pants open, wanger hangin' out, and he's cryin' like a baby."

The detective takes a pad and pen from his overcoat pocket and begins writing. "Did he say anything?"

"Oh, yeah. Blubbered and moaned. Somethin' about it bein' bigger. He was swingin' his thing around like a string of pearls." She chuckles, a cold and somehow dreary sound. "If he was talkin' about his pecker, he was crazy, 'cause it wasn't that big. But it was sick, with big sores."

The detective turns to the young uninformed officer who arrived before him. "Well?"

"The door was bolted on the inside," the officer says quietly. "We had to break in. Eight floors up. Nobody coulda got in."

"Yeah. Figured as much. No surprises here."

"Well, sir. There is one thing."

* * *

He burst into his little apartment, slammed the door and threw the bolt. Tearing off his coat, he let it fall to the floor and hurried to the kitchen, shoulders still quaking with sobs. He pulled out a drawer, almost dropped it, began searching, clanging through the cutlery until he found it. He pushed the drawer back in and held the knife in his hand.

"Oh, God," he breathed, panicking because it was stirring, beginning to whisper before it screamed.

He ripped his jeans open as he left the kitchen and they fell down around his knees. He stopped, kicking his shoes off, stepped out of the pants, and hurried into the living room, his fist tight around the handle of the knife. He paced back and forth, back and forth, crying, scared, because now it was beginning to speak, to scream. His eyes clenched and his head tilted back as he fell into a chair. He did not want to look down because he knew he would see it, knew it had found its way out of the dirty undershorts and was growing, stiffening even more. Ugly. Diseased.

It told him, roared at him, to put down the knife. He did not listen. As he fought to ignore the painful voice, tears squeezed from his closed eyes. A scream tore from his chest as he began hacking.

Hacking and hacking…

* * *

"What?" the detective wants to know, frowning at the officer. "Some head case chops off his dick? No biggie. When I was in San Francisco, there was this guy who—"

"Sir." The interruption is respectful. "Like I said, no one could get in. It's obvious he did it. But, um… we can't, uh, find it. We've looked. And, um… it's just not here."

* * *

Hacking and screaming, hacking and hacking…

DECOR

MICHAEL CORNELIUS

OLD MRS. HILDEBRAND moved in to the Utley house late on a Tuesday night. And I mean late. I know it was late because the lights from the black van that pulled up in front of the house shined deep into my bedroom and woke me up. Curious, I crawled sleepily out of bed and peeked out my second floor window. I couldn't see much. Even though it was pitch black outside, no one had bothered to turn on the porch light. I could only make out the dim shapes of old furniture being hauled in by a couple of burly guys. There was a lady there, too; she was dressed all in black, but I could see the pale outline of her face and hands against the dark quality of night. The whole scene was pretty weird; certainly not something we were used to seeing around Upper Hollow, that's for sure. But all in all, for me, "pretty weird" was hardly worth staying up for, and yawning, I ambled back to bed and was soon fast asleep.

Of course, by the next morning the entire block was talking about the new neighbor—especially my mother. My mother had long ago elected herself "Queen Bee" of the neighborhood, and the occasion of someone new moving in was just the sort of event she lived for. I am sure she was up with the sun, baking a batch of her infamous cranberry walnut muffins—or as my sister Sooz and I called them, her "spy" muffins. Whenever my mother felt the need to intrude upon a neighbor's life, she'd bake them a batch of her muffins and take them over laced with practiced kindness and a million prepared questions. Whether a death in the family or a new job or a new nose, there was Mother, ringing the bell bright and early, muffins in one hand and the steely sense of righteous determination possessed only by the town's leading gossip in the other. Mother had even started baking her muffins for cases of divorce. My father had once made the mistake of remarking to her that this, he believed, was just a smidge past good taste, which not only caused her to make liver for dinner three nights in a row but also to spread the unfortunately true rumor around the neighborhood that my father, in a pique of what can only be considered morbid curiosity, once had his eyebrows waxed at the upscale salon in the mall. Besides, Mother said, people have to eat breakfast whether they're happy or sad, and Sooz and I knew that for our mother, unhappy people were the hungriest of all.

But at least a basket of muffins was a traditional gift for a new neighbor, so Mother didn't cut too unusual a figure as she strutted across Canterbury Lane and knocked hard a few times on the new neighbor's door. Unfortunately, Mother seemed to be getting the "nobody's home" response, meaning, of course, that her knocks went unheeded and unanswered. When I say unfortunately, I mean that more for the poor saps who don't answer the door than my mother, because such a response usually leads to a round of peering into living rooms and the occasional "Yoo hoo!" being blasted through any open window. *Repeated* unanswered door knocks only make my mother more determined than ever to root herself past the unfriendly silence and worm her way deep into the secrets she will soon become convinced that the folks inside must be hiding. But that's my mother for you; she isn't happy unless she's digging into someone else's life, and I'm just glad when it isn't my sock drawer she's busy eyeing, if you know what I mean.

For us kids on the block, life went on as usual. Summer vacation had just started, and we were out of school. So we only cared if the new neighbor had kids the right age for street kickball, and judging from the antique furniture I'd seen going inside the house last night, I sort of doubted that. Still, any new neighbor had to be a big improvement over Mean Mr. Utley. The old coot had lived on the block longer than anyone else here, and was notorious in the neighborhood for threatening to shoot any stray raccoon, dog, or child that even set one foot on his lawn. I guess every neighborhood has some house that—through the actions of the mean old coot who lives inside—becomes forbidden territory for the local kids. Well, for us, that was Mr. Utley's house. So if I wanted to play a nasty trick on Fatso Higgins or Cooter Mooney I'd make sure to kick their ball deep into Mr. Utley's yard. Neighborhood rule meant that the owner of the ball had to fetch it, so when the ball ended up somewhere between Mr. Utley's poison ivy patch and his sagging old willow tree, they'd either have to sneak in themselves and get it or have their dad go over when he got home from work and ask nicely for it back. Either way, it was totally worth it, because whether they got caught by Mr. Utley or had to send their reluctant fathers over, they still caught holy hell, since no neighborhood dad liked dealing with Mr. Utley anymore than their kids. Of course, I had to be careful and not abuse this fact, since sometimes it was my ball that "accidentally" would go over the fence. The first time it happened, Mr. Utley caught me sneaking out of his yard and shook his fist at me while chasing me down the street with his sawed off Winchester. The second time I fell in the poison ivy and itched for a whole week. The third time I became something of a neighborhood legend when I managed to retrieve the ball safely without being caught by either man or plant. Only trouble was I still caught holy hell from my mother later that night since I had ripped my new jeans climbing over Mr. Utley's wrought iron fence. Not only was there a hole where there shouldn't have been any, but I think my mother had a pretty good idea how I got that hole, and she told my dad to talk me over good for stepping into Mr. Utley's yard again. My dad, however, only gave her a look like he was going to do it, but never did. Later, when he gave me my lunch money for school the next morning, he slipped me an extra fifty cents so I could get an ice cream. I sort of think my dad did that because he appreciated that I was solving my own problems without his help, and that this time, he didn't have to deal with Mr. Utley for me.

So anyway, whatever neighbor we got was certainly going to be an improvement. It was just a matter of someone finding out what kind of new neighbor we had, and, of course, no one was better suited for such a task than my mother. That first day she strutted over with her muffins practically every hour, on the hour. It was almost funny to see her keeping a sharp eye on the clock and then, when the appointed time arrived, watch her check her hair and make-up in the big hall mirror one last time before waddling across the street. On about her fourth trip my father commented under his breath that this was the most exercise she had got in years. And still her persistence was not rewarded; by the time dinner rolled around, those muffins were still in their perfectly-appointed basket on our kitchen counter. After being dragged across the street at least a half dozen times they were starting to look a little the worse for wear, though my dad still caught holy hell for trying to filch one right before dinner.

Still, you can't say that persistence isn't its own reward, or that things don't come to those who keep on trying. My mother must have given up going across the street sometime just before dark; so imagine her surprise when our doorbell rang right around nine o'clock that same night. "Now who could that be?" she said in her "oh-so-delighted" tone that indicated, for once, gossip seemed to be coming to her. She checked her hair and make-up again, then answered the door.

I was sitting in our den at the time, watching re-runs on TV, so I couldn't see who had come in. Normally when I was sitting on the couch I could just sort of crane my neck this way and twist my body the other and catch a glimpse of who'd just come through the door in the big hall mirror. This was always a good tactic whenever it was possible I was going to be getting in trouble with Mr. Utley or either Fatso or Cooter's mom, depending on what I had done to them earlier that day. When I saw one of them standing there, that usually gave me just enough time to try and hide, though sooner or later my mother would root me out and chew my head off for whatever I had done. This time, however, I couldn't see a thing, so I just went back to watching my show.

Fat lot of good that did; about five seconds later I heard my mother calling for me. "Rocky! Rocky!" she bellowed. I rolled my eyes and as slowly as possible got up off the couch and trudged over to the door. It was only then I saw who had come in. It was the same lady I had seen the night before, though I have to say she looked much better in our foyer than she did through the dim haze of my bedroom widow. She was short, young enough, and wearing a tight black skirt and an even tighter shirt that really showed off her best features. I mean, her titties were *huuuge*. I was in love, though since I was twelve, I had no illusions about how long it would last. Still, wait until Cooter and Fatso heard about this.

"Oh, there you are," my mother chirped, as if she hadn't known where I was the whole time. "Rocky," she continued, putting one of her fat arms around my shoulders, "this is Mrs. Scheepers. She's living in the house across the street."

"Actually, it's my mother who is living there," the woman said with a warm smile. She had just the tiniest accent—Mexican? I couldn't be sure, but my father railed that anyone with an accent was Mexican, so it made a kind of logical sense to me—and flashing dark eyes. Her nails were long and red as rubies, as were her lips. Frankly, she looked like a vampire, which, I have to say, was a good look for her. "My husband and I bought the home, but it's for my mother. You see, she is quite old, and somewhat infirm. She recently suffered an illness, and is only now recovering."

"Oh, what's wrong with her?" my mother asked with the tone of a woman about to open a box that holds a fourteen-carat diamond engagement ring. For Mother, a neighbor's tragedies really were a girl's best friend.

"Stroke," Mrs. Scheepers confided, a response that brought a sympathetic and yet somehow satisfied cluck from my mother. If Mrs. Scheepers noticed, she didn't let on. "So we purchased this place for her, to enjoy the peace of the suburbs in her retirement. The city doesn't agree with her much anymore. I'm sure you know how it is," she finished, though none of us knew who was supposed to know how it was or what "it" actually was though, like any twelve-year-old boy presented with a pair of knockers like that, I didn't actually care.

"Oh!" my mother said in a tone that indicated she hoped she was the first individual on the block to be presented with such fresh scoop. "And what is your mother's name?"

"Mrs. Hildebrand. She is, of course, quite a dear, but getting on. She's apt to be a bit dotty at times, and certainly doesn't get around as she used to."

"Well, I'm sure we'd be glad to pitch in and help," my mother said. "There's so much to do when you move into a new home, after all." This little offer got looks from me, Dad, and Sooz—we were sure none of us wanted to lift a finger to do a thing for the old bat, and we were just as sure my mother only wanted to offer as a way to get inside the house and get all the information on the new neighbor she could. "Both the kids are good in the yard, and Don is much handier around the house than he looks." Yeah, right. The last thing my father tried to fix was the pilot on our water heater, and he still had the burn mark on his arm to remind him of how good that went down. Ever since then, we'd proven to be sensible souls who called the handyman at the first sign of trouble.

Thankfully, we could tell it wasn't Mrs. Scheepers' first go around with a busybody like my mother, and we marveled as she masterfully dodged my mother's offers of "kindness." "Oh, thank you so much," she said, "but really, that is too much to ask from such kind, new neighbors. No, my husband and I will see to it that all my mother's needs are met. I only came over to ask you to please do your best to avoid bothering my mother, if you can. She does need her rest in her recovery." And with that Mrs. Scheepers and her gorgeous bozungas turned to go, though not before my mother had signaled to my father to go into the kitchen and dutifully grab the basket of cranberry walnut muffins. Mrs. Scheepers kindly received them and left, though my mother's quick counting seemed to assure her that not all of the muffins had actually left the house, and Sooz and I exchanged a smile, as we felt sure my father would be in for it later.

So that's how the entire neighborhood learned all about Mrs. Hildebrand or, as us kids soon called her, Old Mrs. Hildebrand, since anyone too infirm to get out of their house deserved an insulting moniker of some kind from the neighborhood kids. Still, a sick old lady was hardly big news for us or for anyone, and so soon the neighborhood turned its attention to other, seemingly more important, matters.

In addition to being the "Queen Bee" of Canterbury Lane, my mother also styled herself as the Martha Stewart of all Upper

Hollow. Consequently, any holiday meant parties, decorations, and festivities. And for my mother, this meant not only in her own home, but—and this was where she always told us she felt her true passion lay—my mother coordinated all decorations and block parties for every holiday for the entire year for all of Canterbury Lane. This meant circulating her now-infamous "Home Owner's Association Approved Décor List," a booklet that revealed—in scrupulous detail—all the varying "do's" and "don'ts" of decorating on our block. Of course, my mother never bothered to explain to anyone that she herself comprised the entirety of the local Home Owner's Association. And that her list and block parties and holiday "convergences" were just her special way of being a controlling w-i-t-c-h. Still, people went along and, for some reason, seemed to like it. So when each and every house in the neighborhood pretty much ended up looking just like the other, everyone, especially my mother, was pleased.

Of course some people have to spoil everyone else's good time, and for my mother, her neighborhood nemesis had always been Mr. Utley, whose refusal to even answer his door wearing pants generally rendered friendship lights at Christmastime a distant possibility. Still, with Mr. Utley gone, my mother was thrilled at the prospect of finally adding the last house on the block to her cadre of holiday followers, so when Flag Day rolled around, Mother was quick to act. For Flag Day, every home on the block flew—you guessed it—one simple flag, always hung to the right side of the door. And sure enough, my mother trotted over one evening, in her most patriotic red, white, and blue suit, to Old Mrs. Hildebrand's to present her with her very own pre-approved flag and flag holder combination set. Of course, no one answered her knocks; but Mother left Mrs. Hildebrand the cheerfully-wrapped bundle (in Old Glory paper, no less) and a little note to explain its proper use. However, June 14 came and went, and no flag flew at Old Mrs.

Hildebrand's. Mother was stymied; she was determined to add this house to her collection. Still, she reasoned that no one could blame Mrs. Hildebrand for not giving in just quite yet. After all, she had just moved in, and she was sickly; perhaps her daughter and son-in-law had not visited in time to set up the flag properly? My father also speculated that perhaps Old Mrs. Hildebrand just didn't see Flag Day as a *real* holiday, a question that earned us another round of liver for dinner and likely earned him a good tongue lashing later that night.

Still, Mrs. Hildebrand pleased my mother in other ways. The old Utley house had been growing steadily more decrepit over the years. The place was just a small bungalow, easily the smallest and oldest home on the entire block. Whereas most homes were bi-level brick monstrosities built sometime in the 1970s, Mrs. Hildebrand's house was much older, and therefore, much dingier and, as my mother always said, much more of an eyesore. Still, there were signs early on that Mrs. Hildebrand was intent on having the old place fixed up, at least some. The old wrought iron fence, for example, was repaired, and what was once a twisted mess of rusted metal soon gleamed shiny and bright black new. The gate worked now, too, and could lock, which made retrieving stray kick balls more difficult though, truth be told, without Mean Mr. Utley living there, precious few balls wandered their way into the overgrown yard anymore. My father was heard to remark that fixing the fence must have cost a pretty penny, which made my mother hope aloud that perhaps the Scheepers had "real" money and were certainly the "kind of people" that ought to be invited over for one of her specially made dinners. I always hated it when mother had one of her dinner parties, because it meant I had to spend the day cleaning my room (why, I didn't know, since I doubted Mrs. Scheepers was interested in my baseball card collection or seeing how tidy my closet could be) and dragging up extra chairs from the basement for people to sit on. But, without any way to contact Mrs. Scheepers in the city, mother was stymied there as well, and we were all safe, at least for now.

Flag Day was just the warm-up for summer; the real event was always the Fourth of July. Whereas on Flag Day ostentatious displays of patriotism were disallowed, on Independence Day they were highly encouraged. Décor trumped decorum in our neighborhood. The flashier, the gaudier, the more tasteless, the better. Of course, our red, white and blue displays were as big and brassy as anyone's, but as long as folks flew their flags and somehow marked the celebration, mother was pleased. The evening always culminated in a big barbecue held right there on the street, where the dads all gathered around a few rented grills and the moms all circled around my mother, fearing her wrath enough to feign true bonds of friendship with her. My mother angled every year for a feature on the gathering in the city newspaper, and every year she was firmly turned down. This year, however, her calls to the local features editor finally met with success; flushed with triumph, mother was determined that this would be the most tastelessly garish Fourth of July ever.

Yet alas, Old Mrs. Hildebrand proved to be as stingy a hold out for Fourth of July as she was for Flag Day. Mother visited the house often, left notes, and even one night threatened to stake out the joint if no one would permit her entry. Finally, Mrs. Scheepers came over, as boobalicious as ever. She was full of apologies for taking so long to respond, saying that her job and her mother's health problems had been keeping her so drained lately. But Mother wasn't having a drop of it. She wheedled, nudged, pumped, primed, and even threatened to decorate the house herself. "At least fly the flag, for Christ's sake!" she wailed. At this, I sucked in my breath; a "for Christ's sake!" certainly showed the seriousness of Mother's intent.

But Mrs. Scheepers proved to be a nut too tough for even Mother to crack. She apologized up and down, but insisted that her mother preferred no displays of any kind. "Not even the flag?" Mother asked again, but Mrs. Scheepers just shrugged as she saw herself out the door. "Damned foreigners," Mother grumbled as she left. By this time Mrs. Scheepers and her still-as-yet-unseen husband had clearly turned from the "right" people into the "wrong" people. To make matters worse, Mother's most-desired spread in the local paper was marred by the fact that, in the upper left-hand corner of the neighborhood photo, Old Mrs. Hildebrand's plain Jane house could clearly be seen *not* flying the flag. Mother was steamed; clearly, something must be done.

To us kids, though, Old Mrs. Hildebrand wasn't really much of an issue. She didn't chase us with a sawed-off shotgun, or threaten to call our parents every time we sneezed. Still, there was something a little creepy about her, or so I was told during our last kickball game of the summer. School was starting the next day. And I was determined to go out a winner, so I gave the ball a little extra *oomph* during my last time at plate. Sure enough, the ball bounded over Kitty Parsons' head and landed smack in the middle of Mrs. Hildebrand's yard.

"Go get it!" Fatso yelled at me. He was rolling the ball for the opposing team, and even though rollers never really moved all that much, sweat was still oozing out of every corner of his body.

"You get it!" I hollered back. "It's your ball! That's the rule!"

But Fatso only shook his head. I balled up my fists and charged the roller's mound, determined to make my point one way or the other. But even a sock to the jaw couldn't convince Fatso to go after the ball. "I don't care what you do, Rocky," he bawled. "I'm not going in there, you can't make me!"

"What's your problem, you big baby?" Cooter asked. Fatso had always been something of a cryer, but I had never seen him react like this to just going after the ball.

Fatso sniffled and wiped his snot on his arm. "I just ain't going up there, okay? If you want the ball, you go get it!"

By this time, I was more curious about what was going on with Fatso and Old Mrs. Hildebrand than anything that was happening in the game. Cooter was, too; I could see it in his face. No one else quite felt the same way, however. "Are we playing or what?" Vance Jonson yelled. Vance Jonson was a fourth grader who I knew for a fact was still wetting the bed as late as last year. I decided to throw him our neighborhood kid version of the middle-finger salute (we used our pointing finger, just in case anyone's mom was watching) and pulled Fatso over to the side of the street. Meanwhile, Kitty had long ago gotten sick of everyone jawing about getting the ball and had gone and gotten it herself. So for a while, the game went on without us.

Fatso wasn't blubbering so much anymore, just sort of sniffling to himself. I wasn't sure the best way to figure out what was going on with him, but I should have just left it to Cooter, who always knew how to get to the heart of things. "What the hell is wrong with you, big baby?" he said. Fatso and I both raised our eyes because we knew whenever one of us risked the use of the word "hell" in any sentence outside of church it meant he was pretty serious about what was being said.

Fatso finally stopped sputtering long enough to speak up. "Haven't any of you ever seen her?"

"Who?" I asked, unsure what Fatso was talking about.

"The old lady. Mrs. Hildebrand! Haven't you ever seen her?"

Come to think of it, none of us had actually *seen* Mrs. Hildebrand in person, though the thought did bring to mind the sight of her daughter and her two big front headlights. I'd even adapted an old song, just for her: "Jeepers Scheepers, where'd you get those peepers?" I tried sharing this with Cooter, but he was more interested in what Fatso had to say. "Well, I've seen her!" Fatso said. "Through my bedroom window, late at night sometimes." Fatso's house neighbored Mrs. Hildebrand's on the east. "And I tell you, something ain't right with her."

"Well, she had a stroke," I said. At this point I didn't quite know what a stroke was; I just knew it could mess a person up pretty good.

But Fatso shook his head. "It's more to it than that," he said. "It's—" But here he clammed up again and wouldn't go on.

"Well, what is it?" Cooter finally asked.

Fatso lowered his eyes to the ground. "You guys remember back when she first moved in?" We both nodded. "Well, there was this calico cat that had been coming around at the time. And—well, I had been feeding it some. Giving it some milk and stuff. You know, just to be friendly to it. I mean, you know how my dad is about pets." We sure did. If you believed everything Mr. Higgins said, then Fatso's father was allergic to every animal known to mankind. As a result, Fatso was the only kid on the block who didn't have a pet of any kind, even a lizard. "I was feeding it behind Mrs. Hildebrand's house, because Mr. Utley had died and no one had moved in yet. I thought no one would see me there. Anyway, the day after Mrs. Hildebrand moved in, I went looking for the cat— but I couldn't find it anywhere. Same thing the next day, and the day after that. Then, on the fourth day, I was back behind Mrs. Hildebrand's house, and I saw these bits of fur—calico, just like the cat. And so I got curious and followed them around and I found this spot that was just covered in blood and fur." He looked up at both of us and swallowed hard. "It was my cat, I know it."

I looked at Cooter. He looked at me. We could tell Fatso was pretty shook up about all this, but he could also tell that we weren't buying the bull he was selling. "So?" Cooter said. "It was probably just a coyote, or the Lehmans' dog that ate it."

But Fatso shook his head. "No, I swear it didn't look like that. It looked like—it looked like it had been sacrificed or something."

Now Cooter and I just started to laugh. "Sweet Christ, Fatso," I laughed. "I knew we shouldn't watched that *Friday the 13th* movie last time you came over to my house to spend the night."

But Fatso shook his head again. "No, guys, I swear, sometimes at night I can see her moving around her backyard. I don't know what she's doing back there. There's no lights or nothing, but you can tell it's her. It's like—like she's floating, the way she moves around. Like she ain't touching the ground at all. I swear. It's creepy."

I didn't know if Fatso was trying to pull our legs or what, but I was pretty sure that, as a general rule, human beings were incapable of floating—except, of course, when they served turkey burgers and three-bean salad at the junior high for lunch. On those days, everyone was floating, if you know what I mean. I mentioned this to Fatso and Cooter, and while Cooter thought it was hilarious, Fatso wasn't laughing.

"Shut up, Rocky" he said to me. "Hey, if you guys don't believe me, then come over and see for yourself. Sleep over this weekend. One look at her and you'll know what I mean. Something there just ain't quite right."

* * *

Cooter and I weren't exactly swallowing any of Fatso's fish tales— after all, last year he'd been convinced that this new family that moved in must be terrorists, just because he heard they came here from India; he even called the cops to report them, and looked even dumber than usual when it turned out the family was from *Indiana*, and not India. But any night away from my mother was a good one for me, so we both quickly agreed to a sleepover. We had to do some convincing to get our parents on board—school would have started by then—but soon it was all set up for Saturday night.

We waited in Fatso's room with only his desk light on, "so she can't see us," as he explained, and stared out the window at the shabby little house across the street. I admit that while I didn't give any credence whatsoever to any of Fatso's claims, I felt a certain—excitement? nervousness?—as we hunkered and waited for something to happen. And waited. And waited. At some point I think it struck Cooter and me at the same time that sitting around on a Saturday night and spying on a woman who was probably around a hundred and twenty-two years of age was a damned waste of our time. Of course, if Mrs. Scheepers was visiting her mother at the time, that would have been a whole different ball of wax. But seeing as how she wasn't, Cooter and I rounded on Fatso mercilessly.

"Waah, waah, waah," Cooter said, doing a pretty darned good imitation of Fatso crying his eyes out the other day. "I'm afraid of the old witch next door!"

"Shut up," Fatso sulkily replied, but the cold reality of his humiliation was slowly sinking in. Angry, he picked his baseball mitt off the floor and threw it against the closet door.

"Hey wait," I said, my eye distracted by a light turning on next door. "Something's happening." The light was shining below us, in what looked like a small old kitchen. I strained to see—yes, there she was, there was Old Mrs. Hildebrand in the flesh. And damned if "old" wasn't the best word to describe her. I couldn't see much from where we were up in Fatso's room, but I noticed a tangled mess of iron grey hair and skin more wrinkled than the shirts I shoved to the back of my drawers. "What is she doing?" I wondered aloud as Mrs. Hildebrand shuffled closer towards us. She had reached up into a cabinet and pulled out a large drinking glass. But she didn't fill it with water or anything like that; instead, she went into her refrigerator and pulled out a pitcher of a vile-looking concoction that was red, deep red, as dark a red as anything I'd ever seen.

"Gross. What is that?" Cooter said under his breath. We were all watching real quiet like, wondering what the drink was. We watched as Old Mrs. Hildebrand poured herself a glass and downed it in one, long satisfying gulp. She wiped her face with the arm of her tattered, ratty grey nightgown and rinsed the glass out in the sink. Then she did something none of us expected her to do. She took one of her spindly, spider-like hands, reached into her own mouth, and slowly, almost delicately, began to—

"Ieee," I said as Cooter punched Fatso on the arm. "You brought us over here to watch an old lady pull out her dentures!" he exclaimed, punching Fatso again for added emphasis.

"That's nasty," I agreed, reaching over and punching Fatso once myself, just to show my support for Cooter.

"Wait, you guys, wait!" Fatso said, a hint of excitement raising in his voice as he rubbed his sore arm. "It's going to get weirder—just watch!"

But as we watched, the old lady didn't head out to her backyard in her tattered old nightie and float around as Fatso had promised. In fact, she didn't do anything except turn around and shuffle towards a door at the far end of the kitchen. She opened it up and stepped through, leaving the three of us staring at her empty kitchen and leaving two of us plotting our revenge on the one who made us watch it all in the first place.

"Fatso, you are the biggest wuss of all time," Cooter said crossly. "I can't believe you think anything about that was scary."

"Come on, you guys," Fatso tried defending himself. "What about that drink, huh? That was probably blood!"

"That was probably tomato juice," Cooter snorted. "My grandmother drinks it all the time, though usually with vodka in it, too."

"I tell you guys, something really weird is going on over there," Fatso intoned.

"Well, then prove it," I said, a crazy grin spreading across my face. "Prove it. Go on over there, knock on her door, and prove something weird is up."

Fatso stuck his tongue out at me. "No way, man," he said.

"Why not?" Cooter needled, picking up the challenge. "You chicken?"

"No," Fatso lied.

"Yes, you are," Cooter dug, poking Fatso in his ribs. "Yes you are, chicken, chicken *bawk bawk bawk*!" he added, flapping his wings and doing his best chicken impersonation.

"Shut up!" Fatso replied. "I'm not scared. It's just—it's just too late to go over there, that's all."

"It ain't even ten o'clock," I countered, "and besides, you know she's up. We just saw her."

"And what am I supposed to say, huh? What am I supposed to tell her I'm there for?"

I had to admit, Fatso had me there. But fortunately, Cooter came to my rescue. "I know!" he said. "Tell her you're selling something for school. You know, like taking orders for candy or something. We do that all the time."

I nodded enthusiastically; it was a solid plan. "Yeah, good one, Cooter!" I said.

Fatso could tell it was a good plan, too; that's why he didn't like it. "That's stupid," he muttered. "And what if she wants to buy something?"

"Then pocket the money and tell her it'll come in a few weeks," Cooter said. "She's so old I doubt she'd remember it by tomorrow, anyway, and then we get some extra cash."

We could tell that there was no way Fatso wanted to go over to

Old Mrs. Hildebrand's house, but Cooter and I were too into the idea to let it go now. "Come on," I said. "If you do it, I'll let you ride my bike all day tomorrow." It was no secret that I had the newest, most expensive bike in the neighborhood, part of my mother's never-ending quest to ensure that we looked better than everyone else in every way possible.

But Fatso only shook his head. "Do it and I'll steal you two candy bars from the pharmacy before school Monday," Cooter offered. Cooter had been stealing us candy bars from his uncle's pharmacy on and off for years; I always figured his uncle sort of knew what he was up to, because while Cooter was sometimes smart, he was never very slick. But if his uncle could always look the other way, then I figure, for free candy, so could I.

Yet even the thought of free chocolate couldn't convince Fatso. I took a deep breath; time to play my trump card. "You do it or I'll tell Angela Parsons you looked in her window last Fourth of July and saw her changing after she got soaked by the water balloons her sister threw at her." I could tell by Fatso's enraged look that I had him.

"You swore you'd never tell!" he thundered.

"And I won't," I countered, "if you go over there." I paused, letting the reality of my victory sink in. "All you got to do is knock," I said. "You don't even have to go in."

"What if she don't answer?" Fatso asked.

I could tell he was planning a "ding-dong and ditch," knocking real fast and running away even faster. "No way," I said. "You got to wait over there for—what? Two minutes?" I asked looking at Cooter.

"No, three," he said, enjoying the tortured look on Fatso's face. "She's old, after all."

"How'm I supposed to know three minutes is up?" Fatso whined.

"I don't know," I said. "Just wait until it feels like thee minutes has passed. Do it or I'll tell!"

Threatened with supreme humiliation—not to mention the total ass-kicking that Derek McDaniel, Angela's boyfriend, would give him—Fatso reluctantly got off his bed and put on his sneakers. Cooter and I took prime seats by the window and watched as Fatso slowly appeared outside the wrought iron fence of Old Mrs. Hildebrand's house. He paused out there for an awful long time, and for a few minutes Cooter and I felt sure he was going to chicken out, but finally Fatso worked up enough courage, moved past the gate, up the rickety old wood steps, and knocked on the big wooden front door.

He waited there—ten seconds, twenty, thirty. A minute passed, then a minute and a half. We watched the old house closely, but no lights came on indicating that Old Mrs. Hildebrand was moving about anywhere in the house. I figured the whole operation was going to be a total bust when, just through the hazy light coming off from the Higgins' house, we saw the front door open.

The look on Fatso's face was priceless. Even from so far away we could tell he was scared out of his wits. Cooter and I struggled to hold all our laughter in so that we wouldn't miss a minute of it. "I wish we could hear what was going on," Cooter whispered as we watched Fatso trying desperately to explain to Old Mrs. Hildebrand why he'd come over so late on a Saturday night.

Suddenly we saw the porch light go on, and then the light in the living room where Mrs. Hildebrand must have been standing. That was strange—we didn't see anyone moving toward the light switch. Well, maybe it was close to the door, or maybe she had one of those clapping contraptions. Still, even more surprising was when Old. Mrs. Hildebrand moved aside and Fatso—nervously looking about and practically pissing in his pants—walked on in.

We couldn't help it. Cooter and I just about busted a gut

laughing. This had worked out better than we could have hoped! I couldn't imagine what story Fatso was telling Mrs. Hildebrand now, or what story he'd have to tell us when he got back. Maybe—just maybe—he'd even come back with a little money. That'd be cool. The chuckles dying down in our throats, Cooter and I turned back to the window to watch some more.

The lights were out. All the lights in Mrs. Hildebrand's house— even the kitchen—were out. Cooter and I stopped laughing real quick. We looked at each other, feeling real nervous. Cooter was the first one to speak. "He's probably almost home," Cooter said. "He'd need only be there a minute."

"Yeah, you're right," I said. It made sense. "He'll be back in a second."

Only he wasn't back in a second. Nor a minute. In fact, ten minutes passed, then twenty, then thirty. Cooter and I got real uneasy quiet. We kept stealing glances at the house next door, but it was pitch as the night, darker inside than it was outside. We fidgeted nervously. We didn't know what to do. We didn't want to tell Fatso's dad what we'd been up to because we didn't want to get Fatso—or us—into any trouble, but after forty-five minutes passed we figured we had to do something. It was late now, and I felt sure Mr. Higgins would be asleep, but that didn't matter. I was just about to head downstairs to wake him when the bedroom door began to slowly open.

It was Fatso.

For a moment the two of us just sat there, stunned into quiet, as Fatso walked into the room and sat down on his bed. Finally, Cooter spoke. "What... what... where you been?" he sputtered.

Fatso had this glazed look on his face, as if he was staring at something far off in the distance, and he was calm, way too calm, since Fatso was normally one of the most nervous people I knew, but other than that, he seemed completely fine. He was almost better than fine; if anything, I swear his face looked cleaner now then when he left.

"Where the hell you been, man?" Cooter asked again, using our special "word" for emphasis.

Fatso just looked at him stupidly, and when he finally spoke, he sounded as far away as he looked. "I don't know what you mean," he said thickly. "I've just been visiting with Mrs. Hildebrand. She gave me some cookies." He gave a mighty yawn and got into bed. "Come on, guys," he said. "Let's go to sleep."

* * *

Four days later I pulled Cooter out of the lunch line to have a confab inside the second-floor boys' bathroom.

"We have to tell someone," I whispered to him, though since everyone else is at lunch, I don't know who I am worried will overhear us talking.

"Tell someone *what?*" Cooter said. I knew he was just playing dumb, since I knew he knew *exactly* what I was talking about.

"About Fatso!" I said anyway.

Cooter looked me square in the eye. I could tell he was freaked out inside just like I was, but he wasn't going to let on at all. "What about Fatso?" he countered. "There's nothing with him!"

"Yeah, well, that's the problem," I retorted. "Usually, there's always something wrong with Fatso. He's always going on about something his dad did or whatever else is wrong with him. You know how he is!" It was true. Fatso was an unrepentant whiner; always had been. Whether about how his teachers didn't like him, or how his dad got mad at him for nothing, or how some part of him or the other was hurt or sore or swollen to the point of being ten times its original size, with Fatso, it was always *something*. Most kids'll tell some kind of whopper to get out of gym class every once in a while. But Fatso once told Mr. Carson, our gym teacher, that he had arthritis and couldn't play volleyball that day; the sad thing was, Fatso actually believed he did have arthritis, but Mr. Carson didn't buy any of it for a second. He told Fatso sure, he could skip playing volleyball for that day—and then made him run laps around the track for the entire gym period. It may have given Fatso something else to complain about, but he sure learned his lesson.

Only now, Fatso wasn't complaining about anything. In fact, he was barely talking. Most of the time he just sat there, staring ahead blankly, as if most of him wasn't even there. In class, the teachers didn't notice at all; heck, they were usually grateful when one of us was quiet and not causing any problems. But all the other kids noticed, especially the ones on our block who were used to Fatso never shutting his trap. The curious looks that had started on Monday had turned to whispers by Tuesday, which had turned to out-and-out questions by today; that was how come I'd pulled Cooter out of lunch and into the bathroom.

But Cooter wasn't having it. "Rocky, there is nothing wrong with Fatso and nothing to tell. What are we gonna do, go up to his dad and say, 'Hey, Mr. Higgins, your son acted good in school today so we think there's something wrong with him?' And what are we supposed to say about Old Mrs. Hildebrand? That she gummed him into silence? Don't be stupid, Rocky." And without another word Cooter barged out of the bathroom and headed back down for his tomato soup and grilled cheese sandwich.

I stayed behind, running it all over in my head. I had to admit that Cooter had a point. Even if we did tell someone, what would we say? We didn't see anything actually happen. And in a day or two, Fatso would be back to his normal, complaining self, and Cooter and I'd probably send him back over to Old Mrs. Hildebrand's just to shut him up again.

Only it didn't quite work out that way. It took a couple of weeks, but someone besides us kids finally noticed that Fatso had stopped talking. This meant visits to the doctor, and then the school shrink, and then, on a rainy Thursday morning, we noticed Fatso hadn't been in classes all week.

I raised my hand. "Mrs. Cornelson," I asked our teacher, "what happened to Fatso?"

Mrs. Cornelson gave me one of those indulgent looks teachers always give students when they have to share delicate information. "Toby," she said, using Fatso's real name, "has been moved to Special Education." I think my jaw must've hit the floor at two hundred miles an hour. Special Ed? I tried catching Cooter in the eye but he acted like his shoe was all of a sudden real interesting and avoided looking at me for anything. Fatso in Special Ed? What the hell had the old bat done to him?

I tried talking to Cooter again after the bus dropped us off on Canterbury Lane, but he wasn't having any of it. "Just drop it, Rocky!" he said, storming off to his own house. I sat there in the middle of the street, just staring at the old Utley place, wondering what had happened to Fatso in those walls. The house looked so plain, a little run-down but just so ordinary...it didn't seem like anything bad could happen in there at all. I got so lost in thought I didn't move until Derek McDaniel drove up on me, beeping his horn hard and scaring the crap out of me as he pulled into the Parsons' driveway.

When I got home, my mother was full of the news of Fatso's "demotion," as she called it. I guess I should have been impressed that Fatso's dad managed to keep it secret from her as long as he had, but now the entire neighborhood was sure to be talking about it. My mother had all sorts of details, too, about his new classes and the sudden drop in his I.Q. Course, when I asked my mom *why* Fatso had been moved to Special Ed—what had caused it—she just shrugged her shoulders. "I don't know, dear," she said, giving me that same stupid look Mrs. Cornelson had that afternoon. And then she went on and on, but I had stopped listening. I felt pretty sure I knew *how* it had happened to Fatso. I just didn't know what. Or why.

* * *

It's a common rule amongst our neighborhood that adults generally don't have a clue about what is really going on. Not compared to us kids. None of the adults knew that Farley Smoletz was going to leave his wife until it happened; but us kids knew two weeks beforehand, since his son overheard him talking to his new girlfriend on the phone. And none of the adults knew that Mrs. Parsons drank half a bottle of vermouth everyday before her kids came home from school until she went off to rehab; but us kids knew, because her kids told us. That's how it is in nice neighborhoods like ours. Even my mother, for all her status as the biggest gossip around, didn't know anything like the secrets we kids did. Even those we didn't share—even those we couldn't tell—everyone else still knew. We just felt it, down deep, on some level, and we knew. We knew what was going on.

So as a consequence not one kid on Canterbury Lane was about to set foot onto Old Mrs. Hildebrand's front porch, even if Cooter and I'd never told anyone what went down the night we stayed over at Fatso's house. From that point on we made doubly sure no kick balls ever ended up in her yard, and anyone selling Girl Scout cookies or candy for band or magazine subscriptions for the chess club never tried knocking on her door. I guess we had already learned the hard way that when some place seems sinister, it's best to leave well enough alone.

Of course, some adults never learn, my mother being chief among them. The leaves were starting to turn and that meant fall was upon us. And fall meant Halloween. After Christmas, Halloween was my mother's favorite decorating time of the year. There was nothing she loved more than to see every house on Canterbury Lane covered with pumpkins and dried corn and ghosts and goblins and witches—or, as my father called them, "Your mother's relatives." Of course our house was always the one most plastered in Halloween paraphernalia, but mother made sure that every house on the block had *something* to mark the holiday. Two years ago this super-religious family—the Coopers—moved in. They were the kind of religious people who think Halloween is some sort of pagan Satanic devil celebration and therefore do not celebrate it any way, not even to give out sweets to the kids out trick or treating (they actually gave us little religious pamphlets instead, which Fatso used to pick his teeth when some nougat got caught between two molars). Well, my mother worked on those folks non-stop until they finally agreed to put up one measly little pumpkin on their front porch to celebrate "the change of the seasons"—that was the bull puckey phrase my mother used to finally sell them on it. Sure enough, on Halloween night, some wag decided it would be fun to go to their house and smash their pumpkin all over the front door. I swear I asked every kid on the block three times if they did it, and they all said no. Now don't hold me to this but I also swear that I saw my mom sneak out of the house on Halloween that year real late, after she'd figured everyone else was asleep (I was having trouble falling asleep on account of the sugar rush I was feeling from having already ate half my candy.) Now I'm not saying my mother actually did smash the Coopers' pumpkin, but they got the message and had moved out before Christmas.

So this year my mother had just as much a challenge as before —to get Old Mrs. Hildebrand to somehow participate in decorating for Halloween. Mother waited until two weeks before the day—that's when folks were actually allowed to decorate on our block, only two weeks before the day (to Mother, anything else was just too tacky)—put on her best suit and her favorite "spooky" vampire bat pin, and fluffed her hair one last time, determined to convince Old Mrs. Hildebrand that it was time to either put up— decorations, that is—or be prepared to be taken down. But when my mother opened the door, she saw, to her shock, that all her efforts were for naught—because Old Mrs. Hildebrand had already decorated for Halloween. The old bat hadn't exactly gone over the top—there was just one item marking the holiday on her porch—but boy, for one item, it really packed a punch. Old Mrs. Hildebrand had put up one of those life-sized witch dummies that hang from a rope by their neck. This one was dressed in long grey and black robes that hung down past where its feet would be. A big, pointed black hat covered its face, but patches of ratty, tatty grey hair could still be seen poking out from underneath it. There was something about that dummy—something about the way it swayed so heavily, the way a stiff wind just got it moving slowly back and forth—that scared the socks right off me. Mother, I could tell, was pleased—she felt like she had finally got through to Old Mrs. Hildebrand. I could tell she was already planning where Mrs. Hildebrand would put her nativity in her yard for Christmas.

Every day for the next week I had to walk past that dummy twice, on the way to get onto the school bus, and then again coming home. And every time I walked by I shivered. I couldn't help it. Every other kid on the block felt the same way. But the parents were pleased as punch. Maybe this meant Old Mrs. Hildebrand was feeling better and was ready to join the neighborhood proper. Us kids snorted. Next thing we knew, our parents might actually be inviting the old bat over for tea or dinner parties.

Of course, leave it to my mother to start the trend. "Rocky," she said to me one day as I got home from school, only two days before

Halloween. "Do me a favor, and take this invitation to Mrs. Hildebrand."

"Invitation for what?" I asked, incredulous.

My mother gave me her exasperated why-did-God-ever-decide-to-punish-me-with-such-troublesome-children look. "For the annual Halloween Extravaganza."

I snorted, but kept it to myself. The annual Halloween "Extravaganza" was a revolving party where the adults would go, after the kids were done trick or treating and tucked safely in their beds, and enjoy hard cider and cinnamon doughnuts. This year Fatso's family was hosting. "Mom, the old bat ain't gonna go to something like that. She doesn't even ever leave her house," I said, though that made me think of Old Mrs. Hildebrand floating in her backyard, her tattered grey gown flapping in an unfelt breeze as she stalked her prey. *Okay*, I thought, *enough scary movies for you.*

My mother gave me another exasperated look, this one punctuated by a big sigh. "Rocky, when you are more mature you'll realize that for old shut-ins like Mrs. Hildebrand, just the fact that they were invited is enough. Now do as I say."

I balked. I didn't want to go over, even now, when it was still somewhat light out. "Make Sooz go. Why do I have to do everything?" I whined, hoping that my mother would get sick of asking me and think that giving up was the best possible route to preserving family peace.

"Your sister is watching Toby for the Higgins family," she said. "You know he can't be left alone right now. Here," she added, holding out a neatly addressed envelope—calligraphy was one of my mother's hobbies.

I still didn't want to go. And I knew I only had one recourse left open to me. "Why don't you get off your fat ass and do it yourself?" I said, sounding much braver than I felt. There. I had done it. I had insulted my mother and cussed in the same breath.

No way she was going to let this slide. I was going to be sent straight up to my room without supper. And someone else could deliver the invitation to creepy Old Mrs. Hildebrand.

My mother's eyes flashed. Oh, crap. Now she was *pissed*. "Rocky!" she yelled. "How dare you—how—" It wasn't often that I rendered my mother speechless. "You are in big trouble, mister!" she finally sputtered. "You are to go straight up to your room without supper and think about what you said—" Yes! Victory! "—*after* you deliver the invitation. Now go!" Crap. I still had to go over there and now my mother was super pissed at me.

I reluctantly pulled on my coat and stepped onto my porch. Of course, I could just pretend to deliver the invitation. I could just lose it on my way and come back home. But I knew my mother would be watching me. And right now, I was feeling just a bit more afraid of her than I was of Old Mrs. Hildebrand. So stuffing my hands and the invitation in my coat pockets, I marched sullenly over to Mrs. Hildebrand's house.

I paused in front of the wrought iron gate, just as Fatso had. Is this what he felt? Was whatever had happened to him about to happen to me? I looked around to see if anyone else was around, to see if there was someone else I could say "Hi" to, just to feel normal again, just for a minute. But no one was there. Canterbury Lane was deserted. So I turned back to Old Mrs. Hildebrand's house. I couldn't keep my eye off that horrible dummy, swaying slowly, slowly back and forth, even though now I didn't feel any breeze at all. Why did my mother have to have this thing for holiday décor? Who cared what anyone's house looked like? As long as the people inside were nice and didn't care if you messed up their lawn a bit when playing hide and seek, then who cares what decorations they had up? I could feel my mother's eyes on me, and I slowly opened the gate door and walked into the yard. It felt like it took me a hundred years to get from the gate to the bottom step of the rickety old porch. The entire time my eyes never left that swaying dummy, moving back and forth, back and forth, moving on some power all its own. As I got closer I realized with no small amount of dread that the dummy looked a little like *her*—like Old Mrs. Hildebrand. Same sort of hair, same sort of ratty, tatty grey robe. I went up one step, invitation clutched in my hand for all I was worth. *This is so stupid*, I thought. *There's nothing wrong with the old bat. She's just some old lady. All you got to do is drop this in the mail slot and run. That's all. There's nothing to be afraid of. Nothing at all. Not even that dummy.* But I was afraid. I was. *Don't be stupid*, my brain yelled, trying to reason with the more cowardly parts of me. *She's just an old lady who had a stroke and wears dentures. She didn't do nothing to Fatso. She ain't gonna do nothing to me. Neither is that dummy. Just go. Just do it and run. Just go. Go. Go.*

But I had to check out one thing first. The dummy. I had to see —to see its face. I don't know. I just had to. Just had to. So I stole up real quiet like. Just down kind of low. The dummy pushed against me. It was heavy—much heavier than I ever would have imagined those things could ever weigh. The face. It was covered by the hat. I reached up—so slow, my hand shaking like anything. Had to see it. I moved the hat, took it off so slow so no one'd notice what I was doing. I just had to see that dummy's face. Had to.

I saw the face all right. But it was no dummy.

It was Old Mrs. Hildebrand.

I had only seen her for a few minutes from Fatso's bedroom window, but there was no mistaking that wrinkled old mouth and that iron grey hair. But now, up close, I could see her eyes—eyes that weren't normal, eyes the color of rubies, or the color of blood. And they was looking right at me. And then I saw—the last thing I ever saw—was her mouth, and what she had behind those dentures —teeth, sharp teeth, rows and rows and rows of sharp, sharp teeth.

And then I screamed.

PARTY TIME

MORT CASTLE

MAMA HAD TOLD HIM it would soon be party time. That made him excited but also a little afraid. Oh, he liked party time, he liked making people happy, and he always had fun, but it was kind of scary going upstairs.

Still, he knew it would be all right because Mama would be with him. Everything was all right with Mama and he always tried to be Mama's good boy.

Once, though, a long time ago, he had been bad. Mama must not have put his chain on right, so he'd slipped it off his leg and went up the stairs all by himself and opened the door. Oh! Did Mama ever whip him for *that*. Now he knew better. He'd never, never go up without Mama.

And he liked it down in the basement, liked it a lot. There was a little bed to sleep on. There was a yellow light that never went off. He had blocks to play with. It was nice in the basement.

Best of all, Mama visited him often. She kept him company and taught him to be good.

He heard the funny sound that the door at the top of the stairs made and he knew Mama was coming down. He wondered if it was party time. He wondered if he'd get to eat the happy food.

But then he thought it might not be party time. He saw Mama's legs, Mama's skirt. Maybe he had done something bad and Mama was going to whip him.

He ran to the corner. The chain pulled hard at his ankle. He tried to go away, to squeeze right into the wall.

"No, Mama! I am not bad! I love my mama. Don't whip me!"

Oh, he was being silly. Mama had food for him. She wasn't going to whip him.

"You're a good boy. Mama loves you, too, my sweet, good boy."

The food was cold. It wasn't the kind of food he liked best, but Mama said he always had to eat everything she brought him because if not he was a bad boy.

It was hot food he liked most. He called it the happy food.

That's the way it felt inside him.

"Is it party time yet, Mama?"

"Not yet, sweet boy. Don't you worry, it will be soon. You like Mama to take you upstairs for parties, don't you?"

"Yes, Mama! I like to see all the people. I like to make them happy."

Best of all, he liked the happy food. It was so good, so hot.

He was sleepy after Mama left, but he wanted to play with his blocks before he lay down on his bed. The blocks were fun. He liked to build things with them and make up funny games.

He sat on the floor. He pushed the chain out of the way. He put one block on top of another block, then a block on top of that one. He built the blocks up real high, then made them fall. That was funny and he laughed.

Then he played party time with the blocks. He put one block over here and another over there and the big, big block was Mama.

He tried to remember some of the things people said at party time so he could make the blocks talk that way. Then he placed a block in the middle of all the other blocks. That was Mama's good boy.

It was himself.

Before he could end the party time game, he got very sleepy. His belly was full, even if it was only cold food.

He went to bed. He dreamed a party time dream of happy faces and the good food and Mama saying, "Good boy, my sweet boy."

Then Mama was shaking him. He heard funny sounds coming from upstairs. Mama slipped the chain off his leg.

"Come my good boy."

"It's party time?"

"Yes."

Mama took his hand. He was frightened a little, the way he always was just before party time.

"It's all right, my sweet boy."

Mama led him up the stairs. She opened the door.

"This is party time. Everyone is so happy."

He was not scared anymore. There was a lot of light and so many laughing people in the party room.

"Here's the good, sweet boy, everybody!"

Then he saw it on the floor. Oh, he hoped it was for him!

"That's *yours*, good boy, all for you."

He was so happy! It had four legs and a black nose. When he walked closer to it, it made a funny sound that was something like the way *he* sounded when Mama whipped him.

His belly made a noise and his mouth was all wet inside.

It tried to get away from him, but he grabbed it and he squeezed it real hard. He heard things going snap inside it.

Mama was laughing and laughing and so was everyone else. He was making them all so happy.

"You know what it is, don't you, my sweet boy?"

He knew.

It was the happy food.

A DEEPENING HEART

THOM BRUCIE

OFTEN, DURING TIMES of desperation, only his love for Miss Agnes Perser kept Nathan Branchwell on the right side of sanity, and one day, the Rev. Perser would give permission for Nathan to marry her. The more he missed Agnes, the more Nathan wished for the Civil War to end. The men had gone nearly five months without pay. Rations arrived with little regularity, and the soldiers began to spend more of their time and ammunition on rabbit and squirrel than on battle. Uniforms became torn, unwashed, and often devoid of rank or insignia. The men simply knew by face who was private, who was sergeant. This was the general condition of the men of the 110th Pennsylvania on the night of October 19, 1864. They had been camped nearly four weeks near Kernstown, Virginia, and Nathan sat alone watching the jittery flame tips of his fire. The quiet of darkness settled over him, and his thoughts slipped unexpectedly into a peacefulness he had not dared in years. The gurgle of the stream and the soft breeze rustling the grass soothed him. His breathing felt liquid and transparent, as if he were connected to the currents of water and the currents of air, and all the simple breaths he breathed reminded him of life and of growing things like hay and sunflowers in a garden.

Nathan reached the decision to join the volunteers after he spoke with the Reverend.

"I want to marry Miss Agnes," he said to the Rev. Perser.

"I can't allow it," the Reverend said.

"Why not?"

"It's the time, my boy. War. Uncertainty. I want my daughter to enjoy a comfortable home. You have no stake, Nathan. Nothing to offer."

"What can I do?"

"I don't know."

They stood quiet a moment. Then the Reverend mused. "Men honor gold," he said. "Whatever should happen, gold will last."

"Some men find their fortunes in war."

"Some men do, yes."

"I will."

Reverend Perser studied him.

"Please, sir."

"I cannot make such a decision for you, Nathan, but if you return from the war with gold enough to stock a young farm, I believe the good Lord will bless your efforts. With that, I would grant a union between you and my daughter."

Nathan accepted his admonition, and of those irregular times when the soldiers did receive their thirteen dollars in monthly pay, he traded his paper money for gold. He offered three times the face value of any gold coin. It was a time of general madness, so his mild idiosyncrasy caused little concern, and men sought him out, for three times the money meant three times the whiskey and sometimes a woman's favor. Over a period of three and a half years, Nathan traded for and saved two hundred dollars, four fifty-dollar gold pieces.

How much would two hundred dollars buy at the end of the

war?

Nathan felt certain he could afford one milk cow, two Morgan horses, a double harness and a plow, a shovel, a hay fork, and all the seed for a first planting of beans, corn, and hay. Besides these he added a double-handled saw and two axes, one chopping and one finishing, so he could fell the trees and shape them into a two-room cabin. He was certain to find a down mattress, pots, kitchen utensils, and such cooking provisions as flour, lard, and salt to last the first year. Finally, with good neighbors, he would stand a barn of a weekend, pen in some chickens, fence in a hog, and still manage to bury two of the gold coins. Surely, the Reverend would honor his promise.

Suddenly, the gallop of a horse disturbed Nathan's reverie. He watched the rider kick the sides of the animal all the way to the Captain's tent. This bothered Nathan, because he respected animals and liked them. Since he cared for the stock, he knew the horse would be lathered and sore, and Nathan would be up late caring for it.

Captain Hollingsworth jumped from his chair, and the rider saluted. Nathan watched the men gesture, their arms and heads bobbing shadowy behind the glow of the Captain's fire. What news did this night rider bring?

Captain Hollingsworth commanded the 110th Pennsylvania. He had not distinguished himself in battle, but he courted power, and his commander, Colonel Geoffrey MacGeorge, was a man who remembered favors. Captain Hollingsworth spent much time cultivating the Colonel's ear, hoping that at war's end, the Colonel would reward him with the rank of Major. The Captain suspected that Washington and Richmond were close to resolving their differences, and he knew he needed one last opportunity to impress the colonel.

In the morning, word spread: a major battle, a decisive battle, perhaps a concluding battle threatened. No one knew specifics, but the rumors of war bring tension, and weary expectation mingled with the coffee and the talk.

Captain Hollingsworth called for the tracker, Manning, two sharpshooters, Steadman and French, and Nathan.

"Men, Colonel Mac George has put me in charge of a scouting party. We won't engage, just survey. I have a sense he'll reward any good news we bring him." Then he turned to Nathan. "Branchwell, I want you along to watch the stock in case of an injury. They must be ready for quick rides and hard terrain."

"What are we looking for, sir?" Manning asked.

"I don't know. And I don't know what we'll find." Before he dismissed them, he said, "Gather gear and supplies. We leave in two hours."

They took a southern tack, using the protection of forests along the hills. Late on the second afternoon, they rode into a tree-line where the air turned pungent.

"What's that smell?"

"Quiet," Hollingsworth said.

They slowed their pace, but the horses struggled against the reins. The men heard no unusual sound, but their ears strained in an effort to interpret the uneasiness they felt. Suddenly, they all stopped. Ahead of them, through the branches and leaves, they saw a battlefield, a small, unknown location, quiet and eerie with motionlessness. Captain Hollingsworth dismounted. He handed the reins to Nathan. The captain signaled the others to follow him. Each, in turn, slipped from the saddle and gave their reins to Nathan. Nathan pulled the horses together behind a tree.

"Shhhh. Shhhhhhh," he whispered.

The tree line followed the contour of the hillside opening to a small clearing with a stream which flowed away from them. Each man took a position crouched behind a tree. They waited, listening, watching for movement, but nothing moved, and no sound came from the field. Nathan kept the animals quiet, but they didn't like the acrid smell.

Manning circled left for half an hour. He found no signs of life. Captain Hollingsworth panned the field with his looking glass again and again. Finally, he decided the meadow contained no threat, and he ordered the men out of the trees.

Their senses remained alert, but even for these men who had come to know depravity, the stench and silence of this dead place restrained them. Their voices fell momentarily dry, like talcum. Death stretched before them without end. In the heat, bloated carrion stunk like vinegar. Cannons lay muzzle first into the mud. Ghostly bodies leaned as if asleep, and no one could distinguish blue uniform from gray. Their ears began to fill with a quiet buzz of flies—blowflies, horseflies, and black flies, and at once the men recognized that the gray film which dulled the red earth was alive. They watched the hypnotic undulation of maggoty decay. Nathan huddled within the hot breath of the horses, and although flies found their salty hides, the horses, knowing Nathan, stayed calm. Minutes dragged with the miserable slowness of the sun, and nothing stirred—not squirrel, not rabbit, not man.

Hollingsworth turned his thoughts to the Colonel. How would he react to this event? It seemed final, as no battle before had felt. Hollingsworth knew he would have to find something exemplary for his report, but nothing exemplary remained among the carnage, only the pitiful silence of exhausted savagery.

Suddenly, a mule brayed. When they heard it, each man strained to determine its origin. Again, the pathetic bray sounded, painful and unhappy, and with it the sucking sound of a boot or a foot or a hoof pulling against mud.

"There," Nathan shouted, and he ran the twenty yards, jumping over cadavers and splintered trees to a muddy bank. The others followed to a low gully, the slow running water in its basin stained purple. A Confederate stamp on the mule's strap identified it. The mule looked young, recently pressed into service. The wide black eyes of the beast looked full of puzzlement.

"Help me get it to its feet," Nathan said.

"Wait," Captain Hollingsworth said. "It's a Reb. Leave it be."

"It's a mule," Nathan said.

"It's a Reb mule," the captain repeated.

"Let me save it."

Nathan reached for the rein and tugged, but the brute could only show its teeth and bray. Nathan struggled, but mud and exhaustion held the beast, and it would not stand. Nathan turned to the others. "Help me," he said.

Steadman and French moved to help.

"Stop," Hollingsworth said. "I said it's a Reb, and a Reb it stays." He drew his side arm and cocked the lever.

"It's not our enemy, Captain," Nathan said. "It's a mule, a live thing among all this dead."

"That's dangerous thinking, Branchwell. You should know better."

Hollingsworth pointed his pistol at the aggrieved animal, but Nathan stepped between them.

"I can't let you, sir. I can't."

"Don't make me shoot you over a dumb Reb mule. Step aside."

Nathan looked squarely into his commander's eyes. The Captain did not blink.

"I'm asking you not to shoot it," Nathan said.

"You or the mule," Hollingsworth answered.

Nathan clenched his teeth and decided to back away. As he took a step, Hollingsworth fired, and Nathan jumped. The bullet missed Nathan, but dirt sprayed onto his boots.

"Sir," French called. "Are you sure this is what you want?"

"He disobeyed an order."

"But, sir, it's Branchwell."

Nathan's nose flared, and he kept his eyes on the trickle of smoke that eased from the barrel of Hollingsworth's Colt, and for a moment, no one spoke.

Finally, Hollingsworth said, "Mount up. There's nothing to report here."

Nathan did not move. "What about the mule?"

Hollingsworth walked toward the horses. "Mount up," he said. As he swung into the saddle, he looked at French. "Shoot the Reb," he said.

"Wait," Nathan said. "I'll pay."

Hollingsworth reined his horse.

"There are four of you. I've saved four fifty-dollar gold pieces. If you help me with this mule and let me take him home, I'll give them to you. One for each."

"I'll take a gold piece over a dead mule any day," French said. "What's the loss if one Reb mule lives?"

Hollingsworth dismounted and nodded his chin in the direction of the mule.

Nathan leaned down and grabbed the mule's reins. The mule curled its lip, braying and jerking its head. Steadman and French pushed the haunches, forcing the animal to stand. Gray mud oozed under the shifted weight. A dank pool of dark water filled the hollow left by the emaciated body. Nathan motioned with his eyes, and Steadman unstrapped the broken supply baskets from the mule's back, leaving the tie straps. Nathan held the reins and whispered to it.

"Calm now. Calm," he said.

Manning pulled one hoof from the glue-like mud, and French pushed. The frightened mule lifted one leg, then another. Finally, it stood on firm ground.

Nathan found a wound at its rear leg near the stomach. He thought the lead might have grazed the flesh and not entered it.

"It's free," Hollingsworth said. "Pay us."

Nathan examined their greedy eyes. As he reached for his pouch, he realized the cost of this mule—his gold, his farm, perhaps even his marriage. He could not renege. Even if he shot the mule himself, the others would take his gold. A battlefield oath cannot be undone.

The pouch felt heavy and full of promise. As he drew the strings apart, the men moved closer, every eye on the coins. One at a time, he paid their fee: Hollingsworth, Manning, Steadman, and French.

Nathan kept his original enlistment orders at the bottom of the pouch. After handing over the last gold piece, he removed the paper. It was creased and yellowed, but he had preserved it all these long years. To his own surprise, he tore the paper into small pieces and let them drop around his feet.

"We're done with this war," he said. He pulled the reins to lead the mule. "We're going home."

He moved to the horses, untied his haversack, grabbed his musket, and walked away. He headed north in search of water and perhaps some rest. He did not say good-bye, nor did he flinch when Hollingsworth called after him. Instead, he wondered if Miss Agnes Perser would consider one rebel mule wealth enough for marriage if the man who possessed it loved her.

The sun turned okra, and a thin twilight fog began to form. Nathan coaxed the mule with soft encouragement, even though the stout neck sagged and the eyes began to lose their glisten. Nathan tried to comfort the animal by rubbing its jaw and feeding it a hard-tack cracker. The wound bled again, but not seriously, Nathan judged. Still, a bleeding wound stirs concern. After perhaps two hours, he stopped at the top of a hill. They had traveled far enough from the slaughter to smell pine pitch, and the water in the stream ran clear over bluestone and pebbles. He could see the battlefield, but from a distance. The distance gave him courage enough to ignore it and to begin what might be called a healing as reality moved slightly toward memory.

They walked down into a green gully to camp. Nathan tied the reins to a rope, and he tied the rope to a tree so the animal could graze. The mule stood silent, as if it still carried supply boxes and it hadn't slept in a day or two.

Nathan boiled water for coffee. He did not eat. He rubbed his hands in the fire's warmth, and he wondered about the value of the mule, the gold it cost, and the queer decision to forsake the war. He imagined the conversation with his father. His father would say, "Brute appearance calls it foolhardy, but in ten years you'll know its value." Then Nathan imagined his father would return to his field work. Perhaps he would never speak of it again.

The loss of gold seemed fundamentally unsound. But what price a life? His mother, he knew, would value the life. Comfort, to her, came in a smile and a thankful embrace. She would be happy that Nathan returned home alive. Whether he returned with gold or with a mule she wouldn't care. But that's a mother's love; it holds no count in the business of men.

A breeze rustled the weeds, and Nathan finished the coffee with a gulp. He felt tired, and he began to ache in the way only a man who has escaped war can ache, bone-deep and permanent. He thought how the end of this journey would bring him home. Then he closed his eyes. He imagined that his father would stop his work to watch Nathan's approach. His mother would smile and wave and call his name. And he would see Agnes.

As he thought of them together, he slept nearly four hours without waking.

When he did awaken, it took several seconds before he remembered where he was and why. He turned to see the mule in the moonlight. He stirred the coals of the campfire, added broken twigs, and coaxed the weary embers back to flame. He went to the mule and stroked its mud-caked hide. "I'll rinse you in the daylight," he said. He looked across the back of the mule to the hill-line admiring the calm of the night-lit tips of high grass. It was the first time since leaving home he was alone.

The mule brayed. The fire crackled. The night solitude carried the noises in echoes. He went to his bedroll and made a pipe.

The mule moved a little closer to the tree, but Nathan could not tell if it had grazed. Come light, he would hand feed it and bring it to the water for drink. Then he would wash the mud from it to begin its rejuvenation. He planned his route north, almost a straight walk, barring renegade militia and federal search parties. He would walk slow, stopping to rest the mule. He might need to work a day at a willing farm for food. Even under the worst scenario, he calculated he'd be home in three weeks. The thought of it made him smile. Home. Home and Agnes.

He slept again.

At dawn, the mule brayed and woke him. Nathan took the mule's bray as a good sign; perhaps it wanted water or feed. While the sun moved along the horizon, Nathan rose to attend the mule. He undid the rope to lead the animal to the stream. It brayed again, but Nathan shivered at the sorrowful sound.

"What?" he said to it, touching the jaw, patting the haunch. The eyes looked hollow and dry, beginning to turn opaque around the edges.

"You'll be fine," Nathan said. "Come on."

He tugged the rein. The mule trudged without resistance to water's edge, its ribs shadowy along its hide. It did not bend to drink. Nathan cupped a handful of water and rubbed it around the beast's lips and tongue. Droplets fell from its whiskers back into the stream, and the mule bent after them to drink.

Nathan patted its neck. "Good," he said.

Nathan bent too and rinsed his mouth. Then he drank.

He left the mule untied; it would not run. He went to the fire and added kindling and pinecones to the embers. He sat in the dewy sunrise, the smoke from the campfire a comfort of pine scent and ash. The mule moved warily to graze and chewed the grass more like a cow making cud than a horse-breed chewing feed, slow and repetitive, almost melancholic. He thought the mule looked haggard. Perhaps the emotion of the battlefield kept him from recognizing its state. Could it have been his frustration with death that led him to the reckless choice he now possessed? Why did he save the animal? Why did he pay such awful price for its life? Surly, Agnes would ask him these very questions.

"Why, Nathan? What drove you?" she might ask.

He knew what he would tell her. One thing only drove him. Love. It felt like an incorrigible piece of knowledge, yet true and agreeable, like his love for her. He had to save the beast. It had survived the war, and Nathan knew it represented both his own survival and the survival of their love. That's what he would tell Agnes. He looked upon the sad, silent beast, and in that moment, he loved it—as a symbol, as a living thing, as a hope.

Nathan drew on his pipe and exhaled a firm stream of smoke. He poured coffee into the metal cup and sipped gingerly allowing the heat and sour grounds to ease past his tongue. The warmth seeped into his stomach, and the heat of his belly and the heat of the cup against his hands warmed him.

The Rev. Perser would also ask Nathan about his decision. Rev. Perser was a man of principles, a godly man, a man obligated to rigid rules—the singular moralities of Christian faith and the simple exigency of money in a commercial economy. Would he accept love as an item of barter?

"Perhaps not," Nathan answered. "What then?" he asked into

the steam of the cup. But he had no answer to that.

Many rules die in war, and traditions too, but a daughter's responsibility to obey her father does not die. If Rev. Perser forbade Agnes's marriage because Nathan had no money, she would obey. What then would Nathan do?

The sun began to heat the air, and Nathan decided to break camp. Perhaps an answer would come to him. He doused the fire with the remaining coffee and took the pot and his cup to the stream to rinse them. He led the mule by the rope. After he washed the utensils, he drank again and splashed his face. When he rubbed his eyes clear, he realized the mule had not moved. Nathan went to it then and coaxed it to the edge of the water, but the mule struggled and halted at the mossy recession of the bank.

Nathan noticed the wound was bleeding again. He pulled the reluctant animal into the stream, and the water flowed around their legs in swirls. Nathan drenched his shirt and wiped the animal's wound clean. Then he washed the beast from head to haunch, dripping water back into the stream from its back and its legs. He cupped water to the mule's mouth and the wounded creature licked at it with its thick tongue, but it would not lower its head to drink on its own. It shook its muscles to remove the water from its hide, and droplets splashed Nathan's face and arms.

Nathan felt refreshed, almost invigorated. The chilly water cooled his skin and blood rushed pink under it. The mule stood in patient silence.

"All right, mule," Nathan said. "You're clean now. We can move on."

It's not a good idea to hike with wet feet inside wet boots, but Nathan suffered an urge to keep moving. They progressed with slow steps, the sun ahead of them as they traveled easterly and north with the stream. The mule began to limp noticeably, and Nathan's feet began to rub against the sides of his boots.

"My toes are wrinkling," he said out loud. "We better make camp early."

He found a small area of brush and fallen leaves. Ferns and dark green bushes with tiny, white, star-shaped flowers made the place look restful. The stream hit a series of rocks and a slight drop in elevation caused the falling water to add a melody of comfort to the site. Nathan found a fire-site near two trees and a lichen-sided boulder.

He led the mule to some long grasses, but it did not eat. Nathan unstrapped the haversack and the Springfield. He took a paper plug and a pellet from the leather shot bag and loaded the musket.

"You might not be hungry," he said to the mule, "but I am. And I'm going to eat."

He patted the ribcage above the bleeding wound, turned, and walked into the trees to scare up dinner. The afternoon heat felt good on his tired muscles. He knew that the sun and a fire would dry his socks and his boots if he found dinner quickly. He came upon a decaying log, and when he kicked it, a rabbit jumped from underneath. Nathan fired quickly. The rabbit flipped once and dropped.

He lit the fire, skinned the rabbit and put it on a stick to let it skewer. He stretched his socks on a smooth stone and hung his boots upside down on two sticks near the fire.

He went to the mule. Its long ears hung like melting wax and its stubborn head fell, subdued.

"I'm sorry you got shot, mule."

He patted its neck. As he did, the scent of sizzling rabbit wafted into his nose. He inhaled deeply, allowing the green woods and the leaf mulch and the rabbit oil to fill his head.

"Some things are supposed to die, like that rabbit, so I can eat," he said. He grabbed the mule's ears, one in each hand. "And some things are supposed to live because they mean something. And you mean something. Do you hear?"

Nathan left the mule and strode to the fire. The tension in his stomach increased, but he confused uneasiness with hunger. He took some of the white corn meal from the flour sack, mixed water into it, and flattened the dough onto a fry pan.

"A corncake will taste good with rabbit."

Nathan turned the rabbit. Then he decided to turn his socks. They were beginning to dry, but the toes were stiff from the mud, so he had to rinse them again. He twisted each one, shook them, and replaced them on the warm stone. The corncake began to fry around the edges, and the rough doughy smell began to sweeten. He set the coffee pot to boil, and lit a pipe. He took a deep inhale and released the smoke up and away from his face. As he did so, a mosquito bit his skin and he slapped it and killed it. Its engorged belly splattered red.

"Blood for blood," Nathan said and took his pipe again.

The comfort of the moment led his thoughts to Agnes, and he smiled. Somehow, he felt that she would understand his choice as a predilection in favor of life. He closed his eyes to see her, and she appeared as if real. Her long auburn hair surrounded her face and hung across both shoulders, straight and shiny like rippling water. Her brown eyes sparkled when she smiled, and he could see in them the fond yearning and youthful hopefulness that kept Nathan human during the muddy years of war.

"Will you marry me?" he asked.

"Will you marry me, Miss Agnes?"

"Agnes, will you marry me?"

He practiced the proposal so that when he asked in person she would have to say yes.

But the practice turned bitter as he imagined Agnes hesitating. "My father…"

The image collapsed, and Nathan opened his eyes to the hazy

beginning of sunset and coffee boiling out of the pot. He pulled the pot away from the fire, shook the fry pan and leaned the rabbit higher to let the heat cook the inside meat more thoroughly.

Nathan tapped the ashes from his pipe, then poured hot coffee into his tin cup. He lifted a twig from the fire to re-light the pipe when the mule brayed. Nathan turned his head in time to watch the mule collapse awkwardly like a dog sitting on its own tail. He dropped the stick, put his pipe on the ground, and ran to the mule. Its legs were crumpled under its body, and its great head looked forlorn. Harsh breaths snorted from its nostrils. Blood oozed from the tiny wound at its side.

"You're going to die, aren't you?" Nathan said. He sat near its head and watched the ribs swell and fall in hard cadence.

"I can't save you, but you know I tried." Nathan looked away from the mule. "I can't do anything more," he said, his head still turned away from the great, round eye of the beast.

When he turned back to the mule, Nathan realized suddenly that the long, black eyelashes made the thing look human, as if the eyes themselves could plead. Nathan exhaled. "I suppose there is one more thing I can do," he said. "I can make your passing easier."

Nathan went to his gear and brought the Colt .44 to the mule.

Nathan insisted that killing the mule constituted an act of love, an act internal and correct, a pitiful act of kindness in a harsh time —for where is the essence of a man if not in his capacity to love? He put the barrel into the mule's sad ear.

"I love you," he whispered, and pulled the trigger.

The gray sting of gunpowder burned his nose. He sat with the mule for a long time, until the smell of burning rabbit meat and overcooked corn meal reminded him of his surroundings and the other realities of his time.

He rose up then on his bare feet and walked to the fire. He took the burned rabbit and bit into the charred, ashen flesh. It tasted black and dry, and it satisfied his hunger deliciously. He flipped the burnt corncake into the fire, and the orange and blue flame that erupted from its center delighted him. He took another bite of rabbit and turned his face toward the motionless mule.

He thought for a moment about the absence of gold with which he would return to Agnes, but he did not worry about it, for now he knew what he was capable of in the name of love, and Rev. Perser would know too, one way or another.

HUMAN RESOURCES

GREG CHAPMAN

NERVES:

They twisted James' gut, turned his skin slick with sweat, set his pupils dilating, his heart drumming in his chest—he thought he was going to burst.

It's just a job interview, he kept telling himself as he sat in the foyer of Scully and Bonham, one of the country's largest recruitment agencies. The firm was considered the cream of the crop: their goal to find the right person for the right job; for brokerage firms, law firms, hospitals, the military and almost everything in between.

James, a biochemistry graduate from Caltech, was hoping to secure a research spot with Aeon Industries—the most prestigious genetic research facility on the eastern seaboard. He had driven more than three hundred miles for this chance and he didn't want to screw it up now.

He suddenly realised his right leg was shaking, a common occurrence when he was nervous. His anxiety was his greatest weakness; he knew about cellular regeneration and mitosis like the back of his hand, he could break a virus down to its basic DNA, but tell him he had to do a job interview and he just crumbled under the pressure of it all.

A leggy brunette, dressed in a fine grey wool skirt and suit jacket was sitting across from him, smirking in his direction. When James smirked back his top lip inadvertently snagged on his teeth, setting his grin on an odd angle, which only made the girl laugh.

"You haven't done many of these have you?" she said.

"What?" James said.

The girl tugged a loose strand of hair behind her ear, placed her black leather organiser in her lap and looked at him with a pair of gorgeous blue eyes.

"Job interviews," she said.

James checked the room to see if anyone was watching him. "Does it look that obvious?"

"Yes, I'm afraid it does," she said. "I imagine that you'd have that same look of helplessness on your face as you walked down the aisle—or become a father."

James frowned. "Wow, that's very insightful—if not personal."

She looked away. "Sorry—it's a bad habit I have—speaking my mind."

"Oh," James said, feeling even more uncomfortable.

She stood and offered her hand. "Angela," she said. "Angela Freeman."

James shook her hand. "James Richards."

Angela sat back down and methodically straightened her jacket and smoothed down her skirt. "So James—what job are you here for?"

"Researcher at Aeon Industries."

Angela blushed. "Me too," she said, seeming taken aback. "What a coincidence."

James swallowed as his nerves resurfaced. "Yeah, wow," he said. "Who would've thought?"

"So what did you major in?"

"Sorry?"

"What was your major? What College? I've got a Masters in Molecular Biology from MIT."

James couldn't believe it. She was sizing him up; seeing who the better applicant was. As nervous as he may have been, James was no fool; he wouldn't fall for her little play.

"Caltech," he told her. "Biochemistry, Masters."

Angela raised her eyebrows, impressed. "Caltech. Nice," she said. "Talk about your stiff competition."

James scanned the foyer again. There was no one else in the room, but he and Angela. He prayed for the receptionist to come and collect him for his interview now, just to have the upper hand over his new opponent.

"We must be the only applicants?" he said.

Angela nodded. "Looks that way."

"Do you know much about Aeon then?"

Angela picked at a corner of her organiser and shrugged her shoulders. "Not much—just that they're the leaders in genetic research, with a dozen or more government contracts. They made a twenty billion dollar profit last year." She leant forward to whisper. "Apparently they've found a way to clone living tissue and siphon stem cells from spinal fluid, but that's just conjecture. Still, it'd be pretty amazing if it were actually true."

James adjusted his tie and accidentally kicked his briefcase, knocking it over with a loud slap on the tiled floor. The receptionist stared daggers at him. His misfortune made Angela laugh once more. It infuriated James, because it only made her look more attractive.

"Are you okay?" she said. "You look like you could use a drink?"

"I'm fine," he replied, stifling anger. He thought of her last remarks and said: "All those details are on their website you know —apart from the claims about cloning. I wouldn't start spouting rumours in there if I were you."

Angela's smile was fiercer this time, deprecating. "Well, I'm not you am I?" she replied. "What makes you think you're better than me anyway?"

"Look, I'm not going to do this with you, okay," he said. "We've both got a chance at this job—so let's just say let the best man win, okay?"

"Or woman."

"Yeah, whatever," James said, his anxiety being exchanged for frustration, a sensation he was most grateful for.

"What blood type are you?" Angela said, seemingly oblivious to his rebuff.

"Excuse me?"

"What blood type are you?"

"What sort of a question is that?"

"Aeon expects all of its employees to undertake regular physical screenings and health checks, including, blood and urine testing"—that's on their website too," Angela said, smugly. "I've heard they actually encourage their scientists to donate their own samples: tissue, bone marrow, semen—"

James grimaced. "You've got to be joking, right!"

"Oh, that's just another one of those rumours I heard," she replied.

James was about to retort when the receptionist's phone suddenly rang. James and Angela watched as she answered, replied "Yes, ma'am," put down the receiver and walked out from behind her desk to stand with her hands behind her back, before James.

"Mr Richards, the panel is ready for you now."

James was on his feet and hot on her heels, briefcase in hand. He tried to block Angela's wild claims out of his mind; he knew she was just trying to spook him to get him off his game so he would blow the interview and leave the door wide open for her. But he

GREG CHAPMAN

wouldn't give her the satisfaction. He turned to see if she was watching him and indeed she was, with her blue eyes narrowed.

"Good luck," she said.

And her voice followed him all the way to the interview room door.

* * *

There were three on the panel.

Two men and one woman; one of the men was much older than the other, at least seventy years of age, his hair thinning, face gaunt. The suit he was wearing, although expensive, looked three sizes too big for him. The other, younger man was clean shaven, his hair slicked down, all precision and style. The pair looked wealthy —very wealthy and James was certain they were executives from Aeon. The woman looked slightly out of place and James could only assume she was with Scully and Bonham.

"Good morning Mr Richards," the older gentleman said, before coughing into a handkerchief.

James swallowed. "Uh, yes, good morning," he replied, not sure who to keep his eyes on. The two men seemed to ogle him, while the woman offered him a smile.

"Would you like a glass of water?" the woman said.

"Yes, thank you."

The woman stood and walked to a nearby drinks cart, to side of the panel table. She carried a jug and a glass to where James was seated at a table opposite.

The panel had their own jugs of water and as James poured himself a glass, they poured their own. Still the two men watched him intently. Of course they would be wondering what he would say, how he would act. Would his personality match his resume? There was so much to consider that James could feel the onset of anxiety returning. He swallowed the contents of his glass and poured another.

"Are you ready to begin?" the woman said.

James licked the moisture from his lips. "Yes."

"Well, thank you for coming today," she began. "My name is Caroline Keating, and I'm the Human Resources Manager for Scully and Bonham and these gentlemen are from Aeon Industries. But I'll let them introduce themselves."

The old man cleared his throat and stifled another hacking cough. "My name is Gerard Gore and I am the Chief Executive of Aeon Industries."

My God, James thought. *Gerard Gore, the Gerard Gore, founder of Aeon Industries.* He couldn't believe he was going to be interviewed by Gerard Gore.

Mr Gore gestured to the younger man and said: "This is Colin Meyer," Gore told him. "He is the Chief Operating Officer of my Research Division. If you get the job, you would be working for him."

James nodded in understanding as Gore handed back to Ms Keating.

"So," Ms Keating said. "We're going to ask you some questions. You'll have about five minutes to answer each question with a total of thirty minutes. Then at the end you will have the chance to ask us some questions."

"Okay," James said.

"I'll ask the first question," she said. "Tell us about the paper you wrote to achieve your Masters Degree from Caltech. I believe it was on Mendelian Genetics?"

"Ah, yes, I questioned the effectiveness of the Punnett square method in determining potential combinations of gametes for a given cross."

As James revealed the intricacies of his paper, he noticed Gore and Meyer were deep in quiet conversation, all the while watching him and listening to him intently. Their concentration upon him was unsettling and James felt as if he was being undressed by the two men. He stammered and his response ground to a halt.

"Take your time," Ms Keating said, smiling. "If you'd like, we can ask you the next question and you can come back to the first later?"

"Uh, yes, perhaps that would be best." James said.

Gore let out a loud cough as if he was struggling for breath. His aide, Meyer, reacted quickly and handed the old man a glass of water. He drank deeply, his wet gulps echoing about the room. James suddenly felt thirsty and emptied his own glass.

"Do we need to take a break?" Ms Keating asked to which Meyer replied with a shake of his head.

"All right, then," she said. "James, tell us what you can bring to Aeon industries."

"Uh, a strong work ethic for one thing," he said. "I believe that, in science, perseverance is the key and not being afraid to take risks. I mean look at Barry Marshall and Robin Warren's determination to find the bacteria that causes peptic ulcers. I'm not saying I'm as great as those men, but in Aeon's hands I could be."

James' monologue attracted the attention of Gore and it seemed to give him the strength to rise above his breathing difficulty. James imagined he had emphysema from the ragged nature of his cough —he could hardly believe someone as frail could be running a multi-billion dollar research facility. Yet there was a fire behind the old man's eyes that made James shiver.

"How do you feel about the creation of synthetic cells, experimentation with human embryos?" Meyer said, startling James.

"Um, there are major scientific benefits in testing embryos, but then there are also considerable benefits for stem cell research as well."

"So..." Gore croaked. "Are you saying... that you feel embryonic testing is wrong?"

"No, I believe there is a strong case for both," James replied. "We shouldn't discount one method just for the sake of a few billion Catholics."

Gore laughed, but the effort set off a fresh bout of coughs. Still, the old man and his aide couldn't help but smile at him.

"That's very good," Gore said, wheezing. Then he turned to Ms Keating. "I think we've heard enough—ask Ms Freeman to come in now please."

James's face blanched. How could that have been enough time? He'd only just begun.

"I'm sorry," he interjected. "But is that it? I thought I had thirty minutes? I'd hardly call this a thorough job interview."

Meyer was still smiling; James's frankness seemed to impress him. James felt he could no longer look him in the eye; it was too discomfiting.

"Don't I get the chance to sell myself?" James said. "What if I have some questions about the position?"

Gore smiled from behind his handkerchief and then waved it in mock surrender. "By all means Mr Richards, ask away, there are no secrets in this room." Then he turned to Ms Keating. "But please, Caroline if you could still ask Ms Freeman to join us."

James was flabbergasted as Caroline left the room. "How is this even ethical?" he said. "You can't ask another applicant to walk in on someone's interview."

But Gore ignored him. "Go on, Mr Richards, ask your questions."

James felt bile rising in his throat, a wave of anxious nausea. "Well, what sort of work will I be undertaking at Aeon—if I were to get the job?"

Meyer interlocked his fingers. "High-end genetics—or to be more specific—organ replication and regeneration."

James recalled Angela's words outside; the ridiculous claims she made. Suddenly he wasn't so sure she wasn't telling the truth. Nothing made sense anymore. The world around him was softening at the edges, blurring, fading. His mouth felt dry and his mind was off kilter; like he was feeling the effects of intoxication.

"Organ… regeneration…" James tried to say.

Out of the corner of his eye he saw Angela Freeman enter the room. She was still smiling that derogatory smile, but for some reason it looked like a snarl, or a laceration. Her face was in and out of focus and when she spoke it sounded as if her voice was booming from a great chasm behind him.

"How's the interview going?" she said, but not to James.

"Oh, he's doing very well," Mr Meyer told her.

Angela stood with her arms folded and studied James as he struggled to stay sitting in an upright position. He knew now he was feeling the effects of a powerful hallucinogen, the substance severing the link between his body and mind. His subconscious was trapped inside a mind that believed it was being poured down a drain.

"He's quite harsh, isn't he," Angela said to Meyer. "I'd say there's a bit of self-loathing there."

James could hear her talking about him. How could she be allowed to judge him—she was just another interviewee. Then the awful truth struck him and his enfeebled mind almost shattered under the weight of it. She was with them; with Aeon.

"What did you give him?" Gore asked.

"Ketamine. We mixed it with the water," Meyer said.

"Oh, excellent," Gore said. "So tell me about him—what's his blood type?"

Angela turned to the old man, so much pleasure in her smile.

"AB negative. Can you believe it? This is the one we've been waiting for, sir."

"Oh, God," Gore said. "So he could be the one?"

Meyer put a hand on the old man's arm; James thought he saw two vipers rearing up to attack each other where they were sitting.

"There will still be some more tests to run; bone marrow, spinal tap—"

"Ooh, a brain scan," Angela said. "I'd love to get a look at his brain. He could be perfect for you, Mr Gore. He was the most suitable out of all the candidates."

Gore looked James up and down and there was a glint of lasciviousness there, but not of sexual desire, rather something deeper, darker. James wanted to get up and run, but the drug overpowered him. He must have had three glasses from the contaminated jug.

"What... have you... done to me?" he muttered to them.

Angela cocked her head to the side and frowned, pitying him. She walked over to him, her body coalescing in the air, like oil in water. Then he felt her arm around his shoulder and his skin burned.

"Do you see Mr Gore, there?" Angela whispered, yet her voice was like a thousand knives in his ear. "How old do you really think he is?"

James' eyes were locked on Gore; they were unable to move anymore. The old man must have been seventy, but the longer he stared at him, the older he seemed to become. His face cracked and drooped, the eyes sunk deeper into his skull. All of a sudden he looked like a man who'd lived for one hundred and seventy years.

"How do you think he stays so young, James?" Angela said.

James skin was soaked with sweat, his pupils were absorbing too much light and his heart; well it pounded so hard and so fast, each beat threatened to send his whole body into convulsions. Gore was no man, he was a monster and Aeon Industries was keeping him alive.

"Not often, but every once in a while, Mr Gore needs... to get some work done," Angela told him. "It might be a new heart, or a new liver, perhaps a new circulatory system. And you can't just go out and buy those things in a store. Besides Mr Gore's organs shrivelled up and died decades ago so we have to use other ways and means."

James flinched as Mr Gore stood and walked over to him and caressed his face with bony, dry fingers.

"It's like transplantation," Angela explained. "But we don't simply take your organs out and put them into Mr Gore. No it's more intricate than that. We put Mr Gore inside you."

James screamed for help, but there was no chance of that; he could see by the smiles on Meyer's and Ms Keating's faces that he was just wasting his time. So he stopped screaming, but the din rang on in his head.

"Think of it as if Mr Gore was a puppet master and you were his puppet," Angela said.

"And what a lovely boy you'll be," Gore told him. "Welcome to Aeon Industries, Mr Richards."

Then Angela leant down and kissed James' cheek and pins and needles spread across his face.

"There's no need to be nervous, James," she said. "You've got the job."

THEY RESTARTED THE MILL AT KILLINGTON

BOB MOORE

KILLINGTON STRADDLED A STREAMBED between two anonymous wooded hills. It appeared quite suddenly to drivers, as our sign, shot full of holes anyway, was buried in foliage much of the year. The village was four short streets' worth of old buildings and houses, all sagging at least a little. Killington Road, a two-laner off Route 78, descending the wooded slope and entering the village, is fed by four streets and ran by the Killington Mill, long since abandoned. The road climbed up into the woods, leaving this tiny hollow shell behind.

The mill was what put us here. A mill now in pieces, the metal wheels rusted and seized, the wooden arms rotted and broken, decrepit-looking and incomplete, some chunks of once-useful equipment having been carted away when it was worth something. The sturdy wooden timbers braced by steel supports were spattered with droppings from the birds that roost in the scaffolding. They flew in through any one of a hundred-some broken window panes.

And, of course, there's myself, Hugh Crane, and Emma

Thigpen and Calvin Lasalle, and our families buried on the upper slope. Emma's around the bend, an old weaver herself who now talked daily to her dead sister and mother like they were all still having coffee together. Calvin stayed busy keeping his little shop open against the day some stranger wanders in for a paper or cup of coffee. Me, I was like Emma, retired from the mill. I read a lot.

It was very quiet here, which is why we could hear it and feel it when it started, very gently, the first Monday after spring, very softly, like a pulse returning.

* * *

Two nights ago I heard it the first time. A whooshing noise came into my bedroom window on the night air. It's March, so my bedroom window is normally closed, but I craved fresh air so I opened it, and heard it. The rhythmic ululation echoed in the hollow, a delicious mystery to me for a moment; it stirred memories I didn't recognize, and I listened for a long while in my bedroom, looking out into the dark. I recognized it when I smelled something as familiar and as outdated as the whooshing sound—the smell of the coal the mill burned for heat.

From my window the mill is downhill in the streambed. A huge silhouette, tonight I saw smoke rising from its central chimney. I thought it had caught fire—kids have set it now and then—but this smoke had no flame. It didn't gust through broken windows, it puffed from the chimney: the smoke of industry, not vandalism.

After an hour, as suddenly as it began, the sound stopped. The smoke blew away and the chimney was cold and empty. Only when the smoke was gone could I return to sleep.

* * *

Emma was out front next morning when I stepped out to get my paper, arching her neck and savoring a scent. The sooty residue of coal smoke drifted by. "Mornin', Hugh," she smiled at me, "lovely day, ain't it?"

"Mornin' Emma." I'm not very talkative.

"Was good to see the mill back workin', wasn't it?" She smiled.

"You saw that, did you?" I asked, suspicious of my own wits as well as of hers. "What you mean, back workin'?"

Leaning over to pick up a fragment of newspaper littering her tiny front plot, she straightened up her stick-thin frame, gritting her dentures in a passing spasm of pain. "Just what I said. They musta started a night shift last night. I heard 'em start near midnight, went 'til near seven. You can see it better'n I can from your end. You must've seen it, didn't't'cha?"

There's maybe thirty souls left in Killington Falls, only a handful of us still in the row houses near the mill. I never seem to get farther than Cal's store. Life would get very dull if the last few souls I knew decided I was too contrary to talk to. So I nodded agreeably. "Oh sure, I saw. Yep, hope they keep it up." And with an exchange of smiles, I left her to her litter-policing and I went for my paper.

Calvin Lasalle has the worst coffee in New England and the closest paper, so I buy the paper and ignore the coffee. Pushing open the heavy screen door he has half-covered with advertising stickers for Coca-Cola and Marlboro and Sara Lee and all the other crap he sells,the bell he hung on it when his hearing started going announced me. I hate ringing it, because I'm not talkative, but there's no choice if I want my paper. 'Ring'. "Mornin', Hugh."

"Cal," I acknowledged; he was busy with a pencil and a scrap of brown paper bag, standing in front of his first aisle of fruit pies and donuts.

"How many men you think they're gonna be hirin' with the mill startin' up again?" he asked, an unaccustomed air of excitement in his voice. "I'm orderin' more papers and I might expand to take care of the morning crowd. Barber shop next door's been closed five years, I can probably rent it cheap."

Calvin lives over his shop, which is three blocks from my house. He couldn't quite see the smoke from there, but he clearly had smelled it, and heard the looms. Now he was pacing up and down his aisles, counting the Twinkies twice, adding figures he'd scratched on the bag with the only pencil I've ever seen him with— Blackhawk Number 2, half an eraser. "Yea, I recall back when they were goin' three shifts, I'd go through ten, twelve pots of coffee in an hour. Lots of donuts, too. You think that yogurt stuff is still popular? My cooler isn't workin' too good."

He was chattering, not waiting for an answer to one question before asking the next, babbling excitedly like a boy going to the fair. I could understand Emma slipping out of her mind for a moment, she having been half-slipped for a few years already. And I had heard and seen and smelled something from the mill last night. But vandals were probably responsible for that. Cal was alert and still running a business and now he was talking like it was 1949 again. "Cal," I hedged, "'fore you start givin' the grocery store a run for their money, how much have you made so far from the new mill workers?"

He looked up from his figures, irritated at my interruption. "Hell, Hugh, I ain't stupid." Then he thumbed the NO SALE key on his old register and ejected the cash drawer. "You know my usual day, past five years I don't clear twenny dollars in a mornin'." He stepped aside to show me his cash drawer. It wasn't seeing more money in his cash drawer that stopped my mouth, it was the money I saw. Cal had collected a twenty, and three two dollar bills. I leaned down to see those two-bit papers and their year of issue was 1932. "Cal, when did you pick these up?"

Frowning at me like his time was being frittered away by a senile fool, his voice was tested condescension. "Just after seven, Hugh, when the night shift left." After leaving with my paper I thought to ask Cal what the workers had bought, but headed back to my house instead.

In my front room I have my mother's pictures, family snapshots of us as children, as parents, as soldiers. And I kept one of myself taken on my retirement. Finally I found the one of my father standing at his loom. It's hard to say why or how this picture was taken, as the mill was no photo studio. My father is dressed in a collarless shirt, suspenders holding up his pants. Clean shaven and wearin' his specs, he was fifty but looked boyish. Standing next to him is a woman, another man behind her. I noticed today that that second man had only three fingers on one hand. Not uncommon, those industrial accidents.

In the afternoons, when it's clear out, I usually go up the hill to the cemetery and spend some time with Mom and Dad and my friends there. I'm not talkative and neither are they, so I can spend hours in their quiet company. But today I headed downhill, to the mill.

The road was deserted today, as is its usual. The buildings next to the mill are all boarded up and empty, just like the mill. Its front gate was badly rusted but I got it open. Weeds grew tall through gaps in the old brick walkway; one sprouted in the middle of the doorway. The gentle splashing of the stream below was a sweet sound you couldn't hear when the mill was running. Today I heard the stream just fine. So I hoped Calvin hadn't put any money into expansion, and I turned around and went home.

But even though it got chilly when the sun set, I left my kitchen window open. When I walked by it en route to my second beer after the evening news, I looked out down the hill between the boarded-up buildings, and saw smoke billowing vigorously from the center chimney and, tonight, from the north chimney as well. And then the clattering of the weaving machinery came rolling up the hill. That clattering was the town's pulse, a huge metronome to which we all worked. It is among my earliest childhood memories. Sixty years later, you'd think I'd be happy, sentimental over hearing the clanking of the mill. But I had been there today and it was an empty, abandoned shell.

Never got to that beer. I stayed in the house with the windows shut and the blinds drawn. Still, I could feel the mill rattling the floor. I turned on my old TV but it has poor vertical hold and the vibrations made it scroll and scroll until I couldn't stand to watch 'Jeopardy' no more. So I turned on the radio to get a little news. "A third island in the Marianas chain was reported cleared of Japanese resistance today. The announcement, from the Office of War Information... and that General Mac Arthur will clear the entire Marianas... May first." I must've gotten one of those historical reenactments, I guessed, so I kept turning the dial. Got lots of dance music—good stuff, not this rocken roll noise. After two more news stories told me about the progress our troops were making in the Marianas I just turned off the radio and turned out the light, and felt the town's pulse thump. At dawn it stopped, and I finally nodded off.

* * *

Tonight all three chimneys puffed. Still black as the night, I wondered why they needed heat but no light. Never did learn the answer to that. I watched it for a long while, feeling it through my feet, through my hands when I leaned against the window sill. Fear is not an emotion I put up with. I refuse to worry about breaking my bones, or catching flu, and I eat whatever I like. But by the third night of the mill's rumbling I was afraid.

Not of the mill, for I grew up with it and can't fear it, but of someone from the mill. If the mill had come back, I wondered, who had come back to work it? A little later I got my coat on and went.

* * *

The gate, a ten foot iron barrier, was open, as was the front door. John Frances Gates was in there, I could hear him. Tall and powerful, more strapping a man than was needed for watching the time clock, Gates also kept out union organizers. We all hated him, for various reasons. One was that men paid him a penny for the privilege of having their cards punched. Some paid him more, to punch the correct time when they ran late, some habitually. If you refused, he clocked you an hour late for three days. If you still had a job after that, then he would wait outside for you, or be at your house first light, or find you in an empty place. Then he could put you in the hospital. The owner may have known, but Gates was clever, nothing was ever done.

Gates' other dig was to assign men to the trap. The trap was the gearing mechanism that converted the stream's flow to power the looms. It required regular greasing and to have fibers cleaned out. Besides being messy, it was dangerous, for the owner refused to shut down the looms other than for ten minutes at noon, the time he gave us to eat lunch. In ten minutes' time the worker had to squeeze into the gearing trap, a space the size of a car with the maneuvering options of a telephone booth, and slather grease on three main gears and six main bearings. You could just barely get it done and get out in ten minutes. Because at 12:10 the drive wheel was engaged again.

Gates was responsible for warning the man inside that he had only a minute to get out. But sometimes he went out back for a quick snort, or tried to make time with one of the women weavers.

Most guys got themselves out, and a few more lost fingers, one a foot, when the machinery started turning all around them. Two, young Johnny McLelland, and an older guy from Poland, only came out in pieces. You see, the machinist was under strict orders to start up at 12:10 and he couldn't see the trap from where he was. So it was up to Gates. Sometimes the bastard was there, and sometimes not. You can guess getting on Gate's bad side got you sent to the trap. I went three times, then he got angry with someone else.

Tonight I could hear him inside when I went in.

"Crane!" He was leaning back in his chair, his black hair an unruly mop, and a toothpick in his teeth. Smelled too. The shock of seeing him made me glance at my hands, old man's hands, wrinkled and callused and a little bent with a couple of knuckles swollen from arthritis; they reminded me that I was an old man, retired, and that this was all clearly a hallucination, but they were trembling. "You're late, Crane!" He half smiled. "Set you right for ten cents," he growled in a lower voice. He tossed the briefest of glances at the double doors onto the mill floor where the foreman was.

I looked behind me to run out to the empty roadway, but saw instead five other men waiting their turn to be clocked in. "What's the hold-up?" asked the last one out. Someone mumbled to him, something about 'Gates' dues', and the complainer was quiet. They looked at me expectantly. My hands trembling, I looked again at Gates, who was looking sour at me for dawdling.

"Shit or get off the pot," he ordered. My mouth opened but I couldn't speak. Then he sneered at me, fed my card into the clock until we heard it 'clunk'. "You're late, Crane! Need a man for the trap today, and you're it!"

I walked on through the double doors, wondering if the old rotten timbers were unsafe; if I were sleep-walking I could still die in a dream should I find a rotten timber. But as I passed through the doors I saw that the looms were all fully assembled, clean and running, tended by rows of workers. "Crane!" It was Needlenose, the foreman. Frowning and tapping his wrist, he pointed angrily at a small gap in a row facing the fourth loom. "Get to it!"

Funny how old skills come back to you. Watching the swinging wooden arm feed a sliver of fiber and pushing the bar that tightened each row, snugged it into the cloth, I fell right into the rhythm of it. Completely forgot I was dreaming. Must have come to work very late, though, must have been eleven-thirty, because just as we started working on the batch and I had gotten the rhythm back into my bones, the whistle blew.

A powerful hand grabbed my shoulder. "Let's get started!"

At the end of the mill floor was the trap. It was accessible through a small door, waist-high, that I had to creep through on hands and knees. I balked at the opening. This was when I needed to wake up, to find me in my bed up the hill. But there I was—and he shoved me. I was almost inside when he shoved a bucket of axle grease in after me. "Hurry!" I remembered to grab thick handfuls of the grease with both hands. With only ten minutes, neatness didn't count. The long iron rods went fifteen feet into darkness, and there were big gears, a foot wide with teeth three inches deep, every three feet; they had ground Johnny McLelland to hamburger in less than a minute. I inched along, amazed that my knees and back held up. Fistfuls of grease gobbed on the heavy metal gears, hot from the morning's work, I was at the end of the gears and my grease bucket was empty, and for the first time I felt myself breathe.

It was turning around that I couldn't get myself to do. First left, then right. Wasting precious time, I thought, just back yourself out! Snagging myself on each gear as I felt my way out backwards, I could just see the dim light of the opening right behind me when the gears groaned. The teeth rolled around me as they chewed on their fresh ration of grease. A tug on my unfastened sleeve—beginner's mistake!—and my arm was pulled hard into the maw of two massive gears; I tugged back, couldn't get the shirt to tear. Instead, it knocked me off my knees, pulled me towards it. My feet flailed and kicked another gear, nearly getting snagged on metal teeth. Then my sleeve tore, which gave me a chance, and I twisted and somehow wriggled out of the shirt before it pulled me in. The shirt quickly wrapped around the gears. Waiting for a moment, I caught the sleeve next turn around and pulled the shirt out; Gates once sent a man back in after he lost his pants to the gears—"I sent you in to clean 'em out, not jam 'em up. Get those pants out! Jam up those gears and you'll be out of a job!"—and backed my way out, into the quiet, dark cavern of an abandoned mill.

It was empty again, moonlight pouring in through the ruined roof, the old floor empty of the looms and of the workers I'd seen going into the trap. Just an abandoned mill, just me in it. Peering back into the trap, I saw an empty cavern; the gears were the first harvest of the salvagers. Still, I was breathing hard, my shirt was a stiff rag of grease, well-imprinted with teeth marks, and I was drenched with sweat. Outside I felt cold as the sweat chilled on me. Trudging back up the hill, I felt my muscles tightening, and when I reached my front door I could barely grasp my knob, turn it, and pull the door open to get inside. Going upstairs to bed was out of the question. I sank onto my couch.

Next morning my muscles ached. I got up and looked out my window. Down the hill stood the boarded-up mill, dead chimneys, and the air was still. Then I found my shirt on the floor, chewed up by greasy teeth. "What the Sam Hell is goin' on?" I asked my reflection in the bathroom mirror. "Gates' grave is up the slope. I know exactly where it is, by that low stone wall I always hoped would fall on his plot. Could go piss on it right now, if my pecker didn't hurt too!" Then I took a deep breath. "God, I hurt." That was when I first felt scared, of the mill.

* * *

"Hugh," Cal acknowledged. "Running late today, aren't you?" His TV was gone; he was listening to an old radio today. I almost asked him if the TV was on the fritz, but felt less talkative than usual.

"Not feelin' too good today, Calvin," I admitted. "Stiffening up."

"Trip into the trap'll do it every time," he joked. "Lost your shirt, eh? That bastard Gates," he added in a softer tone.

He had changed his shop. The shelves were a lot barer. And somewhere he'd found some old nostalgia pieces—Gold Star regalia, and a sneering cartoon of a near-sighted Japanese soldier —but none of that prepared me for my newspaper.

'MARIANAS CLEAR—PHILLIPINES WILL BE FREE BY CHRISTMAS'. Outside a car went by and I caught a glance at it —rounded fenders, running boards, about a '38. Then a woman came in, in a frayed coat I could see her apron beneath, and pulled from her purse a ration book to buy milk and bread.

A ration book?

Cal took the book, tore out two coupons and handed the book back and took her money, and I followed the woman out. Killington Road actually had a little traffic this morning, and I heard people's voices in the street. Walking back, I had to nod to three people who greeted me, but who I didn't remember. And when I reached my row house, I had a new neighbor. He was outside, daubing paint on his mailbox, but doing a clumsy job of it. His painting hand was minus two fingers.

* * *

The mill continued its thrumming last night. This morning Emma beamed at me when I stepped outside. "We got new neighbors,

Hugh, have you met 'em?'"

"Not just yet, Emma."

"Mill's hirin' a daytime shift. Ain't it wonderful to see the town comin' back?" She was wearing the house coat I never saw her out of.

"Emma," I decided to try, Calvin being too far gone, "what year is this?"

Frowning at me, she asked, "You feelin' okay? I hear you got sent into the trap. Did you get hurt? Hit your head?"

"No," I shook my head, "I didn't get hurt. But I remember seeing John Kennedy being inaugurated. Do you?"

She blinked, as though a friend had just spoken to her in a foreign language, and she tried to understand, but couldn't. "What?"

The last test I could think of. "How's your mother?" Mrs. Thigpen had died of cancer in 1944, a slow, attriting cancer.

"She's comin' home next week," Emma suddenly masked worry with a smile, "feelin' better. We're hopin' for the best."

* * *

So the town went mad without taking me. The mill is going every night now, and from what I hear they'll be going in daylight soon. That would probably be the end of me. There would be no escaping it. Which is why I decided to burn it down.

I have a kerosene heater and I keep a ten gallon can of fuel in the basement. It's very heavy, but I had nothing else to torch the place with, Calvin refusing to sell me gasoline without a damn ration coupon. So I hefted the can that afternoon and headed off down Killington Road to the mill.

Daylight made the old mill easier to approach. The stream splashed away, the pigeons cooed in the rafters. Cobwebs abounded, and I was quite alone when I began slopping the kerosene out of the can, splashing it onto the bone dry timbers of the mill floor. I carefully poured a stream alongside one wall, the kerosene disappearing into the wood and leaving just a dark stain. When I paused to glance up and rest my back I could see blue sky through the huge holes in the roof, burned there by other fires and beaten there by neglect. Good, I thought, I'll need the ventilation. I finished pouring the stuff, upending the can and letting the last few drops land on Gates' table. The floor would burn, as would the inside walls. The bricks would stand, but that's it. Maybe next week I could rent a bulldozer and finish the job.

Then I stood in the doorway, found my matches in my pocket, struck one, lit the pack, then threw the handful of flame into the shadowy cavern. It landed on a dark stain and yellow flame appeared. More flame raced in a line following the dark stain, across the mill floor, traversing the plant. The birds milled about in the rafters, sensing trouble. I waited, as black smoke began roiling up in a bubbling dark cloud, to be sure the old timbers would burn, and when flame spread to areas I hadn't fueled, five minutes had passed and I was still alone. Fire licked at the walls, wood blackened, and pieces of the old roof simmering; the pigeons had long since fled. Relief made me feel tired.

We are now at least twenty minutes from the nearest firehall. On my way uphill I passed no one. I had time to get home and get rid of my kerosene-tainted clothes before the first siren came howling downhill on Killington Road. By that time, of course, the mill was what they call 'totally involved'. It burned for seven hours, an abandoned mill not considered worth risking firefighters' lives for.

At dusk they poured water on the remains so they could get home for supper. Emma and Calvin and I, and a few strangers who follow firetrucks, watched them douse the smoldering brick walls. The roof was gone, as were both floors, and all the inside walls.

Gate's table was gone, and his damned time clock was burnt, useless metal. Neither Emma nor Calvin seemed upset, neither said anything, treating it like a fallen tree across the road, and left with the firefighters. A photograph printed in most Civil War histories, of flour mills in Richmond after the shelling, shows brick walls in ruins. No roof, in most cases not even a complete wall, the building had been reduced to two-dimensions. The picture is usually labeled 'total destruction'. Well, that's almost exactly what my fire did to the Killington Mill.

* * *

It started again that very night and it hasn't stopped since. More a skeleton now than a ruin, it's hard to believe I can still feel the looms running when I can see through the mill to the woods on the far side. Hard to acknowledge that the clunking of the looms makes me tremble in broad daylight. I haven't really slept since.

They came knocking on the door today. I can't go back to work, but they seem to expect me. I'm staying inside and trying to figure out how to get out of town. I won't go back to that mill. I'm too old to run a loom and I can't go back in the trap. My body and mind are eighty-seven now. When they came for me today I told 'em I was sick, which was true. But they probably won't leave me be much longer.

When night fell I stepped out, into the alleyway, and hoped no one could see my suitcase. Running away at eighty-seven. I shouldn't have waited so long to try it; Emma, of all people, heard me. Opened her door, stepped outside, and called to me. "Hugh! You okay? I knocked this morning when they told me you didn't show up for work—" then she saw my suitcase. "Where you think you're goin', Hugh?" Her voice was part mother, part disciplinarian, part prison guard. "You got to go to work, Hugh."

"Emma!" I hissed, and stepped toward her. "I'm not a mill worker anymore. I'm retired. I'm eighty-seven years old!" She was impassive. "Please! I just want to go up the road, up to Route 78, and catch a ride. Please don't tell any—" she disappeared inside, and I could hear a telephone dial turning. "Damn you, Emma!"

Needlenose and Gates were waiting in the middle of the road as I tried to get out of Killington. It's the only road, and I couldn't find my way up the hill through the woods in the night. Should have tried, though. They stuck me back on the third loom, again, which isn't so bad, but Gates growled at me that I'm doing the trap for the rest of the month.

Nobody ever did the trap for that long, and lived.

I'm getting out of here. I'm eighty-seven years old, I swear. 🦇

LORSCAPEDIA

EDWARD AHERN

THE RIVER COURSED below them, deeply ravined and overhung with firs and hardwoods. Light glazed the surface only in the midday hours. Julie and Philip leaned against the sides of the covered bridge, staring down into the water through gaps in the framing, looking for fish.

Julie pushed away from the weathered timbers. "Okay, it's pretty. But it's too cold and fast to swim in, and if I did you'd yell at me that I was disturbing the salmon."

"I probably would. "

"You fish ten hours a day. I've tried to fish with you and don't like it, so I'm mousetrapped. No cell phone reception, no TV, no internet." She stepped back onto the planking. "The neighbors never seem to be out during the day and only speak French anyway. What the hell am I supposed to do?"

She started walking away from Wade back through the bridge toward the house. As she cleared the bridge she turned around to make sure he was following. The name board was spiked into the wood above the bridge opening. Sevierville. The name had more letters than the village had houses.

"Julie, hang in a little longer." He quickened his step and caught up with her. "We drove thirteen hours to get here. You like to hike, you could explore the area and take pictures while I fish."

Ten seconds of silence.

She wrapped her hand halfway around his bicep. "Philip, look around. The river banks are overgrown. The road on the other side of the river is deserted except for logging trucks that come blasting through at seventy. The railroad tracks behind the house run from no place to no place. The other side of the tracks is overgrown forest." She inhaled slowly. " All right, look, I'll try a couple walk arounds and take some pictures."

They stepped up the gravel road into a pocket of eight houses nested between river and railroad tracks. The houses were all of a Nineteen Teen vintage, built by the railroad company as a way station that trains no longer stopped at. The railroad still owned the land and the houses, and leased the houses for thirty-year terms.

Philip's small house, two bedrooms bigger than a hut, rested on a stone foundation that had settled with decades of freeze and thaw, leaving floors uneven and walls out of true. The wooden siding had warped enough to leave cracks for insects. Small patches of wet rot let occasional mammals get in without too much gnawing.

Philip had gently prepped Julie for the experience during the long drive up from Connecticut. They had taught at the same school for two years but had become lovers only that spring. Neither admitted to what they suspected—that two weeks together with few diversions would give their relationship a pass/fail.

"We'll be roughing it a little, but it's got indoor plumbing, electricity and a propane stove. That's easier living than a lot of places used to be in Canada. You're tough and used to roughing it, so we should be fine. I'll teach you how to play cribbage. The locals aren't too fond of me, but we don't need them."

The floor boards muttered softly as they returned to the house. "Look Julie, why don't you take the car this afternoon and go into St. Christophe. It's the closest village. You'll get a better sense of the region."

"Are there any craft shops?"

"Ah, no. There's a church of course, and a dépanneur, a convenience store. A gas station, and a farmers' supply store, I think. But it's a lot more open and sunny. And there's cell phone reception.

Julie saw only two cars on the 12 kilometer drive to St. Christophe, both parked alongside the river. Fishermen. The dépanneur was off the road in a gravel pull out area big enough to handle logging trucks.. As she pulled onto the stones her cell phone began flashing and making noise. She parked and started catching up with her messages. It didn't occupy much time—her friends knew she was out of the country and had stopped trying to contact her.

The dépanneur had a huge overhead sign but was no bigger than a three car garage. Once inside Julie glanced over a minuscule selection of convenience foods. Half the store was devoted to fishing tackle and a large assortment of beers. A portly woman sat behind the register.

"Bonjour."

"Bonjour. Do you speak English?"

" A little, if you speak slow."

Julie glanced over the store. She saw nothing she wanted to buy, but knew she needed to spend time in there. "Do you have wine?"

"Wine, yes, in back." The woman stirred. "You are driving through?"

"My friend and I are staying at his place in Sevierville." Julie stepped back to the shelf. She was big boned and angular. At not quite forty, she worked to retain a youthful grace. Philip was her first serious relationship since her early thirties.

The few bottles of wine were on end and dusty. Two kinds of white, one kind of red. French generic wines, not from the U.S. Julie took a bottle of white wine to the woman at the register.

The woman made no move to ring up the sale. She looked up at Julie slowly. "How long you stay there, in Sevierville?"

"Two weeks."

"The others who live there are not like you. What do you know of them?"

"Almost nothing. I sometimes see them at dusk and very early morning, but almost never during the day. I've only spoken to one of them, Gaston. Do you know him?"

The woman paused. "Gaston, yes. He speaks for the village. You should leave Sevierville soon, take a real vacation in the region."

"My friend loves it there. He fishes the salmon pools every day, all day."

"But he is with you every night?"

"Yes."

"Good. Still, you should leave soon. Sevierville is not a place you should stay." The woman rang up the bottle of wine and handed it to Julie without putting it in a bag. She leaned toward Julie and said softly "Outsiders are not welcomed in Sevierville. You should not rouse them."

At a loss, Julie said nothing and left. As she returned to the covered bridge she waved to Philip, but he was intent on his fly casting and did not notice her. Once resettled on the lumpy sofa she picked up a book and tried to read it but was unable to focus without the gentle white noise of television or music. She grabbed her camera, walked out the back door of the house and took seven paces to the railroad tracks. Right or left? Right up the tracks toward the other houses in Sevierville. The railroad tracks were in full sunlight, but the sun had already started to drop behind the steep hillside.

The trains all seemed to whip through the village after midnight and before dawn, whistles blasting. There would be no trains this afternoon. She started counting the cross ties as she stepped over them. At the eightieth tie she reached the next house in the village, at the hundred and sixtieth was Gaston's house. Shades were drawn on all the windows of the houses. Beyond Gaston's house barely perceptible foot trails slithered from house to house. The foot paths converged behind Gaston's house, disappeared at the railroad bed and reappeared as a narrow trail that meandered into the woods.

Julie skidded down the embankment and walked one foot ahead of the other along the narrow trail toward the woods. After a few yards of alder and aspen the forest closed in. Dense, old growth trees, never cleared. Dead fall was everywhere in various stages of rot. Branches hindered but didn't obstruct the trail so Julie went on, pushing them aside as she went.

She was perhaps a quarter mile down the trail when it steepened upward. Julie grabbed at the branches to help her climb. In the dim light, intent on climbing, she almost stumbled into a vertical drop. As she swayed to regain her balance she sucked in a breath of rank air. Julie focused her eyes downward into a pit. The bones, skin and heads of many salmon, large fish that were illegal to keep. Fur and bones from several animals, deer and muskrat or beaver, and maybe squirrels.

But the smell was not as bad as it could have been. The meat, guts and sinew were missing, leaving only bones and skin, scales and horn. Julie took out her camera and began snapping. The flashes in the dim light made it hard to see what she was recording.

Poachers, she thought, *they're poaching game.*

The trail ended at the midden. Julie clambered back down the embankment and worked her way out to the railroad tracks. As she cleared the trees the bright sun filmed her eyes and when she could focus Gaston's head was visible on the far side of the tracks. She started and almost slid back down the embankment.

"Gaston you startled me. How are you?"

"It is smart that you do not go back to the garbage pit. Animals, even bears come sometimes to eat from the refuse."

"So many dead things Gaston. Does the village eat only game?"

"Best that you do not go there again. It is dangerous." He noticed her camera. "Did you take pictures?"

She hesitated a bit too long. "No Gaston, why would I take photographs of rotting hide and bones."

Gaston was thoroughly covered despite the summer warmth— long sleeved shirt and pants, dark sun glasses and Panama hat. His frame was square and thick but not fat—no belly bulge or neck wattles. His fingers were spatulate and coarse, with thick, dirty nails.

"It is best for you to concentrate on fishing, like Philip. Or take a trip through the Gaspe. We don't like meddlers."

Julie didn't wait ten seconds. "Gaston, I'm not going to pry into your business, but I have as much right as you do to explore the area." She turned and walked back a hundred and sixty railroad ties to their house. When she looked back Gaston was gone.

Philip came back after darkness had made fishing impossible. For all her annoyance, Julie was cautious. Her anger was less important than trying to keep him in her life. Until they were sitting down to eat a stew built from leftovers.

"Did you know there's a huge pile of dead animal remains in the woods near Gaston's house? They must be poaching. Gaston told me to never go back there."

"He's right. You shouldn't have gone there. And whatever you do don't mention poaching to any of the villagers, and especially not to anyone outside the village."

"Philip, you sound afraid. There must be an anonymous poaching hot line you could call."

"God damn it Julie, don't even think about talking about them outside the village. These people can be dangerous. Before I bid on leasing this house one of the other locals threatened to break my arm with a shovel. And when I did bid and was the high bidder the same guy threatened to burn the place down rather than let me into the village. I had to sit down with this man and Gaston and agree to not ask questions and leave them completely alone. They barely tolerate me as it is."

"Philip, listen to yourself. If it's that uncomfortable, why do you stay?"

"The fishing. I'm all alone on one of the best holding pools on the river. I leave them alone, they leave me alone."

Julie pressed her lips together and kept them that way until they went to bed, in almost complete silence, *Philip tell me we can get out of here.*

The first of the trains arrived a little after midnight. The high speed engine noise pushed through the hollow, quickly followed by a horn blast that the engineer prolonged from the first house in the village through to the last. The house quavered with the train's passage.

The third and last train bellowed through at false dawn. The horn was still echoing when Julie half awake, heard a shrill squeal and a crunching thud. She lay still, hoping Philip was awake, but his slurred breath meant sleep.

Julie turned back and forth for an hour and at 5:30 got up, dressed, grabbed her camera and went out to investigate. She turned left on the railroad ties, downstream. The track curved left along the river and Julie looked down the river and saw several of the villagers. She snapped a distant picture, their dirty looking faces staring back at her before turning away. Julie lost sight of them as she continued along the curve, A few minutes later she came upon two men and a woman huddled over a brown bundle alongside the track. As she drew closer she realized it was a yearling moose, crumpled up with compound fractures.

One of the men had a hunting knife and was skinning the moose. And something else had happened. Some of the flesh was not cut, but had been torn away in gobbets from under the hide.

The three villagers' faces were red, as though embarrassed.

"Bonjour," Julie said and got measured "Bonjours" back in reply.

"What happened?' she asked and immediately felt stupid for not asking a better question.

"The train hit the moose," replied the man with the hunting knife.

"So why are you cutting it up?"

"They will come soon and put lime on the moose, then we cannot eat it. So we cut up moose and bring the pieces home to eat."

" But something has already eaten at the moose. Look where the meat has been torn away."

"Maybe coyote."

The hunting knife returned to work, slicing hide from meat. Julie put camera to face and started taking picture of the moose and the butchery. The woman moved to stop her, but was grabbed by one of the men. All three threw heated French words at each other.

One of the men, named Claude perhaps, stepped up close to her, knife still in hand.

His lower face, odd, it's streaked with red.

"Not a pretty thing for you to see. You should go back to the house. Now."

The other man and woman had joined him, blocking her view

of the dead animal. Their jaws were also streaked.

"Look, I'm not going to report that you're butchering the animal. If you don't eat it the coyotes and bears will."

It was the wrong thing to say. Their expressions hardened and closed.

"Leave now," the woman rasped.

The sun was beginning to clear the embankment and fir trees across the river. As she turned to go Julie noticed that the three villagers were also glancing at the rising sun. Very shortly after Julie had returned to the house they passed by on the tracks, carrying haunches and chunks of meat on their shoulders, staining their clothes.

Weird, it's as though they cannot abide the light.

Julie climbed the narrow stairs and shook Philip awake.

"We have to get out of here."

Philip groped for consciousness. "It's—what day is it—oh yeah, Thursday. I thought we'd agreed to play tourist this weekend?"

"Today. Now. I have to get away from this place."

Philip looked at Julie through clearing eyes and realized she was agitated. "Okay, mental health day." He made a quick pot of coffee, shaved and followed Julie out the door.

They drove for an hour to the nearest town, Beausejour. Julie told him about the moose in high pitched tones.

"These people don't have money, Julie, no real jobs. They're on the dole for the entire winter. It's no wonder they make a meal of a dead moose."

"And not just moose. They're poachers, Philip. There's that garbage pit in the woods that's full of fish and animal remains. They never fish during the day, so they must be taking the salmon illegally at night, nets maybe or spears."

"What else do you think you know about?"

"And not just know about. I've got pictures of what they were doing, and the garbage pit!"

"Did they see you taking the pictures?"

"Sure."

Philip said nothing for a long time. Then, "I have to think Julie. This could be bad."

"Why do you need to think? They're thieving animals, or worse."

The day was notable for its silences. There was nothing of interest in Beausejour, no arts and crafts shops, no interesting churches, no quaint architecture. They ate lunch at one of two restaurants, a roadside diner. A provincial specialty, pea soup, was watery.

Julie tried to get beyond intermittent small talk, but Philip was preoccupied, almost frightened-looking. They returned early to the house in Sevierville and Philip went down to the river to fish the remaining hours of sunlight.

She tried reading, but the magazines seemed inane, not relevant. Bored, she took out the digital camera and went back through the shots. She and Philip as they were leaving Connecticut. Philip fishing. Her washing dishes in the kitchen. And then the midden. The pictures were much sharper than her recollection of the offal pile. Definitely salmon skin and bones, bones of small mammals. But some other bones too, much too big to be a small mammal, almost human sized. What would happen, she wondered, if the poachers in the village met another poacher while netting at night?

And the pictures on the tracks, in the first, distant pictures their three mouths and chin were, not dirty, but deep red, much redder than when she sighted them again more closely. Had they been eating at the moose? Raw meat bordering on carrion?

Julie was afraid, and then angry. As she was working herself up she saw Philip returning from the river. Gaston walked over to intercept him. They talked with animation, in what looked like anger. Gaston handed Philip a bottle and turned back to his house.

She met him at the door.

"Philip, my pictures, I..."

"Look what Gaston gave us! I think this is pretty good wine. He gave it to me even though we had been arguing about you."

Julie shouted over his words. "Listen Philip, there's something wrong about these people! They're some cult, some weird carrion-eating group. I think they were eating raw meat right off the carcass, just using their teeth! We have to get out of here."

" Jesus, Julie. What... Let me think a second."

Philip measuredly took out a corkscrew and uncorked the bottle of wine. Chateau Lynch-Bages. He vaguely remembered the name as being an exclusive Bordeaux. He poured two glasses and brought them over to the kitchen table.

"Sit down, Julie. I think they hate you for disturbing them. It's maybe even dangerous for you to stay. We'll pack up and drive away tomorrow. Meanwhile we may as well drink Gaston's wine."

They talked for a few minutes, sipping the wine, before losing consciousness.

Julie woke up in darkness, naked, to hear a train's shrill horn and feel the rumbling of its passage. She was sitting on a dirt floor and her arms and legs were tied.. "Philip," she called and then, more loudly, "Philip Help!"

"Julie where are you? I'm tied up!"

They scuttled toward each other in the darkness, pressing together side-by-side for warmth. Faint light finally seeped through chinks in the wooden flooring over head. They were huddled on the floor of a root cellar. The hard packed dirt was cold and granular, with embedded stones and husks that pushed against them. They were tied with plastic strips, and had lost sensation in their hands and feet.

After they had been yelling for help for a quarter hour Gaston came down into the cellar.

"Gaston," Philip said, "what the hell are you doing? Let us loose!"

"I will be doing many things with you—but not let you loose."

Julie interjected. "Gaston you can't…"

Gaston casually backhanded her, splitting her lip and loosening a tooth. He was very strong.

"Do not interrupt. We cannot allow you to take what you think you know away from here. It has taken us too long to find this place. Our choice is either to kill you or to see if you could become one of us. We are few, so decided to see if you can change.

"Isabel and Georges will come down soon. Do not bother to struggle. They are much stronger than you."

Gaston went back up a flight of rickety wooden steps. Later that morning a man and a woman came down the stairs, speaking French.

Georges studied them both. "Je pense que la femme sera mort dans deux ou trios jours."

"Tu n'a pas raison. La femme est beaucoup plus tenace que son ami."

Isabel and Georges walked behind Julie and Philip and grabbed their arms with muscle bruising firmness. They leaned down and casually bit the captives' right shoulders, chewed and swallowed the small chunk of skin and then spit into the wound. Philip and Julie yelped and tried to writhe away from the bites but were held motionless. Isabel and Georges left without comment.

"Philip, my God, they bit us! Why?"

"To infect us I guess. And we're left here to let the infection develop."

"It's freezing. No food, no water. Do you think you can get loose?"

"I tried, but I can't, I can't!"

Toward dusk Gaston came down the stairs with two buckets. He dragged Julie and then Philip over to opposing walls in the cellar, where shackles had been mounted. He shackled them both and then cut their bindings. From one bucket he took out chunks of over aged meat and threw them on the dirt in front of them both. He poured water from the second bucket into the first, without rinsing out the remaining bits of meat. The water he put next to them.

"To live you must eat as we eat. Eat quick, before the maggots get to it. it. We compete with the maggots."

"Gaston, please, you can't do this to us. You know us, we won't talk."

"You must eat or die. If you vomit up the meat, eat it again, like a dog does."

Julie and Philip left the food untouched. Flies gathered on the meat, undoubtedly laying eggs that would quickly be maggots. Night arrived and was too cold to sleep through. They tried and gave up on getting out of their shackles. They were both developing a fever.

The next morning, dehydrated, they drank the earthy tasting water. The meat lay untouched before them.

"Philip, if we don't eat we'll starve. Maybe we should try and eat some of the meat before it gets any gamier?"

"Can't you smell it? I don't think I could keep it down."

"We should try. I don't want to starve to death."

Julie picked up one of the least dirty gobbets of meat, waving off the flies. The smell was not as bad as she had feared. It tasted, not fresh, but like hung game, deliberately off. She continued to nibble and was surprised to see that she had eaten almost half of the meat.

Philip had been watching her. He too picked up a chunk of

meat and started chewing, but almost immediately wretched, spewing bile from an empty stomach.

"Philip keep trying, you have to stay strong."

"I can't get it all the way into my mouth before I gag."

"Please Philip, you'll die if you don't eat."

They sat in silence for a while, then Philip swiveled to face her. "I'm sorry I brought you here. I thought it would bring us together, but I may have only killed us both."

"We'll get through this Philip, and when we do I'm going to make sure that they pay."

Gaston returned later that day, bringing more meat and water. Julie ate all her meat. Philip tried again but couldn't keep from vomiting. Julie's stomach was writhing , reshaping to its diet of bad meat. Despite having eaten all the chunks of meat and gristle she was still hungry.

"Julie, Jesus. I'm sorry Julie. I would never hurt you."

"I know. Do you remember that Japanese restaurant where you wanted me to eat eel and I refused?"

"And I smacked my lips when I ate it just to rub it in."

"We've had good times Philip."

They continued to talk, just now and then, not of what they were now facing, nor what would happen tomorrow, but of the things they had done together—not sexual, but shared.

After Gaston has thrown out the meat on the third day Philip called over to her.

"Julie, I've tried but I can't swallow the meat. I'm going to throw the chunks over to you. I know you're hungry."

"You can't, you'll die if you don't eat. Try again."

Philip grabbed one of the chunks provided that day. The meat was rancid and after two quick chews he spit it out and went into dry heaves. He grabbed another chunk and started to throw it over to her.

"Stop Philip. If you have to, throw me the oldest chunks. I think I can get them down. Save the least rotten meat for yourself."

Philip grabbed several of the older chunks and pressed them into a ball which he tossed over to her. Julie picked out the maggots. They didn't disgust her, they just seemed—too fresh, too alive to be interesting as food. After a few tentative bites she ate quickly through the ball of meat, hunger overwhelming any repugnance.

By the fourth night Philip's fever had worsened. His sucked air in spasmodic gasps. And while Julie was sleeping, without another word to her, he died. When she woke, Julie could only look across the cellar at him, laying motionless, half on his side.

When Gaston later came into the cellar with his two buckets, he glanced briefly at Philip, and then put the bucket of meat back on the steps.

"Gaston, please, Philip's dead. You have to bury him!"

"Yes, dead, but of use."

Gaston unlocked Philip's shackles and dragged his body to within Julie's reach.

"You are not yet one of us. You will need more meat for survival and for change."

He left the water bucket and took the meat bucket away with him. "I will return tomorrow with water. Water only."

In the gathering dusk Julie squatted down next to Philip's body and wrapped her hand half way around his still muscled arm, as she used to. A few flies were already hovering.

My poor Philip. If I bury you with my hands I will only dig you up when the hunger gets bad enough. God knows what I'm becoming, but I swear to you, one day I will dine on Gaston.

BRIDGE OVER THE CUNENE

GUSTAVO BONDONI

BOTOSO WAS SINGING some innocent rhyme about the horrors of the great change at the top of his lungs. It was a new phase, and Lara was fervently hoping that it would pass as quickly as the rest had.

It seemed only last week that the little five-year-old had contented himself with running around inside the stockade, happy to let his universe be defined by the log walls. But, suddenly, he'd become obsessed with the world outside. First, he'd gone through a period of curiosity about the Pale Ones, never going to bed unless he'd first been told a story about them, and the things that had happened during the change. He'd cover his head and pretend to be terrified, but never had nightmares, and always came back for more.

Then, seemingly simultaneously, every little one in the village had begun to sing the songs that their parents had sung. Songs about the Pale Ones, songs about the change. It was incredible how these songs, that had been buried for years, reemerged all at once. Nonsense songs, but their verses contained references to the horror of the times.

Lara noted that her son was looking at her quizzically. But he was silent at last, which was a relief. She could get back to mending the shirt.

"Mama," his thin voice piped up. "Do you think I could be the headman, some day?"

"Of course, dear," she replied absently.

"Just like Simao Zaboba?"

"Yes, dear."

He wandered off, and she breathed a small sigh of relief. There were clothes to mend, thatching to do. And he could be a demanding child sometimes.

* * *

He'd done this for all of his adult life. His predecessors had done the same. It was as natural as life on the veldt, and had been part of the cycle of life even before the great change, and would be part of it after the Pale Ones were a faded memory.

Simao Zaboba was at peace with himself, with the bright noon sun and the fresh June breeze whispering through the trees. He knew enough to be thankful for his role in the natural cycle. Twice a month, the offering was made, and twice a month, it was accepted. A pig on the full moon, valued for its brains, a goat on the new moon, desired for its blood; and safety, even a measure of protection, for the village all month long. It had always been thus, although in the times of his grandfather, the offering of a chicken or a cow were made on a less regular basis, to other, less tangible, spirits. But even those sporadic devotions must have had some effect, since the village had survived nearly unscathed, while others… well, others had been absorbed into the nests.

Today, he was leading a well-fed goat on a leash of metallic rope, enjoying the three-hour walk to the neutral zone across the river. Today was a clear day, and he could see forever, but knew that he would never see one of the Pale Ones during the day. Like all spirits that had once been day-walking humans, they were nocturnal creatures.

The bridge was a rickety affair, long poles lashed together with vines. His father had told him that the Cunene had once been bridged by dozens of concrete structures designed to last for generations. But these had been torn down in a desperate, failed attempt to stop the plague from spreading north to Angola. The village had avoided the change only because it was so far off the beaten path. By the time they'd been rediscovered, the Pale Ones had evolved, and had even reached the point where they could be reasoned with. Spirits were like that.

As they approached the neutral zone, the goat began to show signs of nervousness. It seemed to sense, somehow, that hundreds of its brothers and sisters had perished very nearby. Close enough that the smell of death was still present.

Or maybe it sensed something else. Something hungry.

Simao was unconcerned. He dragged the now openly resisting, panicked animal towards the clearing the way he'd done hundreds of times before. The stained ground and scattered bones seemed to give the animal added strength, and it left four furrows in the dust as its feet slid along.

He reached the tree and looped the end of the metallic rope around the trunk. As always, he double-checked the clasp; the consequences of the goat escaping were too ugly to contemplate.

Leaving the grunting goat straining against the unbreakable rope, Simao walked, as he'd done countless times before, back towards the village.

He wasn't expecting to see little Botoso crouching behind one of the bushes, because he'd never been there before. And that was probably why he didn't.

* * *

Botoso knew he was in trouble. He had no idea how in the world he was ever going to get back to the village. He had no idea where the village was. This was the first time he'd ever been outside the stockade without his mother or one of the other village adults to take care of him, and the sun was setting redly over the horizon.

But he wasn't frightened. He told himself that a future headman would never be frightened just because night was about to fall. He would laugh the night off, and keep walking until he found the river. He new the river was near his village.

He also knew that he would make a great headman someday. He was smart and compassionate. After Simao Zabobo had left the clearing far behind, Botoso had emerged from hiding and immediately noticed that the headman had forgotten the goat. The boy knew how important goats were to the village—he was old enough to know that the village's very survival depended on the supply of goats.

So he worked at the clasp tying the goat to the tree and began his walk back the way he'd come. At some points, it was difficult to decide which way he had to go, since one patch of low grass or clump of trees looked just like the next, but he wasn't worried. A headman would never get lost.

But he had. And now the sun was all the way down, and it was hard to see where he was going. The goat, sniffing the air, had been getting more and more restless, and, suddenly, it gave a mighty jerk and broke free of Botoso's five-year-old grasp, dragging the leash off into the darkness.

Botoso gave chase, following the tinkling of the metallic cord until an unseen hole in the ground sent him tumbling onto a patch of thorns. He lay there silently, listening to the tinkling which grew fainter and then died out, and to the night, which was suddenly alive with scurrying and wildlife sounds. He knew that some of those sounds weren't alive.

He told himself that he wasn't afraid, but the tears that streamed down his face seemed unaware of it.

* * *

Lara was frantic. She'd been waiting for Simao Zaboba outside the village ever since she'd realized Botoso was missing. Now, off in the distance, she could make out a dark, tiny speck coming towards the village from the south. She knew, she had to believe, that the speck, as it grew nearer, would resolve itself into two figures, a large, thin one, and a slightly rotund smaller speck less than half the height of the first.

As the speck grew into a smudge, her hope waned, but then she rallied. *The headman probably made Botoso walk behind him, as a punishment. That's why she could only make out one figure approaching in the afternoon glow.*

But even that hope soon faded. She ran out to Zaboba, stood before him, clutching his arm, getting her breath back and finally panted, "Did you see Botoso?"

The headman looked her over, perfectly still, his impassive gaze showing no emotion. "There was no one on the path. How long has he been gone?"

She hung her head. "I'm not really certain. I looked for him, to eat the midday meal, and he was nowhere to be found. We looked all over the village." Lara was holding back teas now, desperate, her nails digging into his motionless forearm.

Zaboba looked at her knowingly. She felt that he could see through her, that he knew her deepest secrets, that he knew she was holding back. Finally, she could hold back no longer. "I think he followed you," she sobbed, and broke down completely.

"This is grave news," Simao said. "Go gather the elders." He pushed her gently towards the village, and walked slowly after her as she ran, stumbling, to do his bidding.

Other than Simao Zaboba, there were four village elders, and they all looked gravely on as she explained her plight. Finally, Satumbo, a toothless old man, by far the oldest man in the village, broke the silence. "A boy lost in the night is a job for the father," he said.

"My husband is dead."

"The uncle, then."

"He had no brothers."

"Then the boy is lost. The village cannot risk the men we have. No wife will let her man go. There is no way we can defend ourselves from the Pale Ones outside our walls in the night. The night belongs to them, and if we violate that agreement, we forfeit our lives."

Simao Zaboba spoke unexpectedly. "I will go," he said. "I know where the boy is. The mother must come as well. She will have a choice to make."

Lara swallowed. Nothing was more important to her than her son, but what Satumbo said was true: the night belonged to the Pale Ones. She was suddenly imagined herself being torn to shreds, her bones cracked for their marrow, her blood drained from her body, her brain sucked from her skull through a hole in the top of her head. But then the image in her mind changed, and she saw Botoso there in her place.

"I'll go," she said.

"You will go alone," Satumbo replied. "Simao Zaboba is much too valuable to the village."

"No, I am not. I am just a silly old man whose only value to the rest is that he leads a goat to a dangerous place once a fortnight.

And besides, I will certainly return tonight. I speak the language of the Pale Ones."

"The Pale Ones will kill you when they see you."

"It may be so, but I don't think so. They have changed since your childhood. And even since mine. I will be all right." He turned to the still-open gates of the village, retracing the steps he'd taken to return to the village that afternoon. He didn't look back to see whether Lara was behind him.

And he didn't seem at all surprised when she appeared beside him. Only Lara knew that she almost hadn't come. Only she seemed to have noticed that no matter how confident the headman had been of his own return, he'd said nothing about her.

* * *

It was a typical night. The veldt was cool and the sounds seemed somehow louder than they did from inside the village compound. That was ridiculous, of course; the open-topped wall of logs wouldn't have done much to filter the sounds of the nocturnal animals—the hoot of an owl, or the scurrying of rodents, or the buzz of insects. But it still seemed that the sounds were louder out here without the wall.

They'd been walking, their way illuminated only by the starlight and the knowledge of Simao's feet which had tread this same path for thirty years, for two and a half hours. At first, she constantly called out for Botoso, but, as they neared the bridge, Simao Zaboba told her to be quiet. Sound carried a long way on these grassy plains, and soon, the sound would carry all the way to the nest.

He didn't know where the nest was located, exactly, but he suspected that it was just a little beyond the clearing in the neutral zone—a clearing that was less than half an hour away on foot.

The night sounds seemed to get louder and louder the farther they got from the village, as if the animals, far from the noise and smell of human habitation, grew bolder. But Simao knew it had less to do with the actual noise than the fact that he was listening harder, trying to distinguish the sounds that didn't belong to the night. The sounds that meant that there was a something out there walking noisily on its two hind legs—something that hadn't been designed to prowl in the darkness, despite having originated near there very same plains millions of years before.

Something that, despite not being human, would have the arrogance and fearlessness that had, until the great change, allowed humans to walk the night knowing that no matter how much noise they made, no matter what they stirred up, it could be dealt with.

But now, with the few surviving humans huddling behind thick walls or in underground bunkers as soon as the sun went down, only the Pale Ones walked the night that way. They could be easily heard by someone who knew what to listen for. And it wasn't long before Simao Zaboba distinguished the telltale sounds. His heart sank when he realized that the noise of multiple Pale Ones milling around was coming from the clearing where he'd left the goat that afternoon. It came from their destination.

He looked over at Lara, but she seemed lost in her own thoughts and not to have heard anything out of the ordinary. Her features were set, and she was grimly putting one foot in front of the other. She thought that he would know where to look.

She was right. He knew exactly where the little boy would be, but he dreaded what they'd find once they got there. He began to hope that they would be intercepted before they arrived, dreading each step. Soon, his fear had grown to the point where he was only reluctantly putting one foot in front of the other. By the time they were a hundred paces from the clearing, Lara was dragging him along.

Even in the dark, he could tell the clearing was crowded. Darker shapes could be made out in the darkness, and Simao Zaboba felt as though someone was running cold hands up his spine.

"Welcome," a voice said out of the darkness in front of him.

Lara jumped, but Simao had known it was coming. The word had been spoken in their harsh guttural language, the language that the villagers feared and reviled. They called it Palespeak. The Pale Ones themselves called it English—it had been the tongue of the southern land before the change. Only the headman and a few others could speak it.

The voice went on, "We suspected you come soon." It was a ragged, sighing voice—as if it had been unused for so long that it had to be dug up from deep within the Pale One's thorax. And yet, the speech was clearer than what he'd heard when, as an apprentice, he'd accompanied the old headman to make the agreement that exchanged an occasional goat and pig for their lives. During that meeting, the Pale Ones had spoken in grunts and single, almost incomprehensible words—and it had been impossible for them to understand any but the most rudimentary concepts.

Simao knew that how he responded could make the difference between life and death, but he also needed to understand the situation a little better. "I make fire to see," he said, glad he'd practiced his Palespeak all these years, despite never having had to use it.

His pronouncement was met with hissing and an unseen step forward from his right. Zaboba tensed, but the original voice replied before any action was taken against him. "Small fire," it said.

"Small fire," he agreed. One of his precious, irreplaceable matches was used to light a torch.

The clearing was bathed in flickering yellow light. The Pale

Ones looked much worse for the wear. Nothing with skin as tattered and decomposed as the inhabitants of this clearing had any business being animate. Their once-mahogany skin, already pallid from the change, had become even more gray with the years. They looked like dolls made of stained rags.

Zaboba looked around desperately, searching for a smaller figure. His gaze was attracted by a commotion behind the nearest Pale One.

"Mama!" a high-pitched voice screamed, and suddenly a small brown bullet shot from the shadows and buried itself in Lara's stomach. She cried and bent over to hug him, protecting him with her arms. "Thank you, thank you," she was saying, to no one in particular, without thinking about it, just repeating the mantra—happiness and disbelief mixed.

"Thank you," Zaboba told the Pale One in front of him.

The other acknowledged, inclining his head. "We no eat little ones. Little ones grow, turn big ones. Bring us food. Other nests eat little ones, eat big ones too. Other nests die out. No food."

Zaboba was shocked at this. He couldn't believe what he was hearing, couldn't believe the sophistication of the Pale One's thought processes. But he had no time to dwell on it then. "We leave now," he said, bowing.

"No."

Zaboba realized that the semicircle of Pale Ones in front of them had expanded, and was now a complete circle, ahead and behind. They could not leave unless they were allowed to. There was no way they could break through that line unscathed—and even a scratch meant the end of human life, and the beginning of a twilight existence as a Pale One. He turned calmly back to the spokesman.

"We no have food," the Pale One said.

And suddenly, Zaboba lost his calm. He understood that what

had been his worst fear, in the back of his mind, had actually come to pass. He knelt beside little Botoso and, trying to keep the fear and urgency from his voice, said, "Where's the goat?"

And Botoso, sensing the fear, began to cry. "It ran away. I tried to catch it, but I fell." And, finally, accusingly, "You forgot the goat."

Zabobo turned back to the Pale one.

"We no have food," it repeated. "Give food."

Lara turned to him, eyes wide, understanding. She seemed on the verge of panic, so he calmed her down. "Do not worry," he said. "I will stay. I am an old man, almost fifty summers. The village does not lose much."

Gratitude flashed on her face, but was almost immediately replaced by doubt and then fear. "But how will I find my way? It is still a long time until dawn. What happens if we get lost?"

"You must not become lost."

"What happens?"

"If you get lost, you will both die." He cursed the moonless sky. Even the small illumination from the barest crescent might have made the return trip possible. "Once you leave the neutral area, you are fair game unless you are on a clearly defined path towards the village. If you are anywhere else, other members of the nest will take you, since they have no way of knowing you are from our village."

And Lara knew it. She cried softly, silently, as she accepted what she must do. Botoso, who had lifted his head to see what was troubling his mother, suddenly crying again as he found himself transferred to Simao's care.

Simao took a tight grip of Botoso's hand. He knew the boy would have to be kept in check.

"Will you take care of him?" Lara said.

Simao nodded.

"What will become of him, an orphan? His options will be few."

"His options," he replied, "will be one. He has seen the Pale Ones, and it seems he will survive the encounter. He will be headman. I will take him on as an apprentice."

Pride flickered across her face, but lasted only a fleeting instant. She had remembered that she would not be there to see it. "Tell them," Lara said.

"One will remain," he told the leader of the Pale Ones, who nodded in reply.

A rustling sound behind caused Simao to turn. The Pale Ones behind had disappeared.

"Ones who go, go now."

Simao Zaboba took a tight grip on Botoso's hand and began to walk towards the village. At first, Botoso came readily, but then realized what was happening.

"Mama!" he said.

But it was too late by then. The circle had reformed, with them on the outside. The headman dragged the resisting boy towards the village. He was even thankful for the boy's calls for his mother, as they somewhat drowned out the screaming. At first, a single cry of protest, then a series of long, drawn out screams of agony which grew hoarser and hoarser. The final scream was a ragged cry, mercifully cut off in the middle.

The boy seemed to understand; his struggles stopped.

But the sick feeling in Simao Zaboba's stomach wasn't caused by the sounds of a pretty young mother being torn to edible chunks behind them. It was caused by the knowledge that the Pale Ones had, in their way, discovered farming—or at least a way to get small but sufficient quantities of live food without having to hunt for it. At present, they needed the village to supply their meat, but how long would it take them to figure it out for themselves? After that, the village would serve no purpose other than as a breeding ground for their favorite dish—or, worse, the site of one spectacular nighttime binge.

His reverie was broken by a slurping and panting noise from the feeding ground behind. He shuddered and hoped it would fade soon.

But sound carries a long way over the veldt.

KNOTT'S LETTER

JASON A WYCKOFF

DEAR MR. BENNER,

I regret to inform you that your son is dead. While I know this report is difficult to hear and the tragedy it relates is difficult to bear, I suspect you are not surprised by the news. Perhaps you and Mrs. Benner have reconciled yourselves to the idea already, as it has been nearly a month since Kirk disappeared in the Adirondack Mountains. The authorities might have indicated to you that Kirk's disappearance was reported to them by Tim Knott—I am he. You had probably never heard my name before then as I befriended your son after you and he became estranged. You may wonder what information I possess that I would be the one writing to inform you of your son's passing and not a legal authority. The truth is, I knew at the time I reported Kirk's disappearance that he was most likely dead; when a few nights more passed without his return from the woods, I accepted my friend's death with certainty. I have waited this long to write to you because I wrestled with whether you should be informed of the details of Kirk's last day. I decided it was unfair not to share what I knew even if what I had to reveal was unpleasant, and even if I had to admit some culpability in Kirk's death.

Let me explain: if it weren't for an offhand comment of mine, though we might have yet again pursued the Sasquatch, we might not have done it in the unfortunately successful manner in which we did. I expect your reaction to my mention of that "mythical" animal might inspire you to throw out this letter right away. I hope that you do not. I know that your son's ardent study of cryptozoology was at the root of the arguments that led to your estrangement. I need to tell you that when Kirk mentioned you and Mrs. Benner, while he might vent some frustration over your stubbornness in the matter (a trait you must admit you shared with your son), he would more often lament that your relationship had disintegrated as it did, and he spoke kindly of the two of you and of his youth in Virginia. I hope you will remember the love you felt for your son in those days and continue reading. I think I might be able to show you that, while his passing was untimely and terrible, he did not "waste his life" on his exceptional pursuits.

Perhaps I should tell you about myself briefly, to help you understand from what viewpoint I write. For as long as I can remember, I have had an interest in those subjects often referred to as "paranormal"—though that label tends to find itself applied to an unwieldy amount of phenomena. My belief on any of these subjects was never much more than rumination; I had long ago come to accept that none of these phenomena could be satisfactorily "proven", not only to a skeptic, but even to myself. I found that I still enjoyed entertaining the possibilities these phenomena presented; it was fun for me to think about them, and exciting to color the world I lived in with their mystery, even if I expected it never to be any more than that. One secret I kept even from Kirk is, my interest results from the discovery that cryptozoology is a very *pleasant* study: you get to spend a lot of time outdoors, hiking and camping and generally appreciating nature, often in the company of interesting and enjoyable people. I admit I only shared their excitement at the discovery of a "footprint" by proxy, and I was never defeated when a search was "uneventful". You may wonder how I hope to establish the veracity of my narrative by admitting to mild duplicity; I mean only to show that my "beliefs" never clouded my judgment or perception.

I should say something here as well about Kirk's mindset: I mentioned earlier that the term "paranormal" was very generally applied and used in reference to some things that perhaps it should not. Soon after meeting Kirk I learned that he *strongly* opposed grouping cryptozoology with ESP, ghosts, aliens, and the like. He believed that cryptozoology is solely a biological study and refuted any inference otherwise. He was searching for animals—if average people thought the animals for which he searched "fantastic", then that was their limited perspective keeping them in the dark until he could prove them wrong. I'm sure you recognize the argument. I hope you won't be insulted when I say part of the miscommunication between you and your son may have been the result of your thinking being more like *mine*—lumping the biological with the mystical—albeit with a different prejudice.

Forgive this lengthy introduction. I think you'll soon see that, without it, you would have dismissed out of hand what I have to write. You may still. Also, I may not have prepared you adequately for the horror I must detail. I hope you understand that I wish to write without hyperbole and reveal the unfortunate truth without embellishment.

My disastrous revelation (which seemed so obvious to both your son and I after I shared it that we couldn't believe it hadn't occurred to either of us before) came about from the two of us sitting in my living room and watching yet another cable program about some region's Bigfoot or hairy man or what have you (Kirk and I both preferred to utilize the term "Sasquatch" universally regarding these creatures because we thought the misapplied plural of either of the former to be ridiculous). In addition to eyewitness accounts dramatized with low-budget re-creations, the program featured the usual group of enthusiasts trekking through the woods searching for the animal, setting motion-sensor cameras to capture images, and howling "primate" calls into the chill night. Also on the show were the cynics, invariably represented by a university professor in a lab setting and a park ranger interviewed with his back turned symbolically against the great stretch of wilderness and possibility behind him; these players echoed the argument of every counterpoint "expert": If Sasquatch exist, we would find corpses and bones, and there was no point believing any such creature existed until such proof could be found.

My epiphany seemed too plain to relate any way except casually: "They're *both* right," I said, "Why are we (cryptozoologists) always following tracks, looking for a living, moving creature—or hoping that one might cross our path almost at random? If the proof we need is a dead Sasquatch—his bones—then that is what we should be looking for. Instead we refuse to answer the cynic's question—'where are the bones?'—because we can't seem to find them. But if, as we both believe, that Sasquatch *is* real—"

Kirk caught up with my line of thought. His reaction was much more expressive than mine. He jumped up from the couch and slapped his forehead, staring wide-eyed from beneath his hand. "They are taking the bones! By God, you're right! We've wondered if they might be intelligent—why shouldn't they have burial rites? Primitive man began burying his own at least 130,000 years ago! You're right, you're right!" He grabbed me by the collar and shook me joyfully. "We need to find their graveyard!"

So our course was set. Of the many locations where sightings are regularly reported, we chose to investigate the area around Whitehall, New York, in the Adirondack Mountains. We chose this location because not only had it proven to be reliable from year to year regardless of season, but because it had been reputed to be especially active during migratory months in spring and autumn. I was anxious to get back out to the wilds after a particularly sedentary winter, so our timing seemed to me very fortuitous. Given its reputation, you may be surprised to know that neither of us had yet investigated the area. Upon looking at a map, I was somewhat doubtful of the region we proposed to search: To the North, East, and South, Whitehall is not far removed from significant population centers—hardly an inviting habitat for a reclusive creature. But to the West is Black Mountain, and beyond that, Lake George, so there seemed at least some hope that we were on the right path. I'll admit that my heart sunk to see that the Adirondacks' celebrated "46 Peaks" lay much further West. I was tempted to propose (somewhat selfishly) that the beast would be more likely to be found further from civilization, deeper into the mountains, and that *that* should be our destination, but Kirk believed in the merits of the repeated eyewitness accounts around Whitehall. The question then became, if there are Sasquatch living in the area, there ought to be Sasquatch dying in the area as well—so where are their remains?

First we considered whether there should be any other method of disposal. We soon dismissed this idea: immolation would bring park rangers to investigate the smoke, and would still require the disposal of the bones afterward; ritual exposure would leave the same problem; weighted submersion remained a possibility, but it seemed unlikely the practice had been so effective that no remains had ever washed ashore. We decided that at least some of the remains must be buried, covered, or otherwise deliberately situated out of sight.

Burial meant disturbed earth. If the body was buried unmolested, this meant a *lot* of disturbed earth (Sasquatch are typically estimated to be 7 to 8 feet tall). Could a grave of this size exist without discovery? Certainly. Despite man's best efforts, there yet exist great tracts of near-pristine wilderness. Still, if a *society* were to bury many of their dead *together* (as ritualized burial rites or disposition of the dead suggests), then a sanctified area unlikely to be discovered by normal traffic would best serve. We asked ourselves, what is holy ground to the Sasquatch?

I should mention another subject of contention in our Sasquatch hunt: caves. While some interesting stick-and-reed structures have been found by "Bigfoot" enthusiasts over the years, our discussions about where to find dead Sasquatch reminded Kirk and I that little thought had been given to where we might find the creature in repose—in his den. Recognizing the issue, we both confessed that willful ignorance may have hampered that discussion, as the most obvious answer is that Sasquatch make their dens in caves; obviously, so do bears. Although the American Black Bear is somewhat more "manageable" than his brown cousins, it is still a dangerously bad idea to upset one in his den, especially if he is hungry arising from torpor (contrary to popular belief, bears do not truly "hibernate"), or protecting her young. We decided we would not investigate any caves on this expedition. That was our spoken intent; I think we both knew we were sharing a lie.

We considered that if Sasquatch was duplicating humans' reverence for the dead, perhaps we should assign him our spiritual aesthetics, as well; we decided finally to search difficult-to-scale ridge plateaus. If that course failed to yield results, from that vantage we could survey the surrounding country to plot further searches. For my concerns, the plan was perfect; I was thrilled at the prospect of long hikes and difficult climbs.

The night before we embarked on our expedition we stayed at a hotel outside Lake George, about twenty miles from Whitehall. There we met David DeSoto, a member of one of the local societies whom we knew, liked, and trusted, and who was equipped and competent with professional video and audio equipment. It was only at that meeting that we disclosed to David our hypotheses and the details of our plan. He reacted with the enthusiasm we'd hoped for. I won't give a gratuitous detail of our assets; suffice to say we were experienced outdoorsmen who had learned to be prepared for a wide variety of contingencies without overburdening ourselves. I have thought, without anger, that Kirk's friendship with me might have been emboldened by my ability to finance our "adventures"—it was never an issue between us and I never once suggested it should be otherwise. It may, of course, elicit some anger from you—to know that I provided the support for Kirk to continuing chasing his "follies". I hope you will consider that I did it only out of genuine admiration for your son and dedication to our mutual interests.

Our plan was to spend three days and two nights in the Adirondacks over the arc of mid-week, to avoid as much human traffic as possible (though we thought it unlikely we would have much contact as the nights are still very cool this time of year). We notified park authorities of our presence and gave them a vague area for our intended location. On Tuesday morning we drove through Whitehall (something in our appearance must have marked us as other than normal hikers as a few locals sneered openly at us, while others waved, hailing the return of another Sasquatch "hunting season") and across South Bay, parking close to the bay shore. Our first impression was that we had seriously overestimated Black "Mountain". It was deliberate ignorance on my part, trying to keep the "adventure" in my experience. Even a cursory Internet search would have better prepared us, but I find it more fun to speculate on the unknown than to face an ever more plainly documented reality. Confronted with that reality, I was disappointed. To hike Black Mountain is to enjoy a gradual climb on well-trod and marked paths. Don't get me wrong: It was entirely pleasant, and we tried to enliven the hike by ignoring the paths as much as possible and choosing the most difficult ascent we could (to the amusement of another group of hikers—we weren't alone even on this cool, spring Tuesday), but my heart yearned for something more. I don't mean to be poetic; I only attempt to convey the state of mind we all shared that compelled our decisions later that day and the next. If only to give the full image of our experience, I'll relate that the weather was perfect; it was cool enough to hike comfortably in heavy pack, and sunny enough that we could enjoy the warmth of the diffuse bleed through the narrow conifers. We half-heartedly searched for tracks as we went; the forest floor is covered with a pad of needles, twigs, and leaves that yields to your foot and is unlikely to record any animal's passing. Besides, as I said, we weren't looking for the creature itself—though perhaps that desire crouched in each of us despite our aim. How terrible it is now to think upon that naïve thrill of anticipation.

Despite moving slowly through a haphazard, serpentine ascent, we reached the summit easily shortly after midday. The last hundred feet became steeper and rockier, which enabled us to feel at least some small sense of accomplishment when we stood at the top and looked at the beauty of Lake George below and the Adirondacks beyond, then back the way we came across to the Green Mountains in the East. We sat and lunched. We discussed revising our plans for the remainder of our expedition. We agreed that Black Mountain was unlikely to give up any dead—any remains, however interred, would likely have been discovered by her swarming enthusiasts long ago. If the sightings near Whitehall were to be believed, that meant the witnesses had seen creatures in transit. We took this to mean we should continue our search nearby. We looked across Lake George to the far side and immediately reached unanimity that we would go across the next day. We would begin at the tip of the Tongue Mountain Range and follow the ridge north.

Our plans set, we had little left to do that night but descend the lake side of the mountain in the same undisciplined manner as we ascended and stroll along the coast line to investigate whatever we found worthwhile before setting up camp. We expected we could have just gone back to the car and the hotel for the night without missing anything exceptional, but none of us was as discouraged as that—indeed, spirits were high. I think by then my love of the experience without expectation had begun to rub off on Kirk; I like to think it was one of the reasons he valued my company.

Imagine our excitement, then, when, late in our descent, towards late-afternoon, we came across a low shelf carved into the rock with deep shadow waiting underneath. Our earlier conviction to avoid caves crumbled instantly; we decided to investigate. David began taping; I cautioned the others to wait while I hastily assembled the composite rifle I had stored illegally in my pack. Kirk took point as we eased towards the hole, armed with only a can of bear mace and a flash light. As we got closer we were struck by the smell coming from within: a kind of skunk smell, and death smell, neither overpowering the other. There was something in the smell that was repulsive to me beyond the actual scent. Goosebumps rose up on my arms. I scampered around to one side of the cave mouth and lay flat on my stomach to be able to take a shot if need be while Kirk bent double to dip below the shelf lip. I could see by the beam from his flashlight that the cave opened slightly taller on the inside, but it did not appear to be deep.

"We're clear," Kirk called, and I relaxed, only to tense again when he followed with, "Wait."

Kirk stayed in my view, circling around into the cave and training his light back towards the near wall, where I couldn't see. As he inched forward, I kicked my toes into the dirt and swiveled my body to a more central angle view of the cave. Kirk was looking at a spot on the ground behind a short outcropping of rock.

"What do you see?" David asked from behind me.

"Bones," was the reply. Kirk holstered his mace and disappeared behind the outcropping. He quickly came back into view, cradling something in the crook of his arm. I sank back from the cave as Kirk emerged. In the sunlight, we examined what he'd retrieved from the cave: bones, and a circular tuft of fur of some sort.

"Look." Kirk handed me what was undoubtedly the bone from a bear. I saw why he thought the find intriguing: There were teeth marks on the bone.

"What is that?" David asked about the tuft of fur.

"I don't..." Kirk began, and then remarked "Ah," as he held the object between thumb and forefinger and let the flap dangle down so that we could see the dry pad of a bear's paw.

Though there was no appreciable danger, and though the kill was clearly not recent, we moved on from the area quietly and quickly.

It was Kirk who spoke first. "Like a grizzly."

I nodded back to him. The brutal scene we'd just left is not exceptional—in Western Canada or Alaska. Grizzlies will eat black bears, sometimes taking advantage of the latter animal's slower emergence from torpor. Of course, Grizzlies do not live in the Adirondacks. And black bears have no history of cannibalism. The possibility remained that scavengers had found the bear's carcass and cleaned it. I think that we, who so often only begrudgingly acknowledged alternative theories that debunked our hypotheses, were quick to take comfort from this possibility.

Sometime later we came upon a clearing with a good view up the mountain and across the lake. We studied what we could see of the mountains on the far side, eager for tomorrow's hike. The discovery in the cave had rejuvenated and excited us; now, the awe of the picturesque view humbled us and made us pensive. We decided to split up and reconnoiter one hundred yards in three directions to search for any sign of recent wildlife activity. Having satisfied ourselves of our relative safety, Kirk and I set our camp for the night while David shot the gorgeous view below and recorded the quick creep of the shadow across the lake and up over us.

We ate and we talked. We considered whether our discovery in the cave indicated any threat to our well-being. The obvious interpretation was that if a Sasquatch did kill and eat a black bear then, yes, Sasquatch represented a real physical threat under certain circumstances. However, we were unaware of any lethal attack against a human. Claims of "threatening" activity, particularly against those indoors in an otherwise uninhabited area, were well-documented, but seemed to indicate an attempt to scare the victims rather than harm them. We had to acknowledge that people go missing every year in the American wilderness, never to be heard from again, so that the lack of a recorded fatal attack against a human did not necessarily mean such an event had not occurred. Still, we all agreed that Sasquatch's notorious smell, of which we took some mild remnant to have lingered at the cave long after any creature's presence there, should provide us with warning. And there were the sounds the beasts have been purported to make which none of us had ever heard adequately described where we would recognize them from those descriptions, but which we all felt we would recognize if heard.

David wondered if there were caves of sufficient size in the area to house one family or several of the creatures; it would seem a large underground network might be necessary for even a small population of the species to maintain their secrecy while providing adequate shelter. None of us was sufficiently knowledgeable about geology to answer the question. David wondered further if such caves might be accessible through underwater entryways, and that the necessary immersion in potentially fetid waters went some way to explain their stench. Kirk ruminated on one of his favorite theories, if one he, himself, found unlikely, that Sasquatch was not a primate at all, as was commonly believed, but of ursine descent. Not wanting to spoil his good humor, I, as per usual, withheld from pointing out that an interdimensional origin or alien allegiance would explain away some of the "problematic" aspects of Sasquatch's existence.

Satisfactorily exhausted, we decided it would be unnecessary, and possibly detrimental to the next day's work, to rotate a watch through the night. David was worried he didn't have sufficient battery life to leave his video camera going through the night for the unlikely possibility of capturing any activity, but he did have a digital audio recorder available that he left on to record the first four hours of the evening. I'll state again: We had no expectation of encountering the creature and that was not the aim of our expedition.

We awoke with the sun—late, as we were situated on the west side of the mountain. We stretched out muscles stiff from exertion and the cold. We breakfasted in appreciative silence, looking down toward the valley. David ate distractedly, looking at the dirt while he listened on ear buds to the sounds recorded during the night. Finally, we broke camp and made a quick descent to the water's edge. We were directly east of the tip of the "tongue". Kirk revealed the contents of his pack: an inflatable boat. Anxious to be across the lake, we took turns pumping the compact bellows with our feet until the boat was ready. We must have looked quite a sight crossing the lake: three men huddled together in a small, vinyl dinghy, furtively paddling their way over the dark water lolling lazily in the spring country morning. Indeed, though my intent may have matched my companions, I would not have minded taking a longer course across the water; I have often thought that no one is as at peace as when he is on water.

But we were soon across and landed on the far side. As we set out, just beginning our ascent up the rugged shore, David called excitedly for us to stop. As he stared vacantly at a nondescript spot of earth, the cause of his excitement was apparent: he'd heard something on the tape from the previous night.

"What is it?" Kirk and I asked.

David held up a finger to "wait", and his eyes bulged wide. He stopped the recorder, passed the nibs to Kirk and commanded him, "Listen."

Kirk listened, as did I in turn. Cool as it was, the night had been silent of insects. There was little to muddle the "vocalizations" we heard on the tape. We were familiar with night bird and owl calls and were able to immediately dismiss that identification. The sounds were short, but purposefully sustained howls that I hated to admit could only be adequately described as "primate calls". They had the resonance of a full-throated creature, but something in their nature struck me as deliberately restrained, as if to communicate discretely, unlike the undirected "where are yous?" indicated by most animal calls. The sounds I heard were primarily in my right ear. Suddenly, a softer (presumably more remote) echo repeated in my left ear.

"Is this a stereo recording?"

David nodded emphatically, smiling. "It's a call and response!"

I needn't tell you a prompt discussion delayed the beginning of our hike. We even considered crossing back over the lake to Black Mountain. But David listened repeatedly to his recordings and concluded that the response call might have carried across the water from the side on which we were currently situated. And, of course, we tried to hold to our expedition's initial purpose, which was unrelated to the pursuit of a live creature. We tried to take our findings as encouragement we were in the right area to achieve our goal of finding Sasquatch remains; it was no easy task to restrain our enthusiasm and not redirect our aim. Eventually we decided to stick to our (admittedly revised) itinerary and hike north-northeasterly up and along the Tongue Mountain Range ridge.

There is little I can say about the remainder of that day's hike that would be other than poesy. It was wonderful to be with friends, and to be out in the open. The views were spectacular and I made a note to return in the fall when the leaves were changing. I regret that I don't think I'll have that chance. Even with all that happened there—the macabre ritual we witnessed and the horror undoubtedly visited upon my two friends—I can't hold a grudge against the land itself and the beauty that nature can display for us. I have been fortunate to see so many great displays. I have witnessed the sublime harmony of this world and I forgive that animal eats animal in their dens and hollows and under skeletal trees in moon shadow. Perhaps these are the thoughts of a man reconciled to his fate. Enough. I'll continue my narrative.

At the summit of Five Mile Mountain, we had another discussion: Should we more meticulously examine the area we'd already traced, which lay opposite Black Mountain and which may have been the base of the "response" we'd heard on the digital recorder (but which had not presented us with any particularly inspiring locations), or should we continue north? I reminded the others that we'd have to re-trace our path anyway if we wanted to pick up the boat, which indicated to me we should cover more ground before camping and reversing course in the morning. The others agreed. We dipped into a valley and crossed Route 9 North. I remember seeing a lone, white car going east.

We hiked up Catamount Mountain. Towards her summit, the trees clear away. Several large plateaus step down irregularly on her north face. To the east is Jabe Pond. The air remained clear and cool, but some sense of ominous discovery touched each in the party. We recognized that this area was logically heavy with potential, but, more, we felt it psychically. I hope you'll understand that I mean this without embellishment and that you will put aside any reservations you might have in the matter. Excitedly but deliberately, we surveyed the plateaus. We saw no physical evidence demonstrating the presence of any Sasquatch in the area, but we did discover smoothed and flattened paths crisscrossing the area that indicated some activity. Unfortunately, the prompt discovery of hatch-marked rocks seemed to indicate a track or record for hikers. I wondered why the marks were not more specific or intelligible; they seemed mostly meaningless, little more than random scratches. I considered they might be a code understood by locals. Our growing impression that this area, too, was frequented by humans took some of the wind from our sails. Yes, we all felt "something", but an experienced investigator learns that there are a multitude of reasons this can happen, not the least of which is wishful thinking. Often that sense of expectation simply dissipates with the initial cause unrevealed. We continued north and circled Spruce and Beech Mountains before returning to Jabe Pond to eat our dinner. The sun was soon to disappear behind the ridge to our west. We were disappointed not to have discovered anything further, but were satisfactorily tired. We decided to set up camp back up the side of Catamount Mountain—it would be colder, as we would be more exposed, but we reasoned that we would be better positioned to place any "calls" we might hear during the night if we were stationed at a higher altitude. Deeming it unnecessary to camp at the summit of the mountain, we set up on a plateau just above the tree line on the northeast face—from here we could watch the pond area as well as the sides of the mountains opposite and the valley between them and Catamount. We rested comfortably as outlines of mountains dimmed and disappeared. I dozed off.

I have no idea what time it was when Kirk shook me awake. As you will see, when I fell unconscious it was still dark, and when next I woke it was daylight, so the events that follow could have happened at nine o'clock or five o'clock or anywhere in between. Kirk squatted over me, holding a finger to his lips to indicate silence. I was struck by how light it was—we had planned (as always) for a full-moon expedition, but the crispness of the detail in Kirk's face is yet etched upon my mind. Then the smell hit me and I nearly vomited flat on my back. I spun on to my side as deftly and quietly as I could, and somehow managed to suppress the gag reflex. The smell was similar to what we had encountered at the bear's den—skunk and death in equal measure—but there was more to it now than just the dynamically increased amplitude. There was also a sharply-spiced musk that pulled the sinuses disastrously open to the final components: mossy rot (tinged with the sharp "nitrate" smell of peat) and stale urine. It was a blend of smells that was terrible to consider in and of itself, but my physical reaction went beyond simple revulsion and nausea: the warm buzz of adrenalin hummed through my veins. I had heard described to me a reaction not of fight or flight, but one where the onrush of adrenalin causes the body to lose strength and motor function, where one's limbs move clumsily and slowly, uselessly, like in a nightmare. I had never experienced this reaction before; now I was helplessly in its throes—the usual "fight or flight" options were unthinkable. David was hiding his nose and mouth beneath the collar of his shirt. Kirk held his nose between thumb and forefinger, but the gesture wasn't meant to indicate his discomfiture; he was indicating "better we smell them than they smell us". I do not know why the other two were less affected by the stench than I was. I hope you will trust that I am not trying to excuse cowardice. I truly believe there was nothing else I could do to master my will. I am ashamed, nonetheless—I suppose I might have "survivor's guilt". That shouldn't be a worry for much longer.

Kirk put his fingers behind his ear: I was to listen. After my reaction to the stench, I'm not surprised it took me a few seconds more to realize that the still night was repeatedly punctuated by low grunts in several voices. Kirk pointed towards the north face. I struggled as best I could to crawl over to David's location and look over the ledge. The sources of the grunts (and the smell) were located on a lower plateau, clearly illuminated in the moonlight. They were separated from us by a narrow band of trees clinging to the angled face of the mountain, but we could see easily through the screen, as through the slits on a vertical blind rotated "open".

I counted thirteen of the beasts, but there may have been more (presumably women and children) hidden in the shadows away from the clearing. I was terrified and excited to see them. I was oddly disappointed, too, if only because they looked exactly as we had been led to believe they would: the beasts were at least six feet tall, the largest I estimated at over eight feet (there were a couple shorter creatures that hung closely to the "women" that I took to be juveniles, all the adult males appeared to be seven feet tall at least); they stood upright, but with a slight stoop; they were covered with thick, matted fur which I thought to be brown (it was, of course, impossible to be sure in the moonlight), and had the "flat" faces of primates (as distinguished from the more protuberant ursine snout). Their faces seemed darker than their fur. Their eyes flashed (as a cat's might) in the moonlight, but they did not "glow" as had been reported by some witnesses. Their frames and builds indicated great power in the limbs; their movements were likewise "bulky". So there were no surprises in their appearance (besides the fact of them appearing at all), but I will admit to some real fear in seeing the creatures: besides their "normal" appearance, there was yet something blasphemous about their existence, something foul about their very presence on the earth and on that mountain.

Again, this may have been an intimation I felt as a result of physiological response to the stench—I would not doubt if it were.

The behavior of the beasts indicated that this was not a random assembly, but something more, like a ritualized convocation. As we might expect from the season, their gathering appeared to be related to mating. The largest male stood in the middle of the clearing. Behind him the women and juveniles clustered in a group on the edge of deep shadow. Before him a group of five males weaved about each other in a rough half-circle, leaning forward and grunting towards the alpha male before retreating behind and around another in the shifting pack. Finally, one of the males lunged forward at the alpha. Here it became plain that this was ritual, as the "combat" consisted of a series of threatening passes by the challenger deflected by the alpha's exaggerated arm gestures until the challenger bent low and retreated without either creature incurring injury. The males in the pack (with the returned challenger, presumably the "number two" male) squatted on their haunches in their semi-circle. The alpha turned towards the females. Three came forward, one in the center slightly forward of the others who held her arms around the bicep. The male stepped forward and smelled the lead female. A loud, purring growl could be heard; it seemed to begin from the alpha, but was soon picked up by others in the group so that it rolled up to us, a low-toned, undulating and discordant rumble building in intensity. The lead female quavered as if in a trance and fell to the earth, guided down by her attendants. I don't think I need to describe what happened next. I will note only that few animals, even primates, utilize the "missionary" position (as the Sasquatch did). As you might expect, the vocalizations "climaxed" with a triumphant howl from the alpha. Afterwards, he withdrew and knelt, sitting back on his heels, his head bowed. The woman, regaining from her swoon, was helped back away from the clearing towards the shadow by her attendants who petted her head and cooed softly to her. I was so absorbed watching her being led away that I didn't notice when the other males began creeping towards the alpha. Even in the moonlight I could see clearly that they each carried a sharp rock in one hand. Suddenly, the alpha reared back and let forth a terrifying howl that temporarily *blinded* me. My vision regained focus abruptly as the sound ceased in the wet staccato of a blow to the alpha's skull. The "number two" male stepped away from the alpha as its body shuddered. The others leapt forward, grunting with exertion as they struck the body repeatedly until it toppled to the ground.

Somewhere through the fog of nightmare shrouding my brain drifted Kirk's whisper, "Population control."

The strength of Kirk's will transmitted through his dispassionate observation brought my own wits back to bear. He was right—if Sasquatch had long ago learned that aversion to our race was necessary to ensure his species' survival, he would have practiced whatever means necessary to keep his existence secret. Perhaps the reason for this extreme behavior, this sociological evolution, was lost to time even for the creatures themselves, even as it remained effective: no Sasquatch was left to become old and infirm, unable to hide the record of his passing; his species would not allow the circumstance to occur. The patriarchal alignment of their social order explained why the sexual dimorphism remained undocumented, and why juveniles where so rarely seen; clearly the males were the ranging, giant beasts occasionally witnessed in the wild, while the women and children remained hidden away "in the shadows". There remained the mystery of their undiscovered dead. That horrific secret was soon revealed.

The men backed away from the corpse; the women loped forward and bent over it. Short jerks of the shoulders were followed by bent arms tugging back from the fallen. It was only when one of the women stood up to shuffle over and offer the new alpha a flank of steaming meat that I understood what was happening. Large portions of the dead Sasquatch were presented to each of the males. Two of the women then took parts out of view to the "honored" female and the juveniles. After that, the beasts cut portions for themselves at will and ate enthusiastically. This perfect method of disposal and utilization of resources was both loathsome and hypnotizing to watch. It was only when a drop of sweat stung my eye that I recognized my body was demonstrating the early stages of shock. My heart was beating far too quickly. As much as I hated to put myself into darkness at that moment, I shut my eyes and slowed my breathing. I felt Kirk's hand on my shoulder and got some sense of reassurance from his presence. I opened my eyes and looked at my companions. They were clearly shaken, but did not seem to be suffering the same level of distress I was. Again, this gave me some sense of reassurance and helped me regain my composure. I felt my muscles loosen and my perception widen. I was able to look back at the savage scene and watch as the Sasquatch dismantled and consumed their comrade. When the meat had been stripped clean, the bones were sat in a shallow depression dug by one of the women at the base of a flattish, upright rock. Then the new alpha went to the rock and pushed it down. The impact resounded with a dull thud; I felt the faint shockwave course through the ground, into my abdomen. The new alpha ran a finger inside a section of the dead Sasquatch's pelt; he handed the pelt to a woman, stooped towards the rock, and extended his arm to touch it. The woman folded the pelt and placed it in the middle of the clearing. The full company squatted on their haunches, facing the pelt, and bowed their heads in silence. I could hear the faint ruffle of their breath. Kirk, David and I kept deathly still for an hour, watching. One by one the animals turned and padded off down the slopes and into the cover of the trees so stealthily that half their number had gone without my noting their departure. We waited an additional fifteen minutes after the last had left (or an eternity or more, I couldn't say exactly) before shifting our positions ever so slightly to face each other.

"Exposure?" I whispered, guessing at the ultimate fate of the Sasquatch pelt.

Kirk shook his head. "They'll come back. At least one of them. We can't wait for that."

A horrible dread came over me. Despite my generally adventurous nature, despite the nature of the prize and the certain knowledge of what its capture would mean, I said, "No."

Kirk ignored my protest—or, perhaps, he had greater faith in my courage than I had at the time; he may have guessed the physiological effect the stench was having on me.

"You can sight your gun from there," Kirk pointed to a small, twisted shelf up the rock face that was somehow both outcropping and alcove and which afforded a good angle of the clearing and the path my companions would have to take; "We'll take the flashlights and run for Silver Bay, on the lake. Everything else stays."

David was changing the tape in his video camera. "I'll come with you."

"Okay. Hang back a bit," Kirk instructed David as he handed me the rifle case. He looked at me encouragingly, and with just a touch of a smile as if to say "no worries, mate". There was always something in him that made you believe everything would turn out fine, whatever the risk. Up until that night, it always had.

I dutifully assembled the rifle, surprised that I could use my hands with any sort of dexterity. I was beginning to believe everything would turn out fine, too. I scampered up to my position. I lay flat on my front and put the night scope to my eye as I worked my elbows into the dirt. Kirk eased himself down the incline towards the thin stand of trees and the plateau beyond. David followed him, ten yards back. David's face was illuminated by the faint green glow of the LCD screen. Kirk picked his way through the trees carefully. David traced a wider arc, trying to get Kirk in profile as he emerged into the clearing.

Absolute terror gripped me as a breeze tickled the *back* of my head.

Kirk grabbed the pelt and straightened. His head snapped back in my direction. He felt it, too.

The wind grew more forceful as it shifted again, blowing straight into my face. The stench hit me full. My head went light, my vision swam. I think I heard one angry grunt as I lost consciousness.

* * *

The sun woke me. Some instinct in my soul celebrated the daylight so profoundly that I didn't know where I was or care how I came to be there for a full minute. Then the spell was broken and my heart sank. I looked down to the clearing on the plateau and saw several smears of blood seeping into the dirt. I scampered down to our campsite but there was no trace of our having been there at all. I have to assume that my position slightly further up the mountain, aided by a surfeit of luck, enabled me to remain undiscovered in the night, improbable as it seems to me even now. I went down to the clearing carelessly. The awful scent had mostly dispersed; I knew no Sasquatch was anywhere near. It occurred to me then that their scent was another evolutionary advantage designed for isolation; it drove potential witnesses away, or disabled those foolish enough not to flee. It may be that those who survive sighting a Sasquatch are those sensible enough not to engage him. There was no telling if the blood on the ground was the dead Sasquatch's or that of my friends. From the patterns presented, I guessed that it was not solely that of the beast. Of Kirk or David, I could see no sign. I walked to the toppled rock. On it were a short series of diagonal and vertical hatch-marks like the ones we'd seen and promptly dismissed the day before. A grim resolution came over me. I decided that, whatever the fate of my friends, the goal of the expedition would be realized: I would bring back a Sasquatch's bone.

To lift the stone was unthinkable. I soon saw the futility of scratching with my hands at the earth around the rock. I disassembled the rifle and began cutting into the dirt with the barrel. It was difficult work, but I was soon able to squeeze my arm through the hasty opening and feel around at the edge of the shallow pit dug under the rock. Sharp shards of broken bone pricked my searching fingers. I felt the wet knot of a bone's end and stretched further, crushing my shoulder against the rock. Finally I grasped the thing and withdrew my arm, scraping my knuckles as I pulled the large particle free from the hole. I held in my scraped and bleeding hand what I took to be the top end of the femur. The shaft of the bone was crushed and broken shortly after the bone narrowed, about six inches along. Dirty bits of cartilage and tendon still clung to the bone. There was nothing else to do with it but put it in my pocket. I suppose I could have stayed and attempted to excavate further, to recover more samples. But I feared discovery, even though I felt sure none of the creatures were nearby. The strain of the evening doubtless inclined me to leave as quickly as possible. This is probably the reason I didn't think to re-cover the hole I'd dug.

I retraced our route from the previous day back south. It began to rain moderately as I retrieved the inflatable boat and went back across the lake. I dropped the rifle into the lake—there would be questions enough to answer without compounding my problems. I went back over Black Mountain and drove the car to Whitehall, where I secured a room above a restaurant and called the police. You may wonder why I didn't leave from our campsite and go directly to Silver Bay—the police certainly wondered. To them, I professed confusion, intimating at the psychological shock that I surely had suffered from the events I reported. Oh, yes—I told them everything, exactly as it happened, omitting only two matters of possession—the gun and the bone. That is why I didn't seek help immediately—so that I could secure the sample. Certainly, this was the one element of proof that might have inclined the authorities to believe my story, but I didn't want them to take possession of it; I had little doubt that I would ever see it again if they did.

The police escorted me back to the site of the "incident". I saw immediately that the "burial" stone had been shifted and the bones removed. I felt clammy fear curl into my stomach, not because I thought the police would not believe me (I never thought the police would believe me), but because it meant *they* knew the grave had been disturbed. The steady rain that fell throughout the day had washed any trace of blood from the clearing (although, to me, the dirt appeared disturbed and artificially "re-settled", as if they knew to "clean" the affected area). The only possible evidence to support my story were a few bits of broken glass near where I last saw David standing that I thought might have come from his camera (I wondered if the Sasquatch knew the camera's purpose or if they simply collected it with the rest of our possessions).

The authorities told me to remain "in town" while they determined whether or not the disappearances I claimed were hoaxed. Eventually, as you know, a search-and-rescue operation was initiated by the park service; you know also that the operation failed to produce results. I was questioned several more times by various law enforcement agencies, but I never wavered in my recollection of events. I was threatened several times with murder charges, but no charges were ever filed. Different iterations of the story appeared in the various tiers of the media. The disappearances were deemed either too unimportant (until they could be confirmed as fatalities) or too tragic for the mainstream press to incorporate the "wilder" elements of the story. Conversely, those elements, embraced by the "alternative" media, discouraged any serious consideration by the wider public.

It was when things began to "quiet down", when the search was called off, as the news cycle turned, that I began to hear the Sasquatch calling from a distance, bouncing across the South Bay and over the hill down to Whitehall. Possibly only I heard them at first; they came so late in the dead of night that anyone who could still sleep in the dark was likely doing so, those lucky, normal people who could shut their windows with the idea that they were a satisfactory barrier against the things in the night. I was ready to leave before I heard them; I had given up any residual hope for the safe return of Kirk and David, I had informed the authorities where they could find me if they wanted to question me or charge me. Yet, after I heard those "primate calls" arcing through the night air, I could not go. Something in those same instincts that made me so susceptible to their stench told me that they were calling *me*. It was enough, at any rate, for me to stay on another night and to hear the calls coming from a little closer to the town. I began to understand that they were coming—their natural aversion to our species was insufficient to dissuade their anger. After all, I had desecrated one of their graves. Do these subhumans believe in a soul? Do they think I disturbed the rest of their brother's spirit? Perhaps. Or perhaps their anger is more primitive and territorial. The result is the same: I have to return the bone or they will "make their presence felt" in town. The euphemism is inappropriate, I apologize: They will slaughter these people indiscriminately, I am sure of it—I hear the Hell of it in their increasing anger. Their calls have become steadily louder, they creep steadily closer; unquestionably they have advanced to this side of the bay now. Others in the town have heard them and talk nervously. They look on me with distrust or hate. I can't blame them; I have disturbed whatever fragile peace their practiced ignorance has allowed to hold for centuries. It is likely that the price of peace will be greater than this simple shard. So be it: I pray the Sasquatch will forgive me, but I doubt their mercy. I go today to return the bone from whence I stole it. You see the urgency in my relating these facts to you now, as the opportunity might not be had later—I go again, following your son one last time.

I hope you will take the enclosed vial and present it with a copy of this record to the zoology department at the university of your choice. The vial contains marrow taken from the Sasquatch's bone that they can use to extract a DNA sequence. I do not think the beasts will know I have engaged in this betrayal of their secrecy. In truth, I do not hate them, even for what they have done. If they are animals, they are faultless; if they are more, then they deserve empathy. I would almost prefer them undisturbed, but our world encroaches ever nearer, and they will eventually, probably someday soon, be discovered. I hope Kirk's sacrifice will be recognized appropriately when that time comes.

With sincere condolences,
Tim Knott

A copy of Tim Knott's letter was retrieved from his laptop's hard drive by an enterprising member of our society making inquiries into the disappearance of our fellow member, David DeSoto. Attempts to contact Mr. Benner elicited hostility. Benner indicated only that he made no attempt to reply to Tim Knott's letter, and made no inquiries as to Knott's whereabouts or well-being. He also denied the existence of the purportedly enclosed vial. 🦇

LIFECAST

CRAIG SPECTOR

BY THE TIME the temperature hit ninety-nine degrees, Philip Thomas was completely insane.

He sat by the table in the cramped, airless confines of his kitchen, sweat pasting his *Dawn of the Dead* T-shirt to his back and sides. A white plastic egg timer sat on the table before him, ticking off the seconds. He still had some time to go, but he was getting impatient. The phone would be ringing any minute, sure as shit. It ought to be ready by now.

Phil cracked the door of the oven and peered in at the contents. Waves of heat leached out, adding a horrible stench to the already unbearable air of the kitchen. The contents of the oven stared back, unseeing.

Ready enough.

Inside, nestled in a baking pan, was an exact alginate replica of a human face. In the past hour, it had dehydrated considerably, shriveling from its normal adult size to that of a child—two, three years, tops.

And getting younger by the minute.

Phil stared into the oven. It was an act of madness for several reasons, perhaps the least of which being that it was August in New York, which was a very good time to be somewhere else. Another high pressure system had stalled over the entire eastern seaboard, and it had turned the concrete canyons of Manhattan into the world's largest convection oven, baking the unfortunate inhabitants into a miserable, short-tempered stupor. Nights were no better, as the accumulated heat of the day radiated out from the walls, the streets, everywhere. On his block alone—a dreary strip of brownstones slicing across Avenue D in an area of the East Village that passed clear through trendy into simple squalor—there had been two shootings, three stabbings, and more fistfights than he cared keep track of. All related, directly or otherwise, to the heat. It was felony weather, every brutal second ticking off like a time bomb waiting to blow.

Phil could relate. He was feeling a bit murderous himself lately.

And inside the oven, the alginate was still shrinking.

He smiled; showtime. When he closed his eyes, he could almost hear the screams.

Philip Thomas was a tad young to go over the edge; on the down side of twenty-two, with a lingering air of adolescent awkwardness that belied what experience he had. But he made up for his youth, with talent and intensity and an obsessiveness that bordered on mania. He was tall, thin, pale and stoop-shouldered from too many bright summer days spent hunkered over clay models and molds in the basement. Gaunt, haunted features shrouded coal-black eyes that picked up every detail and stored them forever, and but the barest hint of facial growth struggled to offset a prematurely receding hairline. He looked like a tuberculous Edwardian poet, if you were feeling neo-romantic, or a twerp-faced geek if you weren't. In truth, he was neither.

In truth, Philip Thomas was an artist.

He stood there, flaking dried bits of rubbery goo off his fingers and checking the alginate's progress with a perverse and resounding glee. Amazing stuff, alginate. It was a makeup artist's best friend: a chalky white powder, actually made from sea algae. Dry, it was inert and generally useless. But add liquid, mix it up, and presto! It became a gelatinous blob, which set to a rubber-like consistency in minutes and picked up the tiniest detail of anything it touched.

As with every other aspect of his craft, Phil took it very, very seriously. In his brief, struggling career he'd slathered veritable mountains of the stuff across the heads or tits or bellies or behinds of one low-rent starlet or has-been actor after another, in anticipation of their upcoming hatchet-in-the-face scene, or wet T-shirt/chain-saw sequence, or chest-burster Alien rip-off, or whatever bit of cinematic Cheez to which Herschel Floyd would periodically enslave him.

Of course, for most applications you generally mixed it with water, but today called for an extra-special effect.

And, except for the smell, blood worked surprisingly well.

Phil winced as a stinging trickle of sweat found his eyes. He slipped on an oven mitt, gingerly lifting the pan up and out of the heat. This was a delicate phase of the process; no sense in rushing things.

He carried the pan out of the kitchen and into the living room, where the heat went from unbearable to merely suffocating. Demons, mutants, and mangled limbs greeted him from every surface of the room, throwing monstrous shadows across the walls and ceiling. They were his creations and his friends: the great horned troll adorning the mantelpiece of the bricked-up fireplace, and the dwarfish minions flanking it, all cutting-room floor fatalities from *Voodoo Vacation;* the pair of hacked-off shredded arms which looked so real in person and so ridiculous in *Class of Splatter*

High. The human-faced spider-thing, with eyes of glistening marbles, that sadly spun its web across the mirror over the mantle, a pre-production reject from *Invasion of the Maggot Eaters.* Screaming skulls and mutant body parts adorned the bookshelves; even the cupboard at the end of the room held the headless female torso from *Slaughterhouse Slumber Party,* replete with pitchfork tines protruding below the breasts in neatly-spaced holes.

"Evening dear," he said, laying the pan on another cluttered table. He flicked on his work light and began inspecting the cooling features. This was serious. Every crease, every wrinkle had to be absolutely perfect, even if the ritual didn't strictly require it.

The face in the pan was Herschel Floyd's, taken from the plaster positive Phil had made for *Chainsaw Cheerleaders.* In sleazoid, Hitchcockian imitation, Herschel's ego asserted itself via cameo appearance as the exploding head during the obligatory bone-squat make-out scene, thus achieving immortality while compelling some feckless bimbo to quaff the big-veined man-thing in take after take. The positive from which the mold was taken was propped on the table, facing him: eyes closed, mouth frozen open like Mr. Bill in Hell, bearded jowls drooping, looking altogether more like a deathcast than a lifecast.

"Both, actually," he said to the face. He held up the negative, a bowl-shaped shell of the original with the features on the inside. The alginate's shrinkage had left the features looking more like a pissed-off raisin than a man: all pinched in and wrinkled, its little mouth a puckered sphincter in the center.

"Your true character revealed, Hersch ol' buddy." He looked at the shrunken form. "I do good work, yes?"

There was no reply: its lips were sealed.

"Aw, poor little fellah." Phil took an X-acto knife and rectified the problem. "That's better, isn't it?" He twisted the alginate slightly, forcing the tiny mouth into a hideous tiny grin. "I've got big plans for you, you know." He addressed it in his best Mr. Rogers voice. "Can you say 'san-tah-*ree*-ah?'" The tiny face nodded in his grasp.

"I knew you could."

Phil Thomas had paid his dues—films that were low-budget, more often no- budget, forcing him to make miracles out of next to nothing in the worst of all possible circumstances. He'd been abused and jerked off, conscripted into constructing the requisite monsters and mayhem out of foam latex and chicken wire, squibs and stage blood and pure heart-sweat, all in the hope of that one big break.

Three years into the business, and that one big break was still as elusive as ever. But Phil had gotten better. Much better. It was inevitable: no matter how vile or trashy the production as a whole, it was still *his* heart up there, his soul on the screen with his creations.

It was more than just a job, after all.

It was his life.

Phil smiled, laid the alginate face down and began sifting a few cc's of Ultrocal-30 plaster mix into a bowl. "You've no one to blame but yourself, you know." He talked to the mask as he worked, a by-product of habitual solitude. "You shouldn't expect to go fucking with a man's lifelong ambition and go unpunished, should you?" He glared at the mask.

"Of course not."

And makeup had been Phil Thomas's dream ever since he first saw Lon Chaney as the Phantom of the Opera, skulking out of the sewers of Paris and into his living room courtesy of WTAR's Creature Feature matinee. He went apeshit over the Creature from the Black Lagoon. He devoured the drawings in Creepy and Eerie comics before he was even old enough to read the words; in school, he was extremely popular around Halloween and when they needed someone to run the magic show at the Spring Fair, and virtually ignored the rest of the year.

All of which was fine by Phil. He was a loner by nature, given to pursuing his hobbies under his parents' indulgent inattention. Young Philip Thomas liked magic tricks, music, models, monsters.

And movies.

Especially horror movies.

They were the best, the ones that hit everyone right in the yahooties. Philip was culturally weaned in the seventies, at the dawning of the Age of Excessiveness; a time of ruptured ideals and empathy overload, with all the icons fair game and no taboo beyond reproach. A lot of people were shocked at the new explicitness, the brazen disregard for propriety and restraint.

To Phil it seemed the most natural thing in the world.

By the time puberty kicked his glands into gear he'd witnessed thirteen thousand, nine hundred and forty-two murders and/or random killings, in varying degrees of detail, and easily twice that number of maimings, tortures and sexual assaults. He'd seen Linda Blair's head twist clean around as she turbo-fucked a crucifix in *The Exorcist*, observed tongues being ripped out with red-hot pincers as he collected his own set of 'stomach distress bags' from *Mark of the Devil*, yucked it up with *Count Yorga, Vampire* and a veritable host of Hammer horror films by junior high.

By the time he saw the zombies overrunning the shopping malls in *Dawn of the Dead*, destiny called.

Philip Thomas had found his niche.

But, he wanted more than to just sit on the one side of the silver screen as the dark, awesome magic came to life. He wanted to create the illusions himself.

And he wanted to make them flawlessly, perfectly real.

Sloppiness always spoiled the effect: nylon wires hanging out of a creature's back, seams where the latex didn't lay properly, the flat, waxy pallor of an obviously fake head that took an all-too-real axe —such gaffes Philip Thomas could not abide. He was fanatical about details, even unto the tiniest minutiae of continuity. If the killer got sprayed with blood running out of the farmhouse, then the splatter pattern had goddamned well better stay the same when he is next seen running through the woods with a chainsaw.

He would have offered heart and soul to any of a handful of truly great filmmakers, and any of them surely would have seen the extent of his talent. He came to New York because it was the next best place to L.A., and not too far from that oh-so-vital familial support network. So he came to the big city, to hustle and schmooze and weasel his way into the promised land.

And he succeeded, after a fashion. Philip Thomas's hard work did not go unnoticed, and within six months of his arrival, he was hired to assist on his first feature-length film.

"So who do I end up working with?" he asked the stifling air. His creations regarded the query in silent assent. "Do I get Cronenberg? Friedkin? Romero?

"No. Floyd," he answered, the name flat as copper-plating on his tongue. "I got fucking Floyd."

Herschel Floyd, the producer/director-*schmeissmeister*, grand high potentate of Trauma Productions, Inc.—formerly Goldenrod Productions, masters of the technicolor blowjob. That was before, of course—before video supplanted film as the preferred medium for adult entertainment, and the bulk of the porn film industry sank like a mastodon in a tarpit.

In a luckier world, he'd have gone down with the herd.

"But this is not a very lucky world, is it?" Phil asked the face in his hands. It frowned. "Nosiree."

Because Herschel Floyd fancied himself as more than a sleaze merchant. Herschel Floyd was an *auteur*. Herschel Floyd had mutated with survival instincts that would shame a cockroach, shifting into the one genre where people with a little bit of money, even less imagination, and absolutely no talent could still make a killing.

And straight into a crash course with Philip Thomas.

Of course, he'd brought along the same delicate sensibilities that allowed him to spawn such rip-off megahits as *Bondage Bitches in Heat, Beach Blanket Bimbo,* or a host of others. Which meant that Herschel Floyd made tons-o'-bucks, none of which ever seemed to find its way into the next production budget. He drove a black Mercedes coupe with a cellular phone in it, did prodigious quantities of cocaine, and otherwise brandished his zeal in a way that attracted the young, the unconnected, the eternally hopeful.

And when he had gotten the hungry ones assembled, their vision burning to express itself, he did the only thing an *auteur* of his caliber could ever possibly do.

Hack. Chop. Slash.

He glared at the lifecast, blinking back saline beads from the corners of his eyes. "So what else is new? Herschel Floyd: killer of hopes, mangler of dreams. You attach yourself to real talent like a leech and don't drop off until you've sucked them dry." Herschel Floyd's ash-white image remained fixed, immutable. "You humiliate and bully creative people until their only hope of survival is to become a twisted reflection of yourself."

"And worse yet," he added, under his breath and over the growing knot in his throat, "worst of all—

"We let you get away with it."

It was understandable. at first. He didn't know squat about the lurid guts of the dreaded Industry, and had simply tried to do his best. But the work on Slaughterhouse Slumber Party *was ultimately buried by lame editing, a bone-dumb plot, and Herschel's insistence on casting ex-Penthouse Pets and softcore burnouts for the female leads on the basis of their under-the-desk auditions. Of course, the kudos afforded his work in the otherwise scathing reviews in Cinefex, Fangoria, Cineteratologist, and the other FX rags took a little of the sting out of seeing his work brutalized. And, slime though he was, Herschel was smooth, a consummate master of the buttered back-entry. Thus, when Herschel called him to work on Trauma's next project, Phil still had that brittle crust of hope, that this time, this time would be different.*

He should have known.

Toxic Shock Avenger, the terrifying tale of a deformed boy menacing an all-girl summer camp with lethal tampons, was a nightmare quickly becoming a disaster. Phil had driven himself, under Herschel Floyd's aesthetic sword of Damocles, to the point of near-collapse on the project; designing and redesigning the prosthetics for the dreaded applicator scenes, making the Avenger's super-absorbent head seem really believable.

The on-location conditions were, of course, appalling: weeks at an abandoned dioxin dump in New Jersey, where one of the locals bragged that the E.P.A. had declared its inspection results safe because "they only test six inches down, and we bury it two whole feet." One of the actresses—a former Miss November—quit after an unsightly rash broke out on one of her thighs. Meals—if you consider such delicacies as cold, blue-green spaghetti (so congealed that it retained the shape of the spatula a full half hour after it was scooped) food—were served on tables made of plywood sheets laid on recently emptied waste barrels. The relentless heat wave made the prosthetics finicky and the chemicals he worked with unstable; Phil spent half his time inhaling noxious fumes and the other half trying to avoid blowing up.

But it was worth it. The Avenger was scary, dammit, a goddamned masterpiece. The best work he'd ever done.

Until Herschel got hold of it. Gak. Spew. Plork.

The bastard ruined it, somehow: when they screened the dailies, the head came off looking rubbery and stupid, the horror reduced to cheesy laughability.

Herschel blamed Phil. Of course, Phil knew whose fault it really was, whose negligent vision was ultimately responsible for the insipid awfulness unfolding before him. But that didn't stop the creep from screaming, "Who's the incompetent twit that did this shit?"as Phil sank into his seat in the screening room. "Thomas, you asshole! This shit doesn't look real! It's garbage! Jeezus, we're gonna have to reshoot all of this shit! You call yourself a makeup artist?! Jeezus! You're fired! Get the fuck out-ahere!"

Phil had fled then, unable to cope with the abusive tantrums any longer. This was not the first time, but that was hardly the point. Something in him just snapped. The harangue continued on, echoing off the walls, burning in his mind long after he'd gone.

"You call this magic?! I want to see some fucking magic, goddammit!! Get me somebody who can do it right! Now!"

That was two days ago.

"I got some magic for you now, alrightee," he muttered. "This one's so good that even your participation couldn't fuck it up." He surveyed the array of objects surrounding Floyd's lifecast on the cluttered tabletop: the telephone answering machine, a TDK hi-bias cassette, a wooden box drilled with airholes, a pair of heavy-duty rubber-and-canvas workgloves, the large votive candle he'd scored at *Los Campaneros* bodega on Avenue D, and a bowl of Ultrocal.

And, stippling the plaster surface of the lifecast, perhaps the most important ingredients of all. They were very small, unnoticeable to all but the most observant gaze. They'd been plucked accidentally from the bristling expanse of Herschel's face, back when the original cast had been taken. A few stray whiskers, lifted by the pull of the alginate, then transferred again to the plaster positive, where they even now protruded like saplings on a snow-covered mountainside.

Phil looked at the candle. Its inscription read *Siete Potencias Africana*. It had a little picture on it, a crucified Jesus surrounded by a rooster, a ladder, snakes, swords, spears, and skulls, with a wall of fire behind Him and ringed by what Phil presumed were pictures of the seven 'saints': African gods brought by slaves to Cuba, and annexed into legitimacy by the Church. *Chango, Orula, Ogum, Elegua, Obatalia, Yemalia, and Ochum.* The Seven African Powers.

He'd seen the candles every day for years now, crowding the bottom shelf near the door at *Los Campeneros*, wedged between the Nine Lives Super Supper cans and Goya bean section. They were big, gaudy, and ugly as sin, with a cryptic inscription in Spanish on the back, and were every one manufactured by the Blessed Miracle Candle Company of East Laredo, Texas. Just light the candle, recite the prayer, and *bang! zoom!*, your wish would be granted.

Maybe it was the crazy-making heat, which nudged adolescent revenge fantasies clear into the kill-zone. Maybe it was the fact that last night his video store had finally gotten him a copy of *The Believers*, which he'd missed in the theaters because he was too busy slaving for Herschel Floyd, and he loved the scene where the spiders crawled out of Helen Shaver's face. Maybe it was because he recognized the candle even before Martin Sheen did, and it inspired him.

And maybe it was because he knew that his phone would be ringing any minute now, because he just knew that Herschel Floyd knew that Phil was the best; certainly the best Trauma Productions could ever hope for. He'd call, all right, with weaseldick apologies and backhanded compliments and just enough empty promises to suck him back into the fold.

The last time Floyd fired him Phil held out, until Floyd actually agreed to *double* his salary. A big hundred bucks a week—if the checks cleared. Last time, Phil had been sucker enough to take it.

This time, he wanted a little something extra.

He lit the candle and fed the cassette into his stereo, which was his pride and joy and his sole valuable possession. He'd taken the liberty of prerecording the chant, so that he could better concentrate on the moment. Mood was everything. He'd even mixed in a recording of African rhythms he'd found buried in his record collection, as a kind of soundtrack. The sound swelled in the room, and his own voice came back as if from another planet...

"OH SIETE POTENCIAS AFRICANAS QUE SE ENCUENTRAN ALREDEDOR DE NUESTRO SEÑOR, HUMILDEMENTE ME ARRO DILLO ANTE TU MILAGROSO CUADRA A PEDIR SOCCORO..."

Phil giggled; it sounded great. Real spookshow. He donned the workgloves and reached for the box. The weight shifted as he picked it up; from inside came the frantic skittering of tiny claws. Phil checked the dexterity of the gloves: so-so, the fingertips a bit too thick and squared and clubby for any real precision. He managed to pick up the X-acto knife, thinking *I'll be quick about it.* He pried up the lid, reached in and ensnared one of the screeching prisoners. Good reflexes. He pulled it out.

It was a rat: the youngest one, eight, ten ounces maybe, its eyes shiny-bright and black as night. A heckuva lot easier to come by than a live chicken in Manhattan, and a lot more appropriate. He'd caught a few last night, just by setting the box-trap in the back alley. He hadn't bothered to feed them yet; they were panicked and pissed. The one in his hand tried to bite through the offending digits, got a mouthful of neoprene and duckcloth instead. Phil squeezed it so tightly that it screeched in helpless rage and flipped it over onto its back.

"Nighty-night," he offered by way of eulogy.

And he buried the blade in the soft fur of its breast.

"...PIDANLE QUE ALEJE DE MI CAMINO Y DE MI CASA ESAS ESCOLLAS QUE CAUSAN TODOS MIS MALES..." The tape droned, *"PARA QUE NUNCA VUELVAN A ATORMENTARME..."*

Blood pooled instantly around the hilt, matting the rat's fur as its body went all stiff and trembly. Death was a foregone conclusion: the blade was sharp and long enough to crack its sternum like a dirt-gray walnut, skewering the heart-muscle beneath in an invasion of cold-razored steel. It expended a few feeble kicks, and then it was lights out in ratville.

Before this afternoon, he'd never cold-bloodedly killed anything before. The first one he did to make that alginate. It gave him a giddy, queasy rush in the pit of his stomach. This one felt kind of neat.

It felt like he could get used to it.

The gloves were hotter than hell in the already stifling room, causing the palms of his hands to sweat like crazy. He peeled one off, the better to work with, leaving on the other to hold the ratty carcass. He held it over the bowl of Ultrocal and opened its throat, letting the blood squirt down to spatter the mound of powder. There was a surprising amount of it for such a tiny creature; it filled the bottom of the bowl, turning the Ultrocal into a frothy mush.

When it was drained, he laid the corpse on the table, close enough to the box that the others could smell it. They reacted very, very strongly, gnawing and clawing to shove whiskered snouts through the airholes. "Mmmmmm, yummy nums," he cooed. "Soon, soon." The rats were not amused.

Inside the bowl, the plaster and blood were combining.

Outside, the temperature read ninety-nine degrees.

He peeled off the other glove and tossed it aside. His palm was moist with perspiration, as much from anticipation now as from the heat. He mixed the plaster, dipping his fingers deep into the bowl and stirring it into a creamy red paste. When it was done he picked up a pair of tweezers.

"Now, this won't hurt a bit," he murmured, then he thought

about it a moment. "Wait a minute; who am I kidding?" He smiled grimly at the cast, and plucked a few whiskers off its surface.

"You're not going to believe this, but I read somewhere—I think it was *Psychology Today*, but don't quote me on that—that voodoo only requires the tiniest bit of the victim in order to work. A fingernail paring, a drop of vital fluid, a single hair," he held the tweezers up to the light, "each contains all the genetic identification necessary. Neat, huh?"

The lifecast said nothing as he placed the hairs in a crucifix pattern—forehead, chin, cheek, cheek—in the alginate shell. The fresh blood gave off a ripe, heady odor that permeated the still air of the room. The music on the tape throbbed. In Phil's imagination, which was working overtime, he saw it coming: like a black cloud, boiling up on the horizon. Alginate was versatile: you could shrink it, expand it, liquefy it, and remold it into yet another shape, again and again and again. It was infinitely finer than the banal repetitiveness of another dumb psycho-slasher pseudo-plot: he could literally let his imagination run wild. He wondered how Herschel's shrunken face would look grafted onto his armpit, say, or onto the end of his fat wanger.

The phone rang. *Showtime.*

"*Lights…*" he whispered, clicking off the worklamp. The candle's glow remained, wavering like a beacon. "*…camera…*"

The phone rang again.

"*…action…*"

He picked up. "Hello?"

"Phil, baby! Whoa, what's that shit in the background?! Turn it down, guy!"

Phil turned the tape down. A whine of static told him that Herschel was on the car-phone; probably cruising Eleventh Avenue for a new female lead. "Herschel. What a surprise."

"Heh-hey, Guy! We missed you today!"

"I bet you did." Phil began brushing the paste on the alginate shell. "What exactly do you want?"

"I want *you*, babe. On the set tomorrow, bright an' early."

"Forget it." Phil kept brushing; thick, hasty strokes.

"Aw, don't be that way, guy." Herschel's tone was silk-smooth and oh-so-hip. Mellow, even. "You know how I get when I'm under the gun. I get crazy, okay. I say things. But you know I love you. You're the best…"

He was really laying it on. Phil kept right on brushing, coat after coat. The blood-smell was thick in the air. The rats were getting agitated; he could hear them ripping splinters out of the interior of the box. The room seemed to close in around the candle, hot and stifling. The chanting continued, building in intensity.

"…and hey, I'll even double your salary again. Two hundred big ones, kiddo, every week. Accounting will kill me, but hey, you get what you pay for, right? And besides, we really need you here. The Avenger needs you. *I* need you. Trauma needs your magic touch, guy. Whaddaya ssssaaaaay…?"

One of the problems with Ultrocal-30 is that it gets hard suddenly. It has a lot to do with temperature, and timing. Sometimes it could be a real pain.

Then again, sometimes the timing was just right.

"D'ja say something, Hersch?" Phil paused the tape. The voice on the other end was one long, unhealthy vowel movement, spiraling up and up in what sounded like intense pain.

"Herschel? Are you alright? Speak up!"

"*Aaaaaaeeeeeiiiiihhh…*"

He was reminded of the old Warner Brothers cartoon, the one where Bugs Bunny tortures the fat opera singer by filling his throat spritzer with liquid alum, and the opera singer goes "figaro… figaro…figaro" as his head gets smaller and smaller.

It was kinda funny.

For about two seconds.

Then the rush hit: his heart pounding suddenly in his throat, cold sweat breaking out from every pore on his body as he realized this was real, this wasn't just an adolescent revenge fantasy anymore, this was it—he was really fucking *doing* it! He wished he could have a camera rolling, focused in tight close-up to drink in every awful detail. He closed his eyes, head reeling, as the mind-movie came to life…

…*skin, muscle, and ligament pulling taut, stretching his eyelids until the socketed orbs burst, follicles shrinking around the bristle of his beard until each shaft poked up thick as a pencil stub and then shrinking further still, until it was stretched tighter than the sheets on a boot-camp bed; cartilage compacting, skull pressing in to trash-mash the brain, arteries blowing like high-pressure hoses, spraying blue-black blood to put out the fire that was the heat of the power, the heat of the plaster setting in his hands…*

From the receiver came the sound of many things breaking, and a rush of car horns. A breeze stirred through the windows, hot as dragon's breath. Phil's vision glitched back to real-time, sweat pouring off him. Terror and adrenaline comingled, fueling the buzz in his brain. There was power in the room, uncoiling as days upon weeks upon months upon years of frustration came to a head.

"Hey, Hersch, baby!" he howled. "How do you like my new effect, you bush-league douchebag amateur! Is that *real* enough for you?? Do you think it *works*?!"

He was screaming now, his face flushed with excitement and rage. "You want my 'magic touch' huh?! Is that what you want?! Huh?!"

"Well, touch *this*, motherfucker!"

He stood up, the shrunken mask still in his hands, and shoved it into the trap.

"Touch *this*!"

The rodents fell upon the bloody fetish in a feeding frenzy: tearing it to shreds, taking little pieces out of the box, each other, everything. From over the phone came a high-pitched screech, and the sound of tires skidding out of control. More horns, blaring hysterically. Phil cranked the volume of the stereo back up, louder than before; it was the point in the recording where he'd gone a little overboard, snatching at foreign bits of phrases as the rhythm built in intensity, until he was practically speaking in tongues, wailing little more than garbled incoherencies. It made for great soundtrack, true.

But very sloppy ritual.

Phil fell back from the table, as the box wrenched sideways to crash on the floor. The shadows closed in, a hot blanket enfolding him. The phone slipped thuddingly from his grasp, but Floyd's screams carried well.

They were matched, in perfect stereo, by his own.

He realized, in that dreadful instant of ultimate collaboration, that he'd underestimated something fundamental regarding the nature of the dark arts, and the even darker powers he'd called upon: how very much in common they had. They, too, took their craft very, very seriously. They, too, hated to see it abused.

And, they required very little of the victim to work it. A bit of hair, a fingernail, a drop of blood.

Or sweat.

Phil shrieked and lunged toward the big mirror over the mantle, his voice spiraling up and up. It was small consolation for him to consider that a lesser artist probably could not have pulled it off at all. Blunders notwithstanding, he had given birth to the perfect effect; the line finally disappeared altogether.

His dream and reality fused.

From the telephone, a symphony of screaming metal. Before his bulging eyes, a twisted reflection. Flawlessly real.

And perfectly ravenous.

By the time he got both hands to his face, it could fit neatly into the palm of one; by the time the first whiskered snout poked its way through the soft flesh of his cheek, he was too far gone to care.

The rats remained long after the tape had played itself through.

They dined by candlelight, and invited many friends.

ABOUT THE CONTRIBUTORS

EDWARD AHERN

Ed Ahern resumed writing after forty odd years in foreign intelligence and international sales. He's had over two hundred stories and poems published so far, and three books. Ed works the other side of writing at Bewildering Stories, where he sits on the review board and manages a posse of five review editors. www.amazon.com/-/e/B07D1SHRBQ

GUSTAVO BONDONI

Gustavo Bondoni is an Argentine novelist and short story writer who writes primarily in English. He has recently released three science fiction novels: *Incursion* (2017), *Siege* (2016) and *Outside* (2017). He has over two hundred short stories published in fourteen countries and translated into seven languages. Many of the stories are collected in *Tenth Orbit and Other Faraway Places* (2010) and *Virtuoso and Other Stories* (2011). *The Curse of El Bastardo* (2010) is a short fantasy novel. www.gustavobondoni.com.

ᗡ MAX BOOTH III ᗡ

Max Booth III is the Editor-in-Chief of Perpetual Motion Machine, the Managing Editor of Dark Moon Digest, and the co-host of Castle Rock Radio, a Stephen King-themed podcast. Raised in Northern Indiana, he now lives in a small town in Texas where he reviews books for the San Antonio Current. Follow him on Twitter @GiveMeYourTeeth.

ᗡ PATRICK BREHENY ᗡ

Patrick Breheny is an ESL teacher, fiction writer and stage actor living in Bangkok. He has sold stories in the former 'men's mag' market and most recently, his story *Reversatol* appeared in Straylight Magazine. He is currently in rehearsal for a production of Chekhov's *'A Marriage Proposal'* with the Bangkok Community Theater Fringe Festival. He can be found on Facebook and at patrickbrehenyauthor.page4.me.

ᗡ POPPY Z BRITE ᗡ

Poppy Z Brite (Billy Martin) is an American author. Brite initially achieved notoriety in the gothic horror genre of literature in the early 1990s after publishing a string of successful novels. Brite's most recent work moved into the related genre of dark comedy, of which many are set in the New Orleans restaurant world. Brite's novels are typically standalone books that feature recurring characters from previous novels and short stories. http://www.poppyzbrite.com/biblio.html

THOM BRUCIE

Thom Brucie's major works include the novels, *Children of Slate* and *Weapons of Cain*, a collection of short stories, *Still Waters, Five Stories*, and two chapbooks of poems, *Moments Around The Campfire With A Vietnam Vet*, and *Apprentice Lessons*. A number of his stories have been nominated for Pushcarts; he was awarded a Very Special Arts Grant from Fresno State University in conjunction with Break the Barriers, Inc, for the musical play, *Arnold the Alligator*. www.ThomBrucie.com

ROB BUTLER

Rob Butler lives in Reading in the UK and has had more than 30 pieces of short fiction published in such places as *Perihelion, Mad Scientist Journal, Shoreline of Infinity* and *Daily Science Fiction*. Some of his work can be found on his Amazon Author Page: https://www.amazon.co.uk/Rob-Butler/e/B01ELRD8XS/

ANTON CANCRE

Anton Cancre has cultivated feculent word farms for a good few years now, leading to publications in the tens (I know, right?!) and poetry editorship at Recompose Magazine. He also vomits his literary opines at Cemetery Dance and antoncancre.blogspot.com (please don't laugh at the cheap bastard).

MORT CASTLE

In 2018, Mort Castle published two books in English, two books in Polish, and had stories in a number of anthologies including *C.H.U.D Lives!* and *Fantastic Tales of Terror*. In 2019, he will be executive producer of the Shadow Show TV series on the Terror TV channel. In 2020, he will return to his first love, Lucha Libre, once more in the famous mask of Loco Adjunto to destroy all enemies with his signature finisher, "The Reluctant Flamingo." Arriba!

GREG CHAPMAN

Greg Chapman is the Bram Stoker Award®-nominated and Australian Shadows Award-nominated author of *Hollow House* and the author of five novellas: *Torment, The Noctuary, Vaudeville, The Last Night of October,* and *The Followers*. His debut novel *Hollow House* was nominated for a Bram Stoker Award® in 2016. He also received the Richard Laymon President's Award for services to the Horror Writers Association in 2017and is the current President of the Australasian Horror Writers Association. www.darkscrybe.com

MICHAEL CORNELIUS

Michael G. Cornelius is the author of five books of fiction, including the Lambda Literary Award-finalist *Creating Man* (Vineyard Press) and *The Ascension* (Variance Books). He also penned the speculative fiction collection *Tricks and Treats* (MLR Press). His novels have been nominated for an American Library Association Award and an Independent Press Award. In addition, he has published dozens of stories in journals and magazines.

🦇 RAY GARTON 🦇

Ray Garton has been writing novels, novellas, and short stories for more than 30 years. His work spans the genres of horror, suspense, and even comedy. His novel *LIVE GIRLS* made a permanent mark on vampire fiction. He received the Grand Master of Horror Award in 2006. He lives in northern California with his wife Dawn, where he is at work on his next novel. https://www.raygartononline.com

🦇 KENNETH GOLDMAN 🦇

Ken Goldman, former Philadelphia teacher of English and Film Studies, is an affiliate member of the Horror Writers Association. He has homes on the Main Line in Pennsylvania and at the Jersey shore. His stories have appeared in several independent press publications in the U.S., Canada, the UK, and Australia with many more due for publication in 2018. Since 1993, Ken's tales have received seven honorable mentions in The Year's Best Fantasy & Horror.

🦇 NANCY KILPATRICK 🦇

Award-winning author and editor Nancy Kilpatrick has published 22 novels, over 220 short stories, and 6 collections, and has edited 15 anthologies. She wrote the non-fiction book The goth Bible: A Compendium for the Darkly Inclined. Thrones of Blood, her 6-book novel series, is ongoing: Revenge of the Vampir King; Sacrifice of the Hybrid Princess; Abduction of Two Rulers, and soon: Savagery of the Rebel King. https://www.amazon.com/gp/bookseries/B075HDKCB8/ref=st_afs_B07DTJG8YP

BOB MOORE

Bob Moore is originally from Niagara Falls. He is a semi-retired librarian who enjoys writing (horror, history and mainstream) and community theatre. During the warm months he and his wife, Stephanie, and their rescue dog, Penny, live in Massachusetts, where Killington is set, retreating to central Florida when the leaves fall. He has also published two historical novels set in the falls (Stone House Diaries, Where the Gold is Buried). https://www.facebook.com/mudseasoninsolway/

KURT NEWTON

Kurt Newton's fiction and poetry can be found in the following anthologies: *Untimely Frost, Death's Garden, Darkling's Beasts & Brews, Year's Best Body Horror 2017, Year's Best Transhuman SF 2017, Merchants of Misery and Shadows Over Deathlehem*. His short story "*The Coal Mape*" recently won The Screw Turn Flash Fiction Competition. https://www.amazon.com/Kurt-Newton/e/B006VYUMUM.

CRAIG SPECTOR

Craig Spector is an award-winning and bestselling author and screenwriter, with twelve books published, reprints in nine languages, and millions of copies in print. Spector released an original music album in 2017, *Craig Spector: Resurrection Road*, chronicling his journey fighting Stage Four metastatic prostate cancer; followed in 2018 with *Outposts*, and in 2019 with *Kicking Cans*, all part of his Art of Not Dying cycle. A freedom of speech-themed dark fiction anthology, *Freedom of Screech*, is in progress.

༝ TODD SULLIVAN ༝

Todd Sullivan has published short fiction in several venues, including Odd Tales of Wonder (2018), Kzine Magazine (2019), Aurealis Science Fiction and Fantasy (2017), SciFan Magazine (2017), Pole to Pole's *Dark Luminous Wings* Anthology (2017), Expanded Horizons Magazine (2017), Aurora Wolf Literary Journal (2018 & 2017), Hellbound Books' *Big Book of Bootleg Horror Vol 2* (2017), Scarlet Leaf Review (2017), Eastlit Journal (2016), Tokyo Yakuza Anthology (2015 & 2014), and Tincture Journal (2013).

༝ MICHAEL THOMAS-KNIGHT ༝

Michael Thomas-Knight was the author of numerous horror fiction stories, bending the scope of reality one word at a time. Michael's style ranged from classic ghost stories to atmospheric Eldritch tales steeped in mysticism. His work has appeared in numerous publications and anthologies; his novelette, *Skin Job*, part of *Terry M. West's Car-Nex Mythos* series. When he wasn't writing fiction, Michael built vintage monster model kits and reviewed horror movies, books, and items at his blog, Parlor of Horror. http://www.amazon.com/Michael-Thomas-/e/B00CROMK3M/

༝ JASON A WYCKOFF ༝

Jason A. Wyckoff is the author of two short story collections published by Tartarus Press, *Black Horse and Other Strange Stories* (2012) and *The Hidden Back Room* (2016). His work has appeared in anthologies from Plutonian Press and Siren's Call Publications, as well as the journals Nightscript, Weirdbook, and Turn to Ash.

ALSO FROM LVP PUBLICATIONS:

The Pulp Horror Book
of Phobias

Darkling's Beasts & Brews:
Poetry with a Drink on the Side

Subliminal Reality

Dark Voices: A Lycan Valley
Charity Anthology

Final Masquerade

Simple Things

Available at Amazon, Barnes & Noble and
LycanValley.com